KU-076-308

A PROMISE...
TO A PROPOSAL?

BY
KATE HARDY

HER FAMILY
FOR KEEPS

BY
MOLLY EVANS

MILLS
BOON

Kate Hardy lives in Norwich, in the east of England, with her husband, two young children, one bouncy spaniel and too many books to count! When she's not busy writing romance or researching local history she helps out at her children's schools. She also loves cooking—spot the recipes sneaked into her books! (They're also on her website, along with extracts and the stories behind her books.)

Writing for Mills & Boon® has been a dream come true for Kate—something she wanted to do ever since she was twelve. She's been writing Medical Romances™ for over ten years now. She says it's the best of both worlds, because she gets to learn lots of new things when she's researching the background to a book: add a touch of passion, drama and danger, a new gorgeous hero every time, and it's the perfect job!

Kate's always delighted to hear from readers, so do drop in to her website at katehardy.com

Molly Evans has worked as a nurse for thirty years and has taken her experiences as a travel nurse and turned them into wondrous settings for her books. Some of those assignments were in small rural hospitals, the Indian Health Service in Alaska and in the American southwest, as well as a large research hospital and many other places across the United States.

After rambling for many years, the high desert of New Mexico is now where she calls home. When she's not writing or attending her son's hockey games she's obsessed with learning how to knit socks, visiting with friends, or settling down in front of the fireplace with a glass of wine and her two hounds who are never very far away.

Visit Molly at mollyevansromance.wordpress.com to keep up on her latest releases, book events, and what's going on in Molly's life at any given moment.

A PROMISE...
TO A PROPOSAL?

BY
KATE HARDY

MILLS
BOON

Published in Great Britain 2015
by Mills & Boon, an imprint of Harlequin (UK) Limited,
Eton House, 18-24 Paradise Road, Richmond, Surrey, TW9 1SR

© 2015 Pamela Brooks

ISBN: 978-0-263-24721-3

Printed and bound in Spain
by CPI, Barcelona

Dear Reader,

I've always liked friends-to-lovers stories, but this one has a slight twist in that the hero is also the best friend of the heroine's late husband.

And when friendship turns to love when do you dare to take the risk of wrecking the friendship?

A Promise...to a Proposal? is about how Ruby and Ellis take that particular journey—from Ellis promising his best friend that he'll look after his widow to both of them falling in love.

The story's set partly in my bit of the world (or a fictionalised bit of the East Anglian coast), partly in London, and partly in a very beautiful city that I had the privilege to explore earlier this year—Prague. (And I'm afraid I stole the posh dinner my family and I had—the best meal we've ever eaten!)

I hope you enjoy Ellis and Ruby's story.

I'm always delighted to hear from readers, so do come and visit me at katehardy.com

With love

Kate Hardy

Dedication

To Gerard, Chris and Chloe—
remembering the best meal we've ever eaten!

Books by Kate Hardy

Mills & Boon® Medical Romance™

Italian Doctor, No Strings Attached
Dr Cinderella's Midnight Fling
Once a Playboy…
The Brooding Doc's Redemption
A Date with the Ice Princess
Her Real Family Christmas
200 Harley Street: The Soldier Prince
It Started with No Strings…
A Baby to Heal Their Hearts

Mills & Boon® Cherish™

Ballroom to Bride and Groom
Bound by a Baby
Behind the Film Star's Smile
Crown Prince, Pregnant Bride
A New Year Marriage Proposal

**Visit the author profile page at
millsandboon.co.uk for more titles**

CHAPTER ONE

'HERE?' RUBY ASKED.

'It's a sandy beach, we're below the high tide line, the tide's coming in right now and the wind's in the right direction—so I'd say it's just about perfect,' Ellis said.

Well, it would've been perfect if it hadn't been drizzling with rain. But today was what it was, and the weather didn't matter. Just as it hadn't mattered a year ago. The day that had blown a hole in all their lives.

She smiled. 'Tom always did say you were the practical one.'

And the one with itchy feet who could never stay in one place for long.

Except for the last eighteen months, which Ellis had spent in London solely because of Tom, his best friend since their first day at infant school. They'd gone to university together, and trained together in the same London hospital. When Tom had been diagnosed with leukaemia, that had been the one thing to bring Ellis back to England. He'd wanted to be there for his best friend and support him through to the end. Ellis had promised Tom in those last agonising months that he'd be there for Ruby, too, and support her through at least the first year after Tom's death.

Including today.

Which was why he was walking on the beach on a drizzly September day with Tom's parents and Ruby, on the first anniversary of Tom's death, to help them scatter some of Tom's ashes in his favourite place. A place that brought back so many happy childhood memories that it put a lump in Ellis's throat.

'Thanks for looking up all the information for us,' Ruby said. 'I wasn't sure if we had to get permission from someone first or even how you go about scattering ashes.'

'Hey, it's the least I could do. I loved Tom, too,' Ellis said. And when Ruby had first broached the subject about scattering Tom's ashes, he'd known exactly where Tom would've wanted it to be.

He spread a couple of waterproof blankets on the beach for the four of them to kneel on, and took four brightly coloured spades and buckets from a plastic bag.

It might be a dark day, the final goodbye, but Ellis wanted to remember the brightness. To remember Tom as he was before he was ill and to celebrate the close friendship they'd shared over the years.

'I remember you boys doing this when you were small,' Brenda said with a wobble in her voice as she dug into the sand and filled her bucket. 'You both loved the beach. It didn't matter if it was summer or winter— if we asked you what you wanted to do, you'd both beg to come here and make sandcastles.'

The lump in Ellis's throat meant he couldn't speak. He remembered. Days when life was simple. Days when his parents had been as carefree as Tom's. Though Tom's parents, he knew, wouldn't react in the same way as his parents had when it came to the death of their child. Brenda and Mike would talk about Tom with love and keep him alive in their hearts, rather than stonewalling everything.

Working in companionable silence, the four of them made a sandcastle. Just as they had when Tom and Ellis were small boys: only this time Tom's widow was taking Tom's place.

When they'd finished, Ellis produced a flag from his bag—one made from an ice-lolly stick and a photograph of Tom. It was one of his favourite memories: the day they'd opened their A level results together, whooped, and known they were both going to train as doctors in London. For Tom, it had been the next step towards a dream. For Ellis, it had been the next step towards escape from a home that had come to feel like a mausoleum.

'He was eighteen years old then,' Mike said softly as Ellis handed him the flag. 'With the whole world before him.'

How very little time Tom had actually had. Not even half a lifetime.

And how very much Ellis wished his best friend was still here. 'He was special,' Ellis said, his voice cracking.

'Yes. He was,' Mike said, and put the flag on the top turret.

Brenda and Ruby both gulped hard and squeezed each other's hand.

Ellis finished digging the moat round the outside of the castle; and then the four of them took turns scattering Tom's ashes in the moat and covering them over with sand. Ruby sprinkled rose petals on the top.

Then Ellis moved the blankets back a little way, set

up the two huge umbrellas he'd packed in the car when he'd seen the weather report, and uncorked a bottle of champagne.

'To Tom,' he said when he'd filled their glasses. 'And may our memories of him make the smiles outnumber the tears.' Even though right now it felt as if the tears were more than outweighing the smiles, Ellis was determined to celebrate his friend rather than be selfish about his loss.

Mike, Brenda and Ruby echoed the toast, even though their smiles were wobbly and Ellis could see their eyes were shiny with tears they tried to blink away.

Then the four of them sat and watched as the tide came in, slowly sweeping the sandcastle away with the ashes, and tumbling the rose petals and Tom's photograph in the waves.

Afterwards, Ellis drove Tom's parents home.

'Will you come in for something to eat?' Brenda asked on the doorstep.

'Thanks, but...' Ellis tailed off. Even being in this town made him feel stifled. He hated it here. What he really wanted to do was drive as fast as he could back to London. Away from the dark memories.

'Of course. You'll want to drop in to see your own mum while you're here,' Brenda said.

Ellis didn't have the heart to disillusion her, so he just smiled. Today of all days, he really couldn't face his parents. They'd be aware of what he'd just been doing, and they'd be thinking of Sally. And, as always, they'd retreat into coolness rather than talk to him or even give him a sympathetic hug. Even though Ellis understood why—when you'd lost someone you loved so very much, sometimes withdrawing from everyone seemed

like the only way to keep your heart safe from further
hurt—he still found it hard to deal with. He always felt
as if he'd lost more than his beloved only sister, twenty
years ago; he'd lost his parents, too. And although he'd
remained reasonably close to his older brothers, his
choice of career had put a distinct rift between them.
Tom's parents had been Ellis's greatest support through
his teen years, and he'd always be grateful to them for
it. And for Tom's sake he'd look out for them now, the
way they'd looked out for him.

Brenda hugged him. 'Thank you for being there for
us.'

'Any time.' And he meant it. 'Just because Tom's…'
He couldn't say the word. He just *couldn't*. 'Not here,'
he said croakily, 'it doesn't mean you're not still part
of my life, because you are. You know I think of you
as my second set of parents. I always will.'

Tears glittered in Brenda's eyes. She patted his shoulder, clearly too moved to talk, and then hugged Ruby.

'I'll text you when we get back to London,' Ruby
promised.

But she looked quizzically at Ellis when he drove
straight out of the town and back towards London. 'I
thought you were going to see your parents?'

'Not today.'

'Look, don't feel you have to get me back to London if you want to see them. I can always go back to
Brenda and Mike's and wait until you're ready, or get
the train back.'

That was the point. He didn't actually want to see
his parents. Especially not today. Part of him lambasted
himself for being selfish, but the realistic part of him

knew it was necessary self-preservation. 'Another time,' he said.

'If you're sure.'

'Oh, I'm sure,' he said softly. 'My parents are... complicated.'

She reached over and squeezed his hand briefly. 'I know,' she said, equally softly.

In the months since Tom's death, Ellis had opened up a little to Ruby and told her about the tragedy that had taken the sunshine out of his world. How his older sister had taken a gap year before university, teaching in a remote school. Sally had fallen pregnant by accident and hadn't realised it at first; when she'd been so sick, everyone had assumed it was a virus. But by the time they'd realised she was suffering from hyperemesis gravidarum, a severe form of morning sickness, it was too late. She'd grown too weak, developed complications, gone into organ failure and never regained consciousness.

And Ellis's parents had never recovered from losing their only daughter. Their remaining three sons simply hadn't been enough to bring them back from the cold, emotionless life they'd led from that moment on.

Ellis and Ruby drove back in companionable silence, listening to Nick Drake. The kind of mellow, faintly melancholy stuff Ellis had enjoyed listening to with Tom. It went well with the rain and his mood.

Back in London, he parked in the street outside Ruby's house and saw her to the door.

'Thank you, for today, Ellis. I don't know what I would have done this last year without you,' she said.

'Hey, no problem—and you've helped me, too.' He hugged her. Bad move. Now he could smell her perfume, the sweet scent of violets. And she fitted perfectly in his arms.

She's your best friend's widow, he reminded himself silently. No, no and absolutely no. Don't even *think* about it. You do not make a move on this woman. Ever. Hands off.

'I'll see you at work tomorrow,' he said. 'Call me if you need me.'

'Thanks, Ellis.' She reached up and kissed his cheek.

For a moment, Ellis desperately wanted to twist his face to the side so the kiss landed on his mouth. For months now he'd wanted to kiss Ruby. But he held himself back. The feelings he'd developed towards her over the last year were completely inappropriate; plus he risked losing one of his closest friendships if he asked her out. He was pretty sure that Ruby saw him only as a friend, so wanting more was just *stupid*. Especially as he knew he wasn't a good bet when it came to relationships.

His normal job, working for a medical aid charity, meant that relationships were tricky. Either he had long-distance affairs where he hardly ever saw his girlfriend and the relationship ended by mutual agreement because his girlfriend just got fed up waiting for him; or they were short, sweet flings that ended when he moved on to another assignment. Except for his marriage to Natalia—he'd thought that would be the exception to the rule, that maybe he could have the best of both worlds after all. How wrong he'd been there. So nowadays he didn't do more than short, fun flings—where everyone knew the score before they started and nobody ended up disappointed.

When Ruby was finally ready to move on, Ellis knew

she'd want more than just a fling or a long-distance relationship. More than he could offer her. Asking for more than friendship would just ruin a relationship that had become really important to him over the last eighteen months. And to have her solely as his friend was way better than not having her in his life at all, wasn't it? So he'd just have to keep himself in check.

'I'd better go,' he mumbled, and left before he did something really reckless and stupid. Like kissing her.

And he brooded all the way home. His current job as an obstetrician at the London Victoria was only temporary, covering another registrar's maternity leave, and his contract was due to end in a couple of months' time when Billie was due to return. He'd already agreed to do a month's assignment for the medical aid charity, helping to set up a new medical centre in Zimbabwe, when his temporary contract at the London Victoria ended. Going to work abroad again would mean he'd be out of temptation's way and he wouldn't hurt Ruby.

Then again, Ellis had promised Tom that he'd look after Ruby. Until he knew that she was ready to move on and had found someone else to share her life—someone who was good enough for her and would treat her as she deserved—how could he desert her?

It was a tricky line to walk.

So he'd just have to bury his feelings, the way he normally did, and everything would be just fine.

Ruby watched Ellis drive away, feeling guilty. For a moment she'd been tempted to kiss him on the lips instead of on the cheek.

How could she possibly want to kiss another man? And especially how could she have thoughts like that on the first anniversary of her husband's death? How mean-spirited and selfish and plain *wrong* was that?

She closed the door with a grimace of self-disgust.

Plus she knew that Tom had asked Ellis to look out for her. Letting Ellis know that she was starting to see him as more than a friend might make everything go wrong between them. He'd always been such a perfect gentleman towards her. Trying to push their friendship in another direction might mean that she lost him—and she didn't want that to happen. She liked having Ellis in her life. Liked it a lot.

Though she had a nasty feeling that she was going to lose him anyway. Ellis had always had itchy feet, according to Tom, and she knew that Ellis wanted to go back to the medical aid charity. The place where he'd always felt he'd belonged.

Losing Tom had ripped Ruby's heart to shreds. Over the last year, she'd gradually put the pieces back together, and it would be very stupid to let herself fall for someone who'd made it very clear that he didn't do permanent. Someone who didn't want the same things she wanted. Someone she knew she'd lose to his job. Yes, he would come back to England from time to time to see her—but she'd be lonely in London, waiting for him. Yet, if she went with him, she'd end up feeling horribly homesick and missing her family. Neither option was right for her. Which meant that Ellis really wasn't the right man for her, much as she was attracted to him, and she needed to think with her head rather than her heart.

Now they'd scattered Tom's ashes and she was back in London again, Ruby didn't quite know what to do with herself. She wished she'd asked Ellis to go somewhere for dinner with her or something; right now, she felt so *lonely*.

She mooched around for the best part of an hour, not able to settle to reading or doing crosswords. Even cleaning the bathroom until it sparkled didn't make her feel as if she'd achieved anything; she was in limbo.

Then the doorbell rang.

Her heart leapt. Had Ellis come back?

No, of course not. How stupid of her to think it.

She opened the door to see her best friend, Tina, bearing what looked suspiciously like a box of home-made cake.

'With today being what it is, I thought you could do with some company tonight,' Tina said, 'and this.' She lifted the box. 'Lemon cake.'

Ruby's favourite. And Ruby knew without a doubt Tina had made it especially for her. It was probably still warm.

'There isn't anyone in the world I'd rather see right now,' Ruby said, meaning it. Not even Ellis. Because with her best friend Ruby knew she wouldn't have that edge of guilt and faint shame that she seemed to feel around Ellis nowadays, outside work. 'Thank you. Thank you so much.' She hugged her best friend, hard.

Tina hung her coat in the hallway and made herself at home in the kitchen, putting the kettle on and getting the teapot out of the cupboard, the way she and Ruby had done hundreds of times over the years in each other's kitchens. 'So how did it go this afternoon?'

'Really well. It didn't matter that it was raining. Ellis had brought a couple of huge umbrellas and waterproof blankets for us to sit on.' Ruby smiled. 'We made a sandcastle and put the ashes in the moat, covered it with rose petals, toasted Tom with champagne and let the sea wash the sandcastle and the ashes away together.'

'It sounds perfect—well, as perfect as something like that could be.' Tina finished making the tea, put the lemon cake on the plate and cut them both a slice, then handed Ruby a steaming mug. 'To Tom,' she said, lifting her mug and clinking it against Ruby's. 'I'll miss him horribly. But I'll always be glad I knew him, because he was just the nicest guy in the world.'

'Yeah.' Ruby took a sip of her tea to take the lump out of her throat.

'Hey. It's OK to cry,' Tina said softly.

'No. I want to remember him with smiles, not tears,' Ruby insisted. 'He wouldn't have wanted anyone to be miserable.'

'But?'

Ruby and Tina had clicked immediately when they'd met on the first day of their nursing training at the age of eighteen, and they'd been friends for long enough to have a pretty good idea what each other wasn't saying.

'I feel a bit guilty, that's all.' Ruby wasn't quite ready to admit her feelings for Ellis, but she also knew that Tina was the best person she could float ideas past. Someone who'd be honest with her.

'Why on earth do you feel guilty?' Tina looked puzzled.

'Because tomorrow it'll be a year and a day—the last traditional day of mourning—and over those last months Tom said to me quite a few times that he didn't want me to be alone and grieving for him. He said he wanted me to live a happy life with someone who loves me as much as he did.'

'Now you're putting a lump in my throat.' Tina

hugged her. 'Though he's right—you're still young. In fact, at twenty-nine you're practically a baby.'

Ruby laughed. There were all of six months between them, with Ruby being one of the youngest in their academic year and Tina one of the oldest. 'Thirty's not exactly old, Tina.'

'No.' Tina looked at her. 'Rubes, are you saying you want to date again?'

'I love Tom—I always will—but I think I'm ready to move on. Scattering his ashes today felt a lot like closure,' Ruby said. 'But is everyone going to think I'm heartless and I should wait a lot longer before even thinking about moving on?'

'No. Some people will probably mutter about it being too soon,' Tina said, 'but remember that you can't please all of the people all of the time, so don't let that get to you. It's none of their business. You're the only one who can really say when you're ready.'

'I guess.' Ruby bit her lip. 'I just...' She shook her head and sighed. 'Sorry.'

'As you said, Tom wanted you to be happy and he wanted you to find someone else. You have his blessing, and you don't need anyone else's.'

Even if I fell for his best friend?

But Ruby couldn't quite bring herself to ask that. She'd barely admitted it to herself and she still needed time to get used to the idea.

'You know, we've got a new registrar in Neurology. He's a nice guy. Single. New to London. Maybe...' Tina let the suggestion hang in the air.

'Maybe,' Ruby said.

'Don't make a decision now. Just think about it,' Tina

said gently. 'In the meantime, I think we need a feel-good film and more cake.'

'Brilliant idea. Let's do it,' Ruby said, and ushered her best friend into the living room.

But she found it hard to concentrate on the film, because she couldn't stop thinking about Ellis. Ellis, with his haunted grey eyes. Ellis, who had itchy feet but had stayed in one place for the longest time since his training, specifically to be there for her.

Her husband's best friend.

What if...?

CHAPTER TWO

RUBY EXAMINED MRS HARRIS GENTLY.

'So is everything OK?' Mrs Harris asked anxiously.

'I'm happy with how you're doing,' Ruby said, 'but we do have a tiny complication, in that your little one is quite happy being bottom-down rather than top-down. So I just want a quick chat with the doctor to talk through your options for the birth.'

Mrs Harris bit her lip. 'So the baby's in the wrong position?'

'Bottom-first rather than head-first—it's called being a breech baby,' Ruby explained. 'It's a really common position in early pregnancy, but the baby usually turns by itself into the head-first position before birth. Your baby hasn't turned yet, that's all.'

'Does it mean there's something wrong with the baby?' Mrs Harris asked.

'No. It happens with about three in a hundred babies, and there are all kinds of reasons for it, some of them being plain baby awkwardness because they want to do things their way rather than follow their mum's birth plan,' Ruby reassured her. 'I'll just go and get Dr Webster, and then we can talk it through with him.' She squeezed Mrs Harris's hand. 'Try not to worry. There

are a few things we can do to persuade the baby to turn.'
She smiled, and went to find Ellis in his office.

Her heart skipped a beat when she saw him. Ellis
was wearing a charcoal grey suit, a white shirt and an
understated tie rather than green Theatre scrubs, and he
looked utterly gorgeous. He wouldn't have looked out
of place on the pages of a glossy magazine as a model
for an upmarket perfume house.

And she needed to stop herself thinking like this.
Ellis was her friend and her colleague. Asking for more
was just greedy.

She tapped on the open door and leaned against the
jamb. 'Hey, Ellis. Can I borrow you for a second?'

He looked up and smiled at her, and her heart skipped
another beat.

'Sure. Problem?' he asked.

'Complication,' she said. 'I have a first-time mum
who's thirty-seven weeks. Her baby's quite happily settled in the breech position. I know her birth plan is
firmly centred round a natural birth with no intervention.' And she also knew that a lot of doctors would
take one look at Mrs Harris's situation and immediately
insist on a caesarean section. Given Ellis's experience
outside the hospital, Ruby really hoped that he'd take
a different tack and give Mrs Harris a chance to have
the birth she really wanted. 'So I wondered if you'd
mind coming and chatting through her options for the
birth,' she finished.

'Of course I will. You did warn her that babies never
respect their mum's birth plans, didn't you?'

She smiled back. 'I always do.'

'So what are you thinking?'

'We'll start with an ECV to see if we can get the baby

to turn,' Ruby said. 'But, if it doesn't work, I'm hoping that I can talk one of the obstetricians—' she gave him a pointed look so he'd know she meant him '—into agreeing to a trial of labour for a vaginal breech delivery.'

'I think we've only had a couple on the ward since I've been here, and I wasn't on duty at the time,' Ellis said. 'Are the doctors here not supportive of vaginal breech births?'

'Theo's wonderful,' Ruby said. Theo Petrakis, the director of the maternity ward at the London Victoria, believed in supporting his midwives and keeping intervention to a minimum. 'But, as you say, it's not that common—and I need someone who's had a reasonable amount of experience in delivering breech babies.'

'Which is why you're talking to me?'

She gave him her sweetest smile. 'Got it in one.'

'She's a first-time mum, so we have no guarantee that her pelvis is big enough to cope.' Ellis looked thoughtful. 'OK. If ECV doesn't work then—on condition the baby's not too big or small, the baby's head isn't tilted back and I'm happy that the mum's pelvis is going to cope—I'll support you and you can call me in, even if I'm not on duty when she goes into labour. But in return I need a favour from you.'

Ruby's heart skipped yet another beat. What was he going to ask for?

A kiss?

She shook herself mentally. How ridiculous. She really had to stop fantasising about Ellis. This was totally inappropriate. They were at work, and she needed to keep her professionalism to the forefront. 'Sure. What do you want?'

'I'd like you to talk your mum into letting a couple

of the junior staff observe their first ever breech birth.
One midwife, one doctor.'

'Great minds think alike. I was going to ask you if
there was anyone you wanted to come and observe.'
And she really liked the fact that he'd thought of the
midwifery team, too, not just the obstetricians. She
smiled. 'I want to reassure Mrs Harris that we'll try
our best to help give her the birth experience she really
wants, but I'll make it clear that if the baby's in distress
at any point then we might need to give her a section,
so she needs to be prepared for that to happen.'

'Which is again where I'd come in,' Ellis said.

'Just flutter those disgustingly long eyelashes at her.
Actually, on second thoughts, perhaps you'd better not,'
she said. 'You already look more like a movie star than
a doctor.'

'Very funny, Rubes,' Ellis said, but he didn't look
the slightest bit offended.

Which was another reason why she should put this
whole thing out of her head. If she made an approach to
Ellis and he turned her down...Even though she knew
he'd be kind about it, it would still put a strain on their
friendship. On their working relationship. And Ruby
didn't want to take the risk of wrecking either of them.

Maybe it was just loneliness making her feel this
way, and she should take Tina up on her offer of setting
her up with the new registrar on the Neurology ward.

'Penny for them?' Ellis asked.

No way was she going to tell Ellis what she was
thinking about. 'Just my first-time mum,' she said with
a smile. It was true; it just wasn't the *whole* truth.

Back in the examination room, she introduced Ellis.
'Mrs Harris, this is Dr Ellis Webster, one of our regis-

trars. Ellis, this is Mrs Harris. She's a first-time mum, the baby's thirty-seven weeks, and the baby's quite happy in the breech position.'

'Nice to meet you, Mrs Harris.' Ellis shook her hand and smiled at her. 'Ruby tells me that you'd like as natural a birth as possible.'

'I definitely don't want an epidural. I want to manage with gas and air,' Mrs Harris said. 'And I really didn't want to have a section.' She bit her lip. 'But, because the baby's lying the wrong way, does that mean I have to have a section?'

'It's a possibility,' Ellis said, 'but it might be possible for you to have a vaginal delivery. With the baby being breech, it means that the head—which is the biggest part of the baby—is the last bit to be delivered, so it's a little bit more complicated. May I examine you?'

At her nod, he examined her gently.

'As Ruby said, your baby's definitely bottom-down. But we can try to persuade the baby to move. There's a procedure called an ECV, which stands for external cephalic version. Ruby here's very experienced.'

'What happens is that I'll press down on your abdomen and encourage the baby to turn a somersault—a bit like him doing a forward roll inside your stomach,' Ruby explained.

'And it always works?' Mrs Harris asked.

'It works about for about fifty per cent of babies,' Ellis said. 'And if it doesn't work today, then we can always try again tomorrow. Though I should warn you that even if the baby does turn, sometimes the baby then decides to roll back again.'

'So if you do this ECV thing, what about the baby?'

Mrs Harris asked. 'Will he be OK? It's not going to hurt him?'

'He'll be fine,' Ruby reassured her. 'Plus we'll monitor him before, during and after the ECV to keep an eye on him. There is a tiny risk that you might start having contractions, and also the baby's heart rate might go up a bit—usually it settles again pretty quickly, but I do want you to be aware that sometimes the baby's heart rate doesn't settle again, and in that case you'll need to have a section.'

'But it's a tiny risk?' Mrs Harris checked.

'Tiny,' Ruby confirmed.

'All right, then.' Mrs Harris paused. 'Will it hurt me?'

'It can be a bit uncomfortable, yes,' Ruby said. 'But, if it hurts, all you have to do is tell us and we'll stop immediately.'

Mrs Harris looked worried. 'But if it doesn't work, does that mean I'll have to have a section?'

'The baby's a good weight. He's not too big or too small,' Ellis said. 'Though I would want to check that his neck isn't tilted back before I agree to try a vaginal delivery. If the baby's head is tilted back, then I'm afraid you will need a caesarean section, because that'll be the safest thing for the baby.'

'Is there anything else I can do to help the baby turn, or make sure he stays the right way round if you do the ECV? Can I sit or lie in a certain way?' Mrs Harris asked.

Ruby shook her head. 'I'm afraid it won't make any difference.'

'So why hasn't he turned round the right way? Why is he bottom-down instead of head-down?'

'There are lots of reasons,' Ellis said. 'Sometimes

it's down to the position of your placenta. As I said earlier, the biggest part of the baby is the head, so the baby tends to fidget round and make sure he's in the most comfortable position, which means his head will be in the biggest space—in your lower uterus, so he'll be head-down. But if you have a low-lying placenta, then the biggest space is in your upper uterus, so the baby will be bottom-down.' He smiled. 'Sometimes it's just plain old chance. Babies have a habit of doing things their way, and I know a lot of mums who haven't ended up having the birth they'd set their heart on. So all I'd say is please try not to be disappointed if we can't follow your birth plan to the letter.'

'We'll do our best to make it work for you,' Ruby said, 'but Dr Webster's right—at the end of the day, babies can be very stubborn and they'll do things their way.'

'I think this one's going to be like his dad,' Mrs Harris said ruefully. 'Can Ian be here when you try and make the baby turn round?'

'Of course,' Ruby reassured her. 'We can try this afternoon, just after lunch. Will that give him enough time to get here?'

Mrs Harris nodded. 'I'll call him. Thank you. Both of you.'

'I'll see you later this afternoon, Mrs Harris,' Ellis said with a smile.

The rest of Ruby's clinic ran on time. Just as she broke for lunch, she saw Ellis coming out of the staff kitchen. 'Got time for lunch?' he asked.

'That would be nice,' she said.

They headed down to the canteen, chatting companionably. At the counter, Ellis as usual chose the vegetarian option.

'Any excuse to stuff your face with pasta and garlic bread. You're such a carb junkie,' Ruby teased.

'Protein's important, but I've worked in areas where people are so poor and the cost of raising—' He broke off. 'You're teasing me, aren't you?'

'It's very easy to tease you, Ellis—you're so serious,' she said with a smile. 'Look, I know why you're vegetarian and I admire your principles.'

'But you don't share them,' he finished.

She shook her head. 'I'm sorry, but vegetarian bacon is never going to be as good as the real thing for me.'

He laughed. 'You're such a hedonist. Anyway, Rubes, you can talk about being a carb junkie. I've seen you and Tina with cake. It lasts for about three seconds when you two are around.'

'Busted,' Ruby said with a grin.

'Are you OK about doing the ECV this afternoon?' he asked.

'It's fine,' Ruby said. 'I'd really like to bring Coral, our new trainee midwife, in to observe, if Mrs Harris doesn't mind—and if you don't mind.'

'Of course not. You know I agree with you; it's always a good idea to give students as broad an experience as possible.'

'That's one of the things I like about you—you're so practical and sensible. Thanks,' she said.

Practical and sensible. Not how he'd been when he'd married Natalia, Ellis thought wryly. He'd lost his head and they'd both paid the price.

Though Ruby had said that was *one* of the things she

liked about him. He couldn't help wondering: what else did she like about him?

He shook himself. This really wasn't appropriate. Ruby Fisher was his friend. His best friend's girl—well, widow, but that was a technicality. Time to back off. 'I try to be practical,' he said lightly.

'Ellis, I, um, wanted to run something by you,' she said.

She looked worried, and Ellis frowned. 'What's wrong?'

'Not *wrong*, exactly...but today's a year and a day since Tom died.'

Yeah. He knew. He'd spent the anniversary with her on a Suffolk beach yesterday.

'And a year and a day is supposed to be the traditional length of time for mourning.'

He went cold. Where was she going with this?

'I'm never going to forget Tom,' Ruby said, 'but he always told me that he didn't want me to spend the rest of my life mourning for him, and he wanted me to move on.'

Wait—*what*?

Was she saying that she wanted to date again? That she'd met someone? Who? Where? How? Ellis couldn't quite process this.

'And Tina's going to set me up on a blind date with her new colleague in Neurology,' she finished.

Ruby was really going on a date? With someone else? But—but...

'Ellis? You haven't said anything.' She looked even more worried. 'Do you think it's too soon?'

'I...' He blew out a breath. This was a minefield. If he said the wrong thing now, he'd hurt her—and that was the last thing he wanted to do. 'I think,' he said slowly, 'that you're the best one to judge that. Only you know when you're ready.'

But the idea of seeing her with another man made him feel sick.

It was different when she'd been married to Tom. Ellis would never, ever have done anything to destroy his best friend's marriage. But now Ruby was widowed. And Ellis hated the idea of her going out with someone else.

If she really was ready to date again, maybe he could ask her out himself.

But, if she said no, then how could they go back to their old easy friendship, once they knew they didn't feel the same about each other?

He didn't want to risk losing her.

So he was just going to have to suck it up and deal with it. Even if it felt as if someone had just filleted him.

Typical Ellis. Sensible and measured. *I think you're the best one to judge that.*

Which told Ruby without a doubt that he wasn't interested in her. Otherwise that would've been his cue to suggest that she dated him, wouldn't it?

So it was just as well she hadn't suggested anything to him. It would've put an irreparable strain on their friendship, and she valued him too much to risk losing him.

'I guess you're right,' she said. 'I just didn't want people to think that I was the Merry Widow, not caring about Tom. And I feel guilty about wanting to date again.' She felt even more guilty about the fact that she was attracted to Ellis, particularly as he'd just made it clear it wasn't reciprocated.

'You're always going to love him,' Ellis said. 'But at the end of the day life still goes on. And Tom didn't want you to be lonely. He wanted you to be happy. What anyone else thinks is simply their opinion. They have the right to think whatever they like, but they don't have the right to shove it down your throat. You do what makes you happy, Rubes.'

Yeah.

Though sometimes she wondered if she'd ever find that kind of happiness again. If she was being greedy and expecting too much. Some people didn't even have that kind of happiness once in their lives, so what right did she have to expect to find it twice?

Ellis reached over to squeeze her hand, and her skin tingled all the way up her arm.

'Be happy, Ruby. You've got my full support. And if anyone says otherwise, send them to see me and I'll put them straight.'

He sounded as if he were her big brother.

And she'd just have to learn to see him as a kind of sibling instead of the man she wanted to start dating.

After lunch, Ruby called the Harrises in from the waiting area.

'I was wondering—would you mind if Coral, my trainee midwife, came in and observed the procedure?' she asked.

'No, that's fine, love,' Mrs Harris said. 'I'll do whatever you want if you can get this baby to do that forward roll.'

'I'll do my best. Thank you.' She smiled at Mrs Harris.

'I'm going to check how the baby's doing, first, on the ultrasound. If I'm happy with that, I'll give you some drugs to relax your womb—it won't hurt you or the baby, but it'll mean your baby has a bit more room to do that forward roll.'

'All right. Is that nice doctor going to be here?'

'Dr Webster? Yes. He's just making a quick phone call, and then he'll be right here. And I'll go and collect Coral so I can introduce her to you.' Ruby smiled at her. 'Lie back and bare your tummy for me. Though I'm afraid my gel's a little bit colder than it is in the ultrasound suite.'

'I don't mind,' Mrs Harris said, smiling back.

Once Ruby had established that everything was fine, she moved the screen so that the Harrises could see the baby. 'There he is—looking very comfy right now.'

'Hopefully he won't be stubborn and he'll move,' Mrs Harris said wryly.

'I'll give you those drugs now.' Ruby administered them swiftly. 'Make yourself comfortable, and I'll be right back,' she said.

When she returned, Ellis was already there. Ruby introduced the Harrises to Coral.

'So what we're going to do today is an external cephalic version—ECV, for short. The idea is to move the baby's bottom away from his mum's pelvis,' Ruby explained. 'I've already given Mrs Harris some drugs to help relax her womb, and we've seen the baby on the ultrasound. What I'm going to do now, Mrs Harris, is to push firmly on your abdomen to encourage the baby to do a kind of forward roll. It'll take maybe a minute to a minute and a half. As I said earlier, it might be a little bit uncomfortable but it shouldn't hurt. If it does hurt, I need you to tell me straight away and I'll stop.'

'All right.' Mrs Harris looked nervous, and Ruby noticed that she was holding her husband's hand really tightly.

'You might even see him do a forward roll in your tummy, so keep an eye on my hands,' she said with a smile.

Coral came quietly to the side so she could see and, gently but firmly, Ruby performed the manoeuvre, trying to ease the baby into a transverse position before he moved into the head-down position.

But the baby stubbornly refused to move.

After two minutes, Ruby stopped.

'Is something wrong?' Mr Harris asked anxiously.

'No—just that this baby really doesn't want to move today,' Ruby said.

'The longer the procedure takes, the less likely it is to work,' Ellis explained. 'But try not to worry. We can always try again tomorrow.'

They checked the baby again with the ultrasound. 'He's doing just fine,' Ellis reassured the Harrises. He glanced at the notes. 'Actually, his heart rate is pretty much as it was before Ruby started the ECV, so I'm happy for you to go home now, or you can stay in the waiting room until you're ready.'

'If we try again tomorrow and it still doesn't work, that means I'm going to have to have a section, doesn't it?' Mrs Harris asked.

'Not necessarily,' Ruby reassured her. 'Remember what we said this morning. We can still try for a vaginal delivery if the ECV doesn't work next time. We'll just need a bit of patience.'

'If it helps, I've delivered one or two breech babies in the middle of a field before now,' Ellis added.

'In the middle of a *field*?' Mr Harris looked surprised.

'I worked for a medical aid charity for a few years,' Ellis said. 'So I've delivered babies after natural disasters where there isn't even any running water in the area.'

Mrs Harris bit her lip. 'And here I am, moaning about it all, when I know I'm going to have a comfortable bed and all the medical equipment anyone needs! That's terrible. I feel...' She grimaced. 'Well, guilty, now.'

'You really don't need to. This is all new to you, and it's perfectly natural that you're concerned,' Ellis said. 'Actually, I'd be more concerned if you *weren't* worried.'

'I think she should have a section,' Ian Harris said. 'I looked up breech births on the Internet, and they said it's likely that the baby's head will get trapped or the baby will be brain-damaged.'

'The Internet,' Ellis said gently, 'is full of scary stories. It's the same with magazines—they're going to tell you all about the unusual cases and the dramatic stuff, because it's the drama that sells copies. They won't tell you that most women have a perfectly safe, normal delivery. As Ruby says, you just need a bit of patience with a vaginal breech birth. I believe in being hands off and letting the mum set the pace, and I only intervene if there's a problem.'

'So I won't have to have an episiotomy?' Mrs Harris asked.

'Hopefully not. We'll see how it goes,' Ellis said. 'Though I will say that if your labour isn't progressing after an hour, then I'll recommend a section. In my experience, when labour doesn't progress, it means there's a complication and you need help.'

'All right,' Mrs Harris said.

Ruby could see that Mrs Harris was biting back the tears, and sat down on the bed beside her to hold her other hand. 'We'll do our best for you, I promise,' she said softly. 'We're on your side. All we're saying is that if it doesn't work out quite the way you want it to, then please don't blame yourself. You've given it your best shot and that's more than good enough.'

'OK.' But Mrs Harris still looked close to tears.

Ruby hugged her. 'Hang on in there,' she said. 'It's going to be fine.'

CHAPTER THREE

MRS HARRIS CAME in with her husband the next day for another attempt at the ECV. 'I've been feeling a bit off, all day,' she said. 'I woke up in the middle of the night with a bit of a tummy-ache. Obviously I must've eaten something that didn't agree with me last night.'

Or maybe, Ruby thought, it was something else causing that tummy-ache. She had a funny feeling about this—and her funny feelings were usually right.

'Come and lie down, and I'll examine you before we try the ECV again,' she said.

Mrs Harris had just settled back against the bed when she grimaced. 'Sorry. That was another twinge.'

Ruby examined her gently. 'Has anyone mentioned Braxton-Hicks to you?'

'The practice contractions, you mean?'

'They're the ones,' Ruby said.

'Yes—but I don't think I've had any.' Mrs Harris's eyes widened. 'Hang on—is that what the twinges mean? I'm having a practice contraction?'

'Given that you're three centimetres dilated,' Ruby said, 'then, actually, I think this is the real thing.'

'But I'm only thirty-seven weeks! It's too soon for the

baby to be born.' Mrs Harris bit her lip. 'Do you think it was that ECV thing yesterday that's caused this?'

'Possibly. Or it could be that your baby's just decided that his birthday's going to be today,' Ruby said with a smile. 'Don't worry about him being thirty-seven weeks. Not that many babies are born on their official due date—some are a couple of weeks before, and some are ten days or so late. By this stage your baby's lungs are definitely mature enough to cope with being born.'

'So will I have to have a section?'

'Hopefully not,' Ruby said cheerfully. 'I'm just going to get someone to call Dr Webster for me. And I need to give you a scan to see exactly how the baby's lying.'

'Cold gel again?' Mrs Harris asked ruefully.

'I'm afraid so,' Ruby said.

She came out of the cubicle and asked one of the auxiliary staff to find Ellis for her, then went back to see the Harrises and do the scan. She turned the screen so that the Harrises could see it. 'And here we can see one baby getting ready to be born. His head's tucked forward, just as I'd want it to be, and he's in what we call the frank breech position—that's the least complicated one, with his legs straight up in front of him.'

'So I can try for a normal birth?' Mrs Harris asked.

Ellis arrived in time to hear the question. 'I examined you yesterday and I'm happy that your pelvis is big enough to cope with having the baby. He's not too small, so there's a lower risk of having problems with the cord; and he's not too big, so he's not going to get stuck. I'm happy with the position he's in, with his head nicely tucked forward—so, yes, we can do this.' He smiled. 'As I said yesterday, I believe in keeping things natural as far as possible, so I'm not immediately going to say you'll have to have an episiotomy and forceps to help you deliver. It might end up that way, but we'll do our best to help you have the birth you want. Though I do want to remind you that if your labour doesn't progress, any delays mean that the baby's likely to be in distress and you'll need to have a section. No heroics, OK?'

'Agreed,' Ian Harris said firmly.

'Agreed,' Mrs Harris said, though she didn't sound quite so sure.

Ellis smiled at Ruby. 'Dilation?'

'Three centimetres.'

'OK. It's going to be a while yet before your baby arrives, so I'd suggest walking about a bit—the gravity will help him move down,' Ellis said.

'Would you mind very much if Coral—the trainee midwife you met yesterday—and one of the junior doctors came in to observe?' Ruby asked.

'No, that's fine,' Mrs Harris said. She squeezed her husband's hand. 'We're going to have our baby today, Ian. I can't believe it.'

It was a couple more hours before Mrs Harris was ready to start delivering the baby. Coral, the trainee midwife, and Lance, the new first-year doctor, came in to observe and Ruby introduced them both to the Harrises.

'Being on your elbows and knees will be the most comfortable position for you, as well as being the most effective position for delivering the baby, because you can move about a bit,' Ruby said. 'And resting on your elbows rather than your hands will protect your wrists.'

'Unless you really want an epidural, I'd recommend having either gas and air or pethidine as pain relief,' Ellis added, 'because an epidural will slow everything down.'

'I don't want a section,' Mrs Harris said, 'so I'll manage with gas and air.'

'Good on you,' Ellis said.

'The main thing to remember about a breech birth,' Ruby explained to Coral and Lance, 'is that you keep your hands off and be patient—you don't want the mum clenching her muscles if you touch her.'

'You intervene only if it's clear that the baby needs help,' Ellis said. 'Which is why we're using a foetal monitor to keep an eye on his heart rate.'

Ruby encouraged Mrs Harris to breathe through the contractions.

'I can see the baby now,' she said at last. 'When you have the next contraction, I want you to give a nice big push for me.'

The baby's buttocks arrived first, and then with the next contraction and the next push the back and shoulders were visible.

Ruby glanced at Ellis. As always when she delivered a baby with him, she noticed that he was almost misty-eyed. Ruby was, too; the moment a new life came into the world was so very special, and it was such a privilege to share it.

And Ellis was a particularly good doctor to work with; he was supportive, he listened to both the mum and the midwifery team, and he didn't try to rush any of the mums straight to Theatre at the first sign of a complication.

At the next push, the baby's legs came down.

'Well done,' Ruby said. 'You're doing just great. His legs are down, now. Keep breathing for me.'

The baby's shoulders and arms came out next, and

then Ruby glanced again at Ellis. At his nod, she moved into position, ready to catch the baby.

'Almost here. Next contraction, give me the biggest push you can. Scream if you need to. Shout. Whatever you want to do, that's fine. Just push,' she said.

And finally, the baby's head emerged.

'The baby's not crying,' Mr Harris said, looking panicky.

And the baby was blue. At a first glance, Ruby would give him an Apgar score of four—very low.

'It's fine,' Ellis reassured Mr Harris. 'I know right now this looks very scary, but this is totally normal for a breech birth. Do you want to cut the umbilical cord, and then we can get this little one warmed up a bit and ready for a cuddle?'

Thankfully it was enough to distract Mr Harris; Ruby swiftly clamped the cord and Ellis gave the scissors to Mr Harris to cut the cord while Ruby wrapped the baby in a warm towel.

Ruby then took the baby over to the warming tray for warm air to be blown on him.

'Do you want me to sort out the baby while you deliver the placenta?' Ellis asked.

She smiled at him. 'Yes, please.'

By the time she'd delivered the placenta, she was relieved to hear plenty of crying coming from Baby Harris, and she heard Ellis say, 'I'm pleased to say your little boy's pinked up very nicely indeed. He's got an Apgar score of nine.'

Ruby knew that last bit was aimed for her, and she felt the strain between her shoulders disappear. Everything was fine. And, better still, Ellis also hadn't mentioned anything about hip dysplasia, which could sometimes be a problem with breech babies.

Finally, Baby Harris was in his mum's arms, skin to skin, and took all of three sucks for his first feed before falling asleep.

Ruby examined Mrs Harris. 'I'm pleased to say that you don't need any stitches,' she said. 'You did absolutely brilliantly. Congratulations to both of you.'

'We could never have done it without you,' Mrs Harris said. 'I was so scared we'd have to just do what the doctor said.'

Ruby smiled. 'They're all pretty good here, actually.' She lowered her voice to a stage whisper. 'Though Ellis Webster is a bit special. But don't tell him I said that, or his head will swell so much that he won't be able to walk through the door for a week.'

Mrs Harris laughed.

'Let's get you settled down in the ward,' Ruby said, 'and you can get to know your baby.' She stroked the baby's cheek. 'He's beautiful.'

'Do you have children?' Mrs Harris asked.

'No.' She and Tom had thought very seriously about it, but then Tom had been diagnosed with leukaemia and it had never been the right time to discuss it again after that. 'Maybe one day,' she said wistfully.

And how odd that a picture flashed into her head. Of herself, tired yet glowing with happiness and holding a baby. And of Ellis sitting next to her, holding her hand and stroking the baby's head.

Ridiculous. And totally inappropriate.

Ellis was her friend, and *only* her friend. And she had a date lined up on Saturday night with a completely different man, the new registrar on her best friend's ward. She really shouldn't be thinking about that kind of thing.

Ellis didn't see Ruby over the weekend. He wanted to call her, but he knew she was going on a date with a colleague of Tina's. So he needed to back off. To give her a chance to get to know the guy and enjoy dating again.

Even though what he really wanted to do was to scoop her over his shoulder and carry her off to his lair.

Ridiculous. He knew that Ruby saw him only as a friend. So he was going to have to ignore this stupid antsy feeling. She deserved to feel happy again. It was just a pity it meant she'd find that happiness with another man rather than with him.

So on Monday lunchtime, he summoned his brightest smile when he saw her. 'Want to go grab a sandwich?'

'That'd be nice.'

He waited until they'd sat down in the canteen before he asked, 'So how was your date?'

'Fine.'

Her smile was a little too bright. 'But?' he asked.

She wrinkled her nose. 'He was a nice guy, but I don't think he was ready to date again yet.'

Was that Ruby's way of saying that she'd just discovered she wasn't ready to date again yet, too?

He battened down the hopes as she continued, 'I don't think he's quite over his divorce yet.'

'Ah. Baggage.'

She gave him a rueful smile. 'I guess we all have baggage when we get to this age.'

'Mmm.'

'Look at you,' she said softly.

Oh, no. He really didn't want to discuss that. He didn't like talking about his feelings. And he definitely didn't want to talk about his baggage. Ruby knew he was divorced, but he hadn't told her the whole messy story.

'Tom always said you'd never settle because you were trying to save people, to make up for the way they couldn't save your sister.'

'I guess that's part of it,' he said. 'Though I always wanted to be a doctor, even when Sally was still alive.' After Sally's death, he'd vowed to work abroad rather than stay in an English hospital, and it had caused a rift with his brothers; they couldn't understand why he risked himself the way he did, and they'd told him they didn't want to lose him the way they'd lost Sally. But, however much he'd tried to talk them round, he hadn't been able to make them see that he wanted to save all the other potential Sallys, and to do that it meant working abroad. 'And it's not why I became an obstetrician, either. I always planned to work in emergency medicine, like Tom. But then I did a rotation on the maternity ward and I fell in love with it—that special moment where you witness the miracle of a brand new life.'

'That's why I became a midwife, too,' she said softly. 'It never, ever gets old.'

'And it's even better in a world where things are sticky and you really feel that you need a miracle to happen and make things better. That first little cry...' Every time, it made him misty-eyed and glad to be alive, all at the same time.

'You still have itchy feet, don't you?' she asked. 'I know you're going back to the medical aid charity in a couple of months.'

'It's been arranged for a really long time,' Ellis said. And he did want to go back. The trouble was, he also wanted to stay in London. But he wasn't sure if he could—not if Ruby started dating someone else and it got serious. He'd promised Tom that he'd be there for Ruby, and he'd keep his promise; but he wasn't sure that his promise could stretch to watching her date another man and being happy about it. 'Anyway, we weren't talking about me,' he said, trying very hard to wriggle out of the subject. 'We were talking about your date.'

'I guess it was a case of nice guy, wrong time,' she said with a shrug.

'Would he be the right guy at a different time?' It was a bit like prodding a bruise, but Ellis wanted to know.

'Probably not,' she said. 'There wasn't that spark between us. Whereas the first time I saw Tom…'

'Yeah. I know.' He reached across and squeezed her hand briefly.

Mistake. Because every nerve-end in his own hand tingled at the contact.

He knew about sparks, all right. Ruby most definitely made him feel that spark. His feelings for anyone he'd dated before just paled by comparison—including his ex-wife. But Ruby was vulnerable, she was still missing Tom, and she was still probably not quite ready to move on. Adding his job to the mix…In his book, it all made her very firmly off limits.

'Hey. If you're not busy with a date at the weekend, maybe we could do something together,' he said lightly. 'There's that new action film.'

'You want me to go and see a guy-flick with you?' She laughed. 'Ellis, much as I love you…'

As a friend, he reminded himself sharply.

'....action flicks really aren't my favourites.'

'Hey, this one has a plot,' he protested.

'As if,' she scoffed, still laughing. 'All right, if you're so desperate to see it, I'll go with you. But it's on the understanding that I want ice cream *and* popcorn.'

'Deal,' he said. It wasn't a *date* date. But it would be enough. Because he didn't have the right to ask for more.

CHAPTER FOUR

IT WAS A busy week on the ward. Ruby's favourite day of the week was spent delivering twins in a birthing pool; the water birth was calm and peaceful, and it was a good experience for Coral, as well as being exactly what the mum wanted.

Saturday afternoon turned out to be dull and rainy, so she went to the cinema with Ellis to see the action flick. As promised, he bought her popcorn and ice cream; although the film wasn't really her cup of tea, she still enjoyed his company.

After going to a tiny bistro for pasta and a bottle of red wine, Ellis saw her home.

'Want to come in for some coffee?' she asked.

'I'd love to. Thanks.' He smiled at her.

When they were both sprawled comfortably on the sofa with a mug of coffee, Ruby said, 'Tina says I shouldn't give up on the dates just yet.'

'She's planning to set you up on a blind date with another of her colleagues?' Ellis asked.

'No. She suggested I try one of those online match-making sites.' She looked at him and raised an eyebrow. 'What, you don't approve?'

'It's not like going on a blind date with someone

who's a friend of a friend, which means you sort of know them already, or at least know that they're OK. With a dating site, you're planning to meet a total stranger,' Ellis said. 'And people don't always tell the truth on those things. They can put a photograph up that's years out of date and claim to like a lot of interesting things, just to get someone to pick them for a date.'

'Maybe the odd person would do that—odd in *both* senses of the word—but most people don't do that sort of thing. Don't be such a cynic. And think about it, Ellis. Once you're our age, most of your friends are in a relationship and so most of their friends, which means you know hardly anyone else who's single. Apart from through friends or work, how else are you going to meet someone?'

'I guess you have a point,' he said.

She paused. 'Actually, you know, you could try it.'

'What?'

'Putting your profile on a dating site.'

'Why?' He looked at her in bewilderment.

'Because you haven't dated at all in the last year or so.'

'Yes, I have,' he protested.

'Here and there. Nothing serious.'

No. Because he didn't do serious relationships. Not since his divorce. He preferred to keep things light and uncomplicated, and he'd concentrated on his career rather than his love life. Not to mention the fact that he'd been fighting off inappropriate feelings towards Ruby for months. 'I've been busy,' he prevaricated.

'Ellis, you really don't have to put your life on hold for me,' she said gently.

He froze at her words. Did she *know*?

'I know Tom asked you to look after me, but that shouldn't be at the expense of your own happiness.'

He relaxed again. Clearly she was just thinking of his promise to Tom, and she didn't have a clue how he felt about her. Which was just as well. Because he didn't know how she felt about him—or if she could ever come to see him as anything more than her late husband's best friend. 'I'm fine as I am,' he said.

'But don't you get lonely, Ellis?'

'From time to time I do,' he admitted. 'But I have good friends and a job I love. That's enough for me.' And if he kept telling himself that, eventually he'd end up believing it.

At work on Tuesday morning, Ellis had a written request from the court. Something he really wasn't expecting. And something he really wanted to talk to Ruby about.

He went in search of her. 'Got a minute?' he asked. 'There's something I want to run by you.'

'Sorry, I've got wall to wall appointments this morning,' she said. 'And I'm running late. Can I come and grab you at lunchtime?'

'Sure—there's no immediate rush.'

Except at lunchtime Ellis had been called away to help at a difficult birth, and when he was on a break in the afternoon Ruby was in the middle of delivering a baby.

In the end he ended up meeting her after work for a drink.

'So what did you want to run by me?' she asked.

'I had a written request for information this morning,' he said. 'From the court.'

'The court?' She blinked. 'That sounds ominous.'

He shook his head. 'Nothing that should worry anyone in the department—it isn't a negligence case or anything. It's to do with a baby you and I delivered about a year ago—little Baby Edwards. Sadly, his parents have split up, and Billy Edwards wanted a paternity test.'

She grimaced. 'That's sad—and even sadder still because it's probably not that unusual nowadays.'

'This case is definitely unusual,' he said. 'That's why the court wrote to me. The results came back and showed that Billy Edwards is the baby's father.'

Ruby looked puzzled. 'So if he's the father, which proves the paternity, why did the court write to you?'

'Because it turns out that Grace Edwards isn't the baby's mother.'

Her frown deepened. 'How come? Was she an IVF mum with a donated egg?'

'No. I looked up the paperwork today. Conception and pregnancy were all without any complications or intervention. Grace Edwards only had a section because the baby was getting distressed.'

'So if her former husband was definitely the father and the egg was hers, then surely Grace has to be the baby's mother? I mean, that's basic biology, Ellis.'

'You'd think so—but the genetic tests say not. And DNA doesn't lie.'

'Maybe there was an error in the tests?' she suggested.

He shook his head. 'They did a second set of DNA tests, just to make sure there wasn't some kind of error in the first set. The results show exactly the same thing: Baby Edwards is genetically related to Billy, but not to Grace.'

She blinked. 'This is surreal. How is that even possible, Ellis?'

'That,' he said dryly, 'is why the court's written to me. I'm going to discuss it with Theo Petrakis, but I wanted to talk to you first, to see if you remembered anything unusual about the birth.'

'No. I mean, I'd probably have to reread the paperwork to refresh my memory, because I can't remember every detail of every single baby I've ever delivered over the years.' She frowned. 'But I guess all midwives would remember births that have any out-of-the-ordinary features. I don't remember this one being an unusual case.'

'I'm going to have a chat with one of the genetic counsellors, too. Just to see if I'm missing something,' Ellis said. 'Because there definitely feels as if there's a piece of the puzzle missing. I just can't work out what.'

'Well, if you want a wing-woman, come and grab me,' she said.

Any time, he thought, but stopped himself before he said something stupid. 'Thanks.'

The following weekend, Ellis and Ruby were sitting on the balcony of his flat overlooking the park, enjoying the unseasonably mild evening and a bottle of wine.

'Tina was nagging me again this morning about signing up for the dating website,' Ruby said. She wrinkled her nose. 'Though I don't think I'll ever meet anyone who matches up to Tom.'

'Of course you won't, but it's still relatively early days,' Ellis said.

'So it's too soon to date again?'

'Only you can answer that,' he said. And even though he wanted to tell her to look right under her nose, he was going to do the supportive thing. The *right* thing. 'We could always make a list of what you're looking for from your perfect man.'

'You'd help me do that?'

'I guess Tina would probably be better at that than I would,' he said.

'But you could give me feedback from a male point of view—which my best friend, being female, can't,' she pointed out.

'OK. Let's do it the old-fashioned way—pen and paper, first.' He went into the living room and fetched a notebook and pen. 'What do you want to do first?'

'My profile, I guess. How do I describe myself?' she asked.

The most beautiful woman in the world. Not that he was going to say that out loud. But with that elfin crop and those huge blue eyes, she reminded him of Audrey Hepburn. Though there was nothing fragile and Holly Golightlyish about Ruby. She was strong. Brave. Gorgeous.

He looked at her. 'Pretty, petite midwife?'

She groaned. 'No, because then I'll get all sleazy stuff about men wanting naughty nurses in super-short uniforms. I don't want to have to deal with that.'

'How about pretty, petite professional?' he suggested.

'And that's three Ps in a row—it looks wrong.'

He laughed. 'Make that four and add "picky".'

She laughed back. 'I guess.'

'I know. Pretty, petite medical professional seeks...' He paused. 'So what are you looking for, Ruby?'

'Someone taller than me,' she said.

'That's not exactly difficult, given that you're all of five foot two,' he teased.

She cuffed him. 'All right, we'll skip height. And, actually, looks aren't really that important.'

'So you don't want a guy who looks like a movie star?'

'Well, no woman with red blood in her veins is going to turn down a man who looks like Brad Pitt,' she said. 'But, seriously, it's personality that's more important.'

'Good sense of humour?'

'But not someone who does constant wisecracks—that'd drive me mad. And I don't like people who make someone else the butt of their humour all the time; I think that's mean-spirited.'

'Serious, then.'

'But with a nice smile and a sense of fun.'

'As I said, picky. Serious male with a nice smile and sense of fun.' He paused. 'Do you think you should add "professional" in there, too?'

'Could do.'

He wrote it down. 'What else?'

'Not a sports fiend. I don't want to spend my week-ends freezing cold at the side of a football pitch. Some-one who likes films, a wide range of music and long walks.'

'OK. And what are you looking for? Friendship? Romance?'

'Both,' she said. 'I want to be friends as well as lovers.'

Yeah. *So did he.*

'Friendship leading to potential romance,' he said.

'You sound as if you've done this before. Or read a lot of personal ads.'

He smiled. 'I can assure you, I've never dated any-one through a personal ad. It's usually someone I've met through work.'

'But you haven't dated that much since I've known you.'

Partly because he didn't do serious relationships; and partly because he hadn't met anyone who made him feel even the slightest way that Ruby made him feel. It wasn't fair to date someone when you knew you couldn't give the relationship a real chance. When your heart was held elsewhere. 'I've been busy,' he said blandly.

'Maybe now's your chance to try it. We'll do your profile, next,' she said.

'Hey—I'm not planning to join a dating site,' he protested.

'Fair's fair,' she said. 'If I'm doing this, so are you. Hand over the pen and paper.'

He gave in.

'So. TDH doctor.'

'TDH?'

'Tall, dark and handsome.' She rolled her eyes. 'Come off it, Ellis. Even you must know that one.'

'Along with GSOH,' he deadpanned. 'What everyone says in their profile.'

'You're serious and deep,' she said.

He grimaced. 'Which makes me sound boring.'

'No, you do have a sense of fun—it's just that sometimes you need teasing out of your shell. Serious and deep,' she repeated, 'with principles.'

'And now I sound like a character from a Victorian novel. The one who doesn't get the girl because he's stuffy.'

'You're not stuffy, Ellis.' She grinned. 'Principles and dimples.'

'Dimples?' He looked at her, mystified.

'When you smile. You do know I've heard some of

the mums on the ward sigh over you? As well as all the female staff?'

'No, they don't.' He groaned. 'OK. We need to stop this, right now.'

She shook her head. 'Uh-uh. We're doing this. What are you looking for, Ellis?'

He could lie.

Or he could take a risk and tell her the truth.

'Someone bright and sparkly, to make my dimples come out,' he said softly.

'That's better,' she said. 'Vegetarian?'

'No, not necessarily,' he said. 'I'm looking for someone who enjoys food, films and walking by the sea.'

'For friendship leading to potential romance?'

'That sounds about right. So what do we have?' He shifted so they could both see the notepad, and flicked back to the page he'd written on.

'Pretty, petite medical professional seeks serious professional male with a nice smile and sense of fun, who likes films, music and long walks, for friendship leading to potential romance,' he read aloud.

She took the notebook from him and turned over to the next page.

'TDH doctor, serious and deep—with principles— seeks bright, sparkly female to make his dimples come out. Looking for foodie film-buff who enjoys seaside strolls, for friendship leading to potential romance.'

He groaned again. 'I hate that bit about the dimples. It sounds really pathetic.'

'Tough. It's staying. Your dimples are cute.' She flicked back to her list. 'You know, Ellis, this list could be describing you.'

His heart skipped a beat.

Was this the chance he'd been looking for? Was she telling him in her quiet, understated way, that she'd consider dating him?

'And my list,' he said softly, 'could be describing you.'

They looked at each other, and it felt as if the air was humming.

Should he make a move?

If he did and she reacted the wrong way, he could always blame the wine tomorrow morning, apologise profusely, and rescue their friendship.

And if he made a move and she reacted the right way...

'Maybe,' he said, 'neither of us needs to put an ad on the dating site.'

She didn't pull away or look horrified at the idea.

So he leaned forward and gave in to what he'd wanted to do for a year or more. He touched his mouth very lightly to hers.

CHAPTER FIVE

RUBY'S MOUTH TINGLED as Ellis's lips brushed hers very lightly. Warm. Sweet. Exploring rather than demanding. Gentle. Every kiss, every touch, made her want more.

She'd dreamed of this moment, but the reality was something else. Full of delight—and full of terror. Delight, because now she knew that the attraction she felt towards Ellis was mutual; but terror, because if this all went wrong she knew she'd lose him from her life, and she didn't have the strength to cope with losing anyone else right now.

When he broke the kiss and drew back, his eyes were dark. With worry, guilt or both? she wondered. Because she couldn't tell a thing from his expression. And she was racked with panic.

'Sorry. I shouldn't have done that. I…' He broke off with a grimace.

'No.' She reached across and took his hand. 'Ellis. You and I…we're friends.'

'Yes. Of course.'

'I like being with you,' she said carefully.

'Uh-huh.'

Now he sounded as if he'd gone into polite and neutral mode. So did he think this was a mistake? Or was he worried that she thought it was a mistake? Maybe she needed to take the risk and be totally honest with him.

'You tick every box on my list. But if I date you...' She took a deep breath. 'It scares me, Ellis. You don't tend to date women very often, and when you do the relationship doesn't last for very long. And you're going back to the medical aid charity in a couple of months.'

'For a month's assignment, yes,' he confirmed. 'As you know, I'm helping to set up a new medical centre in Zimbabwe.'

'But isn't that...' She looked at him wide-eyed. There was so much unrest in the country. It was a huge risk.

As if he guessed what she was thinking, he said quietly, 'It's an area that's fairly remote and really in need of help. Especially obstetrics. There are so few medics, and so many fatalities that could easily be prevented.'

Which she knew was a huge draw for him. Even though he'd said he hadn't become an obstetrician for his sister's sake, she knew that he wanted to make a difference, the way someone should've made a difference for her. Of course he needed to be there.

But was he going just to set it up? Or would he stay for a few months after that?

'And what happens after your month's assignment?' she asked.

'I don't actually have an answer for that right now,' he admitted.

Ruby said nothing, but Ellis could see the worry in her eyes. She was clearly thinking that if he dated her, she was going to end up being hurt when he left.

Hurting her was the last thing he'd ever want to do. And even though right now he really wanted to kiss her again—kiss her until they both forgot the world outside—he knew he had to do the decent thing. The unselfish thing.

'OK. Let's forget all about this and stick to being just friends,' he said.

'Yes. No.' She shook her head. 'I don't know. I wasn't expecting this.'

'I'm sorry.'

'I'm not. And I am. And...' She grimaced. 'I'm not making any sense at all, am I?'

'No, you're not,' he agreed, and she noticed the slightest glint of humour in his eyes. Though she knew he was laughing with her rather than at her.

Time for another burst of honesty, perhaps, she thought. 'I wanted you to kiss me just now,' she told him.

His face was completely inscrutable now, and she had no idea whether she was fixing a problem or making things even more of a mess.

'But, at the same time, it scares me. I can't afford to lose you from my life, Ellis. And your relationships never last for very long. You said yourself that you've never settled for anyone, not even your ex-wife—and you're going away again soon and you don't really know if you're coming back.'

'I haven't settled down because I've never met anyone who really made me want to settle down, not in the long term,' he said.

She hadn't pushed him about the details of his marriage, though he'd made it very clear when they'd talked in the past that he wasn't still in love with his ex. But when he said he'd never met anyone who made him want to settle, did that also include her? Ruby wondered.

Or could she be the one who could make him feel differently about settling down?

'Plus you're Tom's best friend,' she said. 'And I feel guilty.'

'Did you feel guilty about dating Tina's colleague?' he asked.

'No,' she admitted.

'So what's the difference between dating him and dating me?'

'Because I know you.' Because Ellis *mattered*—though she didn't quite want to admit that. And because the world needed people like Ellis, people who were prepared to be selfless and make a difference. Asking him to stay would be so selfish of her.

'You could,' he said, 'pretend that you don't know me. Pretend that I'd just answered your ad.'

She was still holding his hand; he rubbed his thumb gently against her palm. 'Ruby. You said you wanted to date again. But at the same time it scares you, right?'

'Right,' she admitted.

'Because you're worried it will go wrong?'

If he'd asked her the question about anyone else, she would've said no. But where Ellis was concerned, she worried that it would go wrong. That she'd lose him back to the medical aid charity—that his month's assignment would turn into two, then six, then a year... That he'd quietly vanish from her life, just as quietly as he'd walked in and become her rock when Tom was diagnosed with leukaemia. Leaving her lonely again. And feeling guilty for feeling lonely, because she knew what he did was important, and in the scheme of things her loneliness was the proverbial hill of beans.

'I don't know,' she said, feeling more confused than she had in a long time.

'What shift are you on, on Friday?' he asked.

'Early.'

'Then why don't we give it a try on Friday evening?' he suggested.

'Have an actual date, you mean?'

'Uh-huh.'

She took a deep breath. 'Doing what exactly?'

'Dinner, maybe. Dancing. Whatever you'd like to do.'

Would there be more kissing? Her body flooded with heat at the idea.

'Ruby?' he asked softly.

Could she be brave and take the risk—date the man she'd started to think of as more than just a friend? And could she squash the guilt she felt about dating again? She swallowed hard. 'Provided we go Dutch, OK.'

'No. If I ask someone out to dinner, that means I'm paying,' he said firmly. 'And there aren't any strings attached, if that's what you're worrying about. Dinner is just dinner. End of.'

'Then do I get to pay next time? To keep it fair?'

He frowned. 'I'm more than happy to pay for your dinner, Ruby. I'm not expecting you to...' He blew out a breath. 'Well. That's not how I operate.'

She knew what he wasn't saying. He wasn't expecting her to sleep with him in exchange for her dinner. The problem was...she did want to sleep with him. And that made her feel even more awkward and guilty. What was wrong with her? Was it just that it had been a while since she'd been physically sated? Was this some crazy hormonal thing? Or was it more than that? The whole thing left her feeling like a confused mess. 'I guess.'

'So will you have dinner with me on Friday, Ruby?' he asked softly.

'I...'

'We'll take it light and easy. We dress up a bit, eat nice food, drink lovely wine, then maybe go dancing if you'd like to.'

It sounded so good. Everything she wanted. But did she want more from this relationship than he did? And why was she so drawn to Ellis anyway—when she knew he loved his job working abroad, always on the move, and she wanted something different? If she looked at it sensibly, Ellis was the last person she should date. He didn't want the same things out of life that she did. He'd been brilliant, a total rock since he'd come back to London for Tom, but she knew he couldn't put his life on hold for ever. That wouldn't be fair. And their real lifestyles weren't compatible, with him moving on all the time and her staying in the same place.

To cover her confusion and her worries, she asked, 'Can you even dance?'

'That's for me to know,' he said, 'and you to find out. Provided you wear high heels and lipstick.' He brought her hand up to his mouth and kissed the back of her fingers, looking her straight in the eyes as he did so. And it sent desire licking all the way down her spine. How had she never noticed before just how hot Ellis was?

'Friday,' he said. 'I'll pick you up at seven. And I'll see you at work tomorrow.'

Dating Ellis.

The very idea put Ruby into a flat spin.

And she couldn't get those kisses out of her head.

The way his mouth had felt against her skin…Her whole body tingled at the memory.

She still couldn't quite believe that she'd agreed to this. And, worse still, that she'd actually told him she was attracted to him and he ticked all the boxes on her wish list for a partner.

He should have run a mile. Especially given that he didn't date much and his relationships never lasted long. And, given that he was planning to leave England again in a couple of months and he wasn't totally sure that he was coming back, he shouldn't be interested in her. He should've brushed everything aside.

But he hadn't.

He'd actually asked her out.

And he'd said that she fitted his wish list, too.

This could be perfect. Happiness she'd never expected to find again—and with a man Tom would most definitely approve of, because he'd loved Ellis like a brother.

Yet it could also be the worst mistake she'd ever made. How awkward would it make things at work if things went wrong between them? He wasn't just her friend, he was one of the colleagues she liked working with most.

And what would happen when he left? Could they make a go of a long-distance relationship, or could they find some sort of compromise? Or would it end up being a total mess?

She was going to have to be very, very careful.

In the middle of a busy morning on the ward, Ellis got a call from one of the ultrasonographers. 'Ellis, can I have a second opinion?'

'Sure. What's the problem?'

'I'm not happy with the baby I'm scanning right now. I think the baby's showing signs of anaemia—the blood flow's a bit too quick for my liking.'

Ellis knew that meant the baby's blood was likely to be thinner, with fewer red blood cells—and that might mean the need for surgical intervention to correct the anaemia. 'How old is the baby, and who's the mum's midwife?' he asked.

'The baby's twenty-six weeks, and the midwife's Ruby.'

The best person he could've hoped for. She always developed a real rapport with her mums. Ellis loved working with her—which was probably the best reason for him not to date her and risk that working relationship. He pushed the thought away. 'OK. I'm coming now, and I'll see if I can get Ruby to come with me.'

She was in the middle of a consultation, but agreed to come along as soon as she was done.

The ultrasonographer introduced him quickly to Mrs Perkins. 'Dr Webster's just come along to give me a second opinion,' she explained.

As soon as Ellis looked at the screen, he agreed with her assessment: the baby's blood flow was definitely too quick.

'Is something wrong with my baby?' Mrs Perkins asked, looking worried.

'At the moment it's just a precaution, so try not to worry,' he said. 'It might be that the baby's a little bit anaemic, but we can to do something to sort that out. Do you mind if I look at your notes?'

As soon as Ellis saw Mrs Perkins's blood group, he had a pretty good idea of what the problem was. 'Your blood group's rhesus negative,' he said. 'And I can see here that you've been having anti-D injections.'

She nodded. 'They're not the nicest things in the world, but it's worth it to keep the baby safe.'

Clearly it had been explained to her that if the baby's blood group was rhesus positive, her body would develop antibodies that would cross the placenta and attack the baby's red blood cells, causing anaemia. Injections of anti-D would stop her body developing antibodies.

Except, by the look of it, the anti-D hadn't worked. So there was a little more to this than met the eye.

'And your husband's blood group is rhesus positive?' he asked.

She nodded. 'That's why they said I had to have the anti-D, because the baby's blood was likely to be rhesus positive as well.'

At that point, Ruby came in. 'Hello, Helen.' She smiled at Mrs Perkins and squeezed her hand. 'How are you doing?'

'I'm fine, but they think my baby's anaemic.' Mrs Perkins bit her lip. 'And I had all the anti-D injections. I didn't miss a single one.'

'I know.'

'There is one circumstance where the anti-D doesn't work,' Ellis said quietly, coming to sit on her other side. 'I apologise in advance if this brings back any bad memories, and I know your notes say that this is your first baby, but have you ever been pregnant before?'

'I don't think so,' Mrs Perkins said.

'It might be possible,' Ruby said gently, 'that you didn't realise you were pregnant—that maybe your period was a bit late and you put it down to stress, and then your period was heavier than normal.'

'I...' Mrs Perkins shook her head, and a tear trickled down her cheek. 'This is so stupid. I can't remember.'

'It could have been a long time ago,' Ellis said. 'But it's really common for women to be pregnant, not realise it, and lose the baby before they have any idea they might be pregnant. If that happened to you, it's very possible that your body was already sensitised to the antibodies, so the anti-D wouldn't work for you.'

'So it's my fault the baby's anaemic?'

'Not at all,' he reassured her, squeezing her hand. 'You did everything by the book. It's just one of these things. But I would like to do some more tests, Mrs Perkins. I'd like to take a blood sample from the baby.'

'How does that work?' she asked.

'I take a tiny, tiny sample from the baby with a needle—it's not so nice for you, because it means putting a needle through your abdomen into your womb,' he said. 'The same way an amniocentesis is done.'

She shook her head. 'It doesn't matter about me. I just want the baby to be all right.'

'I promise you, we're going to keep a close eye on you so you don't have to worry,' Ruby said.

'We can do the sample right here, right now—or we can wait for someone to come and be with you, if you'd rather,' Ellis said.

'I want Joe,' Mrs Perkins said. 'My husband. He was supposed to be here for the scan, but there was an emergency at work and he got called in.' Another tear trickled down her cheek. 'Or am I putting the baby at risk by waiting?'

Ruby put an arm round her shoulders and hugged

her, and Ellis handed her a tissue. 'No, you're not. It's absolutely fine to wait until your husband can be here before we do the blood test,' he reassured her.

'What happens if the baby's anaemic?'

'I don't want to frighten you, but severe anaemia can cause the baby's heart to fail, or even mean that you have a stillbirth,' he said gently. 'But we can tell how much of a problem the anaemia is from that blood sample, and if necessary we can give the baby a blood transfusion.'

Mrs Perkins looked shocked. 'You mean I'll have the baby today? But I'm only twenty-six weeks! That's...' She shook her head. 'Surely I can't have the baby now?'

'No, you won't be having the baby today. I mean we can do a transfusion through a needle while the baby's still in your womb,' Ellis explained gently. 'We'll do it under a local anaesthetic so you won't feel it, but it does mean you'll need to stay in overnight, and we'll need to do this every couple of weeks until the baby's born. But the transfusions will stop the anaemia.'

'I'll call Joe for you, shall I?' Ruby asked.

Mrs Perkins nodded. 'But if the baby's anaemic, how come I didn't feel any different? And I've made sure I've eaten plenty of leafy green veg, and I eat lean red meat twice a week.'

'It's honestly not anything you've done,' Ellis reassured her. 'And that diet sounds about perfect for you and the baby. Try not to worry. And I'll see you a bit later this afternoon, OK?'

The baby's blood sample showed a worrying level of anaemia, so Ellis and Ruby went to see Mr and Mrs Perkins.

'Is our baby all right?' Mrs Perkins asked.

'The sample says the baby's anaemic, but as I explained earlier, a blood transfusion will fix that,' Ellis said.

'So the baby gets a transfusion while still inside Helen?' Mr Perkins asked. 'Isn't that dangerous?'

'It's invasive, yes, and you're right that the procedure gives a very small risk of miscarriage or early labour,' Ruby said.

'What if the baby doesn't have the transfusion?' Mr Perkins asked.

'Then the anaemia will get worse and it could cause other problems.'

'Such as?' Mr Perkins asked.

'The baby might develop heart problems. And I'm sorry to say that, in the worst case scenario, the baby could be stillborn.'

Mr Perkins went white.

'My advice is that, although it's an invasive treatment, the baby needs the blood transfusion, and the advantages outweigh the risks,' Ellis said gently.

'If we say yes, how does it work?' Mrs Perkins asked.

'We'll give you a local anaesthetic to numb the area so you won't feel it,' Ellis said. 'And we'll give you a sedative to relax you, plus a sedative to the baby to make sure that the baby doesn't move during the procedure.'

'That means you won't feel the baby moving for a little while afterwards,' Ruby said, 'but that's perfectly normal and the sedative will wear off for both of you within a couple of hours.'

'We'll do an ultrasound scan to show us where the baby is,' Ellis continued, 'and then we'll give the baby a few millilitres of blood through a needle in the umbilical cord—that means the blood's absorbed better.'

'And it's a one-off?' Mrs Perkins asked.

'We'll give you weekly scans from now on,' Ellis said, 'to see how the baby's doing—but it's quite likely that the baby will need a transfusion every two to four weeks until birth.'

Mr Perkins looked at them, wide-eyed. 'Whose blood does the baby get?'

'It's donated blood, fully screened—type O rhesus positive,' Ellis said.

'I'm O positive. Can I give the blood?' Mr Perkins asked.

'I'll check with the haematologist, and you'll need to have some tests before they can say yes, but if it's OK with the haem team then it's more than fine by me,' Ellis said. 'From now on you'll be under my care and Ruby's, so you'll always see us when you come to the hospital—and if you ever have any worries at any time, I want you to ring us or come and see us, OK? Because that's what we're here for—to look after you and to reassure you if you're concerned about anything, no matter how small it might seem.'

'OK. We'll do it.' Mrs Perkins bit her lip. 'When does the first one happen?'

'Today,' Ellis said. 'And I'd like you to stay in overnight, just so we can keep an eye on you.'

'I agree,' Mr Perkins said. 'If anything happens, Helen, you'll be in the right place.'

'But the chances of anything happening are really, really small,' Ellis reassured them. 'Is there anyone you need to call?'

'No—but can I stay with Helen while it's being done?' Mr Perkins asked.

'Of course you can,' Ruby said.

To Ellis's relief, the haematology tests meant that Mr Perkins was able to donate the blood. The procedure only took a couple of minutes, and he and Ruby talked the Perkinses through every single step, making sure they could see the baby on the screen and pointing out the baby's heart beating to reassure them that the sedative wasn't a problem.

'As Ruby said earlier, it takes up to three hours for the sedative to wear off,' Ellis reminded them afterwards. 'Don't worry if you don't feel the baby moving for a little while. I'm going to prescribe antibiotics to make sure you don't get any infection. But if you feel hot or any kind of pain, or there's any redness or bleeding around the area where I injected you, tell the nursing staff straight away, OK? And I'll be in to see you later.'

'Now that's something you couldn't have done in the middle of a field or an earthquake,' Ruby said to Ellis softly when Helen Perkins had gone up to the ward to settle in. 'And you loved every second of it, didn't you?'

'Cutting edge stuff, you mean? Yes, I did,' he admitted. 'What I like most is being able to make a real difference.'

And now he'd seen that he could make a real difference working in a London hospital just as easily as he could working for a medical aid charity, Ruby hoped that would mean he was more likely to come back to London after his assignment.

'Are you still OK for Friday?' he asked.

She nodded. 'I'm still OK.'

'Good.'

To her shock, he leaned over and kissed her swiftly on the mouth.

'Ellis!' she said.

'Just checking,' he said softly. 'See you later. I want to go and make sure that Helen Perkins has settled in OK.'

And she'd just bet he'd ring in later that evening when he was off duty, just to make sure. It was the kind of man he was. A good man, one who cared deeply.

But the idea of actually dating him still thrilled her and terrified her in equal measures. It could be oh, so good between them. But what if his month's assignment made him realise how much he loved moving on? What if his itchy feet came back? Would he expect her to go with him? She didn't want to leave the London Victoria; she loved her job here. Yet she also knew that Ellis loved his freedom. So one of them would have to make a sacrifice. She didn't want Ellis to have regrets or feel trapped because of her; that wasn't fair. If he came back after his assignment, it had to be because he wanted to be with her, not because he felt any obligation towards her or to Tom. Ruby didn't want Ellis to give up everything for her sake, and she had a feeling that Ellis wouldn't want to make her give up everything for his sake, either.

So maybe she should call off the date. Push the attraction to one side and be sensible. Find someone else—someone who was quite happy to stay in London.

The problem was, the attraction between them was growing stronger by the day. Especially since she'd discovered that it was mutual and that Ellis didn't think of her as just a friend.

Maybe, then, she should just stop thinking. Let it happen. And hope that it was going to work out.

CHAPTER SIX

RUBY WAS GLAD of a super-busy day on Friday so she didn't have time to think about her date with Ellis that evening.

When she got home after her shift, she spent ages working out what to wear.

He'd said high heels and lipstick. Which meant dressing up. She tried on every dress in her wardrobe, and in the end she opted for her favourite little black dress, teamed with high heels.

She'd just finished doing her make-up when the doorbell went. She glanced at her watch. Dead on seven. So it wasn't a neighbour or an unexpected delivery; it was Ellis.

A shiver ran down her spine. She felt ridiculously nervous. There was no reason for it: this was Tom's best friend, a man she'd known for eighteen months and who'd been there for her at her darkest hour. A man she knew she could rely on. So she shouldn't be in the slightest bit edgy about seeing him.

Yet tonight was different—their first date—and it felt as if butterflies were doing a stampede in her stomach.

She opened the door. He looked breathtakingly

handsome in a dark suit, crisp white shirt and silk tie. His smile was slightly shy as he handed her a bouquet of pink roses.

'I thought red ones might be a bit over the top,' he said.

She smiled back at him. 'Thank you, Ellis. They're beautiful. I'll just put them in water. Come in.'

'You look lovely.'

Was it her imagination or did he sound as nervous as she felt?

He bent his head to kiss her cheek, and somehow they ended up clashing heads.

He gave her a rueful look. 'Sorry. I didn't mean to hurt you. I, um...' His voice faded, as if he didn't have a clue what to say to her.

'It's fine,' she reassured him. More than fine, because it told her that he was just as nervous about this as she was.

As she found a vase and put the flowers in water, he leaned against the kitchen worktop. 'I've booked dinner at a place not too far from here. It's a nice evening, so would you like to walk or shall I call a taxi?' Then he glanced at her shoes. 'Ah. Scratch that. I'll call a taxi.'

'Well, you did tell me to wear high heels,' she reminded him with a smile. 'But no, you're right. It's a nice evening, so we can walk. Let me grab a pair of flatter shoes, and I'll change into these ones again when we get there.'

On the way to the restaurant, his hand bumped against hers a couple of times. When she didn't pull away, the next time he caught her fingers in his, and held her hand the rest of the way to the restaurant. It was the lightest, sweetest contact: and it sent a tingle all the way through her.

Though it also put her head in a spin and she didn't have a clue what to say to Ellis. On a normal night, she would have chatted away to him about everything under the sun; but tonight she had to resort to talking about work. 'I hope Helen Perkins is getting on OK.'

'I'm sure she is. It's worrying for parents, though, when something like that happens.' He grimaced. 'I have a feeling this might be one of the rare cases when I suggest an early section, for the baby's sake.'

'I'll back you,' she said. 'Better to be slightly disappointed at not sticking to your birth plan, than to be… Well.' They both knew what the worst-case scenario was in cases of foetal anaemia. The kind of birth that broke her heart because it felt as if all the light in the world had just gone out, and there was nothing you could do to make the loss easier on the parents.

'Yeah,' he said heavily.

When they got to the restaurant, Ruby changed her shoes and handed her bag and coat in at the cloakroom. But, on the way to their table, she tripped. To her horror, she heard a snap and when her foot wobbled she had to grab Ellis's arm to stop herself falling flat on her face. Clearly she'd just broken the heel of her shoe.

'It's just as well we walked so I have another pair of shoes with me,' she said wryly. 'I'll go back to the cloakroom and get them.'

'I'm sorry,' he said.

'It's not your fault. It's me being clumsy. I'm sorry. Don't wait for me. I'll join you at our table.' She slipped off her shoes and walked barefoot back to the cloakroom. So much for dressing up. And those heels had been her favourite pair, glamorous black patent leather which actually managed to be comfortable as well as pretty.

She tried her best to push the disappointment aside and joined Ellis in the restaurant.

Once they'd ordered their food and a bottle of New Zealand Sauvignon Blanc, it was Ellis's turn to be clumsy. He leaned over to top up her glass of wine, and ended up knocking it all over the table. The tablecloth was soaked, and some of the wine landed in her lap.

'Oh, no.' He looked horrified. 'I'm so sorry.'

'It's OK. It'll soon dry off. Anyway, it's white wine so it'll come out in the wash. It's not as if you spilled red wine over a cream lacy dress or something.' She smiled at him. 'I think that makes us one-all in the clumsy stakes tonight.'

'I guess so,' he said wryly, 'but I *am* sorry, Rubes. This was meant to be a nice evening out.'

And so far it had pretty much been a disaster. Anything that could've gone wrong had actually gone wrong. 'It doesn't matter,' she reassured him.

The waiter changed the tablecloth for them and reset the table, but he didn't look pleased about the extra work or try to make conversation with them as he sorted out the table. And then it seemed an endless wait for their meal to arrive; Ruby noticed that people who'd been seated after them had already been served with their food—which was odd, because she and Ellis had both ordered something simple, not something that would take a huge amount of preparation or a long time to cook.

Ellis was clearly thinking the same thing, because he said, 'I wonder if they've forgotten us?'

Though they couldn't ask because there wasn't a waiter to be seen in the dining room.

'I'll go and find someone,' he said. 'Back in a tick.'

He came back looking apologetic. 'It seems our order slipped off the pile. They're sorting us out now.'

'Never mind,' she said brightly.

And when the food finally came, Ruby didn't have the heart to tell Ellis that her chicken was tough and her vegetables were soggy. Though, from the way he picked at his food, she was pretty sure that the meal he'd chosen was just as badly cooked.

'Would you like a dessert and coffee?' he asked politely.

'Thank you, but I think I'll pass,' she said.

'Me, too,' he said. 'I'll get the bill.'

The bill took an excruciatingly long time to come, but eventually Ellis managed to pay for their meal.

This had to be the worst date ever.

So much for sharing a nice dinner out and then going dancing. The food had been awful, the service had been worse, and as Ruby had broken the heel on her shoe he didn't want to suggest dancing and make her feel awkward.

And he didn't have a clue what to say to her as he walked her home. Which was crazy, because he'd always been able to talk to Ruby.

Maybe this was a sign, he thought, that they shouldn't do this. The last thing he wanted to do was to end up hurting her when things went wrong between them, the way his marriage had imploded. She deserved better than that.

'Would you like to come in for coffee?' she asked when they reached her front door.

On a normal evening he would've said yes and spent time chatting to her. Tonight, he just wanted to go home before something else happened to increase the strain between them. 'No, I'd better let you get on,' he said.

'Well, thanks for this evening,' she said with a bright, bright smile.

Ellis knew she was being polite, because it had been truly awful. Even the dates of his teens hadn't been this bad. 'Pleasure,' he said, even though it hadn't been.

He didn't kiss her goodbye, not even on the cheek; he just gave her an awkward smile, waited until she'd let herself in, and left.

And he was still feeling bad by the time he'd walked home. In the end, he gave in and texted her. *I'm so sorry about tonight. It was a total disaster.*

His phone beeped almost immediately with a reply. *Not your fault.*

Wasn't it? The problem with her shoe wasn't his fault—but the restaurant most definitely was. He should've checked the online reviews first, because they would've highlighted that the food was awful and so was the service.

His phone beeped again. *If you were as nervous as I was, I think it all went wrong because we both tried too hard.*

Nervous?

Yeah. He'd been nervous, all right. Worried that he was going to mess everything up. Clearly she'd felt the same. And he'd barely managed a proper conversation with her. They'd ended up talking shop. How pathetic was that? He knew he could talk to Ruby about anything under the sun. They didn't need to rely on awkward conversations about work.

Time to put it right. He picked up the phone and called her.

'Hey, Ellis.'

'Hey, yourself. You're right, Rubes. I was nervous, too. Which is stupid, because we've known each other for so long.'

'I guess.'

'If we'd just gone out together as we normally do—' as friends, though he didn't say it '——we would have laughed it all off. But you're right. Because it was a date, we had all these expectations of what it ought to be like, and I guess we made it difficult for ourselves.'

'Uh-huh.' Her voice was expressionless.

'Maybe,' he said, 'we could try again. But this time we should keep it simple and take the pressure off.'

'What do you have in mind?'

Pretty much what they'd talked about when they'd made those ridiculous lists for that dating site. 'I'm working a late shift tomorrow, but I thought we could have a walk somewhere nice on Sunday morning, if you're off duty—and also depending on the weather, because it's not going to be much fun if it's bucketing down with rain. And then we can find somewhere to grab lunch.'

'That sounds great,' she said. 'What time?'

'Meet you at yours at ten? Oh, and no high heels.'

She laughed. 'Definitely not, if we're going for a walk. OK. See you then.'

Ellis felt a lot better by the time he rang off. And better still when Sunday dawned bright and sunny—a perfect late September morning, with a blue sky and the sun burnishing the bronze, reds and golds of the autumn leaves.

He rang her doorbell and waited for her to answer.

This time when he kissed her cheek, there was no clash of heads, no awkwardness. It felt *right*. He could smell the soft floral scent she wore and his mouth tingled where it touched her skin.

She'd looked gorgeous in high heels and a little black dress on Friday night, but she looked just as gorgeous this morning in faded jeans, a blue silky long-sleeved top that brought out the colour of her eyes, and flat walking shoes. A pocket Venus, Ellis thought, all curves that he wanted to gather closer—but he'd try and take it easy today.

They caught the Tube through to Kew, where Ruby insisted on paying for their tickets to the gardens. 'You bought dinner on Friday, so I'm paying. No arguments.'

'Only on condition that you let me buy you lunch,' he said.

'That's a deal,' she said with a smile.

He enjoyed waking through the gardens with her to the Arboretum, where they explored the treetop walkway. His hand brushed against hers several times and then her fingers curled round his; the light contact made him feel all warm inside. This felt so much more natural than their posh date on Friday night. Maybe, just maybe, they could get this thing to work.

They stopped in one of the cafés for a lunch of hot soup, artisan bread and cheese. It was much simpler than Friday's food, but came with much better service; this time, he relaxed with her and could enjoy her company instead of worrying what would go wrong next.

They wandered through the glasshouses together, hand in hand, then headed back outside to crunch through the fallen leaves. Ellis found a conker fresh out of its shell beneath the chestnut tree and presented it to Ruby with a smile. 'It's the same colour as your hair.'

'Thank you. That's very poetic, Ellis.' She smiled back at him and put the conker safely in her pocket.

That smile undid him. He couldn't resist pulling her into his arms and dipping his head to kiss her. He brushed his lips lightly against hers, once, twice; then she caught his lower lip gently between hers.

Odd how a single kiss could put his head into such a spin.

He wrapped his arms more tightly round her, and her arms were wrapped round his neck, holding him just as tightly. His eyes closed as she let him deepen the kiss, and it felt as if the late afternoon sunshine was filling his soul.

When he broke the kiss, her pupils were huge and there was a slash of colour across her cheekbones. He wanted to tell her how beautiful she looked, but the words felt flat and not enough, so he stole a last kiss and hoped she'd guess what was in his head.

Finally, when the light started to fade, they headed back on the Tube to her flat.

'I'm not ready for today to end just yet,' Ruby said on her doorstep. 'Will you stay for dinner?'

'I'd like that. I can be your sous-chef, if you want.' He knew his way around Ruby's kitchen; he'd cooked quite a few meals there towards the end of Tom's illness, to give Ruby a break and make sure that both she and Tom had something nutritious to eat to keep their strength up.

'That sounds good to me.' She rummaged through the cupboards, found a bottle of white wine and held it so he could see the label. 'I know it's not chilled, but is this OK?'

'More than OK,' he said with a smile. 'And this time I'll try not to knock my glass over.' Funny, it was easy to laugh about their disastrous date now. At the time, he'd been mortified and felt as gauche as a teenager, but he had a feeling that this was going to become a favourite story for both of them in years to come: the night of the Worst Date Ever.

'Is risotto OK with you?' she asked.

'More than OK—I love risotto,' he said.

She poured them both a glass of wine, and Ellis chopped the vegetables while she made the base for the risotto. Working with her in the kitchen felt as natural as working together at the hospital. As if this was meant to be...

They ate at the kitchen table, and it was perfect. The right food, the right company, the right ambience. Especially as Ruby produced posh ice cream for pudding, and even posher shortbread to go with it.

'Today's been really lovely,' she said when they'd finished eating and done the washing up.

'I've enjoyed it, too. I'd better let you get on, though.' He'd taken up the whole of her day already. Any more would be greedy.

'I'm not actually doing a lot—all I plan to do is curl up on the sofa and watch that dance competition show on the television,' she said. 'You're very welcome to stay and join me, if you don't have anything better to do.'

How could he resist?

Especially when they ended up sitting with her on his lap and his arms wrapped round her.

'So which is your favourite kind of dancing, ball-room or Latin?' he asked.

'Ballroom, I think. I love it when the woman is dressed like a princess and they dance a dreamy waltz.' She laughed and sang a snatch of 'Moon River'.

'I didn't know you could sing,' he said, surprised.

'Not that well,' she said. 'I've got a limited vocal range. Tom says—*said*,' she corrected herself, 'that I only manage that one because Audrey Hepburn's vocal range was tiny, too, and "Moon River" was written especially for her to be able to sing it.'

'You remind me a bit of Audrey Hepburn,' Ellis said, tipping his head to one side. 'All pixie haircut and huge eyes. Well, except obviously your eyes are blue.'

Ruby looked pleased. 'She's one of my favourite actresses. I love her films—and Grace Kelly's.'

Ones with happy endings? That was something he couldn't guarantee for her. Not wanting to break the mood, he said nothing and just kept holding her.

The next dance was a waltz—but this time not the dreamy, princessy sort that Ruby had said she liked. It was a dark, edgy and sensual...

'That's amazing choreography.' Ruby fanned herself. 'Oh, to able to dance with someone like that.'

The temptation was too much for him. 'Dance with me?' he asked.

'Now?' She blinked. 'Hang on. Are you telling me that you can dance like *that*?'

'I worked on an assignment for the medical aid char-ity with an Argentinean doctor,' he said, 'and she taught us all how to tango. And that dance on the TV just now was much more like a tango than a waltz.'

'Ellis, you always manage to surprise me.' She gave

him a slow, sensual smile that made him catch his breath. 'I'd love to.'

'Go and put some high heels on,' he said, 'and I'll push the furniture back a bit to give us some space.'

'I can't believe you're going to tango with me in my living room.' She was all pink and flustered and absolutely adorable, and Ellis ached to kiss her.

By the time she'd come back, wearing high-heeled shoes, he'd moved the furniture to give them more of a dance floor and connected his iPod to the Internet, to find the music the couple on the television had just danced to. He muted the sound of the television, but he left the picture on.

'Ready?' he asked. At her nod, he said, 'Just follow my lead.'

The music was sexy and intense, like the dance itself, and her eyes were so dark they were practically navy.

Ellis loved every second of having her in his arms, leaning close and making her sway with him in the corners.

At the very end, he bent her backwards over his arm. Her throat was bared to him, and he couldn't resist kissing his way along the arch of her throat.

'That,' he said huskily, 'was what Friday was supposed to be.'

He could see the pulse beating at her throat; the dance had clearly affected her just as much as it had affected him.

'Ellis, I...just, wow,' she said, her voice deeper than usual and slightly breathy. 'I had no idea you could do that.'

'We had someone on the team who could play the

guitar really well. He used to play while Sofia taught the rest of us to dance,' he said.

'It never occurred to me that you'd have time off, time to have fun together. I thought when you worked with a medical aid charity, it was intense and full on.'

'It was, but we still managed to find some good times—even in the middle of a disaster zone,' he said. 'And that helped us get through the rougher times at work. The days when our skills just weren't enough.'

'I can understand that,' she said. 'Ellis, can I be greedy and ask if we can do it again?'

He'd really have to resist the urge to carry her off to her bed afterwards. But he'd find the strength, if it meant pleasing her.

He put the music on again, and exaggerated the moves of the dance so their bodies were closer still, this time. Though he resisted kissing her at the end. There was only so much his self-control could take, and kissing her again would definitely make it snap.

'That,' she said softly, 'was amazing. Thank you.' She smiled. 'You're a bit of a dark horse, Ellis Webster.'

'Maybe. Let's watch the rest of the show,' he said, and settled her back on his lap on the sofa.

When the show finished, he kissed her lightly. 'And now I really do have to go. I'm on early shift tomorrow.'

'Thank you for today, Ellis. I really enjoyed it.' She kissed him back. 'Can we, um, do this again?'

'Date or dance?'

'Both,' she said.

He smiled. 'Let's sort out our off-duty tomorrow. And maybe we should make another list, this time of places we want to go.'

'Top of mine would be Hampton Court Maze,' she

said promptly. 'I've never, ever been there. Considering how long I've lived in London, that's atrocious.'

'Then we'll do that, the next day we both have off,' Ellis said.

'Provided it isn't raining,' she said with a grin. 'I have a feeling that the maze won't be as much fun if we get drenched through.'

'Agreed.' He kissed her again. 'Sleep well. And I'll see you at work tomorrow.'

CHAPTER SEVEN

RUBY LAY CURLED on the sofa with a midwifery journal, not really concentrating on the articles because she was still thinking about Ellis.

She'd had no idea that he could even dance, let alone dance well. He'd really made her pulse speed up when he'd twirled her round and bent her back over his arm like that. And when he'd kissed her throat…She shivered at the memory. Ellis Webster was the first man since Tom who'd made her feel that thrill of attraction, and it threw her.

She turned the page, scanned the headline of the article and did a double-take.

By a strange coincidence, this article might just have a bearing on the court case Ellis was dealing with. She read through the whole thing more carefully and decided that yes, it was definitely relevant and Ellis needed to see this. She went in search of the sticky notes she kept in her kitchen drawer, so she could mark the first page of the article for ease of reference.

The next morning, Ruby caught Ellis during his break. 'Do you have a moment?' she asked.

'Sure. What's the problem?'

'It's a solution, I hope,' she said. 'You know the DNA

tests said that Grace Edwards wasn't the genetic mother of her own baby?'

'Yes.'

'Did you have a word with Theo or the genetics team about it?'

'I haven't managed to get hold of the genetics team, yet,' he said, 'but I did talk to Theo, and he's scratching his head about it as much as I am. Why?'

'Because I might just have a theory. I was reading a midwifery journal last night and there was a case study from America that reminded me of Grace Edwards's situation. I brought it in with me so you could read it. Hang on a sec and I'll get it from my locker.' She fetched the journal and handed it to him. 'I've marked the first page of the article with a sticky note at the top. I might be misreading things, but it also might be that Grace Edwards has the same biological quirk as the woman in the case study—that she's a chimera, so she has two sets of DNA in her body instead of the usual single set.'

Ellis skimmed swiftly through it and raised his eyebrows. 'You know, I think you could be right, Rubes. So maybe Grace started life as a twin, with two separate eggs fertilised by two different sperm. Then, at some point very early in the pregnancy, the eggs fused together and Grace absorbed her twin.'

'So Grace has two sets of DNA and she's also her own twin.'

'Yup.' Ellis blew out a breath. 'Which is pretty mindblowing.'

'According to that article, having two sets of DNA means that your skin might not have the same DNA as say your heart or your lungs,' Ruby said.

'So it's possible that the cells in Grace's ovaries

originally belonged to her twin and not to her. And in that case it means that her twin is the biological mum of the baby,' Ellis said thoughtfully.

Ruby nodded. 'And that might be why Grace's DNA isn't showing as being the same as that of her baby. It was awful for the poor American mum in the article. She had to have someone appointed by the court to be there at the birth of her next child to witness that she gave birth to the baby. And then, when they did the genetic tests, there was no genetic link between the mum and the baby—even though the court witness was able to say that she definitely gave birth to the baby. Then they did some more tests on cells from different organs in the mum's body, and discovered a match for their DNA.'

'In the case of a chimera, you can't predict which cells will have which twin's DNA. So, as you said earlier, you could have a case where someone has skin and blood cells from one twin and organ cells from another,' Ellis said thoughtfully. 'And the only way to find out is to test several different sorts of cells for DNA to see if they match. Rubes, you're a genius.'

'Hardly,' she said. 'I just happened to see a case study in a journal.'

'But you made the connection,' he pointed out. 'At least now I can give the court a professional opinion, and Theo will back me up so we can suggest they do further DNA tests. Can I borrow this journal for a while?'

'Of course you can.' She smiled at him. 'I'll let you get on.'

'Just a sec. When are you next off duty?'

'Thursday.'

'Me, too. How about going to Hampton Court, if it's not bucketing down with rain?'

'Sounds good to me,' she said.

'It's a date,' he said softly, and Ruby felt warm all over.

Wednesday was a stickier day. As soon as Ruby spoke to the woman who'd come in to the antenatal walk-in clinic, she knew this was a case she really didn't want Ellis to deal with—it was something that would bring back difficult memories for him.

'I just can't keep anything down,' Mrs Bywater said. 'I've read all the books and I've done everything they say I should do about morning sickness. I don't cook anything, I have cold foods rather than hot foods and I stick to super-boring bland things that don't smell.' She grimaced. 'But the problem is, *everything* smells. My mum said I ought to come in and see you because this isn't normal and I've been like this for a month. It's not morning sickness—it's morning, afternoon and night, and I'm losing weight when I'm meant to be putting it on.'

'I think you have something called hyperemesis gravidarum. It's a severe form of morning sickness which affects about one in a hundred women,' Ruby explained. 'It can run in the family. Do you know if your mum ever had it, or do you have a sister who's had it?'

'Just a brother,' Mrs Bywater said. 'I don't think Mum was sick like this when she was pregnant, but I do know she had postnatal depression.' She gave Ruby a wry smile. 'I guess I've got that to look forward to as well.'

'Not necessarily, though we will keep an eye on you

and make sure you get plenty of support.' Ruby poured her patient a glass of cold water. 'Sip this slowly,' she said. 'From the urine sample you gave me, I think you're quite dehydrated and I want to admit you to the ward— we'll need to take blood samples and give you some fluid through a needle into your veins.'

'And then I'll stop being sick?' Mrs Bywater asked.

'You're twelve weeks at the moment,' Ruby said, looking at her notes. 'I hate to tell you this, but often hyperemesis lasts until twenty weeks, and some people find that it lasts a bit longer than that.'

'No.' Mrs Bywater gave a sharp intake of breath. 'I don't think I can cope with that. I just feel so *ill* all the time. And for it to go on for months and months...' She shuddered.

'There are some things you can do,' Ruby said. 'Keep a log of what you eat and when you're ill, so you can see if there's a pattern about timing or types of food that you find difficult. Eating little and often is better than having big meals, and when you do manage to eat something you need to sit upright for a while afterwards, to reduce the likelihood of getting gastric reflux.'

'And don't clean my teeth straight after eating, take lots of small sips of cold water or suck on an ice cube, and try and get as much fresh air as possible,' Mrs Bywater said.

Ruby smiled at her. 'You've definitely been reading up. That's all really good advice. I'm going to admit you, at least for today and maybe tomorrow as well, and we'll give you some fluids to hydrate you and replenish your electrolyte levels. And then you can get some proper rest.'

She'd hoped to catch one of the other obstetricians

when she went up to the ward, but Ellis would have to be the first one she saw.

'I think,' she said carefully, 'maybe you're not the right doctor for this particular mum and I need one of the others instead.'

'Why?' he asked.

She lowered her voice. 'Because this particular mum has hyperemesis.'

Hyperemesis gravidarum. The condition that hadn't been treated properly and had led to his sister's death. 'No. Actually, I'm *exactly* the right person to treat her,' Ellis said firmly. Because then he could make quite sure that what had happened to Sally wouldn't happen to this particular mum.

'Ellis, are you sure you want to do this?' Ruby rested her hand on his arm.

He nodded. 'I know you mean well, and thank you for thinking about me. But I need to do this.'

'If you're sure.' She still wasn't sure about this. At all. Surely treating a patient with this condition would rip open old scars?

'I'm very sure,' he said softly.

And she knew he would be totally professional—he always was. Just at what cost to his heart? Pushing away her misgivings, Ruby took him over to the side room and introduced him to Mrs Bywater. 'Dr Webster's very experienced,' she said, 'and he'll be able to help you.'

'Thank you. I...Excuse me!' Mrs Bywater clapped a hand over her mouth, clearly just about to be sick.

Ruby swiftly handed her a kidney bowl. 'Here. It's fine.'

When Mrs Bywater had finished being sick, Ruby

took the bowl away, first making sure there was a clean one to hand if she needed it.

'Poor you,' Ellis said sympathetically. 'Have a sip of water to make your mouth feel a bit better.'

'Nurse Fisher said I might be like this until twenty weeks—or even later,' Mrs Bywater said miserably.

'Unfortunately she's right, but there are a number of things we can do to help,' he said gently. 'Firstly we need to give you some fluids to hydrate you and replenish your electrolyte levels. I'm going to use something called Ringer's solution, because it gives you the extra levels of calcium and potassium. Before we start, though, we're going to check the levels of minerals in your blood so we can make sure we balance everything out for you.'

If the doctor who'd treated Sally had thought to do that before hydrating her, and given her thiamine, she wouldn't have ended up developing the complication of Wernicke's encephalopathy...

Ellis pushed the thought away and concentrated on his patient. 'And you need some rest,' he said. 'I'm guessing that you're not sleeping so well.'

'I'm even sick in the night,' she said. 'And my ribs hurt from being sick all the time. I was even spitting up blood this morning—that's what scared me into coming to the walk-in clinic.'

'Being sick puts a bit of strain in the small blood vessels of your throat,' Ellis said, 'and it causes them to rupture, so that's why you've seen blood. But it's honestly nothing to worry about.' He took the blood sample swiftly. 'We can also give you some medication to help with the sickness.'

Mrs Bywater looked anxious. 'But doesn't that cause problems for baby if I take medication?'

'Anti-sickness drugs did cause developmental issues in babies years and years ago—in the years before you were born,' he said, 'but I'm glad to be able to reassure you that the modern drugs don't affect the baby at all. And the medication will make you feel a lot better—it'll help you to function normally again.'

'All I want to do is feel normal again,' Mrs Bywater said feelingly. 'I don't think I'm ever going to have another baby if pregnancy's always going to make me feel like this!'

'I'm afraid that women who have hyperemesis are more likely to have it in future pregnancies,' he said. 'It just means you'll need to plan ahead to make sure you get the right support and help next time.'

She shook her head. 'There's definitely not going to be a next time. I can't cope with this for a second time.'

'Ruby will finish booking you in,' he said, 'and then as soon as your blood results are back I'll know what to put in the drip. And I promise you, in the next few hours you're going to feel an awful lot better.'

'Thank you,' she said. 'You've been so kind.'

'That's what I'm here for,' he said. 'And if you're worried about anything at all, no matter how little or silly you think the question might be, just ask me or Ruby. Or you can ask any of the team on the ward, because they're all really nice. And we'll make sure you're feeling better as soon as possible.'

Once the blood results were back, Ellis checked the additions to the Ringer's solution with Ruby. 'Given that she's dehydrated, I think we need to warm the area with compresses before we put a needle in, and warm the first litre of fluid so it doesn't come as a shock to her.'

'Good idea,' Ruby said.

He went over to Mrs Bywater and explained what they were going to do.

'Why do you have to put a warm compress on my hand?' she asked.

'It makes your veins dilate a little bit so it's easier for me to put the needle in,' Ruby explained, doing precisely that. 'And it's easier for you, too.'

'Thank you,' Mrs Bywater said.

'That's what we're here for,' Ellis said with a smile. 'I'm going to get you rehydrated, then we'll give you some anti-sickness medication and you can get some well-earned rest.'

After her shift, Ruby headed for Ellis's office where she could see him catching up with paperwork. She rapped lightly on the door. 'Hey.'

He looked up. 'Hey, yourself.'

'I'm taking you for ice cream,' she said.

'Why?'

'Because ice cream always makes things better.'

'I'm fine,' he said.

She put her hands on her hips and stared at him. She knew he wasn't fine. His grey eyes had gone all haunted, and she had a pretty good idea why. Just as she'd suspected, Mrs Bywater's case had brought back all the bad memories for him. He'd helped the patient, but at what cost to himself?

Ellis had been there for her in her darkest days; and she wanted to be there for him, on one of his own dark days.

'OK. You're right,' he admitted at last. 'Give me twenty minutes to finish the paperwork?'

'Fifteen. And no more than that.' She didn't want to give him time to brood. Time to hurt.

He followed her instructions to the letter and they went to a café just round the corner. Ruby bought them both a sundae.

'Was how I felt that obvious?' Ellis asked.

'No, not at all. You were totally professional. I only worked it out because I have privileged information,' she said.

'I guess.' Ellis ate his ice cream in silence, and Ruby let him because she knew it was pointless pushing him until he was ready to talk.

Finally he put his spoon into the cone. 'They thought Sally just had some kind of bug,' he said. 'There had been a virus doing the rounds making people throw up, and she'd had something like it a month or so before. Nobody even considered Sally might be pregnant. She was on the Pill. She took it properly and she wasn't careless; she didn't miss a dose.'

But being sick meant that the medication was less effective, Ruby knew. Maybe Sally hadn't realised that she needed to use extra protection for the next fortnight to make sure she didn't accidentally fall pregnant.

'I don't think anyone out there realised that what she was suffering from was an extreme form of morning sickness.' A muscle twitched in his cheek. 'Unless you've read up on it or you work in the area, you wouldn't know that hyperemesis can start as early as four weeks of pregnancy—maybe even before you realise that you're pregnant. So I get why everyone assumed it was just a bug again.' He blew out a breath.

'They called the medic to see her. He knew she'd been vomiting a lot, so he assumed that she needed rehydrating and gave her IV fluids.' He paused. 'Without checking her thiamine levels first.'

Ruby had a nasty feeling she knew what was coming next, because prolonged vomiting depleted the body's thiamine levels. Rehydration with a solution containing dextrose would deplete the thiamine levels even further, leading to more problems. 'And she developed Wernicke's encephalopathy?' she asked.

He nodded. 'She had visual disturbances and an unsteady gait, and she was disoriented. The classic triad symptoms, in hindsight—but everyone assumed it was just the virus making her throw up all the time that had knocked her for six and made her wobbly on her feet.' He dragged in a breath. 'She ended up with DIC.'

Ruby knew that disseminated intravascular coagulation was where the blood didn't clot properly, and if it wasn't treated the patient could go into shock or even organ failure.

'She went into organ failure,' Ellis continued softly. 'She collapsed and she never regained consciousness.'

'You do know that's not going to happen to *your* patient, don't you?' she asked.

He nodded. 'I've never had any patients out in the field with it, so I haven't lost anyone there.'

She reached out and held his hand. 'So basically when you're working for the aid charity, you're trying to stop what happened to your sister happening to anyone else.'

'That or any other condition.' He paused. 'I guess I know I can't save everyone.'

'Nobody can, no matter how good a medic they are.

Sometimes you just can't save someone, because the circumstances mean that nobody could save them. All you can do is your best, and that has to be good enough because you can't humanly do any more,' Ruby said softly.

'I know.'

Intellectually, maybe, but she could tell he didn't feel it in his heart. 'Obviously I didn't know your sister, but I bet she's looking down on you right now, and I bet she's so proud of the man you've become.'

'I hope so.' He squeezed her hand. 'I didn't mean to go all brooding on you, Rubes. Sorry.'

'Don't apologise. It must be hard when you come across the same condition that took your sister. That's why I didn't want you to see Mrs Bywater.'

'I know, but I'm glad I did—because I feel I've made a difference.'

'Even though it's ripped the top off your scars?' she asked.

He nodded. 'It's harder knowing that if Sally had been given the right treatment she would've survived—but I guess that's true of a lot of my patients. I know I can make a difference. And that's one of the reasons why I love doing what I do. I can stop other families falling apart the way mine has.'

'Tom said your parents closed off afterwards.'

He sighed. 'Now I'm older, I can understand why. They're protecting themselves from more hurt.'

'It must've been hard on you and your brothers, though. Especially as you were so young.'

'They were sixteen and fourteen, and I was twelve.' He lifted a shoulder in a half-shrug. 'We got by. We had each other.'

'I'm glad you're close to them.'

He wrinkled his nose. 'I was. But we fell out a bit after I graduated. They were pretty upset about me working abroad, and they still haven't really got used to it, even after all these years. They think I'm putting myself in danger.'

'That's because you *are* putting yourself in danger—whether you're working in a war zone or in an area hit by flood, earthquake or whatever,' she pointed out.

'I'm still here.' He shrugged it off. 'Anyway, Tom's parents have been like second parents to me. They were brilliant when it all happened.'

'I'm glad—and I'm glad they still have you.'

'And they have you,' he said softly. 'And now, can we please change the subject, Rubes?'

'Sure.' Though Ruby couldn't stop thinking about it for the rest of the evening. The way he'd talked, it sounded as if he wanted to be back at the medical aid charity and he might not want to come back after his assignment. So she'd better be sure not to lose her heart to him completely...

Thursday turned out to be a perfect autumn day, with blue skies and a crispness to the air. Ellis and Ruby caught the train down to Hampton Court.

'What a gorgeous building,' she said as they got their first view of the house.

'Shall we walk round the gardens first, in case the weather changes?'

'Good idea—and I really want to see the maze,' she said.

Funny, as a child, she'd been faintly bored when her parents took her to stately homes, always more keen on spending time in the adventure playground than looking at the plants. Now, she loved strolling through the gardens, enjoying the skill of the designer in highlighting colours and shapes. The autumn colours in the old tilting yard were particularly gorgeous, and she loved the formality of the Privy Gardens with its geometric designs and its statues, and seeing the fountains and the swans on the lake. Walking hand in hand with Ellis, Ruby felt a burst of happiness that had been missing from her life for a long while. And she intended to enjoy every second of it.

'So this is the oldest hedge maze in the world,' she said as she read the information board at the entrance to the maze.

'Apparently it takes twenty minutes to get to the centre.' Ellis smiled at her. 'Are you ready for this?'

'I'm ready,' she said, smiling back.

They took several wrong turns among the yew hedges, and Ellis kissed her in every dead end. Although it took rather longer than twenty minutes to reach the centre, Ruby didn't care; today was all about having fun and enjoying the moment.

'I love all the sound effects they've put in to the maze,' she said. 'When you think you can hear children laughing, or the swish of skirts—it's almost like hearing the ghosts of the past, little glimpses in time of what it might have been like here.'

Ellis looked at her. 'I can just imagine you in Tudor dress. With your colouring, I think you'd have looked fabulous in a rich blue velvet. Like your eyes.'

She stole a kiss. 'Very poetic, Dr Webster. And I can see you in a cloak and a velvet hat. A royal purple one.'

He started to sing 'I'm Henry the Eighth, I am', and she groaned.

'I think I might be creating a monster, here.'

He just laughed. 'Let's go and have a look round the house.'

When they got to the house itself, they discovered that you could actually borrow a red velvet cape.

'I think we ought to do this,' Ruby said with a smile.

'Absolutely,' he agreed.

The rich red velvet suited his colouring, and she could imagine him as a courtier in Tudor times. As tall, as strong and as handsome as the young King Henry VIII himself.

She loved the chapel with its rich blue and gold ceiling, and the tapestried hall where Shakespeare's men had once played. But the bit that really caught her attention was the chocolate kitchen.

'Funny, I always associate Henry VIII with Hampton Court. I never really think about the later kings and queens who lived here,' she said. 'But having a special chocolate kitchen—why on earth would they keep it separate from the other kitchens?'

'This was built for William and Mary,' the guide told them. 'Chocolate was a very expensive drink back then, so it was reserved for the aristocracy. The chocolate maker was one of the highest ranking servants in the palace. He had his own bedroom, which was huge luxury back then, plus he was one of the few people who was actually allowed to serve the king in his private apartments.'

'So was the chocolate they drank very different to what we have today?' Ruby asked.

'They made it all by hand. They roasted the cocoa beans on the fireplace over there—' the guide indicated the area '—and then the kitchen boy took off the shells. They put the cocoa nibs on a heated stone slab and crushed them into a paste with a stone roller, then put the paste into moulds to set into a cake.' He showed them the little cakes of chocolate in cases of waxed paper.

'Was that for eating?' Ellis asked.

'No, bar chocolate wasn't invented until almost Victorian times. The chocolate back then was just for drinking,' the guide explained. 'They'd mix one of these chocolate cakes with water, wine or milk in a pan, then add sugar and spices—the most popular ones were vanilla or chilli. And the king would have hot chocolate for breakfast along with some sweetmeats.' He smiled at them. 'Actually, the palace kitchens have already made the sweetmeats, and we're going to have a demonstration and make drinking chocolate the old-fashioned way for visitors to taste, if you'd like to come back and see us this afternoon. The demonstrations are on the hour, every hour.'

'That sounds great. Thank you,' Ruby said with a smile.

'That's the sort of thing I can imagine you and Tina doing,' Ellis said when they'd moved on to let the guide talk to other visitors. 'Having hot chocolate and sweetmeats for breakfast.'

Ruby laughed. 'I'll have you know that cake for breakfast is one of life's great pleasures.'

'I was right, you are a hedonist,' Ellis teased.

'You bet.' She smiled back at him. 'Life's for living, Ellis.'

'Yes. It is.' His hand tightened round hers.

They continued looking round the house, and went back to the kitchens later in the afternoon for the chocolate demonstration. Ruby preferred the vanilla chocolate, but Ellis preferred the chilli.

'A bit like the Spanish explorers who discovered chocolate,' she said. 'I can see you as one of them. A Conquistador.'

And that was where Ellis really fitted: not in the city, but in a wilder place. So it would be wise not to lose her heart to him, because one day his itchy feet would take him back to where he belonged. He'd teased her about being a hedonist; but she'd never been able to see the attraction of having a holiday in a tent, sleeping on the ground and without running water. In some respects, they were total opposites and this was never going to work out.

But for now, she was going to live in the moment and just enjoy this thing blossoming between them.

On Sunday afternoon, Ruby went shopping with her best friend. Tina was going to be godmother to her sister's baby and needed a suitable outfit, and Ruby had promised to go help her find something.

'It's a shame it didn't work out with Roger,' Tina said, referring to her new colleague.

'He's a nice guy,' Ruby said. 'But I'm not sure he's ready for dating again yet. I don't think he's over his divorce, poor man.'

'So what about you? Did you sign up with that online dating agency?'

'Not yet.'

Tina gave her a narrow look. 'Is there something you're not telling me?'

Yes, Ruby thought, but it was too early to talk about it. There was definite attraction between her and Ellis, but would he ever be ready to settle down? She said with a smile, 'Why don't you try this dress on? I think it'll really suit your colouring.'

'You're trying to distract me. So there *is* something,' Tina said. 'OK. You can spill the beans now, or I'll interrogate you over coffee and you can spill the beans then.'

'That's not exactly a choice, Tina.'

'I'm your best friend, Rubes. Who else are you going to tell?'

'True. All right. I'm seeing someone,' Ruby admitted, 'but it's early days.'

'Who?'

'We both want to keep it quiet,' Ruby warned.

Tina flapped a dismissive hand. 'You know perfectly well I'm not going to tell anyone. Who is it, Rubes?'

'Ellis.'

'Ellis? You mean Ellis Webster?' Tina looked surprised.

'What's wrong with Ellis?' Ruby bit her lip. 'Is it because he's Tom's best friend, so it's not appropriate?' It was something that had worried her—how people would react to their relationship.

'No, it's not that.'

'Why, then?'

'It's because Tom always said that Ellis would never settle down—and he's been back in England for a year and a half or so,' Tina said. 'And isn't he planning to go back to the medical aid charity?'

'He's booked to go out with them for a month in a few weeks' time, yes. But that doesn't mean he'll stay out there. If Billie decides to take a career break, then Theo might offer Ellis the job,' Ruby said.

'And is Ellis ready to settle down in England?'

That was something Ruby wasn't sure about. And, if not, would Ellis feel trapped by her? 'I don't know,' she admitted.

'That's what worries me,' Tina said gently, giving her a hug. 'That he still has itchy feet, and you'll lose him to his job and end up hurt.'

'Or we might both decide we're best off just being friends.'

'Maybe.' Tina paused. 'What do you really want, Ruby?'

'To keep seeing Ellis, and for him to settle here. I've felt like this about him for a while,' Ruby admitted. 'I was going to sign up for that dating agency, but I asked him to give me a male point of view on my list of what I wanted in a date. It turned out that he ticked every single one of the boxes.' She paused. 'And I teased him into doing the same—and I ticked all his boxes, too. So we, um, thought we'd give it a try.'

'Then I hope, for both your sakes, that it works out,' Tina said, giving her another hug. 'As long as he makes you happy. But if he ever hurts you…'

'He won't. Not intentionally,' Ruby said.

'Just don't fall for him too hard,' Tina said softly. 'He's a nice guy, but he has itchy feet—and you don't.'

'As I said, it's early days,' Ruby said lightly. 'Now, are you going to try on this dress?'

Tina let her off the hook and went to try on the dress. But it left Ruby wondering. Was Tina right? Should she start backing off from Ellis? Was she hoping for too much? Or was it just way too early even to be thinking about the future and she should just enjoy the moment?

CHAPTER EIGHT

LATER IN THE WEEK, Helen Perkins was scheduled for another intra-uterine blood transfusion for the baby. Ellis made sure that she was booked in with him, and Ruby made sure that she was there to support Helen and Joe.

Ruby had heard nightmare stories from other nursing colleagues about arrogant doctors with non-existent people skills who never listened to the patients because they always thought they knew best, and seemed to forget that they were dealing with people rather than a textbook case. But, apart from the fact that Theo wouldn't let anyone like that work on his ward, since Ruby had been working with Ellis she'd found that he was a natural with patients.

She liked the way he chatted to the Perkinses, and explained what he was doing at each step and answered every question they had without making them feel stupid. And she really liked the way he stayed for a little while after the procedure rather than rushing off to his next patient, making sure that Helen and Joe weren't worried about anything. Dr Ellis Webster was definitely a good man. And she couldn't quite get her head round the fact that they were actually dating. They were still keeping their relationship to themselves, but Ruby was beginning to believe that she'd been granted a second chance at happiness, with a man who could make her as happy as Tom had.

'Next time you come in for the baby's transfusion,' Ellis said to Helen Perkins, 'you'll probably be the one to tell me what happens next.'

'An overnight stay in the ward, and I have to tell you straight away if I have any pain or fever. And I mustn't worry if I can't feel the baby moving for the next couple of hours, because the sedative takes a little time to wear off,' she said with a smile.

He smiled back. 'I stand corrected—I think you're already my star pupil.' He moved the screen so the Perkinses could see the baby's heart beating and be reassured that all was well. 'One snoozing baby,' he said. 'So everything's just as we expected.'

'Thank you, Dr Webster.' Joe Perkins shook his hand. 'We really appreciate this.'

'I know, but it's my job and I don't want any of my new parents to worry,' Ellis told him. 'I'd much rather you asked me a gazillion questions than went away worrying.'

What if I asked you questions? Ruby thought. Would you answer them as honestly as you answer your patients? Or would it scare you away? But she kept her counsel and accompanied the Perkinses up to the ward.

The following Monday morning, Theo called Ellis into his office.

'Billie wants to come back part-time in a month and a half, as a job share,' he said. 'I'm currently arguing budgets with the suits. At the moment, they're saying no, but I'm looking at my figures again to prove that we need another full-time obstetrician on the team and I'm pretty sure I can make a solid case. I know you're going back to the medical aid charity for a month's assignment, but I'm hoping you're planning to come back afterwards and I'd like to interview you for the job.' He smiled. 'It's a formality, really, simply because I have to advertise the position, but I want to offer you the job. Bottom line, Ellis, you're a good fit in the team. You've got the right attitude towards our patients, you've got much wider experience than anyone else at your level, and you're really good at teaching the younger staff and giving them confidence. I'd like you here for good.'

'Thank you,' Ellis said, inclining his head in acknowledgement of the compliments. 'But right now I don't actually know what I'll be doing in a month's time, and it wouldn't be fair to leave you hanging on.' Would the lure of his former job make him want to stay on for another month? Or would he come back to London to be with Ruby? Would it all work out between them? It was still too early to tell—and he didn't want to make the same mistake he'd made with Natalia, rushing into the relationship only to discover that they wanted different things. Yes, he'd known Ruby for an awful lot longer—but until a couple of weeks ago their relationship had been strictly platonic.

Was Ruby the one who'd make him want to settle?

And what if he let her down, the way he felt he'd let Natalia down?

'Think about it,' Theo said. 'Don't say yes or no right now. Think about what you really want.'

'Thank you.'

'For what it's worth, I think you and Ruby are good together.'

Ellis stared at his boss in shock. Theo *knew*?

The question must have been written all over his face, because Theo said softly, 'She hasn't said anything to me, and nobody's gossiping about you. Don't worry, you're not the hot topic on the hospital grapevine.'

'So how on earth do you...?' Ellis was still too flabbergasted to frame the question properly.

Theo smiled. 'Because I've been there myself, when I started dating Maddie. And I definitely needed a good shaking at one point. Just make sure that doesn't happen to you.' His smile faded. 'And if you do decide to accept the job offer and stay here, remember that nothing, but *nothing*, disrupts my team here.'

'Agreed,' Ellis said. 'Patients are always my priority at work. And I'm professional enough to keep my private life very separate from my job.'

'Good.' Theo shook his hand again. 'We'll leave it open for now, but come and see me when you're ready to make a decision. I want you to say yes to the interview, if nothing else. But when I offer you the job— because I really can't see that any other candidate will be better than you—I also want you to be absolutely sure about it, OK?'

'OK.'

Ellis caught Ruby on her break. 'Are you busy after work?'

'Nothing I can't move. Why?'

'I could do with bouncing some ideas off someone.'

'I'm your woman,' she said immediately.

Yes, I rather think you are, he thought. But does that

scare you as much as it scares me? 'Let's do it over dinner. Is tapas OK with you?'

'Tapas would be lovely.' She smiled at him. 'See you after our shift, then.'

After work, Ruby and Ellis went to a small Spanish bar in the middle of London. She settled back in her seat. 'This place is very nice. I haven't been here before,' she said.

'I looked it up online first, and it has good reviews.' He spread his hands. 'Let's just say I learned from that particular mistake.'

'The Date of Disastrous Proportions. Me, too.' She smiled back at him. 'This is a fabulous menu, Ellis. Shall we order a pile of dishes to share?'

'You're welcome to order meat if you want to,' he said. 'You don't have to go vegetarian for my sake.'

'I'm absolutely fine with veggie food. Though I must admit the Serrano ham croquettes do look nice,' she said wistfully, 'if you don't mind me ordering them?'

'No, that's fine.'

They ordered a mixture of dishes—*patatas bravas*, Manchego cheese and quince paste, Manzanilla olives, tomatoes, bread, a bowl of garlicky wilted spinach, the Serrano ham croquettes that had caught Ruby's eye, and a traditional Spanish omelette, together with a bottle of good Rioja.

Ruby had a feeling that Ellis was brooding about something. And it would be better to face it sooner rather than later. 'So what did you want to talk about?' she asked.

'Theo asked me to see him today.' He grimaced.

'Maybe I should shut up now, before I break a confidence.'

'You know I won't say anything to anyone,' Ruby said. 'And it's pretty obvious why Theo would want to talk to you, given that you're Billie's locum and her maternity leave ends soon. So I assume she's coming back?'

'Part-time,' Ellis confirmed.

She bit her lip. 'So where does that leave you?'

'Full-time until she's back. Then I'm doing my month's assignment with the charity.' He paused. 'Theo's looking to recruit another full-time registrar and he wants me to apply for the interview. He says it's a formality but he has to advertise the job externally as well.'

'I get that.' But this was a crunch moment, Ruby thought. Would Ellis apply for the job at the London Victoria, or would he look for a post in a different London hospital—or would he want to stay with the medical aid charity?

Ruby wanted him to stay—but she wanted him to stay because *he* wanted to stay. She didn't want him to feel trapped.

Face it, she told herself. Be brave. Ask him straight out. 'I know you came back to London for Tom's sake, and you've stayed here since he died because he asked you to keep an eye out for me—but what do you really want, Ellis?'

Everything.

Though Ellis was pretty sure he couldn't have Ruby in his life and go back to the medical aid charity. He knew she loved her job here and she was happy in London, so he couldn't ask her to leave it all behind and go travelling the world with him, never staying more than a few weeks in one place.

He really did miss the travelling and the camaraderie of the medical aid charity team, even though he liked his colleagues at the London Victoria very much. There was that extra edge when he worked abroad, where every second was vital.

An old pop song flickered through his head, asking him if he should stay or if he should go.

It was going to be a hard choice. Either way, he was going to have to make a sacrifice. Stay here in London and be with Ruby and miss his old life; or go back to his old life abroad and miss Ruby.

'This thing between us,' he said. 'It's very new.'

'Uh-huh.'

Her face was absolutely expressionless. He had no idea what she was thinking, though he had a feeling that she was trying not to put any pressure on him. Which made him feel horrendously selfish, because Ruby was clearly trying to put him first. He was trying to do the same for her. Were they working at cross-purposes, here? Or could they both have everything they wanted?

The only way to find out was to ask.

'The medical aid charity isn't just for doctors, you know,' he said. 'They recruit nurses, too. Midwives.' He paused. 'If I went back permanently, would you consider going out with me and working for them?'

Her expression changed, then, to one of total surprise. She clearly hadn't expected that to be an option.

Was that a good or a bad thing?

Panicking, he said, 'Ruby, you don't have to answer straight away. I pretty much sprung that on you.'

'Uh-huh.'

And he was all at sea again, not being able to guess how she felt. Though he could see that she looked wary. And he knew it was a huge decision, not one she could make quickly or lightly. 'Take your time,' he said. 'Just think about it in the back of your head, and we'll talk about it again when you're ready.'

'OK.'

He changed the topic of conversation to something light, and when their food arrived they were able to distract themselves with that. Especially when Ruby ordered churros with a cinnamon-spiced chocolate sauce for them to share, and he had to stop himself leaning over and kissing a tiny smear of chocolate from the corner of her mouth.

'I know the coffee here is probably going to be as excellent as the food,' he said, 'but would you like to have coffee back at my place?'

'Good idea,' she said. 'It'll be easier to talk.'

In other words, discussing something in private.

Adrenalin trickled down his spine. Did that mean she'd made a decision about what he'd asked her? Would she go with him, or would she stay?

He paid the bill and they caught the Tube back to his flat. He made them both a coffee and brought out a packet of buttery biscuit curls.

'Now these are nice,' she said with a smile. 'I'm impressed, Dr Webster.'

'Good.' But even the sugar rush couldn't distract him. He needed to know. Now. 'Have you had enough time to think about what I said?' he asked softly.

'Yes.' She took a deep breath. 'I know it's a really worthy thing to do, and I feel horribly selfish about saying this, but working for a medical aid charity really isn't for me, Ellis. I love my job here and I want to stay relatively near to my family and Tom's. Manchester's only a couple of hours away from London on the train, and so is Suffolk. If I work abroad, I won't get to see any of them very often. I might not even be working in a place where I can get a phone signal to talk to them.'

And he knew that Ruby was emotionally close to her family and Tom's. Of course she wouldn't want to be physically far away from them. It was unfair of him to ask her to change that for his sake.

She reached over to squeeze his hand. 'But I also care enough about you to let you go, if you want to go back. I'm never going to hold you back or trap you.'

But it meant he had a choice to make. Go back to working abroad without Ruby: or stay in London and be with Ruby. He couldn't have both.

'What if I apply for the job in our department, come back to London after my assignment and—provided that Theo offers it to me, because he might find a better candidate—I accept the job?' he asked softly. 'Do we take our relationship to the next stage?'

'Is that what you want?'

'To take our relationship to the next stage?' His fingers tightened round hers. 'Yes.'

'But?'

Typical Ruby, picking up what he wasn't saying. 'But the last time I got married, it all went so wrong. And it kind of scares me. If I give up my job abroad, stay here and try to make a go of it with you, and it all goes wrong...' He blew out a breath. 'I don't want to hurt you.'

'I don't want to hurt you, either,' she said. 'So what happened? Why did you split up? I mean—don't get me wrong, I'm not prying, but maybe if you look at what happened you can learn from your mistakes or something?'

'Maybe.' He sighed. 'I met Natalia when we were both working at the medical aid charity. It was one of those *coup de foudre* moments—you know, you meet someone for the very first time and you feel as if you've been struck by lightning. You just click instantly.'

She nodded.

'We were both assigned to a team helping a community after bad flooding. We had a mad affair. And then one day she was caught in a flash flood. Luckily they managed to rescue her. But she could've drowned. She was the first person I've ever been scared of losing—and I guess I acted on that fear instead of thinking it through and letting myself calm down and be logical about things.' He gave her a rueful smile. 'You always say I'm practical and sensible. I wasn't, then. I asked her to marry me, even though we'd barely known each other for a month, and she said yes. And, two weeks later, the paperwork was all sorted and we got married.' He grimaced. 'In a rush. And that's why Tom wasn't my best man. There wasn't enough time to tell him I was getting married and get him a flight out there.' He looked away. 'And I still feel guilty about that. It was supposed to be one of the most special days of my life—the kind of day I'd want my best friend to be part of, too.'

'Just as you were Tom's best man,' she said softly. 'And you flew back to England for three days, so you'd be at our wedding.'

'The year before I got married. Yeah. Which should've told me that I was doing the wrong thing when I married Natalia. I should've talked to Tom about it and at least waited so he could come and be my best man.' He sighed. 'It was a whirlwind romance and we both lost our heads a bit. We didn't really know each other well enough, and we should've waited a while and got to know each other an awful lot better.' He gave her a rueful smile. 'I assumed Natalia loved the job as much as I did and she'd be happy to keep travelling with me, working in a different country every few weeks and seeing the world and knowing we were making a difference. But she wanted something else.'

'Something you didn't?'

He nodded. 'She assumed that getting married meant I wanted to go back to one of our home countries and settle down. Probably a capital city. Moscow or London—she didn't mind which.'

'But you obviously didn't want to settle.'

'No.'

'And you didn't talk any of this through before you got married?'

She sounded surprised—shocked, even. And she had a point. They hadn't thought it through or talked it through. 'I was twenty-five and I still had an awful lot of growing up to do. I guess, so did she. We ended it reasonably amicably, or as amicably as you can end any marriage,' he added. 'We both realised that we shouldn't have got married in the first place; we should have left our relationship as a mad affair and waited for the right person. We lost touch after the divorce, so I have no idea if she found her Mr Right—but I hope she did. I'd like to think she's happy now.'

'Fair enough.'

Ruby's voice was even, but Ellis noticed that she'd gently wriggled her fingers out of his grasp. Did that mean she'd changed her mind about him—that she felt his track record meant that he wouldn't be a good bet for her?

'So do you know what you want out of life now?' she asked. 'Do you still want to go back to the medical aid charity?'

'Yes, I do, because I love my job,' he admitted. 'But part of me wants to stay with you.' Even though the two things were mutually exclusive. Job or Ruby. That was the choice.

'I've already lost someone I loved deeply,' she said. 'I'm not sure I'm ready to take that risk again. I don't want to lose you to your job. So maybe you and I should go back to being just good friends.'

'Is that what you want?' he asked.

'Yes and no,' she said. 'I want to be with you, Ellis. But I also know you need to follow your heart and I'd never stop you doing that. If you decide to stay here in London when you still have itchy feet, then at some point in the future you're going to feel trapped and you'll start to resent me for holding you back. The whole thing's going to end up—' she grimaced '—and please don't think I'm being bitchy, because I'm just trying to be realistic here. I worry that things between us are going to end up like your marriage did. They'll go wrong, because we want different things from life and we haven't talked it through properly. We haven't given each other enough time.'

'I married Natalia in a rush because I was scared of losing her, and I ended up hurting her because it turned out that we didn't want the same things. I've grown up a lot since then,' Ellis said. 'But I admit that over the past few years I've kept my relationships just for fun, so we all know the score and nobody gets hurt.'

'I can understand that,' she said.

'Since I've met you, it's been different,' he said. 'I know Tom loved you deeply, and you loved him. And while Tom was alive I would never, ever have made a move on you. But somewhere over the last eighteen months my feelings towards you changed. I don't think of you as just a friend, Rubes.'

'So what are you saying, Ellis?'

He took a deep breath. Crunch time. 'I want to be with you.'

'We've known each other for a long time, but it's still very early days with us dating. Supposing we find out we really don't want the same things?' she asked.

'Then we'll talk about it and find a way to compromise. Isn't that what a grown-up relationship's meant to be about?'

'I guess so.' She looked at him. 'And that's what you want? A grown-up relationship? With me?'

'I do,' he said softly. 'Right now, I can't promise you that everything's going to work out. That it's all going to be perfect and plain sailing.'

'Nobody can ever promise that,' Ruby said. 'Because life happens and changes things.'

'But what I can promise,' he said, 'is that I'll always try to be honest with you.'

'That's all I can ask for,' she said. 'And it's enough for me.'

'So, you and me.' He took her hand again, and drew it up to his mouth. 'I can't quite believe this is happening.'

'Me, neither.'

'Ruby.' He leaned towards her and touched his lips

to hers. For a moment she remained tense, and then she gave a small sigh and relaxed into his arms.

This was what he wanted.

Ruby, soft and warm and in his arms. Kissing him until they were both dizzy.

He deepened the kiss, and the next thing he knew he was lying on the sofa, with Ruby sprawled on top of him. His hands had slid underneath the hem of her top and were splayed against her back.

'Sorry. I'm taking this a bit too fast,' he said softly, restoring order to her clothes and then sitting up again, moving her so that she was sitting on his lap with his arms wrapped round her.

'Sorry.' She stroked his face. 'And here we are. Apologising to each other and being super-polite.'

'I've wanted you for a long time,' he said. 'But, as you said, this is still early days. I'm happy to wait until you're ready for the next step.'

'Thank you. Because I want this, too—but...'

'I know. It's scary.' He dropped a kiss on her forehead. 'Can I be honest with you? I really don't want our first time together to be in London. I want it to be somewhere else, where neither of us has any memories.'

'Is it going to be a problem? The past, I mean?'

'No.' He was definite about that. 'I'm not trying to compete with Tom, and I know you're not comparing me to him because we're very different men. And I loved Tom dearly—as much as if he was one of my brothers. But I want something that's just going to be for us,' he said. 'I assume you've already been to Paris and Rome with Tom?'

She nodded. 'They're my two favourite cities,' she

said. 'And Tom and I visited a lot of Italy over the years. Florence, Venice, Sorrento, Verona, the Lakes.'

'Not Italy, then. Or Paris. But somewhere just as magical.'

'How about you?' she asked. 'Where's the most magical place you've ever been?'

'The Australian Outback,' he said without hesitation. 'Uluru—Ayers Rock is amazing, Rubes. It glows red at dawn, and purple and blue at sunset. I've never seen anything like it. And the stars are stunning, because there's no artificial light source. You just look up and see the Milky Way and the Magellanic clouds stretching across the sky. It's one of the most incredible sights I've ever seen.'

'Were you there for long?'

'A few days. I wasn't working—I just took the opportunity to get on a plane and spend a couple of weeks travelling round Australia. I was privileged to go on a tour round Uluru with one of the Anangu people. He showed me the springs, caves and rock paintings, and he told me about the Aboriginal dreamtime stories of the area. And we talked about medicine—did you know they use the sap of the centralian bloodwood as a disinfectant and an inhalant for coughs and colds?'

She smiled. 'I should've guessed you'd end up talking about that sort of thing. You're all about the wild and untameable, aren't you?'

'Only in part. I'm guessing that you prefer cities?'

'Ones with pretty buildings, lots of history and good food. I'm not so fussed about shopping,' she said.

'Maybe we could go somewhere together,' he said. 'Just the two of us.'

Her eyes widened. 'And then we take the next step?'

'Not necessarily. No expectations—the same as going out for dinner with you didn't mean that I expected you to go to bed with me. We just spend a bit of time together and take life as it comes. We'll have separate rooms so there's no pressure. If it happens, then fantastic; if it doesn't, then we'll wait until we're both ready.'

'No pressure,' she repeated.

'Is your passport current?'

'Yes.' She stroked his face. 'Are you thinking of soon?'

'Yup. When's your next off-duty where you have three days off in a row?'

'I'll need to check on my phone. Then maybe we can synchronise it.'

'Sure.' He kissed her lightly. 'And we'll see what happens.'

A few days away together, in a place that had no memories for either of them. A place where they'd make new memories. Where maybe they'd make love for the first time.

Part of Ruby was thrilled. She loved the idea of spending time with Ellis, sharing a new city with him, discovering little cafés and art galleries.

Part of her felt guilty. It still wasn't *that* long since Tom's death. Was this too soon?

And part of her wondered if this was the beginning of the end of her relationship with Ellis. She'd seen the wonder in his face when he'd been talking about the Australian Outback, the longing in his eyes when he'd mentioned the medical aid charity. Would the odd few days in Europe really be enough to keep his itchy feet happy? Or would the lure of his job be too much for him, once he went back for that planned month's assignment?

CHAPTER NINE

TRAVELLING AGAIN. EVEN though it wasn't quite the same—he was going simply to have fun, rather than working to make a difference in the world—the idea of seeing another part of the world filled Ellis with joy. Especially because he was going to share it with Ruby. Somewhere new for both of them.

During his lunch break, he went to the travel agent's to pick up some brochures for city breaks, then left Ruby a text.

Have pile of brochures. Want to come and plan our trip after work?

Sorry, can't. On lates until Friday, then I'm going to Manchester for the day to see my family, was her reply.

He damped down the disappointment.

Sure. Let me know when you're free and we'll do it then.

You could come to Manchester with me, if you like?

As her official date?

He wasn't sure he was ready to go public with their

relationship, yet, let alone go to meet her family as her date. Not until they were both sure about where this was going. He knew how he felt about Ruby, but he also knew that he didn't have a good track record. Until he could be absolutely sure that this was going to work out and he wasn't going to hurt her, the way he'd hurt Natalia, he didn't want to make things too official.

Ellis had met Ruby's family at the wedding and at Tom's funeral, and Tom himself had always spoken highly of his in-laws. But meeting them as Tom's best friend was a very different kettle of fish from meeting them as Ruby's partner.

Sorry, working Friday, he typed back. Maybe next time you go?

Ellis and Ruby were both free on Sunday, and spent the afternoon poring over the travel brochures.

'An ice hotel—that sounds really romantic,' Ruby said. 'And we might get to see the Northern Lights. I'd love that.' Her smile faded. 'That was on Tom's bucket list, too. Except we didn't have the time.'

He hugged her. 'I know. Maybe we'll do that another time,' he said softly. 'This is only a short break, and there's no guarantee we'll actually see the lights.'

'Plus the short daylight hours mean we won't have time to explore any of the cities,' she agreed. 'OK. How about Barcelona?'

'Apparently the Sagrada Familia is amazing. So that's a possibility.' He paused. 'Or maybe Vienna.'

'Sachertorte and Mozart,' she said promptly. 'And it'll be late October when we go, so the Austrian Christmas markets might have started, too. That'd be nice.'

'Or,' he said, 'what about the city of a thousand spires?'

'Where's that?'

'Prague. In the Czech Republic. Next door to Austria.'

She grinned. 'That's where you really want to go, isn't it?'

Yes. He'd seen the pictures in the brochures and known immediately that he wanted to visit the city. But how did she know? 'What makes you say that?' he asked carefully.

'The way your eyes lit up when you said it. Like they did when you talked about the stars in the Australian Outback.'

'Busted,' he admitted. 'I, um, sort of made a list. In my head. Nothing formal, and I wouldn't have made a proper list without you.'

She laughed. 'I didn't think you'd be able to wait.'

He hadn't. The itch to travel, and to plan a trip, had been too strong. He *missed* travelling, seeing new places and meeting new people and learning new things.

She glanced through the brochure. 'All those bridges across the river—Prague's very pretty. It reminds me a bit of Florence, or maybe Paris.'

'And at this time of year there might be a chance of a sprinkle of snow. It could be really romantic.'

'Sold. Let's do it,' she said.

'Great. The hotels all seem to be gorgeous art deco buildings.'

'That's lovely. And, by the way, we're going halves on this trip,' she reminded him.

He sighed. 'We've already had this conversation. You know, about accepting gracefully when it's made clear that there are no strings? I just want to spoil you a bit, Rubes.'

'Buying me dinner isn't the same as taking me away for a three-day break, Ellis.'

'I wouldn't offer if I couldn't afford it,' he said softly.

'We're going halves.' She folded her arms.

'How about I pay for the hotel and flights, and you pay for dinner?' he suggested.

'And entrance fees to wherever we go,' she added.

If it made her feel more comfortable, then he'd agree. 'OK.'

'Good.'

Though her arms were still folded and there was a little pleat in her brow—something he'd noticed when she was unhappy about something. 'I'll try and find us somewhere central,' he said. 'And remember I said I'll book separate rooms, so there are no expectations and there's no pressure. We're just going away and enjoying ourselves, exploring somewhere new to both of us.'

To his relief, the frown faded. 'Thank you, Ellis,' she said softly. 'I appreciate it.'

'I know.' He kissed her lightly. 'And we need a guide book.'

She laughed, and he frowned. 'What's so funny?'

'Given that you're such a seasoned traveller, I expected you to—well, just go with the flow.'

'No. When I get the chance to explore somewhere new, I read up about the place in advance so I can plan what I want to see and make the most of my time there.' He smiled. 'I don't do it quite down to the microsecond, but some places are closed on certain days and it'd be a shame to miss out on them because we hadn't bothered to check up beforehand.'

'OK. I'll pick up a guide book tomorrow lunchtime,'

she said. 'I haven't been away for quite a while, so this is really exciting.'

'What I'm most looking forward to,' he said, 'is spending time with you, chilling out and discovering things together.'

'Sounds good to me. So I take it I need to pack walking shoes and comfortable clothes?'

'And maybe a posh dress, in case we decide to have dinner somewhere fancy.'

She laughed. 'Promise you're not going to spill wine all over me?'

He laughed back, knowing she was referring to their disastrous 'first date'. 'I'll try not to.'

Ellis called for Ruby the day of their departure; then they took the train to the airport and queued up at the flight desk to process their baggage.

'So whereabouts is our hotel?' she asked.

'We're just off Wenceslaus Square,' he said, 'so we're about a ten-minute walk from the Old Town Square, and maybe another five minutes from there to the river.'

'That sounds perfect. Thank you.' She stood on tiptoe and kissed him, and it made him feel warm all the way through.

Once they were through customs and passport control in Prague, they saw a taxi driver waiting by the barriers holding a board with the name 'Webster' written on it in capitals,

'I booked the taxi transfer in advance, to save us having to queue,' he explained.

'Which is why your name's on the board.' She smiled. 'I thought that sort of thing only happened in films.'

'Me, too.' He took her hand. 'But it's fun.'

The taxi driver didn't speak English. 'Thanks to working with doctors of all nationalities with the medical aid charity, I've got a smattering of a lot of languages,' Ellis said. 'Though I don't know much Czech beyond please, thank you, hello, goodbye and ordering a couple of beers.'

'Just as well we have a phrase book, then,' Ruby said, taking it from her bag.

The airport was in the middle of the countryside, and they enjoyed the autumnal views on the way to the city. Prague itself was beautiful, with lots of white four- and five-storey buildings with orange roofs. Everywhere they looked, they could see domes, mosaics and lots of windows.

'This is gorgeous. It reminds me a bit of Paris,' Ruby said.

'Me, too—but look.' He gestured to the skyline; there were lots of turrets and towers with spires, all very gothic and very pretty.

'I can see why they call it the city of a thousand spires. There must be a dozen on that tower over there alone.' She smiled at him. 'I'm so looking forward to this, Ellis.'

His fingers tightened round hers. 'So am I,' he said softly.

The taxi drew up outside their hotel. Ellis helped Ruby out of the back of the cab, then tipped the driver. A doorman wearing a top hat took their luggage, and they checked in at the front desk. The hotel reception was gorgeous, all marble and art deco glass; there was a table in the centre containing huge vases with stunning arrangements of lilies and peonies.

'This is amazing,' she said once they'd got their card

keys for their rooms and were heading up in the lift. 'But, Ellis, this must have cost a fortune. It has to be the swishest hotel in Prague.'

'No, the swishest hotel is overlooking the river, actually. I did ask, but sadly their presidential suite is currently booked by a film star,' he said, and laughed. 'Plus it was ever so slightly out of my budget. This isn't.'

'I wasn't expecting this to be so—well...' She gestured round them. 'It's gorgeous, but I feel bad that you've spent so much money on me.'

'Remember what I said about being gracious. I want to do something nice for you, so let me have the pleasure of making you smile.'

'I guess.' She bit her lip. 'Sorry. Now I'm being an ungrateful brat. I didn't mean it like that.'

'I know. But there really are no strings attached. This is just a couple of days for us to explore somewhere new and have some fun,' he said. 'No timetables and no schedules—though I admit I've reserved us a table here tomorrow night, because they have a band playing and I thought it might be fun to dance together after dinner.'

'That sounds lovely.'

'Let's unpack,' he said, 'and then we can go exploring. How long do you need?'

'Ten minutes,' she said.

'Great.' He smiled at her. 'See you out here in ten.'

The room was amazingly swanky. The bed was incredibly wide and very comfortable, and the bathroom was all gleaming marble and thick fluffy towels. It didn't take Ruby long to unpack, and she was ready to meet Ellis in the ten minutes she'd promised.

'I feel thoroughly spoiled,' Ruby said when she

walked through her door to find him waiting in the corridor.

'Good. That was the idea.'

His grey eyes were sparkling with what she guessed was happiness; the same feeling that was bubbling through her.

He smiled and took her hand. 'Let's go and see the sights.'

The city was beautiful and Ruby really enjoyed walking through the Old Town. There were lots of gorgeous art deco buildings with yellow, pink or white walls, a dome on the roof and huge arched windows.

A crowd of people was waiting outside one particular building.

'That's the astronomical clock,' Ellis said when he'd consulted his guide book. 'It's the oldest working astronomical clock in the world, and it shows the movement of the sun and moon through the zodiac.'

'It's so pretty with all those swirling greens and blues and golds.' She glanced at her watch. 'Does something happen on the hour?'

'Apparently the figures move. Shall we wait and see?'

On the hour, the figure of Death struck the bell, to the cheers of the waiting tourists.

'It's amazing that it's six hundred years old and still working,' she said. 'I'm so glad we came here.'

They walked from the old town square down to the Vltava river, then found a small café overlooking the wide, fast-flowing river where they could grab a sandwich and coffee for lunch.

'Would you like to go on a river trip?' Ellis asked.

'That's a great idea. I hardly ever got to go on a boat

as Tom used to get horribly seasick. Even with travel sickness pills, he couldn't handle a gentle cruise down the Thames.'

'I remember,' Ellis said. 'There was a school trip in the South of France where we were supposed to go out in a glass-bottomed boat and see all these amazing fish, except when we got out of the harbour the water was a bit choppy. I didn't get to see any of the fish either, because I was too busy trying to find extra sick bags for him—the crew hadn't brought enough and suggested that people shared bags, and that made Tom throw up even more!'

'Poor Tom. It must have been awful for him—and not that nice for everyone round him, either.' She smiled at him. 'I'm so glad we can talk about him, Ellis. That it's not going to make things awkward between us.'

'We both loved him,' Ellis said simply, 'so it's an extra bond between us. Of course it's not going to be awkward. And I'd never cut him out of my life and refuse to talk about him.' He knew she was well aware of what he hadn't said: the way his parents were about Sally. 'I want to remember the good times and smile about them. Just as I do about Sally.' And how he wished he could fix it for his parents, so they'd still have some of the joy left in their lives. He slid his arm round Ruby's shoulders and gave her a hug.

He held her hand all the way on the river trip. And his fingers tightened round hers when they passed the lover's bridge festooned with padlocks. 'It seems to be a tradition in a lot of European cities now,' she said, 'to put a padlock on a bridge with your initials on it.'

'Which is a bit more environmentally friendly than carving it into a tree trunk,' Ellis said.

Once they were back on dry land, they walked over the Charles Bridge, admiring the statues and the views of the other bridges across the Vltava. 'I can hardly believe this bridge is nearly seven hundred years old,' she said. 'I loved the story the guide on the boat told us about mixing the mortar with eggs to make it stronger. I wonder if that really happened?'

'Who knows? As you say, it was a good story.'

They wandered hand in hand through the streets. Ruby hadn't felt this relaxed in a long time, and she was really enjoying exploring the city with Ellis, stopping whenever something caught their eye to consult the guide book for more information.

They found a small, romantic restaurant serving local dishes, and the waiter smiled in approval when Ellis spoke Czech to order two beers.

'What do you recommend that's typically Czech?' she asked the waiter.

'*Svíčková na smetaně*,' he said, which turned out to be dumplings and beef in creamy sauce with cranberry compote and sweetened whipped cream.

The vegetarian option was *smažený sýr*—a thick slice of cheese, breadcrumbed and fried, served with potato salad.

'It all looks amazing but not so good for our arteries,' she said when the waiter had gone again.

'I'm pretty sure we'll walk it off tomorrow,' he said with a smile. 'I thought we could go and explore the castle.'

'Sounds great,' she said.

The food was excellent; the dumpling was larger than Ruby expected, made into a large roll and sliced. She liked the tartness of the cranberry as it cut through the richness of the cream. 'I definitely need to join you in walking this off tomorrow,' she said with a smile.

Once they'd shared a pudding—a potato dumpling stuffed with plums, steamed, and served with melted butter and a sprinkle of sugar—they walked back to the hotel, enjoying the way the city was lit up at night.

'This was a brilliant idea,' she said. 'Thank you, Ellis.'

'My pleasure.' He slid his arm round her shoulder, and she slid hers round his waist, enjoying his nearness.

Back at the hotel, they ordered hot chocolate at the bar; then finally they headed to their rooms.

Was this when it was going to happen? Ruby wondered, her pulse hammering.

Ellis kissed her goodnight at the door, his mouth warm and sweet and coaxing.

But then he pulled back. 'Goodnight, Ruby. Sleep well.'

Clearly he wasn't expecting her to invite him in to her room—and he hadn't invited her to his, either. So he'd meant it when he'd said there were no strings, no expectations. Odd how that made her stomach give a little swoop of disappointment.

But maybe he was right. Rushing into anything could be a mistake. And he'd admitted to making a huge mistake, rushing in to marriage in the past. He must feel just as wary as she did.

'You, too,' she said brightly, and let herself into her room.

Once she'd showered and cleaned her teeth, she changed into her pyjamas and climbed into bed. She lay there awake, thinking of Ellis. Wandering round such a romantic city with him, hand in hand; the way he'd kissed her at unexpected moments; and the warmth and sweetness of his arms round her.

What would happen if she picked up the phone and dialled his extension?

She thought about it to the point where she actually picked up the phone and dialled the first digit of his room number. But then she replaced the receiver, not wanting to get this wrong and make things awkward between them.

Tomorrow was another day.

Maybe tomorrow.

Ellis lay awake, thinking of Ruby. Outside her door, she'd looked so vulnerable for a moment that he'd wanted to hold her and not let her go. Yet at the same time he hadn't wanted her to feel pressured. He'd booked separate rooms on purpose, to make it clear that he was happy to wait until she was ready to take their relationship to the next step.

What if he called her now?

What if he asked her to come to his room—just to cuddle up and go to sleep together?

But that would be unfair. He didn't want her to feel obliged, just because he'd paid for the trip. Plus it was still early days between them.

He'd wait until she was ready, just as he'd promised himself. He'd keep cool, calm and collected.

But, oh, he wished...

CHAPTER TEN

RUBY HAD BREAKFAST with Ellis the next morning in the hotel restaurant: a mushroom and cheese omelette cooked by the chef; toast, fruit with yoghurt, and freshly squeezed orange juice followed by a cappuccino.

'This is the perfect start to the day,' she said with a smile. 'And it's nice not to be grabbing a granola bar and a banana and eating them on the way to work.'

'So you like being waited on?' Ellis asked.

She laughed. 'No. I'm just enjoying being spoiled. Weren't those your orders?'

'Absolutely.' He smiled back.

It was another crisp, bright autumn day: perfect for exploring. They bought tickets from a kiosk; using a mixture of guidebook Czech and sign language, they found out where the tram stop was and took a tram to the castle. There was a jolt when the tram turned one corner and she stumbled, not quite sure where to grab on to as there weren't overhead bars or straps like there were on the Tube in London. Ellis caught her before she fell.

'Thank you.'

'No worries.'

It felt natural then to wrap her arms round his waist

and stay where she was until they reached the tram stop for the castle.

They had a beautiful view from the hill.

'According to the guide book, this is the largest castle in the world,' he told her.

Ruby could believe it; there seemed to be courtyard after courtyard, and the walls seemed to stretch out for ever.

They went into the oldest section of the castle and walked up a set of wide, shallow brick stairs. 'I have to say, I was expecting narrow stone spiral stairs,' she said, 'like the ones you get in a lot of English castles.'

He consulted the guide book and raised an eyebrow. 'That's because these weren't for people.'

'Not for people? Who were they for, then?' she asked, puzzled.

His eyes sparkled. 'Would you believe, horses?'

'No way!'

'They used to joust in the Vladislav hall, so the knights would ride up these stairs,' he said. 'Honestly. I'm not teasing.'

When they walked into the hall, she realised that he was telling the truth. It was a massive room, very long, with vaulted ceilings, the most enormous windows and huge wrought iron chandeliers. 'I can imagine it. There's enough room for the knights to joust and people to watch them.'

Afterwards, they strolled through the palace gardens, enjoying the amazing view of the city from the castle walls.

'The cathedral reminds me very much of Notre Dame, with the twin towers and the rose window,' she said as they went into yet another courtyard and discovered the cathedral of St Vitus. Inside, she loved the soaring vaulted ceilings and the Mucha window.

'And there's a bell tower... I know they don't have a grotesque gallery here like they do at Notre Dame, but I still think we have to climb it,' Ellis said.

'Agreed,' she said with a smile.

'You look all pink and adorable,' he said when they got to the top.

'You mean, I'm not as fit as I like to think I am,' she said wryly. 'Especially as you're not even glowing, let alone hot and sweaty like I am!'

'Nope, you're all pink and adorable,' he repeated, and kissed her.

They stood looking out at the views, with Ellis standing behind Ruby, his arms wrapped round her and holding her close. Funny how being with Ellis made her feel like a teenager again.

Almost as if he'd picked up on her thoughts, he asked, 'Can I take a selfie?'

'Sure, as long as you send it to me as well.'

He stooped to press his cheek against hers and took a picture of them both smiling. 'Me and my girl,' he said softly, 'and there's the spire to prove we're right at the top of the cathedral.'

Me and my girl. It sent a thrill all the way through her.

They enjoyed wandering through the rest of the castle, visiting the tiny houses in Golden Lane. Ruby was fascinated by the herbalist's house, with its narrow wooden shelves full of stone jars and bottles, with bunches of herbs hanging up to dry from the rafters. 'This is what we would have worked with, all these years ago,' she said.

'In some of the places where I've worked, it's more than we'd have now,' he said. 'Even hot water can be a luxury.'

Ruby wondered again, would Ellis stay with the medical aid charity? Was visiting a place like this enough to stop his itchy feet returning, or was it making things worse? She didn't like to ask him outright—it felt like an ungrateful question, especially as he'd gone to the trouble to make this break special for her—but she remembered Tina's warning. She'd be a fool to let herself fall for someone who didn't want to stay around.

When they'd finished looking round the castle, they grabbed a *trdelnik* from one of the fast-food stands just outside the castle gates. The rolled dough was made into a spiral, grilled on a stick and sprinkled with sugar and cinnamon. 'This is gorgeous,' she said after the first taste. 'It's like a cross between the crêpes in Paris and the doughnuts you'd have at the seaside in England.'

They walked through the cobbled streets of the Lesser Quarter into Petrin Park. 'We have to see the Observation Tower while we're here,' Ellis said. 'It's a cópy of the Eiffel Tower but about a quarter of the size—though, because it's on a hill, it's actually higher than the Eiffel Tower and the views are meant to be amazing.'

The day had turned windy and when they got to the top of the tower Ruby was a bit taken aback to discover that it actually swayed in the wind. As if Ellis realised what was making her nervous, he wrapped his arms round her again, making her feel safe. 'The guide book was right. The views are amazing,' she said, 'and I think that golden roof is the theatre we passed when we were on the river.'

'And the Dancing House,' he said, pointing out the modern building that looked just like a couple doing the waltz on the other side of the river. 'Maybe we can have a closer look at that tomorrow.'

'Sounds good to me.'

Hand in hand, they walked back to the hotel.

'Our table will be ready in an hour and a half,' he said in the corridor outside their doors. 'Unless that's not giving you enough time to get ready, we could go to the bar for a drink first?' he suggested.

She smiled. 'You know I'm not one of these women who needs hours and hours to do her hair and make-up. A drink at the bar sounds good. Shall I knock on your door when I'm ready?'

'That'd be perfect,' he said with a smile, and kissed her. 'I've really enjoyed today. I'm glad I shared it with you.'

'Me, too—even though that tower was a bit scary when it started swaying,' she said.

Ruby showered, did her hair, changed into the new little black dress she'd bought especially for Prague, and did her make-up. And she felt ridiculously nervous as she knocked on his door.

Ellis was wearing a formal dinner suit and bow tie. She was used to him wearing a suit at work, but this took it to another level. 'You look amazing,' she said, feeling her eyes widen.

'So do you.' He drew her into his arms. 'Right now I really want to kiss you, but I guess I shouldn't smudge your lipstick.'

'You can kiss me later,' she said.

'I hope that's a promise.'

'It is—and I always keep my promises,' she said.

They had a glass of wine in the bar, and then it was time to go into the restaurant. Ruby glanced at the menu and gasped. 'Ellis, it's Michelin-starred.'

'I know, and it counts as part of the hotel bill.'

'It most certainly does not. Our deal was that I'm paying for dinner.'

'You can buy me lunch tomorrow,' he said. 'I'm paying, and you're not allowed to argue. Remember, graciousness.'

She rolled her eyes. 'Thank you. But you really didn't have to.'

Once their waiter had poured the champagne, he brought them both an *amuse-bouche* of ravioli filled with mushrooms and truffles, served with foamed butter.

'This is to die for,' Ruby said.

Ellis smiled. 'What was that in the ad you wrote for me about finding a foodie as a partner?'

She laughed. 'Absolutely.'

The starter was a soft buffalo mozzarella served with rocket and tomatoes and balsamic, light and quivery and beautifully presented. Ellis had beetroot ravioli filled with ricotta and thyme and served with more of the foamed butter, while Ruby had grilled sea bass with Mediterranean vegetables. But the best bit for her was the pudding—crème brûlée, her favourite, and the waiter actually brought a blow-torch to the table along with the dessert. 'There's a tiny drop of brandy on the top so the sugar will be flambéed,' he explained, then set fire to the sugar so it would melt into a hard crust.

'This has to be the best meal I've ever eaten in my entire life,' Ruby sighed when they'd finished.

'From a foodie like you, that's quite a compliment,' Ellis said.

After dinner, as Ellis had promised, there was dancing. A woman with a smoky voice was singing soft jazz, accompanied by a piano, double-bass, and guitar. The lighting was soft and, together with the music, made the room feel very intimate. Ellis swayed with her, holding her close, and Ruby felt as if she could dance all night.

She closed her eyes and gave herself up to the music and his nearness. Right at that moment, she could believe that the two of them were the only ones in the room. And Ellis was an excellent dancer; he led her round the floor so she didn't have to worry about putting a foot wrong.

Finally the singer said goodnight and the band left the stage.

'Do you want to go to back to the bar?' Ellis asked.

'No, I think I've had quite enough alcohol for tonight,' she said. What she really wanted was to ask him to come back to her room with her, but she didn't quite have the nerve to say so; shyness kept the words inside.

'I'll see you back to your room,' he said.

The lift was all mirrors inside, and their reflections stretched out to infinity.

'I could kiss you to infinity right now.' His voice was low and husky, and the words sent a thrill right through her.

'Do it,' she whispered back.

He gave her the sexiest smile she'd ever seen, dipped his head and brushed his mouth against hers. Every nerve-end tingled; she wrapped her arms round him and kissed him back until she couldn't think straight.

There was a soft ding and the lift doors opened.

He broke the kiss, looking dazed.

Somehow they managed to walk out of the lift and down the corridor to their rooms.

He paused outside her door. 'I guess this is good-night,' he said softly.

She could do the sensible thing and say goodnight.

Or she could give in to the demands flooding her body and ask him to stay.

For a heartbeat she was torn between the two. She knew that making love with Ellis would change things between them again, and supposing it changed things the wrong way?

But she'd never been a coward. If things between them went wrong in the future, then they went wrong. Right here, right now, she knew what she wanted. Ellis.

'What if I don't want it to be goodnight?' she asked, her voice equally soft.

'Are you saying...?'

'Stay with me, Ellis.'

'Are you sure about that?'

'Very sure.' She took her card key from her evening bag, slipped it into the lock and opened her door.

Then he scooped her up in his arms and carried her into the room. He nudged the door closed behind them, then set her back on her feet, keeping her body close to his so she was left in no doubt about how much he wanted her.

The curtains were already closed, and there was just the low light of the bedside lamp.

'It feels as if we should have candlelight,' he said.

'This is the next best thing,' she said. 'It'd probably set the fire alarms off if we had candles in here anyway.'

'You're so practical. It's one of the things I love about you.'

'Thank you.' She inclined her head in acknowledgement of the compliment.

'Something else I love,' he said, 'is your mouth.' He traced the curve of her lower lip with the tip of his finger. 'It's a perfect cupid's bow.'

She opened her mouth and drew the tip of his finger inside, then sucked hard.

He gasped and his eyes darkened. 'Ruby, you drive me crazy. I want you so much. I've wanted you for so long.'

'I want you, too.' She reached up and undid his bow tie.

He smiled at her. 'Oh, so this is the way we're doing it, is it?' He spun her round, unzipped her dress, then kissed a path all the way from the nape of her neck to the base of her spine, sliding the dress down her body as he did so.

She stepped out of the dress and turned to face him. 'My turn.' She started undoing the buttons of his shirt. Her fingers were a little clumsy, but it didn't matter; the heat in his expression encouraged her to keep going. He shrugged off his jacket, and she untucked his shirt from his trousers so she could finish undoing it and slide the soft cotton off his shoulders.

'Perfect,' she said, running her fingers over his pecs. 'I've always thought you could be a model for any of the posh perfume houses.' She let her fingers slide down to his abdomen. 'And a perfect six pack.'

'Careful—my ego might explode.'

She laughed. 'You're not an egotist, Ellis.'

'Good.' He drew her closer and kissed her again, his

mouth warm and sweet and very sure. Then he broke the kiss and held her gaze. 'Right now, I want to kiss you all over.'

'Sounds good to me.' Her knees felt like jelly; she hadn't felt this nervous or this turned on in a long while.

'I'm glad. And, just so you know, I intend to take my time.'

The huskiness in his voice made the heat running through her gear up another notch.

He kissed from the corner of her mouth down to the curve of her jaw. Instinctively, she tipped her head back and he kissed his way down the side of her neck, teasing and inciting. She was aware of the pulse beating madly in her throat, and then his mouth skimmed it, skimmed it again, and nibbled and teased until she thought she was going to burst into flames with desire.

Then he straightened up again and traced the lacy edge of her bra with his fingertip, taking his own sweet time. Just as he'd promised.

'Do you have any idea how much I want you?' she whispered.

'I hope it's as much as I want you,' he said.

She smiled, and let him slide the straps of her bra down her arms. At work he was a total professional; nothing ever fazed him and his hands were steady and sure. Yet right now his hands were shaking and his breathing was shallow. Clearly he was as affected as much as she was by this thing between them.

He undid her bra strap and let the garment drift to the floor. 'You're so beautiful,' he said. 'And I want you so much I can't think straight.'

'Me, too,' she said, and lifted a hand to stroke his face. He pressed a kiss into her palm, drew his hands down her sides and then stroked upwards again so he could cup her breasts. His thumbs grazed her nipples and made her shiver.

She slid her hands into his hair; it felt soft and silky beneath her fingertips. Then she kissed him, pressing against him.

He pulled her closer and kissed her back.

Ruby wasn't sure who removed the rest of whose clothing, but the next thing she knew Ellis was carrying her to the wide, wide bed and had pushed the coverlet aside. He laid her down on the sheets; then she felt the mattress dip with his weight as he joined her.

'Ruby, you're so beautiful—everything I dreamed of and more.'

His fingers were feather-light as he touched her, making her skin feel hotter. He followed his hands with his mouth, and she arched against the bed.

'Now, Ellis,' she said. 'Please, now.'

She felt the bed dip again as he stood up and opened her eyes in shock. Had he changed his mind?

Then she realised that he was taking his wallet from his jacket, removing a foil package.

'Protection,' he said. 'And, just so you know, I wasn't making assumptions. Just being prepared.'

'Practical and sensible.'

'Which isn't,' he said as he joined her back on the bed, 'the same as boring.'

No, she didn't think this was going to be boring in the slightest.

She reached for him and kissed him hard.

This time, it felt safe to let the desire ignite. Her head fell back as he kissed his way down her body, exploring the hollows of her collar-bones and the valley between her breasts, stroking the soft undersides and making her sigh with pleasure.

She slid her fingers into his hair as he teased her nipples with the tip of his tongue. Then he drew the hard peak into his mouth and sucked.

'More,' she whispered, and he kissed his way downwards over her abdomen. She shivered. She wanted this so much; she couldn't remember the last time she'd wanted someone so desperately.

He shifted to kneel between her thighs. She felt him lift her foot and kiss the hollow of her ankle. As he worked his way slowly north, she felt as if her bones were dissolving; she was so ready for him.

She felt the slow stroke of one finger along her sex, and it made her whimper with need. And then he bent to replace his finger with his mouth. As his tongue flicked across her clitoris she completely lost it; her climax hit her like a wall.

Ruby was still almost hyperventilating as she finally opened her eyes.

Ellis held her close. 'Well. That was interesting.'

'Ellis...' Her brain felt scrambled and she couldn't even string two words together.

He just smiled. 'It's good to know that I can turn the smartest woman I know into mush.' His smile grew tinged with wickedness. 'But I haven't finished yet.'

'Better be a promise,' she mumbled.

'Oh, it is.' He kissed her again, touched her and stroked her until she was back at fever point, and then she heard the tear of the foil packet and the snap of the condom as he moved to protect her.

And then, finally, he eased inside her.

Incredibly, she felt her climax rising again.

And this time, when the wall hit her and she cried out, she heard his answering cry and felt his body surge against hers.

Afterwards, he said softly, 'I need to deal with the condom.'

'Sure.'

When he came back from the bathroom, he climbed back into bed beside her and drew her into his arms.

'Ellis, I...'

He pressed a finger lightly against her lips. 'Don't speak. Tonight, let's just be.'

And it had been so long since she'd slept in someone's arms. So long since she'd felt warm and safe and cherished.

She reached over to switch out the light, and cuddled into him. And finally she fell asleep in his arms.

Ellis lay awake for a while longer, just holding Ruby.

What had just happened between them had been a total revelation—a connection he'd never experienced with anyone else, even Natalia.

It gave him hope for the future. Maybe, just maybe, this thing between them would work out.

But, at the same time, it brought back all the panic. He'd thought that he loved Natalia, and that she'd felt the same about him. They'd been good together. Yet his marriage hadn't lasted—they'd discovered within weeks that they'd made a huge mistake because they wanted totally different things out of life.

What did Ruby want out of life? Another marriage like the one she'd had with Tom, perhaps, settled and close to both their families? He didn't know if he could offer her that. Would he be enough for her? Would he be able to suppress his wanderlust for her? Had he just made another huge mistake with the potential to hurt someone he cared about?

He smiled wryly. So much for telling her, 'Tonight, let's just be.' Instead of enjoying this moment, relaxing in the warmth and sweetness, he was full of doubts.

Maybe he should take his own advice, just for tonight, and live in the moment. Just be. Tomorrow there would be time for reflection. Tonight, he'd just enjoy holding her asleep in his arms.

CHAPTER ELEVEN

THE NEXT MORNING Ruby woke, feeling warm and comfortable. A surge of embarrassment heated her skin as she remembered last night, and then a flood of guilt washed away the embarrassment.

She felt a kiss against her shoulder. 'Ruby. Chill out,' Ellis said softly.

'How long have you been awake?' she asked, turning to face him.

'Long enough.' He stroked her face. 'What's the matter?'

She took a deep breath. 'You and me. Last night.'

'Problem?' His voice was neutral and his face was expressionless, so she didn't have a clue how he was feeling. Did he regret this? Did he think they should go back to being friends? Did he feel as mixed-up about this whole situation as she did?

'Yes. No.' She closed her eyes. 'I don't regret what we did. But I do feel guilty about it.'

'Why?' he asked gently. 'Ruby, we're both single. We have feelings for each other, and we simply acted on those feelings last night.'

'You're the first since Tom,' she whispered. 'The only one apart from Tom.'

'Which makes me feel incredibly honoured,' he said softly.

She opened her eyes then and looked at him. 'Honoured?'

'Honoured,' he repeated, 'that you chose me. Ruby, there's no need to feel guilty. You're not betraying Tom.'

'It feels like it,' she said.

He shook his head. 'Tom loved you enough to want you to be happy after he died. And you're not trying to push his memory out of your life. It's OK to move on. We've been dating for a few weeks and we've known each other for an awful lot longer than that.'

'I guess I'm being ridiculous.'

'No. You're human. You can't turn your feelings on and off just like that—neither of us can.'

'Are you saying that you feel guilty, too?'

'Technically, you're my best friend's girl,' he said. 'So, yes, in a way I do feel guilty. But I would never, ever have done anything to jeopardise your marriage if Tom had still been alive. Tom's been gone for more than a year now. I know we both still miss him and we always will, but we have to face up to the fact that he's gone. And I think he'd be pleased if we could find happiness together.' He gave her a rueful smile. 'Though I have to admit, he'd probably give me a huge lecture about commitment and making sure I don't hurt you.'

'Right now we can't promise each other for ever,' Ruby said.

'Which is fine,' Ellis reassured her. 'We can promise each other for now. Enjoy the moment.'

'While it lasts?'

'Which might be for longer than both of us think. If we're lucky.'

'I need to stop brooding,' she said wryly.

'And I need coffee,' he said. 'How long will it take you to shower?'

The glint in his eyes prompted her to say, 'That depends on whether I'm showering alone.'

He grinned. 'I like your thinking, Rubes. In fact...'

They were almost too late for breakfast. And Ellis didn't look quite as pristine as he normally did when he emerged from his room with his luggage, ready to go in the hotel's store-room until their taxi arrived to take them back to the airport.

'So, our last day in Prague,' he said when they'd checked out and had the receipts for their luggage. 'Where would you like to go?'

'You're the one with the guide book. Where do you suggest?'

'I'd like to take a closer look at the Dancing House,' he said. 'And there's this café where Einstein used to hang out.'

She laughed. 'And you want to follow in his footsteps?'

'Just for coffee. I think I'll pass on developing theories of relativity.' He laughed back.

They went to see the Dancing House, and Ellis persuaded another tourist to take a photograph on his phone of himself and Ruby in front of the building in the same dance pose. They walked along the river bank, hand in hand, enjoying the autumn sunshine, then found the café on Ellis's wish list. It was all chandeliers and gorgeous Viennese-style cake and coffee; and there were chess sets out on various tables with a note telling patrons to enjoy a game if they wished.

'Fancy a game?' Ellis asked.

Ruby shook her head. 'Sorry, I've never played.'

'I could teach you.'

'Thanks, but I don't think chess is for me.' She raised an eyebrow. 'Something else I didn't know about you, Ellis.'

'Me? I'm an open book,' he said lightly.

The bright morning sunshine had given way to threatening clouds by the time they'd finished their cake and coffee, so they spent the rest of the day in art galleries and museums, before collecting their luggage and meeting their taxi to the airport.

Prague would always have a special place in her heart, Ruby thought. The place where she and Ellis had first made love.

But, once they were back in England—what then? Would they stay close like this? Or would the world get in the way?

And there were other considerations, too. They weren't the only ones to think about.

She pushed it to the back of her head and chatted easily with Ellis all the way back to England.

Though he'd clearly been thinking about it too; when he saw her to her front door, he asked softly, 'So where do we go from here?'

'I don't know,' she said. 'What do you want?'

'Are you ready to go public?'

She wrinkled her nose. 'Don't take this the wrong way, but can I talk to Tom's parents about it first?'

'I think that would be kind,' he said, 'and I agree with you. If they're not comfortable with the situation, then we need to keep it to ourselves a little longer, until they've had time to get used to the idea.'

'Thank you. For understanding,' she said.

'Any time.' He kissed her lightly. 'I guess I'll see you at work tomorrow.'

'Yes. And thank you for Prague. It was special.'

'It was,' he agreed. And for a moment she could swear that she saw sadness in his eyes.

'You're twenty-two weeks, according to your scan, Mrs Falcon,' Ellis said gently.

'I really can't get my head round this.' Anita Falcon shook her head. 'I'm forty-five years old. I'm a professional. I've got a fifteen-year-old. How could I possibly not realise I was pregnant again, until last week?' She shook her head. 'I've seen the newspaper stories about women who don't have a clue they're pregnant until they actually have the baby. I always thought that was crazy—I mean, if you're pregnant you get morning sickness, your periods stop, you have a definite bump and you can feel the baby moving. How can you not *know*? I just…' She shook her head, and a tear trickled down her face. 'Ten years ago, I would've been thrilled. It'd be a dream come true, being able to give Max a little brother or sister. But how can I possibly cope with a baby now, when I have my parents living with me, and my dad has dementia, and my son is going to be doing his exams next June? Not to mention Nick—my husband—might be made redundant next month, so we can't afford for me to give up my job, even if it's only for a few months. And it's so late now that even if I could face the idea of a termination, it's not going to be possible. It's my own stupid fault for not having a clue.' She covered her face with her hands, and Ruby could see her shoulders heaving with sobs.

She sat down next to Anita and put her arm round

her. 'Hey. Don't beat yourself up. There are plenty of reasons why a woman might not realise she's pregnant. From what you've just told me, you're under quite a bit of stress right now.'

Anita rubbed the tears away from her eyes with the back of her hand. 'It's been hard to get the right help for Dad. Dealing with the authorities is like banging your head against a brick wall. We all want him to keep his independence as much as possible, and I wanted to take the strain off Mum—that's why they moved in with us.'

'It's difficult, sharing a home with your parents again after years of not living with them,' Ellis said. 'And it's doubly hard if they're not in the best of health. You're worrying about them, and you're worrying about your son as well—and your husband's job.'

'I thought it was just stress mucking my system up,' Anita said. 'I haven't had a period for four months—but my periods were a bit all over the place before that, so I just assumed I was heading for the menopause. The same as having to get up at night for a wee; I thought it was my age. I went and had a chat with the local pharmacist, and she said she was the same age as me and it was probably nothing to worry about, but do a pregnancy test just to put my mind at rest.'

'Good idea,' Ellis said.

She dragged in a breath. 'Back when I was pregnant with Max, you just had a blue line on the test stick and you had to guess whether it was a dark enough blue to be a positive result. Nowadays, the tests have a screen that tells you how pregnant you are—and the one I did definitely said "not pregnant". So I thought it was OK, that I was right about my system being all over the place with menopause and stress.'

'Sometimes you can get a false negative result on a test,' Ruby said. 'Though you're right. A lot of women hit the perimenopause at your age and your periods go all over the place.'

'I haven't had any morning sickness,' Anita said, 'and I was terrible when I had Max. Even tin cans used to smell and make me feel queasy. Right from the second week to the twelfth, when I was pregnant with him, I had to run to the bathroom if someone came into work wearing really strong aftershave or hairspray. This time, there was nothing. Not the slightest bit.'

'Your body doesn't always react the same way in pregnancy. Some women have horrendous morning sickness with one baby and nothing at all with another. How about your weight?' Ellis asked. 'Has that changed much?'

'I've put on about ten pounds.' Anita grimaced. 'Though I put that down to middle-age spread. And stress. I haven't exactly been eating brilliantly—when the going gets tough, the tough get chocolate, right?'

'Right,' Ruby said. 'Some women don't put on that much weight during pregnancy. If they're doing a lot of exercise—say they're training for a marathon—or they're overweight to start with, the pregnancy might not show for quite a while.'

'Plus, if you have a uterus that tips back the other way—as one in five women do—you wouldn't have noticed a bump anyway for at least the first twelve weeks,' Ellis said.

Anita stared at them, the tiniest bit of hope on her face. 'So I wasn't just being stupid, not realising I was pregnant?'

'You weren't being stupid at all,' Ruby reassured

her. 'And there's a fifteen-year gap between your pregnancies, so your body won't remember what it feels like to have a baby moving around inside. Plus you've been worried sick about quite a lot of things, and you haven't been looking out for the signs of being pregnant. So that'd be why you missed that little fluttering of the baby moving.'

'I did have terrible heartburn last week. I never had that when I was pregnant with Max. I thought it was just a combination of stress and comfort eating, and I knew I ought to be doing something about my weight but I just couldn't face it, not with everything else going on. Chocolate is the only thing that's kept me sane. I couldn't believe it when my GP said he thought I might be pregnant.' Anita bit her lip. 'And I've been eating all the wrong things—soft cheese, lightly cooked eggs, wine. I haven't taken any folic acid, I've been eating rubbish instead of really nutritious food, and...' She broke off, clearly fighting back the tears.

'And you're panicking that you've harmed the baby,' Ellis said. 'But what I saw on the scan was a baby who's the right size for dates, has ten fingers and toes, and has a steadily beating heart. I didn't see anything that would worry me, as an obstetrician. Plus you still have another eighteen weeks or so to eat green leafy vegetables until they're coming out of your ears.'

'You bet I will.' Anita gave him a wobbly smile. 'So I'm not the only woman who's ever done that?'

'Far from it,' Ellis said with a smile. 'And it will take a bit of getting used to. Do you have other family who can support you?'

'An older brother,' Anita said. 'But he sticks his head in the sand about Mum and Dad, so he won't do anything to help me with them. He's always got an excuse not to visit us. And it's not even as if he lives over the other side of the country.'

Guilt prickled the back of Ellis's neck. Over the years he'd had plenty of excuses not to visit his parents. Mainly because he worked so far away.

'Families aren't always easy,' he said feelingly. 'How about your husband's family?'

'Let's just say how much my mother-in-law will enjoy telling people that I'm supposed to be so clever, but I was too stupid to know I was pregnant and too stupid to know how to use contraception,' Anita said wryly. 'But I do have the best friend in the universe. She'll be there for me. And I think, once Max and Nick get over the shock, they'll be there for me, too.'

Ruby squeezed her hand. 'That's great. And you've also got us. Anything you're worried about between your appointments, come and talk to us. We have a walk-in clinic here in the department as well as the regular appointments.'

'Thank you.' Anita took a deep breath. 'I'm sorry I've been so wet. Crying and all that. That just isn't me.'

'Hormones,' Ruby said sagely. 'Plus you have a lot on your plate. In your shoes, I'd be just the same.'

'Really?'

'Really.' Ruby patted her shoulder. 'Right. Let's finish doing your checks, and we'll make another appointment for you in two weeks' time—we want to keep a closer eye on you simply because you're an older mum, not because there's anything to panic about. But if you're worried about anything in the meantime, come and see us.'

'You've been so kind about this. Both of you. I mean,

you have to see this stupid, ditzy woman who doesn't even know she's pregnant until she's over halfway through...'

'Don't put yourself down,' Ellis said. 'Actually,' he added, 'studies show that about one in about five hundred women don't realise they're pregnant until they're twenty weeks gone, so you're not stupid at all.'

'Thank you. Both of you.' She took a deep breath. 'This baby wasn't planned, but it's never going to feel unwanted.'

Later that evening, Ellis and Ruby were curled up together on his sofa.

'That poor woman who came to see us this afternoon,' she said. 'She's got a huge amount to deal with.'

'A late baby's tough for anyone, but she's caring for her parents as well, and she's supporting her son through his GCSEs and worrying about her husband's job. It's hardly surprising she was too stressed to notice the signs of pregnancy,' Ellis said.

'If I was in her situation,' Ruby said, 'I'd have to leave London and go back to Manchester. I couldn't leave my parents to struggle, and I wouldn't want to uproot them from everything that's familiar and make them move to London with me. I'm an only child, so there's nobody else to pick up the slack or share it with me.'

'If it happened to my parents, they'd be difficult about it,' Ellis said. 'I think they'd hide how much they were struggling and they'd stonewall the three of us if we asked any questions.' He sighed. 'I worry about them. So do my brothers. But we can't force them to be close to us or accept more help than they're prepared to take.'

'And I guess when you're working hundreds and hundreds of miles away, rushed off your feet and with a million different things to think about, it helps fill in the gaps so you don't have as much space to worry,' she said softly.

'You mean, I use my job to escape? There's a lot of truth in that,' he said ruefully. 'And I feel a bit ashamed of myself for that. I thought about that when Anita was telling us how her brother makes excuses not to visit. I guess I do, too.'

'Ellis, you're human,' she said, stroking his face. 'We all have our limitations. And you can't save everyone or fix things for everyone.'

'I know.' He kissed her lightly. 'Some things can't be fixed. And you have to put up with the fact that you're doing everything you can, even if it doesn't feel anywhere near enough.'

'I wish I had a magic wand,' she said.

'Me, too. But thank you for making me feel better about it.'

'I haven't done anything.'

'You have. I can talk to you and know you're not judging me. That makes a huge difference.'

'Oh, Ellis.' Her eyes sparkled with tears.

'Hey. Let's change the subject now and talk about something nice.'

'Brenda and Mike are coming up to London, next weekend.' Ruby paused. 'I think it's time to tell them about us.'

'With me by your side,' he said. 'I love Tom's parents. Even if you and I weren't together, I would've probably asked if I could drop in just to say hello to them.' He stroked her face. 'But now you and I are together, of course I want to be there and help you tell them.' He stole a kiss. 'And I'm also hoping that I can persuade you to stay here with me tonight.'

'I don't have anything with me.'

'I have a spare toothbrush, practically all the toiletries you'll need except face cream—and taking one night off isn't going to give you immediate wrinkles—and I can always put your clothes through the washing machine now so they'll be clean and dry in the morning. Your uniform's kept at work, you don't have a dog or cat to go back and feed, and I do a seriously mean scrambled egg on toast. Oh, and freshly squeezed orange juice—and I mean freshly squeezed by me, not poured from a bottle.'

She laughed. 'Very persuasive, Dr Webster. I have no arguments against any of that. I'd love to stay.'

'Good.' He kissed her again. Another step towards the relationship he thought they were both looking for. Another reason to stay in London. At the same time, though, it scared him. He knew Ruby so much better than he'd known Natalie. They were compatible in every way. And yet the doubts were still there. He'd failed at his last marriage—his last serious relationship. Would he fail at this one, too?

CHAPTER TWELVE

'I FEEL RIDICULOUSLY NERVOUS,' Ruby said on the Sunday morning.

'It'll be fine. Don't worry,' Ellis reassured her.

'I guess.' But she couldn't help feeling antsy. She wanted to be with Ellis—but she also didn't want to lose Brenda and Mike. Once they knew she was dating again, would they reject her?

The doorbell rang; Ruby opened the door and Brenda and Mike greeted her with a hug and flowers.

'Oh, Ellis, you're here too—how lovely to see you as well.' Brenda hugged him and Mike shook his hand warmly.

'Can I get you some coffee?' Ruby asked.

'That'd be wonderful,' Brenda said.

'I'll make the coffee,' Ellis offered.

'And I'll put these lovely flowers in water,' Ruby said with a smile.

'When are we going to tell them?' Ruby whispered in the kitchen.

'I vote for sooner rather than later,' Ellis whispered back.

'OK. I'll be brave,' she said.

Once they were all sitting down in the living room

with coffee and posh cookies that Ruby had bought from the deli round the corner, she said, 'There was something I wanted to talk to you about.'

'Of course, love,' Mike said.

Ruby took a deep breath. 'Please don't think I'll ever forget Tom or push him out of my life, but—'

'—you've met someone,' Brenda cut in gently.

Ruby stared at her, surprised. Was it that obvious? 'Um, yes,' she said awkwardly.

'Love, it's been more than a year since he died and you're still young. I'm quite sure Tom didn't want you to spend the rest of your life on your own, missing him,' Brenda said.

'So you don't mind if I see someone?' Ruby asked.

'As long as he treats you right,' Mike said. 'If he isn't good to you, then I'll have a problem with it.'

'That won't be a problem,' Ellis said. 'Remember, Tom asked me to take care of her.'

'Have you met Ruby's young man, then?' Brenda asked.

Ellis coughed. 'Let's just say you've known him for quite a few years, too.'

They both stared at him, and he saw the second that the penny dropped. The surprise in their faces was swiftly chased away by relief.

'But,' he said, 'we didn't want to go public until we knew you were OK with it.'

'We're OK with it,' Brenda said softly. 'More than OK.'

Mike smiled. 'I wish we'd brought champagne now.'

'Actually, I did, hoping that I wasn't tempting fate,' Ellis said. 'Though if you hadn't been OK with Ruby seeing me, then I would've suggested using it to toast our Tom. Shall I go and open it?'

'Absolutely yes,' Brenda said. 'And we wish you both every happiness, we really do.'

Later that evening, Ellis and Ruby lay together on her sofa.

'I'm so glad they were OK about us,' she said.

'Me, too. So are you ready to go public tomorrow?' he asked.

'I think so.' She looked awkward. 'I probably ought to confess that I told Tina, a while back.'

Her best friend. Would she approve? 'And was she OK about it?' Ellis asked, careful to keep his voice neutral.

'Actually, she brought up your itchy feet.' She sighed. 'And she told me not to fall for you too hard or too fast.'

'My feet aren't itchy,' Ellis said, 'but it looks as if I'm going to need to convince you of that—and a few other people, too.'

She stroked his face. 'It's not that I doubt you. But you're used to moving about all the time.'

'I've stayed in London for well over a year and a half now,' he pointed out.

'Don't you miss it, working abroad and seeing different places all the time?' she asked.

'Yes. But I'm pretty sure I'd miss you more,' he said softly.

The news gradually spread round the hospital. Ruby was surprised and pleased that everyone seemed to wish them both well, especially when they made it clear that the personal relationship would make absolutely no difference to their professional relationship.

The next morning, Ellis came over to the midwives' station to show Ruby a letter from Grace Edwards. 'You know you thought she might be a chimera? She had more DNA tests, and they showed that you were right. The court case has been settled now, and she says the relationship with her ex is starting to become more amicable for the child's sake.'

'That's good. I'm so glad it's working out better for her now.'

Ellis stole a kiss. 'Not just for her. Everything's working out. I never would've believed I could be so happy.'

'Me, too.' She kissed him back.

'Tsk, you two, you're supposed to set a good example to your juniors,' Coral, the trainee midwife, teased as she passed them.

Ellis just laughed. 'We are.'

Over the next few weeks, time seemed to go at the speed of light. Ellis and Ruby spent every possible minute together. But finally it was his last official day at the maternity unit. That evening, all the staff from the unit who weren't on duty went out for a pizza to say goodbye to him, and presented him with a special care package for his trip to Zimbabwe—including socks, chocolate and soap, which made him laugh—and a card signed by every single person on the team.

'We want you back, Ellis,' Theo said. 'No pressure, of course, but we want you back. And I'm expecting the answer to a certain question the second you get back on English soil.'

In other words, whether he'd accept the job offer. Ellis smiled. 'OK. Message received and understood.'

'And we want regular texts to know how you're getting on,' Iris, the senior midwife, chipped in.

'Actually, I'm not going to be able to be in touch with anyone while I'm away,' Ellis said. 'This clinic I'm going to in Zimbabwe is so remote that there isn't any Internet access, and there's no mobile phone coverage.'

Ruby swallowed hard. He'd already told her this, so she was prepared for it, but it was still hard to get her head round it.

'So I guess sending us the odd postcard won't be possible either?' She tried for levity.

'By the time I'd found someone to take a letter to the nearest big town with a mail system and buy a stamp for it—well, I'd probably be back here before the postcard reached you, even if I sent it on my first day.'

It finally hit home. No phone, no texts, no emails, and not even a letter. A whole month without contact. She trusted Ellis—she knew he wasn't the kind to cheat—but how did people cope with the loneliness of long-distance relationships like this, when they couldn't even contact each other for weeks at a time? Was this the way her future was going to be?

She changed the subject and teased Ellis along with the rest of the team, but when they went back to his flat afterwards he held her close.

'Rubes, I know it's going to be hard, not being able to talk to each other for a whole month,' he said. 'But if there's an emergency, you know you can call John at the medical aid charity and he'll get someone to radio a message through to me,' said. 'And, if you really want me to, I can pull out of the assignment.'

He'd really do that for her?

She could see the sincerity in his eyes. Yes, he'd give it up for her.

But she couldn't ask him to do that. Especially on the day before he was meant to be going. She shook her head. 'You promised you'd go. I'm not going to make you break a promise.' She just wished there could be another way.

Though the only other way she could think of was for her to go with him. Which would mean letting down everyone at the ward, and deserting her family, Brenda and Mike. She couldn't do that, either.

And giving Ellis an ultimatum wasn't fair; it would tear him apart. She knew he was a man of integrity. He was going back to do the job he loved—maybe for the last assignment. Or maybe not. For his sake she needed to be brave about this. To make him feel that it was okay for him to go—even though watching him leave would hurt like hell. 'Go get 'em, tiger.' She gave him a wobbly smile.

That night, they made love for what might be the last time, and the sweetness was almost unbearable. Ruby just hoped that Ellis wasn't aware of the tears trickling silently down her face as she lay awake in his arms afterwards, pretending to sleep.

The next day, Ruby went to see Ellis off at the airport.

She looked at the kitbag slung over his shoulder as they left his flat. 'I can't believe that's all the luggage you're taking with you for a whole month.'

'I learned to travel light.' He smiled at her. 'Ruby, I *am* coming back, you know.'

'I know.' His assignment was for a month. Of course

he was coming back. But would it be for good, or would it be to tell her that he'd rediscovered how much he loved his job and he needed to go back to it?

'Ruby, I lo—'

She pressed the tip of her finger against his mouth. She had a feeling she knew what he was going to say—and she didn't want to hear it. Not right at this moment. 'Wait until you're back,' she said softly. Until he'd been away from her and had had time to think about it. Until he really knew what he wanted to do—whether he needed to go back to working abroad, or whether he wanted to come back to London to stay. If he could still say it in a month's time, then she'd know that he really meant it.

They travelled to Heathrow on the train in silence, and had a last cup of coffee together while they waited for his flight to be called.

And then the flight to Harare was announced over the tannoy system.

'I guess this is me,' he said. He held her tightly. 'I'll see you in a month. And I'll be counting the days. I'll think of you every single day.'

'Me, too.' She wasn't going to cry. She wasn't going to let him go on that plane feeling guilty and miserable because of her. 'You go and you make that difference to the world. I'm proud of you.' And she was proud of him. Just… she didn't want him to go. 'I'll keep an eye on your flat for you and make sure you've got fresh bread and milk indoors when you get back.' She dragged in a breath. 'And I'll see you in a month's time.'

'I'll ring you as soon as I can switch my phone on and get a signal.' His grey eyes were tortured. 'Ruby. I wish I wasn't going.'

'If you don't go, you'll regret it for the rest of your life. So go. Do what you're brilliant at. Help set up that clinic and make life better for people.' Go with her love, though she wasn't going to say that and put pressure on him. 'Have a safe journey,' she said. Though she wouldn't even know if he did arrive safely. She could check the airport website to see if he'd landed; and then she'd just have to trust that everything went well after that. That any unrest in the country wouldn't affect the clinic. That he wouldn't catch some awful virus. *That he'd come back.*

A whole month without him.

And it stretched out as if there was never going to be an end.

'Ruby.' His voice sounded as clogged as her throat felt.

He kissed her hard. 'I'll be back soon,' he said.

'I know.' Even though she didn't know whether it would be just to say goodbye, or to tell her that he wanted to be with her.

She waited in the airport until his flight had taken off, even though she knew he wouldn't be able to make her out through the window. She just needed to be there until he'd finally gone.

And just why was the sun shining so brightly on the train home? Why wasn't it miserable and raining, the way it felt in her heart?

The following day, Ruby went to see one of their new mums, whose baby had been born at thirty-six weeks and now, at three days old, the baby had a distinct yellow tone to her eyes and skin. For a moment, Ruby wished Ellis was there, because he was so good at explaining things like this to new parents. Then she pulled herself together. Ellis wasn't there; this was her job, and she was just going to have to deal with it.

'Basically the baby has a bit too much bilirubin in her body—that's why her skin and her eyes have that yellow tinge,' she explained.

'What's bilirubin?' Mrs Patterson asked.

'It's a yellow substance the body makes when red blood cells—the ones that move oxygen round the body—break down. Usually the liver removes the bilirubin from the blood—actually, your liver did the job for her while she was still in the womb. Three out of five babies have a bit of jaundice—that's why we do that heel-prick test on the first day, to check her blood. She's quite jaundiced, and Coral tells me that you've had a bit of a problem feeding her.'

'So is it my fault?'

'Not at all,' Ruby reassured her. 'The jaundice explains why she's not feeding well.'

'So will she have to have medication to treat it?'

'Believe it or not, the treatment's a bit of sunshine— but at this time of year there isn't much sunshine around, so what we're going to do is fibre-optic phototherapy,' Ruby said. 'Which is a fancy way of saying we're going to lie her on a blanket which shines a special light onto her back. Her skin will absorb the light and it makes oxygen bind to the bilirubin, helping it dissolve so her liver can break it down.'

Mrs Patterson looked surprised. 'That's all? You just lay her on a special blanket?'

'And we keep checking the levels of bilirubin in her blood until they start dropping. It does mean she's going to lose a bit more water from her body than usual, so we might have to give her some fluid in a drip to keep her hydrated—but basically that's it, and you can be with her the whole time. You can still feed her as normal and change her nappies,' Ruby explained. 'She'll be much better in a day or two.'

'And then she's going to be all right?'

'She's going to be just fine,' Ruby confirmed.

It was true for the baby; and if she kept telling herself often enough that everything was going to be fine, then it would be true for her and Ellis, too.

Ellis was really glad that the pace in Zimbabwe turned out to be punishing. Being so busy that he didn't have time to think about how much he missed Ruby was a blessing—as was being so tired that he fell asleep almost as soon as his head touched the pillow at night. And although he was friendly with the other medics on the team, he didn't socialise as much as he would have done in the old days. Instead, he spent every evening writing to Ruby, in a notebook he'd bought especially for the purpose. He wouldn't be able to send her a postcard or a letter every day, but he would at least be able to give her the book when he returned. So she'd know that he'd meant what he'd said—that he'd thought about her every single day when he was away.

On his last day, he had a radio call from John, the assignment handler at the medical aid charity. 'Ellis, I know it's a lot to ask, but could you stay a bit longer? A couple of weeks?'

Two years ago, he would've said yes without even having to think about it. Extending an assignment was something he'd done quite a few times.

Now, it was different. He'd spent a whole month

missing Ruby and it was like a physical ache. He loved what he did, but the job wasn't enough for him any more. Not without Ruby.

Because he loved her.

Bone-deep *loved* her.

And he needed to be back with her.

'I'm sorry,' Ellis said. 'But no. Don't get me wrong—I love this job, but I've met someone. In London. And now I need to go home. For good.' He was shocked to feel the lump in his throat: London *was* home. Because Ruby was there.

As long as she hadn't changed her mind about them while he'd been away.

'Fair enough,' John said. 'It sounds as if we've been lucky to have you back for the last month.'

'I promised I'd do this assignment,' Ellis said, 'and I wouldn't break my promise.' Even though he'd been tempted to. He'd done the right thing.

'We'll miss you,' John said. 'And if you ever change your mind—even if it's just for a few days—we'd have you back any time.'

'You'll be the first to know,' Ellis said.

CHAPTER THIRTEEN

ELLIS HAD DELIBERATELY given Ruby the wrong date for his return; he'd told her that he'd be back the day after his real return date, knowing from experience how likely it was that his journey home would be disrupted. In the past he'd worried his brothers by turning up later than they expected, and he didn't want Ruby to be anxious about whether something had happened to him when he wasn't in a position to get in touch with her.

The journey home seemed to take for ever—from the journey by jeep from the camp through to the airport in Harare, and then the flight itself. With two layovers, it took the best part of a whole day to fly back to England. And every minute felt like a lifetime.

As soon as Ellis was through passport control at Heathrow, he got his phone out of his pocket. But somehow he managed to fumble it, and it dropped to the floor. When he picked it up, he groaned. 'You've got to be *kidding* me! How am I going to ring Ruby now?'

'Got a problem, mate?' a voice said beside him.

Ellis turned to face his fellow passenger and ruefully showed him the cracked screen. 'I've managed to baby this thing for a whole month while I've been setting up a clinic in an incredibly remote area, but as soon as I'm back here I drop it just once and…' He shook his head. 'What an idiot.'

'Here, use mine.' The man handed Ellis his phone.

'Are you sure?' At the other man's nod, Ellis smiled. 'Thank you very much. I'll keep it quick and I'll pay you for the call.'

'It's fine, mate. I know how I'd feel if I'd been away and couldn't ring my missus to tell her I'd landed safely.'

'Yeah. I told her I'd be back tomorrow because I didn't want her worrying if I was held up. And I just can't wait any longer to talk to her.' He opened the screen to dial Ruby's number, and stopped. 'Oh, no. I don't believe this. I can't actually remember her mobile number. How stupid am I?'

The other man gave him a rueful smile. 'That's where these things fall down, isn't it? We rely on them to remember everything for us, and when they don't work we're stuck.'

'Very true,' Ellis said, equally ruefully. Plus, after more than twenty-four hours spent travelling, he could barely think straight. All he wanted was to go home and see Ruby.

He handed the phone back to the other man. 'Thank you anyway. I appreciate the offer.'

'I hope you manage to get hold of her.'

'I'll find a way,' Ellis said.

Once he'd walked through customs to the airport shopping complex, he found the nearest shop that sold mobile phones. 'How long does it take to fix one of these?' he asked, showing the assistant his cracked screen.

'At least until tomorrow, I'm afraid,' the assistant told him.

Not what he needed to hear. Time for Plan B. 'Okay, how long would it take to migrate all my data across to a new phone?'

'The guy who does that sort of thing won't be in for another couple of hours, and he might already have stuff to do, so I can't say.'

A couple of hours and then unlimited waiting? No chance. Ellis knew he could be back in the centre of London, actually *with* Ruby, in the time it'd take to sort out his phone so he could call her. 'Thanks, but I'll manage. Can I just buy a cheap pay-as-you-go phone to tide me over until I can get this one fixed?'

'Sure.'

Armed with a working phone, Ellis managed to get the hospital switchboard number from the Internet, and two seconds later he was patched through to the maternity ward.

'Hey, Iris. Don't say a word—it's Ellis. Is Ruby there?'

'Yes, she is. I thought you weren't due back until tomorrow?'

'My journey home was a bit smoother than I expected,' Ellis explained. 'What shift is she on?'

'Early.'

'Excellent. Can you keep her there, please? And don't tell her that you've spoken to me. I want to surprise her.'

He knew he was taking a risk. He'd missed Ruby like hell. Hopefully she'd missed him just as much—but on the other hand she might have had time to think about the situation and decided that she couldn't cope with his lifestyle. He knew she didn't want to join him in working abroad; and he knew she was scared that he'd feel trapped if she asked him to stay in London. But, while he'd been away, he'd come to his own decision. One that he hoped would work for her, too.

'I'll do my best,' Iris said.

'Thank you. I'll be there as soon as I can.'

The good thing about travelling light meant that it wasn't too much of a drag to carry his kitbag around. He caught the fast train back to central London, and then the tube across the city to the London Victoria. He paused only to buy the biggest bunch of flowers that the hospital shop could offer, then headed up to the maternity ward.

Iris was at the reception desk. 'Welcome home. Perfect timing—she's in the staff kitchen, and I'm pretty sure she's on her own,' she whispered with a wink.

'Thanks.' Ellis blew her a kiss and went straight to the staff kitchen.

Ruby was leaning against the counter, sipping a mug of coffee; she almost dropped it when she saw him. 'Ellis! I thought you weren't back until tomorrow!'

'Sometimes the flights get delayed—and I didn't want you having to hang around the airport for hours waiting for me, worrying that something terrible had happened. That's why I told you I'd be back tomorrow instead of today.' He placed the flowers on the counter, dropped his kitbag, swept her into his arms and swung her around. 'I've missed you so, so much,' he whispered and kissed her hard.

She matched him kiss for kiss, and her arms were wrapped as tightly round him as his were round her.

When he finally managed to break the kiss, he noticed that her skin was reddened. 'Oh God, I'm so sorry. The beard. I should have shaved first—and had a shower.' He grimaced. 'Sorry. I'm not exactly fragrant.'

She laughed. 'Don't worry. The main thing is that you're here. How long did it take you to get here?'

'Six hours in the jeep from the clinic to Harare, a bit of a wait there, nearly twenty hours from there to Heathrow in between layovers, and then way too long to get back to the middle of London.' He dragged in a breath. 'I was going to call you from Heathrow, but I dropped my phone. Would you believe, it was fine all through Zimbabwe, yet I managed to break it practically the second I was back in England?' He rolled his eyes. 'The guy next to me was really kind and lent me his phone—and then I couldn't remember your number. How stupid is that?'

She stroked his face. 'If it makes you feel any better, I don't think I can remember your mobile phone number, either—I rely on my phone to remember it for me.'

He moved his head so he could drop a kiss in her palm. 'I missed you so much. I know you stopped me saying it at the airport when you waved me off, and I know why, but I need to say it now. I love you, Ruby. I love you so much. And I want to stay here in London with you.'

'Ellis, you've been away for a month. You've been travelling for what, a day and a half, you probably haven't had much sleep, and this is a conversation I think we need to have when you're properly awake.'

Her voice was gentle, but fear trickled through him. Had he totally misread the situation? Had she changed her mind about their relationship while he'd been away?

She fished in the pockets of her trousers and brought out her door keys. 'Your flat is probably freezing cold, and you won't have any food in the fridge—I was going to sort all that out this evening, because I was expecting you back tomorrow and I thought I'd have time to do it tonight. I'll get my spare key from Tina. So why don't you just go back to my place, have a shower and get some sleep, and I'll see you when I get back after my shift? Help yourself to whatever you want from the fridge.'

'Thank you.' He put her keys carefully into his pocket. 'I wrote to you every day while I was away.' He opened his kitbag and took out the small notebook he'd carried everywhere with him. 'I thought it would be easier to write everything in here than carry around loads of bits of paper that I'd probably end up losing.' He handed her the notebook. 'It could be a bit of lunchtime reading for you.'

She went pink. 'You wrote to me every day?'

'Every single day,' he confirmed. 'It was the only way I had to be close to you when I was thousands of miles away.'

'I missed you so much.' Her voice sounded rusty. 'Ellis, I love you too.'

Everything in his world settled and felt right again. They felt the same way about each other—so somehow they would be able to work things out.

He wrapped his arms around her again and held her close. 'You're right, I need some sleep,' he said softly. 'But when I wake up, you'll be home with me. And then we can talk.' He kissed her lightly, then took the notebook back from her, went to the last page he'd written and carefully removed it.

'What are you doing?' she asked.

'When you read this particular page, I want to be with you,' he said. Then he remembered the flowers. He scooped them up from the counter and handed them to her. 'For you. I know they're not the best, but I just wanted to...' Right now, he was too tired to string words together.

'They're lovely, Ellis. You've been travelling for hours and hours and hours, and yet you still made the time to bring me flowers.' She kissed him again. 'Go home. Sleep. I'll see you soon.' She hugged him one last time. 'Welcome back. And I'm so, so pleased to see you.'

Her smile warmed him all the way back to her flat.

Ellis just about managed to shower and shave, though he couldn't quite face making himself anything to eat. He cleaned his teeth, then dragged himself into the spare bedroom—where he'd slept so many times before during Tom's final illness—and fell into oblivion almost the second that his head hit the pillow.

Ruby was glad that she hadn't arranged to have lunch with anyone. Right at that moment, she wanted to be on her own to read Ellis's letters to her. With the notebook stowed safely in her handbag, she went to the hospital canteen to buy a sandwich and some coffee, then found a table in a quiet corner and settled down to read.

The letters read almost like a diary. Ellis told her all about setting up the clinic, what the rest of the team was like, and told her about some of the patients he'd treated. Yet it wasn't just a practical day by day account of his life out there—he also wrote down his feelings. How much he missed her while he was away, how he'd always loved being able to make a difference to the world through his work and yet it just didn't feel right any more being away from London. How he'd looked up at the stars at night and thought of her, then realised they weren't even going to see the same stars because they weren't in the same hemisphere, and it made him feel lonely.

There was a huge lump in her throat. So his feelings for her hadn't changed. He really had missed her while he'd been away—and it looked as if there was a real chance that they had a future together.

Right at that moment, Ruby just wanted to be home with Ellis. Though she still had a whole afternoon until her shift was over. She was kept busy with clinics, but even so the time seemed to drag.

And then finally she was able to go off duty and go home. When she let herself into the flat, everything was silent. She walked quietly through to her bedroom, but Ellis wasn't sleeping in her bed. Clearly he was still being sensitive to her feelings and not sleeping where his best friend had once lain.

Even more quietly, Ruby opened the door to the spare room. Ellis was fast asleep, and she could see the tiredness and strain still etched on his face. Although part of her wanted to wake him up, she knew that it wouldn't be fair; he needed some rest to recover from all that travelling. She could see his kitbag on the floor, so there was at least one thing she could do for him; without waking him, she picked it up and quietly closed the door behind her.

The next thing Ellis knew, there were faint sounds coming from the flat. Clearly Ruby was at home, bustling about and yet trying her hardest not to wake him. Wishing he'd thought to call back at his flat first to get some clean clothes, he climbed out of bed, wearing only his boxer shorts, and bent down to where he'd left his kitbag.

Except there was an empty space where he was expecting to see it.

Had he left it in the bathroom, too tired to carry it in here? But it wasn't there, either.

Ruby must have heard him walking about because she called, 'Hey, Ellis?'

'Hey, yourself,' he said, following the sound of her voice and finding her in the kitchen. 'Sorry, I can't quite remember where I left my clothes.'

She smiled. 'In your kitbag, and at the moment they're most of the way through the washing cycle.'

'So basically I'm wearing the only clothes I have that are dry?' he asked.

'I thought you'd sleep a bit longer and they'd be ready by the time you woke up.' She looked guilty. 'Obviously I've been really noisy. Sorry I didn't mean to wake you.'

'You didn't wake me.' He wrapped her in his arms. 'Ruby, I'm so glad to be home.'

As the words left his mouth, he realised how much he meant it. London *was* home. He hadn't felt like that about a place for a very long time—since before Sally died, really—and it felt strange. Strange, but good.

'I'm glad to have you home,' she said. 'You must be starving.'

'I think I'm still too tired to be hungry,' he admitted. 'Right now, I just want to be with you. Though I could do with a cup of tea.' He glanced down at himself. 'And I'm really not respectable enough to be standing in your kitchen.'

'I gave all Tom's clothes to the charity shop,' she said, 'so I can't offer you anything of his to wear, and I don't think my dressing gown would fit you.'

He laughed. 'And I'm not sure pink's my colour anyway.'

'The best I can do is a towel, if you're cold.'

'I'm not cold. Just...' He paused. 'Maybe a little underdressed.'

'The view's quite nice from where I'm standing.' she said, and he loved the way colour stole into her face.

'The view's very nice from where I'm standing, too,' he said, and kissed her lingeringly.

Between them, they managed to make two mugs of tea, then sat down at her kitchen table.

'Did you read the notebook?' he asked.

She nodded. 'Every single page—except the one you took out.'

'Which I put in my...' A nasty thought hit him. 'Rubes, did you empty my pockets before you put my jeans in the washing machine?'

She went white. 'No.'

'Ah.'

'Are you saying I put your last letter to me through the wash?' She clapped a hand to her mouth. 'Oh, no. I can't have done.' Tears glistened in her eyes. 'Now I'll never know what you said.'

'I remember every word I wrote,' he said softly. 'I wanted to be there when you read them, but maybe it's better this way—with me telling you. I missed you out in Zimbabwe, Ruby. There was this big hole in my life, and my job just wasn't enough any more. On my very last day, John put a radio call through to the clinic, and he asked me if I'd stay on for a couple more weeks. Two years ago, I would've said yes without even hesitating. But this time I said no. Because I wanted to come

home, Ruby. I wanted to come home to you. I wanted
to be with you.'

He slid out of his chair and on to one knee in front
of her. 'This isn't where I planned to do this. I was
planning to find somewhere romantic—maybe somewhere by the sea, or maybe in one of the glasshouses at
Kew with some exotic flowers in the background.' He
gave her a wry smile. 'And I was going to be properly
dressed. But as I was sitting on the plane, I knew exactly
what I was going to say to you, and now I realise that it
doesn't matter where I say it or what I'm wearing—and
I don't want to wait any more. I love you, Ruby. I want
to be with you. I don't want to go back to my old life,
working abroad, because it just isn't enough for me any
more. I've found the one person who makes me want to
settle down—you. And I want to make a family with
you, here in London. You're the love of my life. Will
you marry me?'

She paused for so long that he thought she was going
to say no.

And then, very shakily, she said, 'Yes.'

That was when Ellis realised that he'd actually been
holding his breath.

He dragged in a lungful of air, then got to his feet,
pulled her out of her chair and wrapped his arms round
her. 'Thank God. I thought you were going to say no. I
was so scared you might have changed your mind about
us while I was away.'

A tear trickled down her cheek. 'Ellis, I missed you
so much. And I was so scared that you wouldn't want
to come back.'

'No. I missed you more with every passing day. And
it's never been like that for me before. I couldn't wait to

come home.' He stroked her face. 'And now I'm home for good.'

'Ellis, you don't have to give up your old life completely,' she said. 'I don't want you to have any regrets in the future. Maybe if you went out for, I don't know, a couple of weeks every six months, then you could still do the stuff you love and feel that you're making a difference to the world.'

'Though you've taught me that I can make a difference right here—like I did with Helen Perkins and the intra-uterine transfusion,' he said. He paused. 'You're right, I will miss it sometimes—I've spent most of my career working abroad. But what you've suggested could work.'

'But?' She spoke the word that was echoing through his head.

'I'd still hate leaving you behind. I know I asked you before and you said no, but if I was only going out for a really short assignment once in a while, would you consider going with me?'

'If it's only for a really short assignment, then yes, I could cope with that,' she said.

'Good. I love you.' He kissed her. 'And once my clothes are dry, we'll go and tell the world our news.'

She kissed him back. 'That'll be a while yet. So I think maybe we have time to go and have a private celebration, first.'

'That's one of the things I love about you,' he said with a grin. 'You're full of great ideas…'

EPILOGUE

Two years later

ELLIS SAT ON the edge of the bed in the maternity department of the London Victoria, with his arm round Ruby and his finger being clutched very hard by their tiny, red-faced son.

'Life doesn't get any better than this, Mrs Webster,' he said softly. 'And I love you both very, very much.'

'We love you, too,' Ruby said. 'Don't we, Tom?'

In answer, the baby simply yawned, and they both laughed.

'I'm glad you got back in time for his birth,' she said.

'I nearly didn't. First babies are meant to be late, not two weeks early. Especially when their father is working in the middle of nowhere, several hundred miles away, for just one short week, thinking that he probably had a month until the baby arrived.' He rolled his eyes. 'Talk about timing. I think this one's going to be stubborn as anything.'

'Just like his dad,' she teased.

'Getting to the airport, opening my phone and seeing the text from you that you'd gone into labour…I nearly passed out,' he said.

She grinned. 'Tsk. And all the babies you've delivered, Dr Webster.'

'It's very different when it's *your* wife and *your* baby,' he said, and bent to drop a kiss on the baby's forehead. 'Luckily the woman in front of me in the queue for passport control asked me if I was all right—and when I told her my news, she told me to go in front of her. And so did everyone else in the queue, passing it forward. They all made way for me so I didn't have to wait so long to get to you. The kindness of strangers is truly amazing.'

'It certainly is,' she agreed. 'Though you've done your share of giving and kindness, too. Think of it as what goes around, comes around.'

'I guess.' He smiled. 'I love you, Rubes. And our baby. I can hardly believe we made someone so beautiful and so perfect.' He met her gaze. 'How many times have we heard new parents say that and smiled? But it's true. And I can't wait to take you both home.' Home, to the terraced house with a garden they'd bought together just after they'd got married. 'And for all the grandparents to come and see him—because this baby's going to have three sets. Your parents, my parents, and Tom's—because they're practically my parents too and there's no way I'll let them feel left out.'

Ruby smiled at him. 'That's another thing I love about you. You've turned into a real family man.'

'With a little help from you. You've done a lot to thaw my parents out.' He smiled back at her. 'You've changed my life, Ruby. I never thought I could ever be this happy and settled.'

'And I never thought I'd find this kind of happiness

a second time,' she said softly. 'It felt greedy, expecting too much.'

'No—as you said, what goes around, comes around, and you're one of life's givers. If I make you and baby Tom as happy as you both make me—well, that's all I want.' He kissed her. 'I think everyone on the ward is dying to visit you, so I'm going to let them all come and make a fuss of you while I have a shower and get rid of all the travel dust.'

'And the stubble. Looks sexy, but...' She pulled a face. 'Ouch.'

He laughed. 'Yeah. You say that every time. I love you. And Tom. And I'm so proud of you both.'

She laughed back. 'We're proud of you, too. Go and get rid of the travel stuff. And then you can take us home.'

He smiled. 'Your wish, my love, is my command.'

Home.

And he really was home. For good.

* * * * *

HER FAMILY
FOR KEEPS

BY
MOLLY EVANS

Published in Great Britain 2015
by Mills & Boon, an imprint of Harlequin (UK) Limited,
Eton House, 18-24 Paradise Road, Richmond, Surrey, TW9 1SR

© 2015 Brenda Schetnan

ISBN: 978-0-263-24721-3

Harlequin (UK) Limited's policy is to use papers that are natural,
renewable and recyclable products and made from wood grown in
sustainable forests. The logging and manufacturing processes conform
to the legal environmental regulations of the country of origin.

Printed and bound in Spain
by CPI, Barcelona

Dear Reader,

Thanks so much for picking up my latest Mills & Boon®
Medical Romance™, which has all of my favourite
elements: a great heroine, a fantastic hero, romance and
family.

This one is set in my adopted state of New Mexico,
where green chili is the number one agricultural crop.
After being in this state for so long I've begun to
understand why the state is nicknamed 'The Land of
Enchantment'—because once you live here for a while
you become enchanted and don't want to leave it. I hope
you enjoy the setting I've created and the characters
who make their home here as well.

If you find yourself in the neighbourhood of
New Mexico stop for a visit. You might also find yourself enchanted—as I was.

Love

Molly

CHAPTER ONE

REBEL TAYLOR ROLLED her shoulders against the heat. Sweat tickled and trickled down her back as she crossed the steaming parking lot. It was a very hot day for the first of June, even for New Mexico.

Movement in the backseat of a small sedan drew her attention. As an ER nurse, she was highly trained in skills of observation. Even the smallest detail made the difference between life and death. Frowning, she moved closer to the back window.

Rebel dropped her backpack as she hit full ER nurse mode. "Hello?" She stepped closer and the bottom dropped out of her stomach.

A toddler was strapped in the backseat.

Alone.

"Oh, God." Panic flooded her, and her limbs went limp for half a second. She looked around at the parking lot full of cars but devoid of people. "Help! Someone help!"

Tugging on the door handle brought her no results. The windows in the front were down a crack, but not enough to squeeze her arm through.

The child's cries grew into screams as he pulled on

his hair. What Rebel had first thought was a seizure was the frustration of the toddler imprisoned in the heat.

"Hold on, baby. Hold on!" She jerked her cellphone out of her pocket and called 911.

Dr. Duncan McFee strolled across the parking lot toward the hospital, but had to pass through the lengthy, car-filled parking area. When the doctors' car park was full, he parked with the rest of the staff. Heat bubbled up from the black surface and seemed to take on a life of its own, reaching out to drag passersby down into the dark depths. Days like this, he always wondered why he'd passed on that exotic job offer in the Caribbean. An ocean breeze would have been very welcome at the moment. If the desert had an ocean, it would be perfect.

Up ahead, he noticed a woman with long, luxurious, curly red hair who apparently had locked her keys in her car and was bent on beating the life out of it as a result. He decided to see if he could help the lovely damsel in distress. Not every day presented an opportunity to meet such a stunning woman.

"Lock your keys in?" he asked.

She turned, true panic in her incredibly green eyes, and took in a gasping breath. Duncan frowned. Something was wrong with this lady, not just keys locked in her car.

"There's a *baby* in there!"

"How long has he been in there?" Duncan dropped his briefcase, instantly understanding her panic.

"I don't know, but he's in trouble."

Duncan knew he needed to get that child out of there. Time was the enemy right now.

"Call 911."

"I did, but he'll die before they get here. We've got to *do* something." She hit the heel of one hand against the window in frustration.

Duncan looked around for a rock or anything he could use to break into the car. People started to gather, attracted by their activity. The woman grabbed the closest person. "Go get Security. We have to break into this car. It's an emergency. Go!"

The man raced away into the building.

Frustration mounted in Duncan, and he felt the same emotion emanating from this unknown woman. She was obviously a caring and concerned person, as well as stunningly beautiful. She stuck her fingers through the space in the front window and pulled. The window didn't budge. "Dammit."

Duncan joined her and managed to slide his fingers in alongside hers. "On three, pull. One, two, three... pull." Together they put their muscles to work, but the window simply didn't move. They couldn't get enough leverage on it.

"Dammit! Where's Security?" He glared toward the building, but there was no rescue party racing up the hill. "We're going to have to do this ourselves." One glance in the backseat was all he needed to realize she was right. The baby would die in the next minute unless he was rescued.

And then what they both feared happened. The child had a seizure, its little limbs jerking uncontrollably in response to the high temperature in the car forcing its body temperature too high. The brain could only take so much before reacting badly.

"There has to be something we can use to smash the window." The woman glanced around. "There!" She ran a few feet to grab a landscape rock nearly hidden by shrubbery.

"Give it to me." He took the rock, and she turned her back, but stayed close. With everything, every ounce of strength he had, he smashed the rock into the driver's window, determined to get this baby free. Never again was he going to let someone die in a car. Not if he could help it.

Glass shattered. She shoved the window in with the heels of her hands and released the door lock. "Got it."

Duncan yanked open the back door. In the last few seconds the baby had lost consciousness after the seizure. With quick thinking, she released the car-seat clasp and Duncan pulled the child free.

"We have to cool him quickly." She pulled off his shoes and socks and stripped him down to his diaper.

"Let's go." Duncan raced into the ER with the woman at his side. "Pediatric code! Call a pediatric code," he yelled as they sprinted through the doors, the baby clutched against his chest.

This man was obviously known here and thank heaven for that, Rebel thought as she raced into a treatment room with him, her hand supporting the baby's head.

Once she had her hands on him, she refused to let go, as if her touch could infuse life into him. Staff arrived quickly and took over the scene. Once on the stretcher, the baby was flaccid, his breathing erratic.

"Get an IV in him." Duncan gave orders and the staff were already responding. Performing in code situations was something these people did routinely and were obviously accustomed to working together.

Out of her element and uncertain what to do, Rebel wet a towel at the sink and draped it over the boy's head.

Duncan looked at her with dark brown eyes filled with dangerous anger, and she nearly stepped away. Had she overstepped her boundaries? He didn't know she was a nurse or that she had any medical knowledge whatsoever.

"Good idea. Cool his brain off." He gave a grim nod and continued to give orders, orchestrating the scene. After the boy was hooked to the respirator, Duncan took a stethoscope and listened to the little chest as it rose and fell in synchronization with the respirator. "This will rest him a bit."

Rebel tried not to give in to the awful sense of dread crawling into her limbs and stomach. These heroic efforts may have been too little, too late. The baby had had a *grand mal* seizure, the worst kind. His immature brain had gotten too hot too fast and might not recover from the insult. Even if he survived, he could have lifelong brain damage.

Rebel pressed her lips together as emotion overwhelmed her. Images of her family flashed into her mind. "We didn't get to him in time." He was going to die. Just the way her father and three brothers had.

"We don't know that yet," Duncan said, and clasped Rebel's shoulder in a reassuring gesture that failed to bring any comfort. She knew that no matter how good medical care was, people still died. Her father had been the first, then her brothers. Nothing had been able to stop the disease that had taken them all.

"Time will tell," she said, defeated by the rescue efforts she knew were probably futile. If there were miracles in the world, they hadn't been given to her family. Each of her brothers had died a slow, agonizing death, leaving behind holes that could never be filled.

Duncan looked at her as if trying to read something into her words. "Yes. Time *will* tell." He moved to the side and drew Rebel with him. "Is this your child?"

"What? No." Rebel's eyes widened, surprise on her face. "I just happened to come along at the right time." She looked away. "I guess it was the right time."

"I see. Just doing business in the hospital?" He normally didn't stick his nose into the business of others, but this was an unusual and very traumatic situation. One he wanted to figure out now.

"Actually, I'm here to finish up some pre-employment paperwork. I'm a travel nurse. Start tomorrow."

They moved into the hallway as the staff finished stabilizing the boy to transfer him to the pediatric ICU. There was always hope. There had to be for him to carry on with this work as a healer, a physician, as a human being. If there was no hope, what was the point in even trying? Even when his fiancée, Valerie, had been near death, he'd had hope she'd survive. Unfortunately, he'd been wrong that time.

"Where will you be working?" Curiosity made him ask.

"Here. In the ER." The sideways smile she gave said it all.

Duncan nearly chuckled at the irony of the situation, but held back. This was no laughing matter, and he could see in her expression that she thought the same thing. "Quite a trial by fire you hadn't expected."

"It's the life of an ER nurse."

"Yes, for ER doctors, too. I'm Duncan McFee, one of the physicians here in the ER." He paused a moment and watched her soulful green eyes follow the child as he was wheeled toward the elevators. "How are your hands?" He gestured for her to hold them out.

"My hands? What do you mean?" She frowned and looked down at them.

"Your palms, I mean." He placed his strong hands over hers and turned them over. His touch was firm and warm and a little tingle she hadn't expected rushed through her. "You pushed the glass in with your hands, and I'd like to make sure you don't have any cuts. Glass can go deep before you even know it."

"I did? I don't remember doing that."

"You did." He stroked his fingers over the heels of her hands and her palms, using his sensitive fingertips, looking for any irregularities. "Guess we'll be working together if you stay." He released her. "Looks good. What's your name?"

"I'm Rebel Taylor and what do you mean, *if* I stay?" Rebel raised her brows and leveled her intense eyes on him. "I'm not going anywhere."

"Good. Then I'll see you tomorrow. Don't worry about the paperwork. You can finish up in the morning. Go home and de-stress after this. You need it."

After a deep sigh, Rebel's shoulders drooped. She knew the benefits of letting go or destressing or whatever you wanted to call it, after such an event. Time to take a breather on duty was often a luxury, rather than the necessity it should be.

"Maybe you're right." Conceding felt like weakness, but her mind overrode the emotions. She wasn't officially an employee yet, so she had no real place here.

"I'll walk you out. I have to recover my briefcase anyway."

"I hope it's still there. My backpack is there, too."

She shook her head, having forgotten about it in the rescue crisis. What a pain that would be to replace all of the items in her wallet if it had been stolen.

"I'm sure it is. This hospital complex doesn't have a lot of crime and there were plenty of people around."

As they approached the exit, Duncan turned to her. "So where'd you get such an unusual name? You don't look like a rebel to me."

She smiled, some of the tension lifting, even though she recognized his distraction technique. She'd used it many times on her patients, and she appreciated his efforts for her now. "It was something my father gave me when I was a kid. Apparently, as a toddler, I was *quite* the rebel and the nickname stuck." She gave him a slant-eyed glance. "My given name is Rebecca, but if you ever call me that, I'll slap you silly."

Duncan laughed and some of the tension seemed to let go of him as well.

"Agree." He offered an arm for her to move ahead of him. "I think Rebel suits you better anyway. Rebecca is too tame for all that wild hair." Curiously, that hair made him itch to touch it, feel its texture and softness. Check that. Not gonna happen.

They left via the double doors that whooshed open on quiet hydraulics. They approached the parking lot, now alive with police and security.

"Wow." Rebel looked at the area now packed with fire trucks, rescue vehicles, an ambulance and a police aid directing traffic away from the area. "Guess we'll have to file a report, won't we? And someone's got to find out who that baby belongs to." The person probably worked in the building and had forgotten to leave their child with the sitter.

From behind them, Rebel heard a gasp. A young woman dashed past them toward the car and the police officer putting up yellow tape.

"What happened to my car?"

The officer faced her. "Is this your vehicle, ma'am?" He set down the crime-scene tape and stepped closer to her, the sun glinting off his reflective sunglasses. He removed them and wiped his forehead.

"Yes, what happened?" She gestured to the mess it had become.

"Can I see some ID?"

"Oh, for heaven's sake." She dug into her purse as Duncan and Rebel moved closer. "Someone breaks into my car, and *I'm* the one who has to show ID?" She shook her head in obvious disgust. "I was only at work for half an hour and someone broke into my damned car."

"We broke into your car," Duncan said, his voice soft, and Rebel shivered with anticipation as to what his next words would be.

That confession got the officer's attention, and he looked between Duncan and Rebel, keen eyes putting together the scenario.

"You broke into my car?" The woman looked him up and down, then at Rebel, completely baffled. "Why?"

"Because your son was in there." Even though his voice was as soft as silk, the words were hard to hear.

Rebel took a deep breath and gritted her teeth, certain she'd have knots in her shoulders later. Duncan held her gaze and gave her a nod and she moved a little closer to him. The close proximity brought her some comfort and feeling some of his strength made her realize she was going to get through this difficult situation. With the power this man exuded, she thought she might just be able to get through anything.

CHAPTER TWO

"WHAT DO YOU MEAN, *my son?* Eric's at daycare." She swallowed, her blue eyes wide with fear and uncertainty. She looked between Rebel and Dr. McFee trying to figure out if they were telling the truth or if this was some sort of sick joke.

"No, ma'am. Your son was discovered in the backseat of this vehicle." The officer took her ID from her limp fingers.

"N-no, he wasn't. He's at daycare." She looked at Rebel and Duncan, and then at the car as she put the pieces together and completed the horrifying puzzle.

The back door hung open.

The car seat was empty.

The diaper bag lay upside down on the floor.

She focused on Rebel. "Isn't he?"

"Did you forget to stop on your way here?" Duncan asked as gently as possible.

"Did I forget…? Of *course* I didn't forget." Anger flared in her face, then was quickly replaced by fear. She began to hyperventilate and her grip on Rebel's arms loosened.

"Then you left him in the car on purpose?" the officer asked.

"No! I would never…" Her eyelids fluttered.

"She's going out." Rebel held on to the woman's arms as the purse and wallet thudded to the pavement.

"Go get us a gurney," Duncan instructed the security guard, who ran into the building, and took some of the woman's body weight from Rebel.

"As soon as she wakes up she's under arrest," the officer said, and shoved his shades back on.

"As soon as she wakes up she needs to see her child, so back off." Dark anger flashed in Duncan's eyes, and Rebel held her breath.

"She put her kid in mortal danger. He may die."

"I understand. She's not going anywhere, so you can arrest her later."

For the second time in less than an hour Rebel and Duncan entered the ER with an unexpected patient.

"Can you start an IV?" Duncan asked. "The others are working on a new trauma."

"Yes," Rebel said, ready to be helpful and hide the fear surfacing in her veins. Facing her fears was what had led her to ER nursing, but some days the fear nearly did her in.

Duncan pointed to the counter behind her. "Supplies are there. Get some saline going."

In seconds Rebel had everything prepared and inserted an IV into the back of the woman's hand.

Duncan rummaged in a cabinet beside her. "Aha." He moved closer to the patient. "Make sure that's taped down well."

"Why?"

He held up the small mesh-covered capsule. "Old-fashioned smelling salts."

"Haven't seen those used in years." Thinking outside the box was what kept ER nursing interesting. "Let 'er rip."

The instant Duncan popped the capsule with his fingers, the noxious scent invaded the room. He waved it beneath the woman's nose, and she jerked away.

"Wake up for me," Duncan said, and patted her cheeks.

"Her name is Amanda Walker." The police officer arrived from outside with her belongings.

"Amanda? Amanda. Wake up now." Duncan spoke to her.

Rebel leaned close to Amanda's ear. "Eric needs you."

Amanda's eyelids fluttered, and she jerked away from Duncan's hands. "Yuck, what is that?" She struggled to wake from unconsciousness and coughed.

"Amanda, I'm Dr. McFee, and you're in the ER. Do you remember what happened?" Amanda kept her eyes closed and frowned.

"Eric? What about Eric?" She opened eyes that appeared to have no memory of the recent events in the parking lot. Not unusual. The brain provided wonderful coping mechanisms to assist in dealing with emotionally painful situations. None of them were going to help her now.

"You were on the way to work and what happened?"

"What do you mean? I parked and came into work like I always do." She focused more on Duncan and glared. "Why are you asking about Eric? Did the daycare call?"

"No, ma'am…" Duncan interrupted the officer with a glare. He clenched his jaw, not wanting to verbally castigate the officer when he had a patient on his hands. "No. Daycare didn't call."

"I was… No. Is Eric okay? What's happened?" She tried to sit up. "What's going on?"

Rebel stepped forward and glanced with hesitation at Duncan. He didn't know her, had never worked with her before, so he had no reason to trust her or her abilities as a nurse. Then again, he had no reason not to trust her. He nodded.

Rebel placed her hand over Amanda's with a gentle touch. Compassionate energy pooled around Rebel in such waves that Duncan felt them. This woman was made of tough stuff. So far turning out to be a damned good ER nurse. Gorgeous and smart. Hard combination to find.

"I'm Rebel, one of the nurses. I…discovered Eric… in the back of your car."

"No, you didn't." Amanda shook her head in denial and jerked her hand away from Rebel. "He's at daycare." Amanda placed a trembling hand over her mouth and tears spilled from her eyes as trickles of the truth emerged from her subconscious. "You're scaring me now." Amanda looked around the room, at the glaring overhead lights, at the medical equipment, at the IV in her arm. Then she took a deep breath.

The wail that followed emerged straight from her soul.

The hair on Duncan's neck twitched in reaction to the agonizing cry no amount of comfort could touch. He looked at his newest coworker.

Tears overflowed Rebel's eyes as she stood with hands clenched in front of her. Even the cop turned away.

"N-o-o-o. No. No. No." She hopped off the gurney, her eyes wild. "You people are crazy! His dad *always* drops him off." Her breathing came hard and fast.

"Amanda. Think back to this morning. Was there a change in your routine? Did you deviate…?" Rebel asked questions designed to trigger her memory.

"No!" She pointed a finger at Rebel. "Wait till I call my husband. He's a lawyer, and he'll… My husband… is…sick…today." Amanda collapsed to her knees. Sobs croaked out of her in an unrelenting torrent of realization.

Rebel knelt beside her. "What happened? Can you tell me?"

"His office has daycare." She huffed in a few breaths. "He always takes Eric. *Always*."

"And he's home sick today?"

Amanda nodded, then slumped over onto the floor. "I killed my son! Oh, God, I killed my son."

"Eric is alive, Amanda. He's not dead."

Amanda sat up and grabbed Rebel by the shoulders. "You found him in time?" She hauled Rebel into an exuberant hug. "Oh, my God." Now, sobs of relief overflowed. "I don't know how to thank you."

Rebel placed her arms around Amanda and looked at Duncan. Those beautiful green eyes of hers pleaded for his help and something inside him emerged. Whether it was the trained physician in him, the male protector of women and children, or he was just reacting to the pain in Rebel's face, he didn't know. He just knew he had to respond.

"Amanda, sit up. I'll tell you about Eric, then we'll take you to see him." He assisted her to her feet, protecting Rebel from being overwhelmed. He offered a hand down to Rebel and brought her by his side. His instinct was to place his arm around her waist, to shield her from the pain they both knew was yet to come, knowing the story before it was even told. Instead, he took Rebel's hand and led her to a chair. She was pale and her hand was clammy. Though she didn't look it on the outside, he knew she was having great difficulty with this situation. Officially she wasn't even an employee, and she'd gone above and beyond what was expected of her. She could just as easily have walked away, but she hadn't. What heart she must have.

Duncan placed his hands on the shoulders of the sobbing woman. This was going to bite. "Amanda, pull yourself together. You need to be strong for Eric. Now take a breath and stop crying."

In a few minutes she'd managed to subdue her emotions. Tears still dribbled from her eyes, but she could look at him. That was a start.

As the noon hour approached, Rebel felt about a hundred years older than her actual thirty. Days like this were why people left healthcare. Some days being a nurse just wasn't worth it.

She'd been sitting outside the PICU where Eric had been taken. She didn't know why, but she didn't want to leave just yet. Dr. McHunky had taken the mother inside to see Eric.

Rebel had plopped herself into a chair outside the unit and hadn't been able to get up. Sitting outside an intensive care unit brought back so many overwhelming memories it shut her down. For years she'd been an unwilling participant in her family's inherited illness, Huntington's disease. Watching her brothers struggle to survive had forced her to grow up too quickly, to be too old too soon, to leave childhood behind too early. Events like today sucked her back in time to when she had been a frightened little girl watching her family be taken from her one by one.

The door to the unit swung open, and she shoved aside her past to dive into the present again. That's what adrenal glands were for, right? Surges of adrenaline kept her going from one crisis to another in the ER, and that ability didn't fail her now.

"So, how is he, Doctor?"

"It's Duncan, please." Though he patted her on the shoulder in what was supposed to be a comforting gesture, he looked as if he needed some comforting himself.

"Okay, Duncan. First tell me how he is then tell me how you are. You look like someone beat you with a hammer." Lines of what could be grief or fatigue showed on his face. Though it was mid-morning, he looked like he'd been up all night.

A small smile twisted his lips and a little relief appeared in her eyes. Mission accomplished.

"I *feel* like someone beat me with a hammer." He looked at his watch. "And it's not even lunch yet." He took a deep breath and let it out in a very long sigh. "I'll be okay. I think. Eric's critical, on a vent, the works. I've never seen so many tubes hooked up to a kid that size, and I thought I'd seen it all."

"I'm so sorry." She gave his arm a squeeze, intending to offer him some of the comfort she'd offer to any of her patients and families. His arm beneath her hand was warm and firm. Though this child wasn't related to either of them, he was special and bonded the two of them together.

Duncan turned his dark-eyed focus fully on her, and she gulped at the intensity of him. When he focused on something, it was something else. His dark, dark eyes seemed to have no pupils. His aura nearly reached out to her, like some invisible cloak trying to cocoon her into its warmth.

"And how are you holding up?"

"I'm okay, I guess." She shrugged. "Are you ever okay after an event like this?" She'd been through many traumas in her career as an ER nurse and some patient situations stuck with her, no matter how long ago they'd happened.

"You might want to go home. The paperwork for employment can wait until tomorrow."

"I'm good, really—" Denial had gotten her through many tough situations in life, why not one more?

He gave her such a doctor look, knowing she wasn't all right, knowing she'd been through the wringer today, and knowing she wasn't telling the truth, that she actually felt a flash of shame.

"Rebel. We don't always have time to shake off the vibes from work while in the midst of it. Take the time to relax and shake this off." Duncan spoke like a man who had been on the front line of healthcare for a long time. That kind of experience didn't come without a toll on the body and the psyche.

"Thanks. You're right." She nodded. "I usually like to meet with the charge nurse the day before I start and introduce myself to see who I'm going to be working with. Stuff like that."

Duncan gave a snort as the elevator doors whooshed open. "I think you've had quite an introduction already. The entire staff knows who you are by now, so just go home. I'll tell Herm."

"If you're sure it's going to be okay…"

"It'll be fine." The elevators took them to the first floor, and they exited. "Today is an admin day for me, so I'm going to do the bare essentials and head to the gym. Always helps me blow off the stress of the day."

"My apartment complex has a pool. Maybe I'll take a swim."

"Good idea. Don't forget the sunscreen. At this elevation the rays are more intense. See you tomorrow." He'd hate to see all that luscious skin damaged by the sun. It was beautiful and she obviously worked to keep it that way.

Rebel turned and held out her hand. Duncan took it. "I'd like to say it was a pleasure to meet you, but I'm not sure that's the right thing to say." She met his eyes and held his gaze. This was a very interesting man. Unfortunately, she hadn't come here to be sidetracked by gorgeous doctors. Men and emotional relationships didn't go with her long-term goals, so there was no use in establishing a short-term one either. Men were fine as friends and the occasional lover. Too many times she'd counted on a man and had been disappointed. She needed to be in control and if she were in a relationship, she lost that. Plain and simple.

"How about 'See you tomorrow'?"

"Good enough." They shook hands, and Rebel untangled her sunglasses from on top of her head and walked out into the bright June sunlight, determined to make it to her car before another disaster happened.

Hitching her backpack across one shoulder, she tried not to look at the scene of where they had found Eric. That, like so many other bad memories, already had a permanent place in her brain.

Thoughts of Duncan, however, lingered. How would

it be to work side by side with such a dynamic man? She'd worked in many types of hospitals and clinics, and there had been plenty of handsome doctors to be had, but this one was different. Somehow, deep in her gut, she knew something was different about Duncan, and she itched to know what it was. Could it be that the intensity of the situation they'd just been through was making her see things that weren't there?

She didn't think so, as she'd been through many tough situations with many doctors in the past. Today, however, made her think more about what it would be like to have a man like that around her more often.

Those dark, dangerous eyes of his remained in her mind.

CHAPTER THREE

THE NEXT DAY dawned as bright and shiny as any she'd ever seen.

Until she arrived just before her morning shift to find the ER in complete chaos. This ER was shaping up to be just like most of the ones she'd worked in. Either it was complete bedlam, or the staff were falling asleep from sheer boredom.

She took a deep breath, shoved her backpack beneath the desk and hurried to the first busy room she found. "I'm your new traveler. Someone give me a job."

A Hispanic man strode over to her with his glasses perched precariously on top of his graying hair and shoved a clipboard into her hands. "Here. Run the code. I'll be back in ten minutes."

Gulp. Running a code within thirty seconds of arriving. That was a record, but this was something she was fully capable of managing. She squeezed behind staff members who were performing all kinds of tasks around a patient who had been in a traumatic accident.

She looked at the clipboard. Pedestrian. Hit by a high-speed vehicle, thrown forty feet in the air. Possible neck and spine injuries. Probable head injury. Punctured one lung. Blood in the abdomen.

If he survived, he'd spend the next year in rehab all because someone hadn't looked both ways. She read the cardiac monitor. His heart rate was fast, rhythm good.

"What do you need next, Doctor?" She hadn't met any of the physicians yet, so she didn't know who she was working with.

"Glad you're here, Rebel. Call Radiology. Need a chest X-ray, abdominal films." She knew the voice and a little bit of her relaxed, and a little of her got excited at the compliment. Although she couldn't see his face behind the mask and goggles, she knew Duncan was in charge of this case. The sound of his voice was reassuring and made a funny squiggle in the pit of her stomach at the same time. The man had definitely made an impact on her senses yesterday.

"Got it." She turned to the phone on the wall. Fortunately, there was an extensive phone list posted nearby. After the first call, she checked the monitor again. The heart rhythm had changed. Not looking good.

"Doctor. He's had a rhythm change."

Duncan twisted around and looked at it for himself. "Dammit. I was hoping we could get him to the OR before he crashed. Get a chest tube set up."

She set the clipboard down. "Where are they?"

"There. One of the other nurses pointed to a cabinet right behind Duncan. Rebel squished her way through the bodies in the room to fetch the sterile tray, dropped it onto a portable tray table, opened it, and donned sterile gloves.

"I'm back." The man who had given her the clipboard returned to take over.

"We're putting a chest tube in on the left." Rebel called out the information so he could catch up to where they were in the situation and record it. "Rhythm is V-tach. Rate one-eighty." She prepared to assist Duncan with the procedure. Duncan removed his gloves, and she held out a new, sterile pair for him. A collapsed lung would be deadly along with all of his other injuries.

After insertion, blood poured through the tubing into the collection container and the heart monitor settled down. Rebel drew a deep breath. Yet another save before eight in the morning by a doctor she was coming to have confidence in very rapidly. "Good going, Doc."

The only response was a connecting of glances and a nod. The tension of the code dwindled as the patient stabilized and was being prepared for transfer to the operating room for surgery.

"Rebel, right? What a name. I'm Hermano Vega, but call me Herm. I'm the charge nurse in this madhouse for today. You're with me for orientation. The others can get him upstairs."

Rebel shook his hand, liking his gentle, fatherly demeanor immediately. "Nice to meet you."

"Quite the first day, *no*?" He echoed Duncan's statement from earlier. "Come on. Let's get you settled." He turned and motioned for her to follow. Though she looked back as Duncan removed his protective gear, she went along with Herm. Somehow that man had gotten under her skin, and they'd only met yesterday.

"Great. What sort of torture do you have planned for me this morning?" There was *always* torture involved at the beginning of a new assignment.

Herm gave her a stern look over his glasses, and her gut twisted a little. Maybe she was being too flip too soon. Eek.

"The evil policy and procedure manual."

Rebel relaxed. Yep. This was going to be just like every other ER she'd worked in. Torture with orientation material then release her to the wild.

"You've got the expedited orientation training to go through for travelers. Fire safety, infection control, HIPPA, etcetera. All online now. I'll set you up with a computer terminal then we can talk about your schedule." Schedule. The most important thing to keep staff happy. Aside from payday. And good coffee.

"Got it." She looked around the station. "Is there by chance a cup of coffee somewhere I could snag first?"

"Oh, sure." He gave a nod down the hall. "Grab what you need, then back here for the mind-meld the rest of the day. If you get it all done today, you can go home early."

"Awesome."

Rebel wandered down the hall to the staff-only area and the crazed energy of the main unit eased a bit until she opened the door to the small lounge. Then her heart fluttered when she saw Duncan in his blue scrubs, coffee in hand, leaning against the counter.

His eyes were closed, and he seemed lost in his thoughts. She paused a moment, uncertain whether or not to disturb him, but the smell of coffee called to her.

"Come in. I know someone's there. I'm just perfecting my sleeping while standing up technique."

With a little smile, Rebel entered the lounge. "I thought that's what you were doing. Maybe you can give me some pointers for the next time I work a stretch of night shifts."

Duncan opened his eyes a little, glad to hear her voice free of tension. Obviously she'd been able to let the stress of yesterday go. That was a good thing. Today she looked as gorgeous as she had yesterday. But her hair was up in a clip with little strands handing down to tease her face. He had to resist the urge to push some of that mass back behind her ear. Those weren't the kinds of thoughts he should be having about a new co-worker, but he seemed powerless to resist. He cleared his throat. "Not scared off after yesterday and walking into that trauma today?"

"Nope. You?"

"Nah." His smile was self-deprecating. "I grew up with four sisters, four brothers and twenty-five cousins. I saw more trauma and drama than you'd guess by the time I was twelve."

"I see. That's a huge family." Indeed. Hers had dwindled down to just her mother and herself, with a few cousins in the Mid-West somewhere.

"I'm guessing you didn't come in here to chat, but need some liquid fortitude to get through the rest of the day Herm has planned for you." He raised his coffee cup toward her.

"Psychic, too." She nodded. "I'm impressed by your extensive set of unusual skills."

Playful and flirtatious, she appealed to his lighter side. Duncan shoved away from the counter and poured her a cup of coffee, then handed it to her. "Additives are over there." He indicated the powdered creamer and sweetener selection on the counter.

"Sorry, I'm a creamer snob." She pulled out her own stash of flavored creamer and added it to the mug.

"Good to know." He grinned.

Rebel noticed that Duncan watched her intently as she prepared her coffee. She wasn't accustomed to such attention and she was a little uncomfortable with it.

She'd spent years avoiding the intimacy of relationships, apart from a very occasional and very brief fling. Right now she wasn't certain whether she was appreciative of, or offended by, Duncan's focus.

The silence that hung between them went on for a few seconds too long as she ran out of things to say. Her charm only lasted so long.

"Well, I'd better go before Herm thinks I've run off." She raised her mug. "Thanks." Dropping her gaze away from him, she headed out to the safety of the unit and the dreariness of orientation.

Rebel sat in a corner of the ER away from the hustle and bustle around her, answering the incessant questions of the computer program. *Have you located the fire alarms and fire extinguishers in your area?*

She clicked "Yes," although she was pretty certain she'd just raced by them on the way to the trauma this morning. That counted, didn't it?

Staff occasionally would give her a wave, but no one stopped to chat. She supposed that was best for the moment. The next three months would give her plenty of time to make friends. These relationships were only temporary, lasting only as long as her assignment, then she moved on, to another hospital, another set of temporary friends, to relive the same life over and over again.

This lifestyle was one she'd chosen after losing most of her family to Huntington's disease. There had been no hope for her father or three brothers, and they hadn't even known it. Here, at least, she could save someone once in a while. Like yesterday.

Herm peeked in on her after a few hours. "Had enough yet?"

"Have a barf bag?" Humor in the workplace was a necessity for survival.

"Enough said. Come with me." Rebel followed him to the nurses' station and wondered what it was that he had for her to do.

"Am I going to like this job?"

Herm peered at her over his glasses again. A gesture she was coming to associate with him. Kind of like a beloved teacher overlooking his charges.

"Hard to say, but one set of papers is a follow-up from yesterday and then a scavenger hunt." He handed the papers to her. "The ER is required to follow up on patients to see how successful our efforts have been."

"I'm not quite getting that."

"Did the patient survive the first twenty-four hours, any infections, any further injuries as a result of being resuscitated? Those sorts of questions that risk management people love to drool over."

"Okay, now I'm with you." She took the paper. It was filled front and back with questions. The flow chart from hell.

"See if you can find these departments without cheating, then you can take lunch. Cafeteria's pretty good, coffee shop is close by, then come back up here."

"Got it."

Rebel didn't know how, but she knew the instant Duncan approached them. Whether it was his energy, his cologne or some unknown force she was attuned to, she turned slightly, already knowing he would be there. Maybe it was having gone through the situation together yesterday, but she felt a strange connection to him. She was probably imagining things. Men like Duncan didn't go for women like her. That was for sure. He was too much, too exciting, too dynamic, too over the top for a woman like her.

The same scenario had played out over and over on various travel assignments. Dashing doctor and super-nurse work side by side, saving lives, and one day they discover a new spark that has nothing to do with work and everything to do with the heat crackling between them. She'd seen it dozens of times, but it had never happened to her.

She rolled her shoulders against the twinge of guilt that nestled uncomfortably there. If she was honest with herself, it wasn't that she hadn't had opportunities, she'd run from them when someone had wanted to get close to her. Right now, it didn't matter. Duncan was here to do a job, just like her. It didn't matter how handsome he was or how much her heart fluttered when she thought of him.

In some dark place deep down inside her, if she was really, *really* honest, she'd admit that something about Duncan made her want to stop running, to take a chance on a relationship, see if there was a man who could love her despite the problems of her past, someone who would just love her and not worry about the time bomb ticking inside her. Loving someone again who would then reject her because of something inside her would be her worst nightmare.

Looking down into that place scared her. Made her afraid no one would be able to love her the way she needed to be loved. A man like Duncan made her want to take a chance.

CHAPTER FOUR

"Oh—hi, Doc. Maybe you can help, too." Herm included Duncan in the conversation, and Rebel turned toward him. Yes, he was definitely as handsome in scrubs as he was in street clothing. Possibly more, because scrubs had a way of stripping a person down to their basics—no frills or high-priced clothing to hide behind. From her first encounter with Duncan, she'd concluded he certainly had that. He didn't skimp on his clothing. Not that she minded. She did admire a sharp-dressed man.

"Sure. What is it?" He stepped a little closer, and Rebel's senses squealed. Oh, the man was too close for comfort. Though she could talk herself out of engaging in any sort of liaison with him, her senses reacted on their own volition.

Duncan looked at Rebel. She was tall, nearly as tall as he, and he could meet her clear green eyes almost head-on. Curious that she didn't realize how attractive she was. Maybe she'd been burned, just like him. He gave a mental shake. No one had been burned like him. The arguments, the fights. And then the wreck. That was something he'd never get over. Refocusing, he looked away from Rebel.

"It's a follow-up on the boy you two rescued yesterday. Within twenty-four hours we need to lay eyes on them." Herm muttered a few things under his breath. Probably about more documentation. Seemed it was the same situation everywhere in healthcare. Do more with less.

"Sure. I thought about him most of the night."

"Me, too." Rebel admitted what had kept her from having a good night's sleep, other than first-day jitters and thoughts of Duncan. She took the paperwork, and Herm pointed to the brightly colored map in her hands.

"That's the scavenger hunt. Find these places in the hospital so when you need to know where they are at three a.m., you can find them." He glared at Duncan. "No helping her."

"Who, me?" Duncan placed a hand on his chest and raised his eyebrows and, despite herself, Rebel responded to his light-hearted attitude. It was so essential for their work. How could she not?

"Yes, you. Get out of here for a while and take a break." Herm turned away as another staff member called for his attention.

With papers in hand, Rebel drifted toward the exit and Duncan moved with her. "You'll have to lead the way, I don't even know how to get to the PICU yet." Rebel kept her gaze on the papers, not really seeing the words. She was suddenly atwitter at spending time with Duncan. He was her coworker, but he was also a disturbingly handsome man. And one who smelled like a dream.

"This way." He ushered her with one arm ahead of him, as if he were escorting her. "We'll take the staff elevators to the fifth floor. PICU is up there." Duncan swiped his badge to call the elevator.

In just a few seconds they entered the empty car, and Rebel pushed the button. The idea of staff elevators appealed to Rebel. They helped keep the staff separated from the visitors at important times. Taking a bloodied and battered patient upstairs in view of the public did not make for good surveys. And it also protected patients' privacy.

Nervous, she kept her eyes focused on her papers. They arrived at the PICU and approached Eric's room. Duncan had gone quiet beside her, his energy dark and serious. His anticipation of what they would find was palpable, and she reacted in much the same way.

Nothing was ever quiet in an ICU. Bleeps, alarms, and the noise of respirators, although quiet in and of themselves, together made quite a racket.

A nurse in cartoon scrubs and a bouncy blond ponytail approached. "Can I help you?" She was perky in a way Rebel could never hope to be. Her skin was flawless, and she had applied just the right amount of makeup to enhance her features. She was buxom and curvy, where Rebel barely had breasts. Or at least that's what she felt like sometimes. This was the kind of woman Duncan probably went for, not someone as uninteresting as her. She didn't wear much makeup, her hair kept its own schedule of events, and she didn't have a curves in the places men liked. Even though she had flaming red hair, she thought it was a detractor. Men like Duncan didn't go for women like her, but then again she didn't date, so it didn't matter, and she needed to focus on things other than her dashing coworker.

The nurse's bright blue eyes looked between them as

she spoke, but lingered on Duncan. Rebel could hardly blame her, he was something the eyes could linger on and not become fatigued.

"We have some paperwork to fill out for the ER as follow-up to see how Eric's doing," Rebel said, focusing once again on the task at hand, the only reason she was here with Duncan.

"Oh, you must have been the first responders." A light of sympathy entered her blue eyes. "I heard about your efforts in report this morning." She pouted out her lower lip and placed a gentle hand on Rebel's arm.

"Yes, we were." She looked at Duncan, who seemed impervious to Becky's beauty and sympathetic manner. Maybe he already had a squeeze on the side and wasn't interested in anyone else. She mentally yanked herself back. Maybe it was none of her business.

"How awful it must have been to find him."

"Yes, it certainly was a shock." Rebel showed Becky the form. "Can you give us an update?"

"Sure."

Duncan observed the interaction between the two nurses who couldn't possibly be more different in looks. Though Becky was certainly attractive, his gaze kept returning to Rebel. What an unusual woman she was. Of course, he'd run across unusual women before, but there was something about Rebel that kept taking his mind down a path he'd sworn never to go down again. Romance and dating was something he'd thought had died when his fiancée had been killed. His interest in sex had been on hiatus, but now was beginning to return as he watched Rebel beside him.

"Excuse me. I want to go see him first." He stepped forward, leaving the two nurses to do the paperwork.

Rebel watched as he placed a hand on Amanda's back, startling her from sleep in the chair. He exuded compassion and Rebel swallowed hard, crushing down the memory of being on the receiving end of such a gesture some years ago.

In a few minutes, Duncan returned, the lines in his face serious. "Can you tell me where your intensivist is? I'd like to speak to him or her."

"Her. Dr. Barb Simmons. She's in the charting room behind the nurses' station. Drop-dead gorgeous blonde. Can't miss her."

With only a nod and no lingering glances of interest, Duncan left them.

"Let's see your paperwork. I can help you fill it out," Becky said.

As Rebel stretched out her arm to hand the paperwork to Becky, her arm seemed to go numb, and she lost her grip on the pages. They fluttered to the floor. "Oh, rats!" Hastily, she grabbed them and shuffled them back together. "Sorry about that. Lost my grip for some reason." She knew the likely reason and it frightened her more than anything in the world. She was starting to show symptoms of the disease.

"That's okay," Becky said, and opened her bedside computer chart, distracting Rebel from her self-focus. Becky's fingers flew over the keyboard and pulled up the data on Eric's case.

"Any sense of how he's doing overall?" Rebel asked, nurse to nurse. Experienced nurses developed senses that couldn't be learned in a classroom or in books.

"Well, he's deeply sedated right now." She gave another sympathetic look. "I hate to even give you a guess because patients surprise me all the time. These little ones are so amazing. They spring back when you least expect it." She sighed. "Then again, they take a downturn just as fast." She gave that pout again. Once, Rebel got, twice was just unattractive.

"Thanks." She looked behind Becky. "Can I go in and see him?"

"Absolutely. Just let me know if you need anything."

Rebel could see Amanda half sitting on a chair, half lying on the bed beside Eric. Across the room a man sat with a computer on his lap, leaning back in his chair, fast asleep. "Amanda?"

The mother turned to Rebel, her face splotchy and swollen. "Yes?"

"It's Rebel, the nurse from the ER." She knelt beside the bed and placed her hand on Amanda's back, the same way Duncan had. "I came to see how you and Eric are doing." The words sounded trite. After all, how could any of them be doing after such a life-altering event?

"He's going to die. I know it." Her voice was just a whisper that spoke to Rebel's soul, which had seen so much pain in her own family. Somehow, there had to be hope, even if it was just a little.

Trying to be encouraging without giving false hope was a tricky dance. "I just reviewed his chart with Nurse Becky and things look pretty stable right now." That was the truth. At least for the moment.

"Then why hasn't he opened his eyes? Why doesn't he respond to me?" Frustration shot out of her like electricity.

"He's being heavily sedated. When kids are on the respirator they get wiggly and won't let the machine do the work." That was true, too.

"Why didn't anyone explain this to me?" She raked a hand through her hair in frustration then clenched her fists in her lap. She looked as if she wanted to hit something.

Rebel knew this information had likely been explained more than once, but due to stress of the event she hadn't remembered it.

"Just keep talking to him. He can hear you." Hearing was the last sense to leave before death. People who returned from seemingly unrecoverable events often did, and were able to relate stories of hearing everything going on around them but being unable to respond at the time.

"I didn't know whether he could hear me or not."

"He does. Just give him your love. Just let him hear your voice." That was the one hope she'd held on to when her brothers had died, that they had heard her voice and had known she loved them. "He may not respond to you right now, but he will hear you. It will be your voice he recognizes and responds to. If anything is going to pull him out of this, it will be you."

"Really?" Shocked, Amanda looked at her child, then back at Rebel, trying to determine the truth.

"I've worked with many patients who have awakened from comas, and that's the thing they all had in common. They heard their families and knew there was someone with them."

"Do you think he can…make it?" She pushed her hair out of her face.

"I don't know, but for me to go on as a nurse I need to have some hope." Rebel squeezed Amanda's hands as she echoed Duncan's sentiment and choked down her own emotion that wanted to swallow her whole.

This moment was not about her own grief and loss but about the recovery of Amanda's child. "It's never easy, but don't give up."

"I don't want to…but I'm not getting much support…" she glanced at her husband "…from anyone."

"Men like to fix things and feel powerless when they can't." She thought about Duncan. He was definitely a fixer.

"You are observant." Amanda offered a smile at that bit of wisdom.

She leaned over and spoke into Eric's ear, then gave him a kiss on the forehead, careful not to bump any of his tubes. "Just remember, there is always hope."

Eagerness and a little hope now showed on Amanda's face.

"I will." She stroked Eric's forehead. "I'll talk to him all the time now. Thank you." Tears welled again in Amanda's eyes. "Thank you. You've given me more hope than I've had since this all happened."

Unable to bear the onslaught of emotions dredged to the surface by this situation, Rebel pushed them aside. She backed away before she lost control and turned to dash out the door.

And ran right into Duncan's arms.

CHAPTER FIVE

Duncan reached out just as Rebel crashed into him. The only way he would not bowl her over was to grab hold of her hips and bring her close against him. The papers in her hands flew into the air and seemed to drift in slow motion to the floor.

He pulled her against his hips with one arm and braced them against the doorframe with the other. Eyes wide in shock, she clutched his upper arms with both hands and caught her breath with a squeal.

With her trim frame and lower body weight, she would certainly have bounced off of him and landed on the floor had he not caught her. Now that he had caught her, he found himself in a very interesting position. Holding her was inappropriate, yet letting go of her seemed equally so. She was tiny beneath the figure-erasing scrubs. It was a crime against man to cover up such a beautiful body. He looked down at her and realized that if he'd wanted to kiss her, she was in the perfect position to do so.

He watched as she licked her lips and pressed them together. What an enticing mouth she had. Unfortunately, he had to release her before any opportunity to taste those lips occurred. As a man experienced in the ways of romantic coworker relationships, that was a treat best left unsavored. "Sorry about that. Are you okay?" Reluctantly, he released her. With some amusement he watched a vivid blush cruise up to her neck and into her cheeks. She was not as unaffected as she pretended to be. Interesting. Off limits, but very interesting.

"Yes, sorry about that."

They retrieved her paperwork, and she shuffled it back in place. They left the room with a respectable two-foot distance between them. Duncan had had enough of losing the women in his life. His mother, a sister and his fiancée. The last one had about killed him, and he'd sworn off of emotional relationships for a while to rest his heart and soul. Rebel was the most interesting woman he'd run across in a long time and, still, he hesitated. That last relationship had burned him to the core, and he hadn't really recovered from it. She'd been a colleague, too. He paused, thinking. Perhaps it was time he at least tested the waters again.

"It's Duncan, please. And it was just a little accident of timing. No fault."

She cleared her throat, focusing on the tile pattern on the floor. "So are you going to help me cheat on this scavenger hunt, or what?" She quickly diverted the conversation.

"No." He snorted. As if. But he did like a challenge.

Her gaze flashed to him. "No? So how am I going to get through all of this without dying of hunger or thirst? We are in a desert, you know."

He gave a quick laugh. He liked humor in his coworkers. Made shifts a lot more interesting. And it was safer than where his thoughts had been going. "Isn't there a map on there?"

Now *she* snorted. "If you can call it that. The copier must have run out of toner at an inopportune time. I need a GPS to get through this hospital."

"If you can navigate to the cafeteria I'll buy you some lunch." His stomach had been reminding him of his skimpy breakfast for some time now.

"You're on." She started toward the elevators, and he followed along behind, admiring the view. Puzzled, he frowned as he observed her gait and the way she moved her body.

"What do you do?" Now, more curious than ever, he began to ignore that finely tuned alarm system in his head. Pursuing her might be worth the pain.

She hit the elevator button. "Do about what?"

"For exercise. Working out." He gave her a once-over glance and liked what he saw. "The way you walk and the way you carry yourself is different. I can usually pick out how a person stays fit by the way they move and their body shape. It's a little game I play with myself. Swimmers look one way, runners look another way, cyclists another way, but you I can't figure out." The feel of her body beneath those scrubs had been firm, yet still very feminine. "You aren't a body-builder either." He frowned and tried not to ogle her in public. Administration wasn't kidding about sexual harassment.

At that, a genuine grin covered her face. "Yoga." She stood on one foot and clasped her hands together over her head with the paperwork flattened between her palms. "Like this."

"Yoga?" He glanced over her again, dumbfounded.

"Really? Just yoga? I thought you just sat in impossible situations and chanted to the universe for enlightenment."

Rebel laughed. "That would be meditation. You should try yoga sometime. Strengthens the mind and spirit as well as the body." She resumed her standing position without even a wobble. Show-off.

Duncan tried to mimic her pose and was able to get his hands over his head, but standing on one foot at the same time was *not* happening, and he almost crashed into the wall. Very uncool.

"I'm a more brute strength, linear kind of guy, like running, hiking, that sort of stuff. If I have to think about it too much, I won't do it." He laughed. "Just put me on a bike in a straight line, and I'm good."

"So how do you get back, then, if you just go in a straight line?"

He laughed, liking her quick wit. "Eventually, I stop, turn around and go in another straight line until I'm back where I started."

"You need to expand your horizons, Doctor."

"I like skiing."

"Skiing in the desert—really?" The bemused look on her face betrayed her skepticism at his statement.

"Yes. Ice hockey, too. You'd be surprised what kind of landscape the desert has to offer. We're considered high desert since we're higher in elevation than other desert areas of the southwest."

"Oh, so not like Phoenix or Death Valley?"

"Right. Way too hot for me. Went there for a conference once and about cooked my brain."

The elevator arrived, and they were off on the scavenger hunt. Rebel successfully negotiated her way to the blood bank, lab, central supply, and finally to the cafeteria.

Duncan sniffed appreciably. "I can smell the green chili from here." He closed his eyes, savoring a fond memory. "I'm in the mood for green chili cheese fries, how about you?"

"What's that?" Innocent curiosity showed in that gorgeous face of hers. Stunned, Duncan looked at her. She was *serious*.

"You've never heard of green chili cheese fries?"

"Nope. Or green chili anything." Duncan's jaw dropped, and he swore his heart skipped several important beats. He may have seen stars, but he wasn't certain. "I think I may have a coronary right now." He placed a hand over his chest. "Get the AED."

"Why? What did I say?" Eyes wide with concern, she pressed her lips together. "Did I say something totally stupid?"

"I know you're new in town, but green chili is the number one agricultural crop of the entire state and has been the foundation for my family's holdings for the last two hundred years." He took a breath and frowned. "My grandfather should never, *ever*, hear you don't know what green chili is or it could start another highland war."

"Oh, is that all?" She turned away.

"What?" Stunned, he froze in place.

"Kidding." She gave a sly grin over her shoulder. "Got it. Important stuff around here."

"And, besides that, it tastes really, *really* good."

"Okay, can we get some, then?"

"Absolutely. Your orientation would not be complete without a sampling of green chili cheese fries." Another sign of her adventurous spirit if she was willing to try an unknown food on his recommendation. That was very attractive to him. But he remembered his fiancée had also had an adventurous spirit and look where that had left them. Her dead. Him with a broken heart.

Minutes later, they had a pile of steaming French fries in front of them, topped with green chili sauce and shredded cheddar cheese. The consistency of gravy, the sauce was absolutely amazing, as far as Duncan was concerned, and he was an expert.

"If you don't like this, I'm afraid your contract will have to be terminated."

"Oh, give me a break, it will not." She gave the first natural-sounding laugh he'd heard out of her since they'd met. That was a good sign. This was fun, showing her something she'd never seen or even heard of before. Gave him new appreciation of it, too, to experience it again through her eyes, and his heart lightened.

Duncan watched as Rebel took a fry, dripping in chili sauce and cheese, and put it in her mouth. She closed her eyes as she chewed. What was it about eating a meal with some people that was so erotic? He didn't care as he took in how Rebel's face changed and her eyes popped open, surprise filling those incredible green eyes of hers. His mouth began to water and it wasn't for food but a taste of her. Even against his better judgment, the longer he spent with her, the more intrigued he became. Could he engage in a casual relationship with her, knowing she'd leave in a few months? Could they have a simple, sexual relationship and let the rest go? It was worth thinking about.

"That is spectacular. You're gonna have to get your

own, pal, 'cos I'm not sharing." She slid the plate closer to her.

"I'll tell Herm you cheated." He slid the plate in front of him.

"I did not." The plate returned to Rebel.

"Who's he gonna believe, you or me?" Duncan reached for the plate but Rebel narrowed her eyes and held on to it.

"You are evil. And I believe that's blackmail."

"Then you have to share." He slid the plate into the middle again. "And it's actually extortion." He shrugged at her look. "Got a cousin who's a lawyer."

"Fine. But you know what they say about payback."

"I do. And it is." He grinned and dug his fork into the bliss on the plate, deciding to shove away thoughts of a casual sexual relationship for the moment.

"So you have a hobby farm?"

Duncan tried not to choke at her description. "If you can call ten thousand acres a hobby farm." That was in Hatch, New Mexico alone. Cousins in surrounding areas worked ranches half that size, but every acre produced quality chili in dozens of varieties.

"Shut. Up." Disbelief covered her face.

"I will not. I'm highly offended at that." Not.

"I mean, really?" She paused and looked at the chili on her fork. "Is *this* from your…ranch?"

"Probably. We ship all over the world."

"I'd love to see this place."

"I'd love to show it to you." Showing off the family estate was a piece of cake, and he'd taken a few lady friends there. Unfortunately, once they'd seen the size of his family holdings, they'd changed, expected more out of him and offered less. Sharing the money was part of the reason he enjoyed it. He was just a regular guy whose family had created wealth by working hard. His fiancée hadn't cared, and it hadn't changed their relationship, but she'd been an exceptional woman. She'd been his friend as well as his lover. And he missed that, wanted it again. But was he as appealing on his own without the draw of the wealth? With some women he hadn't known, but it had been a factor over and over again, enough to make him hesitate, less likely to take risks on a woman. Especially with a woman who might not even be around in a few months.

He wanted a woman who had heart and soul and a passion for living that equaled his own. So if he was honest with himself, he wanted the whole package, the soulmate deal, not just a sexy roommate he had nothing else in common with.

"It's obviously not here in town." Rebel's statement brought him back to the conversation.

"No. South of here. Just follow the river and stop before you hit Mexico." A place his heart lived.

"Cool. Maybe someday I can see it. I love to take day trips when I'm on my assignments to see places I never would be able to otherwise."

Just as Duncan put a forkful of the heavenly stuff in his mouth, his phone received an emergency text. He looked at it quickly, then back at Rebel. "Grab the fries. We gotta go."

Rebel took her newly discovered dish with her as they raced back to the ER and back to saving lives.

Two hours passed before Rebel surfaced from the trauma room. What had come in had been a tractor trailer versus motorcycle. Neither had won.

Rebel combed back the hair of the young man lying on the gurney while awaiting the arrival of his parents. He was only twenty-five and brain dead. She hoped his parents would consent to organ donation as there was no indication on his driver's license.

"How are you?" Herm entered the room.

"Okay." She sighed and looked at him. "I was thinking about how many people this one person can help, and he won't even know it."

"It's true." Herm pursed his lips in contemplation for a moment. "If it's a match, it's a match." He rubbed his eyes and turned away from the patient, who was being kept alive on a respirator. "Unfortunately, I've seen too many young folks like this."

"You'd think that it would get easier over the years, but it doesn't. We just learn to get through it, shake it off, and do it all over again." Fatigue swamped her. Herm was a very observant man, and he didn't miss that.

"You're sure you're okay? I can have someone else monitor him for a while and give you a break."

"Nope. I'm good."

"His folks are on the way. Should be here within the hour. You can finish your orientation materials in here and keep an eye on him at the same time, can't you?"

"Sure." Nurses were forever being tasked with multiple duties at one time. Part of the job and part of the way nurses were built.

"Is there something you need to tell me about? If there is, I'm a good listener." He turned his full attention to her.

"No." She placed a hand on his arm. "I appreciate the offer, though." A sigh escaped her. "He reminds me a bit of my brother, Ben. He died a few years ago. Now and then the memories spring up for me."

"I'm sorry, Rebel. If I had known…"

"You couldn't have, and I'll be all right." With a nod, Herm left her to her thoughts.

After the situation was tended to and the parents had given consent, the patient was taken to the operating room. It was a somber time, and she needed some fortitude to get through the rest of the shift.

She entered the staff lounge and poured herself a cup of coffee, wishing for something strong to put into it, like Irish whiskey or coffee liqueur Kahlua. After the last couple of hours she could use a stiff drink.

Just as she was about to have her first sip, the lounge door opened and Duncan entered. He stopped short when he saw her. "Don't drink that. It'll kill you."

"What? It's coffee, not hemlock."

"It's awful." He rummaged in a cupboard over the sink. In just a few minutes he'd put on a new pot of coffee and the brew smelled heavenly. Her mouth even watered. "I keep a stash of the good stuff for just the right occasion."

"And this is it?"

"Seems good enough for me." He gave a sideways smile that made her heartbeat a little irregular.

"Wow. That smells like Jamaica, or what I imagine it to be." She'd never been there, so she could only imagine.

"It does, and that's why I like it."

"I've never been there, but it's on my bucket list for sure." It was a very long list.

"Seriously? Your *bucket* list? What are you, thirty?" He peered at her, trying to figure out if she was serious.

"Yes, I'd like to go there before I die. That's what a bucket list is about, right?" She'd go there and go other places her family hadn't been able to go to. Someday. Before she died. Hopefully.

"You're out of your mind." He stared at her as if she was.

"Why?" She frowned. "Didn't you say you liked Jamaica?"

"Jamaica isn't a place you go before you *die*. It's a place you go in the prime of your life, with a lover on your arm, taking long walks on the beach. Hell, even sleeping on the beach." He shook his head and sipped some more, considering her. "You need to move Jamaica up on that list." He tipped his empty coffee cup at her. "It's for young people. Long days at play and longer nights in your lover's arms. *That's* what Jamaica is for."

Though the description sounded fantastic, she'd put away fantasies of having a normal, loving relationship with a man a long time ago. No man would willingly go into a relationship knowing his partner could die any time, and waiting until she was well into a relationship before telling a man wasn't fair either. It would be starting a relationship on a lie, and she wouldn't do that. "That's all well and good, but I don't have anyone to go with." She shrugged as if it didn't matter to her when it really did. "I don't date, so I'd end up going by myself anyway. It can wait." Something about his description of Jamaica scratched at a door she'd locked long ago. With her family DNA she wasn't a marriage candidate. She'd accepted it. Explaining it wasn't going to change it.

Duncan nearly spilled the coffee he was pouring. "What do you mean, you *don't date*? A woman with your looks, your smarts should be beating men off with a stick. Why wouldn't you have someone whisk you off to Jamaica for a week of passion?" The thought was ludicrous. Even he, who had serious commitment issues, had been to Jamaica with a woman before now.

Rebel glanced away and got fidgety. Uh-oh. He'd offended her.

"It's not something you'd understand, but I just don't date very much." Her smile was tight and that open door to communication they'd been enjoying had just slammed shut. He poured her coffee and brought it to her at the table where she sat.

"You should. You'd live longer."

She looked at him then, doubt covering her face.

"It's a documented fact that people who have a regular sex life live longer than those who don't."

"Now, that's just not true." She flat out didn't believe him.

"Sure it is. Read it in a men's health magazine. Three orgasms a week, and you'll live longer."

Flabbergasted, obviously uncomfortable with the topic, she delayed by adding some milk and sweetener to her coffee. "Yes, well. I'll take that into consideration should the occasion arise."

He sat at the table with her and hid a grin as he pursued the topic against his better judgment. What was it about Rebel that was making him take more risks, want to take even bigger risks, than he had in, like, forever? "As a traveler, you control your own destiny, right? Your own schedule?"

"In theory. I can always refuse an assignment or take a break between. But being a traveler is like being on permanent vacation and having a full-time job at the same time." She shrugged. "I don't take vacations either."

"That's a serious infraction against adding fun to your life." He took a sip of the steaming brew, but his gaze remained intently focused on her. "This is definitely what I remember from Jamaica." He closed his eyes, and instantly an image of walking with Rebel on the beach at night surfaced in his mind. The wind teased her luxurious hair against his skin as he reached out to bring her closer to him. That was too easy, so he opened his eyes.

"Sounds like it was a good experience for you." She wished she could say the same. There was nothing else going on in her life so she just worked. Although some people might call that sad, she saw it as a necessity to get through her painful life. If there was too much extra time she thought too much of her family losses.

"It was." He focused his full attention on her in that probing way she was coming to associate with him. "But what you said concerns me, Rebel." He got all serious then.

"Oh, don't be. It's the way I live my life. Quiet, unassuming, devoted to work." Avoiding emotional intimacy and relationships along the way. They only resulted in loss and she'd had enough of that in her life.

"I get that. You can be all that and still date, maybe add a layer of fun to your life. It doesn't have to be all about work, does it?"

"At this point, it does." She put down her cup. "I'm not comfortable having this discussion with you, Duncan, so can we table it and just have a nice cup of coffee together?"

"Sure." He nodded. "Sure." Wow. That was a very

strong boundary she'd erected around herself in seconds flat. She'd obviously been doing it for some time. Most people were willing to talk a little about themselves, some people talked entirely too much about themselves, but Rebel was a different issue and that intrigued him. He loved a good mystery, and Rebel was cocooned in it.

"You mentioned your family has lived here for some time." She was changing the topic away from herself. That was okay for now, but he wanted to know more about her and one day he would find out. For the moment, he let it go.

"Yes. Although I favor the Hispanic side of my family in looks, the other side is Scottish. If you talked to my grandfather, you'd think he'd just gotten off the ship."

"What do you mean?"

"His grandparents were from Scotland and immigrated here, so he learned English with a heavy Scottish accent." Even the memory of the man made him smile. He was an old codger, but lovable. Sometimes. On occasion. If he felt like it.

"Oh, wow." A small smile curved her lips upward.

"Yes, you should hear him when he gets going on something."

"Like what?" She leaned forward, her green eyes sparkling now.

"Like formal introductions when you meet someone for the first time." He'd had that pounded into his brain over and over as a kid, so it wasn't something he'd ever forget.

"Come again?" Her brows twitched upward.

Duncan set his coffee cup down, cleared his throat as if preparing for a stately oration and struck a dignified pose. "Hoo d'ye expec' people t' remembe' hoo ye are if ye don' intr'duce y'self?" Duncan gave a plausible Scottish accent, rolling his tongue in all the right places.

Rebel laughed out loud and covered her mouth with her hand. "In this day and age? He's still stuck on introductions and proper manners? Are you kidding me?"

Wide-eyed, Duncan gave her a serious look. "Absolutely not. When I was a kid he was tough on all of us when it came to manners. We thought he was from another planet. I now have a highly tuned reflex to open a door if a woman even *thinks* of going through one."

"I'd like to meet this grandfather of yours sometime. He sounds like a kick in the pants." She sipped her coffee and Duncan picked up his cup, too.

"He is. And that's something I'd like to see. You and all that red hair could give him a run for his money." He leaned forward and peered intently at her. "I'm willing to bet there's a bit of a temper hidden down in there somewhere in the right circumstances."

"What are you talking about?" She played it up, wide-eyed, and blinked innocently at him. "I'm just a simple lass of Irish descent."

Duncan barked out a laugh. "Like I'm going to believe *that* anytime soon." He shook his head, enjoying this repartee. "But I'm willing to bet you didn't come in here for a chat about my family history."

"Nope, but that's okay. It's been an interesting chat."

Duncan tilted his head as an even more interesting thought entered his mind. Why not? "I'm going to see him this weekend if you'd like to come along. He won't go see his doctor, so I have to give him the once-over a couple of times every year, make sure everything's still ticking the right way."

"Oh, sure. I'm off this weekend. Sounds like fun." She pointed a finger at him. "But it's not a date, just a field trip."

"Great. I'll pick you up on Saturday morning for a non-date field trip." He looked at his watch then sighed. "Guess I'll let you get back to your reading."

Rebel nodded. "Thanks for the coffee." She smiled, but it was less exuberant than her laughter had been only moments ago and he could see she was fading away. Whatever had happened to her still had enough pull to drag her away.

"Anytime." Duncan watched her go out the door, careful to avoid any coffee spillage. More puzzled and intrigued than he'd been about a woman in some time, he wondered what was going on with Rebel Taylor that she'd left romance, relationships and thoughts of romantic islands behind. She was too dynamic to wither away her youth. How in the world could he help her when she wouldn't cop to what was really going on? One way or another, he'd find out.

That thought stuck with him for most of the day. Rebel was in the prime of her life, had her career path laid out, obviously single without children or she wouldn't be working as a travel nurse.

As he moved through his day in the ER, seeing patients with spring flu or a kid with serious road rash on his right arm and leg after crashing on a bicycle that was too big for him, to writing up notes and reviewing radiology reports, he'd see Rebel in a corner of the nurses' station seemingly engrossed or hypnotized by the computer screen. Probably bored out of her mind.

He'd been pursued by women of many cultures and from unfathomable wealth, but none had captured his interest the way Rebel had. Women in his social circle were generally predictable, demanding, and spoiled rotten, and he wanted nothing to do with that anymore. After the death of his fiancée, he'd changed. The experience had changed him. But he was interested in a trim woman with flaming red hair and sad eyes that made him want to know why.

CHAPTER SIX

TWO DAYS LATER, Duncan's muscles felt every bit of the workout he'd just performed. Running. Swimming. Biking. As if he were preparing for a triathlon. But it was just his way of working off the stress of the job. It wore him out, but filled him up at the same time.

Thank you, endorphins.

No, thank you, yoga.

Duncan prowled his living room after getting something to eat and hitting the shower. Television news was the same old hash with a human interest piece thrown in, so he preferred to read it online. Usually a few miles on his stationary bike or elliptical machine kept his mind focused and helped him to decompress from the day, but not tonight. Tonight was different. Restlessness seized him.

Nothing distracted him from the unusual green eyes that kept flashing in his mind, and the deep sorrow hidden within them. Somehow, the world must have hit on Rebel Taylor's life. She'd assured him there was no ex-husband, about to jump out of her past into her future. So what was it that drove her, kept her going from assignment to assignment without a break? People behaved in predictable ways, and he could figure

them out pretty quickly, but Rebel was not being predictable at all.

Though he'd had a few relationships over the years,
the last one had about done him in. A woman he'd loved
enough to be engaged to had died in his arms. He'd
been unable to help her and that had destroyed him for
months. Now the memory burned in the back of his
throat and prevented him from having another deep
relationship.

Just then the phone rang, and he answered it. His
cousin Rey was on the other end.

"Hey, man."

"What are you up to?"

"Heading down to Hatch on Saturday to see him." He
paused, knowing he was going to get some stick from
his cousin, but they were like brothers, so he could deal.
"And taking a lady friend with me. She's Irish. Should
be interesting."

"A lady friend, eh?" The tone in Rey's voice hinted
he thought she was more than a lady friend. "Irish, eh?
You're asking for trouble." Rey laughed.

"There could be sparks for sure."

"You're tempting fate. Remember the last chick you
took down to meet him? Disaster from the get-go."
Duncan couldn't argue that. Rebound relationship after
Valerie had died.

"This one's different, and she's not a romantic interest."

"Why not? She ugly?"

"No." She was gorgeous.

"Overweight?"

"No." Fit and athletic.

"Smell bad?"

"Hardly." She smelled like a lavender garden.

"Bad breath?"

"Not that I can tell." He hadn't gotten close enough to really know. Yet.

"Then you have some explaining to do, cuz, 'cause she sounds fine to me. Why aren't you interested in her?"

"*She* actually isn't interested in *me*. She doesn't date."

Rey laughed out loud at that one. Duncan could hear the wheeze as he struggled for breath. "That's a good one. Maybe she likes ladies instead."

"No. She's straight for sure, but she doesn't date. Now someone who is as gorgeous as she is should have men standing in line for her, but she doesn't, and isn't interested." He paused a moment. Rey was a cop and had finely tuned instincts. He definitely knew how to read people. "Does that make sense to you?"

"Not to me, but to her it does. Something probably happened to her she's not over yet." Rey snorted. "You're the doctor, not me. Aren't you supposed to know this stuff already?"

"Yes, but it just doesn't make sense." Seriously.

"Not to me either, but you know women, they can change on a dime. Maybe she just doesn't like *you*." He laughed that one up big time.

"What?" Seriously? He was nice, had a good job and—

"Come on, man, lighten up. I'm just kidding. What lady in her right mind wouldn't like you?" He knew all about Duncan's romantic escapades since they'd both discovered girls were cool.

"Sounds like you need to have a heart-to-heart with this lady. If she's like you say, you can talk to her, right?

And if you can't talk to the woman you're in love with, there's something wrong."

"Whoa. I'm not in love with her." But he would admit to being intrigued by her. And very attracted *to* her.

"Maybe she just has a broken heart you need to fix. Some ladies have tender hearts, even the tough ones. You're a doctor, so heal her." There was mumbling on the phone and the sound of children giggling in the background. "I gotta go, bro'. The wife's out with her lady friends tonight, and I have dad duty. Homework, baths, the works."

"Sounds like fun." Duncan knew Rey loved being a dad, and he hoped to be one someday, too. Having grown up surrounded by cousins, he wanted a big family of his own. He had wanted to marry Valerie and be a dad, too. That's what had been the last straw in their relationship. They'd argued. She hadn't wanted children. Period. She'd taken off in her car and crashed. He'd followed behind her and pulled her from the wreckage, but she'd died in his arms.

"So what's your lady friend's name?" More giggling in the background, and Duncan knew his time with Rey was just about up.

"Rebel Taylor." Even as he said it, her name lingered in his mind, and he wanted to see her again. Soon.

"Okay, okay, wait. Her name is Rebel? Seriously? Maybe she was just born bad with a name like that." In his culture superstitions were everywhere, so it wasn't a surprise his cousin said that.

"She's a perfectly nice woman, Rey. She has a proper name but it doesn't suit her at all." The thought of using her given name didn't feel right.

"Then why don't you just ask her? You've never been

shy about getting what you want, even if it's just information."

"I don't know." He ran a hand through his hair. "There's
something with her. A vulnerability or something that's
deep. When I talked about Jamaica, she said it's on her
bucket list to do before she dies."

"So?"

Was his cousin brain dead? "Seriously? Would you
want to wait till you're old to go to a place like that?"

"Good point. That's messed up."

"And she had never heard of green chili."

Silence on the other end for a moment. "You're *serious*?"

"Unbelievable, isn't it?"

"You should marry that woman."

Duncan blinked. "That's a hell of a leap. From 'This
is green chili' to 'Will you marry me?'"

"Well, you know this lady isn't out for your money if
she's never even heard of green chili, and she certainly
doesn't know about the family business." There was a
snort of indignation in the background. "Just need to
find yourself a woman like my Julia. She's the best."

"Of course she is, but you've known her since we
were kids."

"True."

"I'll keep that in mind, should the occasion arise.
For now, I'm just bringing a coworker to the ranch for
the weekend. No big deal."

After signing off with Rey, he did his best to settle down for the night. A pair of haunted green eyes
kept appearing in his mind's eye. There was something,
some pain, some regret, some…something she couldn't

hide. He wanted to help, wanted to take her in his arms and hold her close.

Was it only curiosity holding him captive? Was it the shared experience of rescuing Eric bonding them when otherwise they'd have just been acquaintances? Or was he imagining something that wasn't there, simply because he was lonely?

Flopping facedown onto his bed, he gave up for the night. He didn't know what the answer was, maybe Saturday would tell, but right now he needed some shut-eye.

After a few more days of chaos in the ER and seeing Duncan only briefly, Rebel was ready for a weekend of peace and quiet, with a small side trip to meet Duncan's elderly grandfather. Duncan had called and said he'd pick her up at eight a.m., so she was ready to go.

She flitted around her apartment, waiting for Duncan. Was she out of her mind? Had he really invited her to meet his grandfather? What had she been thinking to agree to that? She didn't meet the families of people she worked with. She didn't even socialize with people she worked with. She didn't know how many invitations she'd turned down or avoided over the last six years of her travel nursing career that had been offered by coworkers.

The echo of their words rang in her mind.

Come on, it'll be fun.

It's just one cocktail.

You work too much.

Why don't you want to come?

They were all well meaning, and she certainly could have made more friends, but people who extended offers like that expected something in return. They wanted something from her. Wanted to get to know her, and that was out of the question.

The doorbell rang, and Rebel's pulse kicked into high gear. If she didn't move, maybe he'd go away. Maybe he'd think she'd forgotten. Couldn't she just say she'd changed her mind or gotten called into work?

"Stop being silly, Rebel. You're a grown woman. You can do this." She opened the door and realized she wasn't being silly at all. Her senses were instantly overloaded by Duncan, the epitome of a sexy Hispanic New Mexican man. A black T-shirt hugged muscles that hadn't been apparent beneath his scrubs. It molded to his torso and defined his shoulders and trim waist. Jeans that were well loved, a little worn around the edges and fit him to perfection. A tan chamois shirt with sleeves rolled up to his elbows, revealing muscled forearms and strong hands. And scuffed cowboy boots that seemed a perfect fit to his heritage and personality.

She swallowed and took in one of those deep yoga breaths she practiced every day. She'd told Duncan yoga was good for the mind, body and spirit. She needed some of that now. Gulp.

"Wow. Don't think I'd have recognized you out of the scrubs." Seriously, and he smelled like a dream. "Come in."

She huffed out a little breath.

This was *s-o-o-o-o* wrong.

She was in *s-o-o-o-o* much trouble.

"Thanks. Same to you," he said, and indicated her state of dress in white clam-diggers that exposed her calves, a Kelly-green top, and her family tartan thrown over one shoulder.

"You do realize you're going to start a war with that." He nodded to the tartan and gave a full-out grin.

"Oh, really? Then I won't bring it." She reached to remove the plaid and gasped when Duncan clasped her wrist tightly in his hand.

"Absolutely not. Don't change a thing." He leaned closer to her and looked down as she could only stare into his eyes. "I wouldn't miss that for anything. It's about time the old man had a challenge."

Somehow she ended up closer to Duncan with his one hand still clutching her wrist and his other pressed against her hip, reminiscent of the position they had been in the other day. Only this time there were no constraints of work, no witnesses, nothing to stop him.

Then his gaze dropped to her mouth. Without thinking, she parted her lips and tilted her face toward him, silently begging him to kiss her.

This was a woman who had no idea how beautiful she was and how that intrigued him. If there was no flash between them, then he'd know they were destined for friendship. But if there was a spark, that could lead them down another, more dangerous, yet much more interesting, path. Needing no further encouragement, Duncan closed the distance between them and pressed a simple, chaste kiss to her lips.

Spark.

Definite spark.

Duncan's mouth was soft and firm against hers and her lips actually tingled. The surprise of the kiss flashed all the way to her toes. Something she'd heard about but had never experienced. Then he moved and pulled her more firmly against him. One hand dove into her hair and held her head as his mouth opened over hers.

Inside she gasped as his tongue touched hers. Oh, God, she was in trouble. Without being aware of it, she moved her arms and clutched his shoulders, easing closer to him, if possible. The glide of his silky tongue nearly made her want to abandon her morals and her clothing, but she restrained herself. She tasted cinnamon on him and the lingering essence of coffee. Two of her favorite things, but right now she didn't care as she gave herself over to the kiss that overwhelmed her senses.

Duncan nearly forgot he was going to just kiss her to test the situation. As she moved closer, bringing her body against his, he realized how well she fitted him from nose to toes. The taste of her was shockingly sweet. As he cupped the back of her head and dove deep into her, he sensed a depth of passion she probably wasn't aware of. Tremors shot through him, and he wanted to abandon the planned trip to take her down the hall to her bedroom instead.

Not a good idea. Yet. He eased back and watched in delight as her eyelids fluttered and surprise covered her face. She was as turned on as he by the surprising power of the kiss. Her lips were red and plump, face flushed and breathing slightly erratic. He imagined he looked about the same. He'd love to see her all rumpled from making love all afternoon but had to grit his teeth and pull away.

She was relieved when he moved back, but at the same thoroughly confused by the kiss. Then again, Duncan wasn't going to be someone she'd date. They were just coworkers and friends.

Who maybe kissed on occasion. That happened, didn't it?

"That was very nice, Rebel." His eyes glittered.

"Uh, very." She cleared her throat and blew out a breath, trying to get herself under control.

He placed a light kiss on her lips and reluctantly withdrew. He clasped her shoulder, then let his hand stroke down her arm and take her hand. "Let's get going, shall we?" He straightened the tartan over her shoulders. "This looks perfect on you."

Despite her experience as a nurse, she was such a babe in some ways. He liked that. Not sure why, but he did. The innocence she exuded was really quite alluring. Her own siren song she didn't know she sang.

"Thanks." With her senses still humming, she grabbed her handbag and locked the door. Duncan took her hand and escorted her to his vehicle. The pickup truck seemed totally *Duncan*. It was black and unassuming on the outside, but inside it had all the bells and whistles one could ask for. It looked like a small airplane. She wasn't surprised when he put on aviator sunglasses.

"We'll be there in a few minutes."

"Where does he live? In a retirement home?" There were probably lots of them in Albuquerque. It was a retirement hot spot.

Duncan snorted, then choked on a laugh. "Him? In a facility? Not on your life. He'd throw himself in front of a bus first."

"More self-sufficient than I imagined, then?" Some elderly lived independently well into their nineties.

Duncan gave her a slant-eyed glance then turned his attention back to the road. "You have no idea."

In short order, they arrived not at a private home, as she'd expected, but at a private airfield.

"He lives at an airport?" Now she was more confused than ever.

"No, he lives in Hatch, like I said. It's about three hours by car, but only about forty-five minutes by plane."

Her stomach churned. "This isn't a good idea. Why don't you just take me home, and we can forget it? Or we could drive." Panic began to set in. How the hell was she going to get out of this? Get into an airplane with him after he'd just given her the kiss of a lifetime? How was she going to sit *that* close to him and not reach out?

"You don't get air-sick, do you?" He parked the truck and got out. She bailed out of her side and slammed the door.

"N-no, I don't think so, but I've never been in a plane that small before." It looked like a toy. Seriously, where was the wind-up device?

"Well, here's your chance." He began to remove the padded covers from the propeller. "You're not afraid to go up with me, are you?" He moved closer to her. "You are. You're uncertain about going up in a plane with a man you just met."

What a relief. He understood, and they could end this now.

"No problem." He resumed his preparations and anxiety resurfaced.

"You're a pilot?" That surprised her. Most people she knew were just what they appeared to be. A doctor or nurse or plumber. Duncan was starting to have more depth than she'd imagined, but that didn't mean she wanted to get into a flying tin can with him.

"I've been flying since I was fourteen. Got my junior license when I was sixteen, flew my grandfather

back and forth from Hatch to Albuquerque I don't know
how many times, then got my full pilot's license so I
could fly day or night. Been flying for almost twenty
years now."

"Uh…that's nice." He was still preparing the plane,
like he thought she was getting into it.

"Don't worry, Rebel. I'll get you there safely, and
I'll get you back safely." He grinned and looked at her
over his reflective sunglasses. "Trust me. I'm a doctor."

Now, that made her laugh, and she relaxed. "I think
that's the cheesiest line I've ever heard."

"Yeah, but it made you laugh and that's a beautiful thing."

He approached her and took her hand gently in his.
"It's going to be okay. You said you wanted a field trip."
He led her to the small plane, opened the door and
assisted her into the passenger seat, tucked the plaid
around her and buckled her in. After securing her door,
he rounded the plane and settled himself in the pilot's
chair.

Duncan helped her to adjust the headphones so they
could speak to each other over the headset and started
the plane. The hum of the engine whined in her ears
and the vibration pulsed through her. Excitement and
eagerness fought with equal parts of anxiety and nausea
inside her as Duncan got all serious and went through
his pre-flight checks.

"Any mishaps over the years?" Although it was wise
to ask, it also felt impolite.

"Only one. Daisy got sick every time." Though he
answered the question honestly, he didn't elaborate and
continued his preparations.

"Oh, I see." A sick, jealous feeling surged inside

her, and she pushed it down. Though he'd kissed her, she didn't have any right to be jealous. Knowing he'd flown another woman multiple times put a damper on the day. Another yoga breath to clear those thoughts. And she ignored the tremor in her hands. It was nothing.

"She hated flying, but once she got her paws on the ground she was a whole new dog. Raced through the fields like a puppy."

"Paws?" That opened up a whole new dimension to the situation.

"Yes, she was my dog. Chocolate lab. Never had another dog like her." A wistful sigh escaped him. "She was a gift from my mother when I was twelve. Said I needed to learn how to take care of a four-legged female before I could ever consider taking care of a two-legged one."

Relief flowed through Rebel and a warm pulse in her chest followed. A dog.

Someone spoke into the headset, and Duncan responded. Rebel remained quiet as they bumped out onto the runway and prepared to take off.

Her heart raced and her mouth went dry. Clenching her hands on the seat didn't relieve her anxiety, but she couldn't help it, just as she couldn't help the grin that exploded on her face when the tires left the pavement and they were airborne.

CHAPTER SEVEN

A TOTALLY GIRLISH squeal erupted from her throat. "Oh, my, this is incredible!" There were so many things to look at all at once out of every window of the plane, she felt as if her head were on a swivel. There was the river, the mountains, cars on the highway, and all kinds of buildings that were growing smaller and smaller.

Duncan's chuckle sounded warm in her ears. "Keep that up and you're gonna barf. Pick one side of the plane to look out of."

That got her attention. So uncool to barf in front of witnesses. "Good to know."

"Look to your right, there's the Rio Grande. Locals say it *without* the emphasis on the e at the end. And I've heard people add the word river at the end. It literally translates to river big, so no need to add river on the end."

"Dead giveaway for tourists, right?" Note to self.

"You got it."

For the next hour Duncan kept her entertained by pointing out the sights below and didn't make her one bit nauseated. She was fascinated by all the knobs and dials he tended to. No wonder his truck looked like a small plane on the inside. He was used to it.

"We're coming in over the property now."

Rebel looked at a beautiful patchwork of red dirt and green vegetation, whirls of dirt kicked up by a tractor adding another dimension to the scene below. The engine changed tone, and Rebel clutched the seat.

"Don't worry, just have to slow the plane so we can land."

"Down there?" She raised her brows and didn't see a thing large enough to land on. "Uh, where?"

He chuckled. "Yes, down there. Don't worry. I've never missed the airstrip yet."

"That's reassuring."

Duncan expertly guided the plane down until they were just a few feet above the dirt. Rebel cringed and closed her eyes tightly, held her breath.

Then a few bumps, the pressure of the brakes pressed her forward into the seat belt and then flung her back into it as they came to a dusty, bouncy stop unscathed.

"You okay?" Duncan asked, and looked at her.

"I'm okay."

Duncan reached toward her, his hands cupping her face as he pushed off the headset. "Welcome to Hatch."

Both doors were flung open from the outside and two young men, bearing a strong resemblance to Duncan, peered in at them.

"Come on, he's waiting for you."

Rebel smiled as she stepped out onto solid ground again.

"Rebel, these are my nephews, Jake and Judd," Duncan said as he introduced them. They rode in a golf cart on a dirt track that paralleled a field of chili. In minutes, they approached a huge, two-story home that reminded her of pictures she'd seen of historic old Mexico. Beautiful, traditional and exotic.

"There he is."

Rebel noticed a hunched-over old man standing on the porch. He raised a hand, and she waved back, though she knew he couldn't see her. The old man appeared to lean on something, and she thought it might be a cane or a walker. With the sun bright overhead, she shaded her eyes with one hand and as they neared the house she realized she'd fallen victim to a trick of light and shadow.

The man was six feet tall and as robust as she could imagine any ninety-year-old could be. Duncan had said he was impressive, and Rebel believed him. The cart stopped at the edge of the patio, and Duncan stepped out, then offered a hand to assist her. "Don't be afraid."

"I'm not afraid," Rebel said, and straightened her spine. "I've taken on many patients his age. I can handle him."

A snort erupted from one of the nephews in the front seat, but Rebel didn't know which one.

Duncan walked beside Rebel with anticipation humming through him. He didn't really know why. They weren't a couple, they weren't even dating. The last time he'd introduced a woman to his grandfather it had ended in disaster. The man had seen right through her and had made no bones about what he thought of her.

They'd broken up the next day.

"So this is the lady friend you were tellin' me about?" he asked, and stepped forward.

"Yes. Allow me to introduce my friend and a nurse, Rebel Taylor. Rebel, this is my grandfather, Rafael McFee, current owner of this impressive empire."

Rafael held his hand out to Rebel, and she didn't

know whether to shake it or curtsy, so she went with a firm grip. She'd seriously have to amend her mistaken assumption he was going to be elderly, frail and *cute*. This man was anything but, and she could see how Duncan had inherited his strong, commanding presence and control.

"It's a pleasure to meet you, sir. Duncan has mentioned you several times." She hoped that was okay.

Without releasing her hand, he gave Duncan a narrow-eyed look. "I'll bet he did." His accent was soft with a mixture of Spanish and Scottish inflections. Rafael tucked her hand into his elbow and led the way to an outdoor patio, a *portál*, if she remembered correctly. "Did he tell you I chased off his last girlfriend?"

Rebel gave a panicked look at Duncan's enigmatic expression, then returned it to Rafael. "No. No, he didn't. But as I'm not his girlfriend, I don't have to worry about you chasing me off, do I?"

"Well, there's still the matter of you walking into my home brazenly displaying the colors of a rival clan, now, isn't there?"

Rebel laughed and patted him on the arm. "Now, that's a whole other issue."

They settled at a large wooden table with chairs made of wood and cowhide, and an older Hispanic woman emerged from inside, carrying a tray of iced tea. She didn't have the manner of a hired member of staff, but carried herself as if she had been around this family for a long, long time.

"I'm Lupe, and I run this madhouse," she said, then turned to Rebel. "Now, be on your best manner."

Rebel raised her brows and Duncan said, "She's talking to him, not us."

"Oh." She paused. "Oh! So you've made a habit of misbehavior, have you?" Rebel asked, innocently setting her chin on her hand and looking right at Rafael.

Duncan tilted back in his chair and roared out a laugh. "I knew this was going to be fun."

The scowl on Rafael's face should have made her cringe, but she only smiled, comforted by Duncan's relaxed demeanor. He was right. It was fun.

"So, tell me, why *aren't* you dating my grandson? Don't tell me he's not good enough for you either." Rafael turned to face Duncan. "Don't tell me she's like that last one. Only seeing dollar signs." He paused, thinking. "Or was that the one before that? The last one didn't make it to the altar either." He slapped his hand on the table and Rebel jumped. "Dammit, Duncan. You're supposed to find a woman you can make babies with. I want to make sure my favorite grandson has his life in order before I die." The scowl on his face was enough to make anyone cringe, but Duncan hardly looked disturbed.

Duncan snorted and reached out to take Rebel's hand for a second. "That's about enough of the grilling." He leaned forward, getting into Rafael's face. "And I've *never* been your favorite grandson."

"Duncan certainly is a fine doctor and a fine man, but the fact is I don't date. It has nothing to do with him." There. She said it out aloud, and she hadn't been struck by lightning. She looked overhead. It could still happen. Looked like thunderheads were coming their way. Outrageously huge ones, racing across the horizon.

"Why not?" The frown grew even more fierce. "Don't you like men?"

"I like men just fine." She glanced down and fiddled

with her glass. "Things just haven't worked out that way for me. So I've decided to let go of that part of my life."

"Why? There must be something wrong with the men you're picking, then."

"Yes. Well." Rebel's insides tightened a bit, not wanting to get into her tragic family history the second they arrived, but it seemed they were on the edge of it.

"Seriously, Rafael. Enough." Duncan defended Rebel. She didn't need that sort of treatment. "Rebel's decisions are her own and it's not for us to pry. She hasn't even had a cup of coffee, and you're jumping down her throat."

"It's not natural, that's for sure," Rafael said, and eased back into his chair.

"If I've offended you, sir, I apologize, but, as Duncan says, this is my own business." She stood and wrapped the plaid around her shoulders as if it would protect her. "You'll have to excuse me for a while," she said, and walked away from the table, back out the gate they'd entered and away from the house. Where she was going, she didn't know, but she needed a breather. Now.

Her strides lengthened until she was almost running away from the house. If she'd worn better shoes, she would have raced, but her flats weren't designed for that. And there were too many rocks and stickers on the road.

Minutes later she heard the crunch of tires on the dirt, but no engine. She kept going, not looking behind her. It was probably one of the field workers she'd seen, and she wrapped her tartan around her shoulders tightly. Certainly wouldn't be Duncan chasing after her. He wasn't the kind to chase.

"Rebel, wait."

It really was him. "No."

"Seriously, please wait." He drove the golf cart closer and pulled alongside her as she huffed along the dirt road. A small rock had gotten into one shoe and now she limped along, pain in every step. But it was nothing to the pain in her heart. She didn't want to have to explain herself to anyone. Her lifestyle was a choice. A personal one. Telling it didn't change it.

The sky darkened further as the thunderclouds raced closer and drops of rain began to fall all around her while Duncan was safe in the little golf cart.

"I'll stop if you'll stop." What a ploy.

"I'm not stopping." It was a matter of stubborn pride now. The Irish always could out-stubborn the Scottish. Or at least that's what her mother had told her. Rebel was about to find out.

"Then I guess I'm not either."

When the skies opened up minutes later and lightning sizzled too close, she jumped into the golf cart. "Let's go. I can be mad at you later."

Duncan guided the lumbering golf cart toward a large barn, which looked really far away. Rain pelted down on them and Duncan began to drive slower.

"What are you doing? Go faster, not slower."

"The battery is dying. Damned kids never plug anything in. We're going to have to run for it."

"Oh, no." She got out of the questionable shelter of the cart and ran alongside Duncan. They were getting closer to the barn when mud engulfed one of her shoes, and she was forced to stop.

"Come on!" Duncan raced back to her.

"I'm stuck!" She was *not* leaving her shoe.

Like any superhero ready to save the damsel in distress, he bent at the waist, put her over his shoulder and ran for it.

Rebel screamed the whole way.

Duncan stumbled into the barn and collapsed into a pile of hay as he lowered Rebel down. Or tried to. It was more of a controlled fall than a gracefully executed maneuver. Seemed like he was always stumbling into something when he was around Rebel.

"Are you okay?" Riding on his shoulder couldn't have been comfortable.

"I'm fine. Just soaked." She pushed her dripping hair up and out of her face. "That storm came up quickly."

"Welcome to monsoon season."

"Seriously?"

"Seriously, but that's not what I mean. I meant okay about what happened back there. He's a cantankerous old buzzard, but that was going overboard, even for him." Duncan slid his hand down her arm until he reached her hand. "I'm sorry. I should have stepped in sooner, but I didn't realize he was going for the jugular until too late."

"It's okay, really. I should be used to people asking me questions like that."

"Well, no, you shouldn't. Your personal decisions are nobody's business, not even mine. Though I don't understand, it's really none of my business." He wanted to, but it was such a waste of life to not fully enjoy it. And for someone as vibrant and lively as Rebel, it was equally sinful in his eyes. Especially when that life could be ripped out from under you at a moment's notice. Like in a car wreck.

"Thank you." Giving herself a verbal shake, she sat on

a bale of hay and patted the space beside her. "Sit down. Why don't you tell me about this monsoon season? I've never heard of it."

Duncan shook himself like a dog. He dropped onto the spot beside her. "It's the rain this time of the year that makes or breaks a chili season." Though he was soaked to the bone, it didn't bother him. He was warming up watching Rebel try to make headway with her hair, which was a wild tangle. He itched to dig his hands into the mass and test it for himself.

"I had no idea." She huffed one last strand out of her face.

Pieces of straw poked out from her shirt, and he reached to remove that. She looked up at him, and she'd never looked more beautiful, more alluring than she did sitting there soaking wet on a hay bale in his grandfather's barn.

"Rebel." He reached out and cupped her face so she looked up at him. "I want to kiss you again."

She didn't say anything, but held his gaze. He wanted her with everything he had in him, but she was much more fragile and vulnerable than he'd known. Hiding behind all that fire and sass was a profoundly bruised soul. He leaned closer, drinking in the sweet fragrance of the hay, the fresh aroma of the rain falling around them, the unique perfume of Rebel's body, and he leaned closer still. Her eyes dilated, and her gaze dropped to his mouth.

He'd only intended to give her a small kiss. But his appetite to taste her had been whetted that morning. When his lips touched hers, she took a deep breath, as if scenting him, breathing his essence, and he was lost.

Wrapping his arms around her shoulders, he brought her fully against him. She tasted sweet, like the rain on his lips. Pliant, she relaxed beneath his touch and parted her lips to his questing tongue.

Lord, the man could kiss. Unable to deny herself this moment, she wrapped her arms around his middle and hung on as he kissed her like he couldn't get enough of her. His hand dove into her hair and cupped her head while his mouth explored hers.

She'd been kissed plenty of times, had had a few short-term relationships that had been purely physical, but she'd never been kissed like this. Warmth began with his lips pressed against hers and spread to her chest and abdomen, inspiring surges of pleasure that made her want to stay in his arms forever.

Duncan could stay here, just like this, wrapped up with Rebel for the rest of the day, the rest of the night. Doves cooing overhead only lent to the atmosphere. Making love all afternoon would be something he'd never forget, but he knew she wasn't ready for that yet.

Rebel wrapped her arms around his neck and drew him closer, aching to have him against her skin. When his hand cupped her breast and his thumb traced her nipple, she knew she was in over her head. Telling him no or pulling away wasn't one of the options she was thinking of right now.

The lights of a vehicle shone in the doorway, and they broke apart.

"Someone's come to get us, I think." Duncan pressed a kiss to her nose and helped her to sit. "Dammit."

The SUV raced down the road and nearly drove into the barn. Rebel watched as Duncan changed, his radar on full alert. This wasn't the usual rescue of people stranded in the rain.

One of the boys burst from the vehicle and dashed into the barn. "Come quick. He's in trouble."

CHAPTER EIGHT

DUNCAN GRABBED HER hand and they hurried through the rain and into the SUV.

"What's wrong?" Duncan leaned forward from the backseat.

"He's having another spell." Jake skipped the road and drove right through the middle of what had once been a promising field of chili, but was now a straight shot to the house.

"Another spell? What do you mean, *another*?"

"Last week he couldn't breathe, but it passed, and he wouldn't let anyone call you."

"Dammit."

"He's so stubborn, he thinks he's invincible."

In minutes the SUV stopped in front of the house. "Go to the plane and get my medical kit from the outside cargo hold."

"Got it." Jake sped away before Duncan even closed the door.

Rebel waited, anxious, for him. He was more serious than she'd ever seen him. Concern for his grandfather was evident on his face and the grim set of his mouth.

"It'll be okay. We'll take care of him." Somehow she wanted to reassure him.

Duncan nodded and led the way inside. Lupe met them at the door. She clutched her hands in her apron. "Where is he?"

"In the den. He can't breathe, *mijo*, just like last time."

Without a word, Duncan strode to the den, with Rebel steps behind him. If his grandfather died it would be because of pure stubborn pride. Or Duncan would strangle him. One or the other. Rafael could inspire the most patient of men to murder.

He sat on the couch, eyes closed, his color a waxy, greenish-yellow. That indicated a cardiac issue. "How long has this been going on?"

"'Bout…half…hour." His breathing came in short gasps, and Duncan could hear crackles in his lungs, even without a stethoscope.

Rebel sat on the other side of Rafael, and she placed his hand in her lap, her fingers on his pulse. "He's clammy, tachycardic, and I can hear fluid in his lungs."

Her demeanor snapped him out of grandson mode and into doctor mode. "Where's Jake? I need that kit."

Lupe dashed to the door. "Here he comes now." She pulled the door open as the young man ran through.

"Here it is." What he set down looked to Rebel like a giant black fishing-tackle box with a red cross painted on it.

Duncan flipped the double clamps on it and opened it to reveal a stash of medications and equipment equal to any ER crash cart she'd ever seen.

"I'm going to call my mother and let her know," Jake said.

"Dear God…not…your mother," Rafael gasped.

"Just go for now," Duncan said, and Jake hurried from the room but lingered in the doorway, his eyes wide.

Duncan extracted a stethoscope from the box, and Rebel fished out a pulse oximeter, a small monitor that fit on a finger to check the oxygen level and whether a patient's condition required supplemental oxygen.

"Sat's seventy-two—way too low." That meant his lungs were full of fluid and oxygen wasn't getting into his bloodstream the way it was supposed to.

"Get an IV in him. There's a butterfly setup on the left side." Quickly, Rebel got an IV access in the back of his right hand.

"Got it."

As she dug into the kit for the proper equipment to administer the medication, she noted that the room had started to fill with people. Lots and *lots* of people. Migrant workers, whose lives and livelihoods depended on this man, showed up and stood at the threshold of the room. Others stood inside the door. All were grim-faced and staring.

Rebel began to feel uncomfortable with so many strangers staring at her. Fumbling with the packing of the IV insertion supplies, she dropped it twice before being able to open it properly. What was wrong with her? She was a skilled nurse, and she could perform an IV setup in her sleep. So why now were her hands trembling like she was a new nurse fresh out of school?

That little voice in a dark place in her heart told her she knew why. It told her she was beginning to get sick. Just like her family had. Just like she'd known she would.

"Do you think someone could make coffee?" she asked Duncan.

His gaze flashed to her, and he frowned. "Seriously? You need coffee now?"

She wanted to whack him one for his lack of insight, but she refrained. Given the circumstances with his distress over this grandfather's sudden illness, she had to cut him a break. He wasn't thinking as clearly as he normally would if he were in the ER with control of the situation. "*N-o-o-o*. It will give them something to do and ease the tension in the room, which is about to strangle me. We also need oxygen. Is there any sort of oxygen machine we could hook him up to?" It would give her a little space to control her own racing thoughts and steady her hands again before she put in the IV.

Duncan closed his eyes for a second as he realized her suggestion was brilliant. "Sorry. You're right." He'd been too focused to see a solution to the congestion in the house. Turning slightly, he spoke to Lupe in Spanish, and then to the people gathered in the room.

Lupe clapped her hands like a drill sergeant and shooed everyone out. One man stepped forward. "I get the oxygen." He raced from the room, plowing through the rest of the crowd now that he had a mission to accomplish.

The atmosphere eased as people filed out, each offering a quick sign of the cross for Rafael's recovery. Rebel could take a deep breath for the first time since she'd sat down.

"I'll take your blood pressure, too." She applied the cuff to his left arm and performed the short procedure. "One-eighty over eighty-five."

"Give him a diuretic."

"How much?" Rebel was already reaching for the vial. The tremor in her hands was less visible, but she still felt it on the inside, down in her gut.

"Twenty now, twenty more in thirty minutes if he doesn't respond."

Rebel dropped the vial in her lap, cursed quietly as she wiped the perspiration from her palms and picked it up in a tight grip.

"Don't worry, Rebel. It's an unexpected situation, but don't worry. Take a breath, and we'll get through this together." Duncan gave a glance at his grandfather, who had not opened his eyes. "We'll *all* get through it."

Finally, she drew up the prescribed dosage in a syringe and administered it through the IV, grateful Duncan was putting the shaking of her hands down to nerves. He couldn't know what she knew. Someday, she knew she was going to get sick, but it was like a time bomb, waiting to go off. Distraction and focus on the task at hand was the way out of her mental chaos.

"This will ease your breathing by pulling the fluid from your lungs, but it's going to make you pee like a racehorse." She gave him the information she'd give to any patient.

"If you…say…so."

"I do." She patted his knee, knowing he needed comfort, even if it was the last thing he'd ask for.

She glanced at Duncan. His gaze was glued to Rafael's chest. She wanted to comfort him, too. This was what she did, what she was good at, and she shoved aside her own tremors to give them her best.

Leaning over, she placed a hand on Duncan's arm until he looked at her. "He's going to be okay."

After placing a hand over hers, he gave a terse nod. Not that he didn't believe her, but as a physician he knew too much. People who knew too much worried even more. They knew what could happen, knew the worst-case scenario, and always went there mentally. Plan for the worst, hope for the best, was her motto. Personally and professionally. She'd had her will made out for ten years now and had purchased life insurance with a long-term care rider for when she became ill. She just hadn't expected it to be now.

A shiver made her twitch and their dash into the rain was starting to reveal its unforeseen consequences. Though the room should have been warm, she felt chilled. The effect of adrenaline only lasted so long and the kick she'd gotten was fading.

Duncan's phone rang. "It's Juanita. One of my sisters," he added for Rebel's benefit.

Rafael clucked his tongue, just as one of the men returned with a very dusty oxygen tank. If it worked, who cared what it looked like? Duncan stood and answered the phone, leaving them to the task of getting the oxygen hooked up.

After pulling a tubing package from Duncan's kit, Rebel placed it on Rafael's nose and turned on the tank. "Now take some deep breaths. Slow and steady."

Amazingly, Rafael did what she said and slowed his breathing, though she knew it was very difficult. "Listen to the sound of my voice. I'll tell you what to do." She kept up the light chatter for Rafael, but watched as Duncan wandered away, listening to Juanita pontificate in his ear.

Lupe entered the room with a tray of coffee and sat it on the table in front of them. "He trusts you, you know?"

Rebel reached out for the warm cup Lupe handed her and added a few drips of creamer, not too picky about the flavor at the moment. "I'm not sure what you mean."

"Duncan. He trusts you, or he wouldn't have left you alone with him." She nodded at Rafael.

"I…can hear…you," Rafael said, and opened his eyes to slits, glaring his displeasure.

"Oh, you." Lupe inhaled a tremulous breath and gave him a light rap on the wrist, then took his hand and held it. "Be quiet, you old goat." The words she said were at odds with the concern and love in her eyes. Rebel was starting to get a clue there was more going on between them than a professional relationship.

Who was she to pass judgment? Her family had been full of oddities. Rafael turned his hand over to clasp Lupe's in his. What a sweet gesture, to see their aging hands intertwined. Something she had accepted would never happen to her. Especially not now, since she'd noticed a tremor. There was nothing to stop her illness now.

Rebel cleared her throat and placed the oxygen monitor back on Rafael's finger. "I'm sure Duncan just believes I'm a competent nurse."

Lupe raised her brows and gave her a look that made Rebel reconsider. "I don't think so, *mija*. I know him. He trusts no one to care for Rafael."

"I see." Another shiver made Rebel twitch. This time Lupe saw it.

"Oh, *mija*, look at you. Sitting here like a drowned rat!"

Duncan wandered in, still listening to Juanita rant on the phone, but his gaze remained sharp and focused on the scene.

"It's okay." She clutched the cup. "The coffee will warm me up."

"Nonsense. You'll have a shower, and I'll make you

both some of my special hot chocolate." She motioned for Duncan to come closer.

"Juanita, get a hold of yourself and take a sedative or something. I gotta go." He closed the phone, but Rebel could still hear the voice on the other end as he cut her off.

"Everything okay?" Though he spoke to Rebel, he watched Rafael.

"His color is better and his breathing is, too."

"And she's soaked to the bone, *mijo*!" Lupe said with great concern.

For the first time since they'd entered the house, Duncan grinned. "Well, so am I."

"Bah!" Lupe waved away his statement. "Rebel needs a shower and dry clothes before she gets a cold." The housekeeper stood, once again in charge of herself and the situation. She took Rebel's hand and led her away. "You take care of things for a while."

Rebel went with Lupe, but cast a look at Duncan, who could only stare as the most interesting woman he'd met in years was being held hostage by his grandfather's girlfriend. They soon disappeared upstairs, and a door slammed.

"Duncan! Get over here. She's right. I have to pee like a racehorse!"

A light-hearted sensation filled him. All was well in the world if his grandfather could yell again. He shivered, casting a longing glance upstairs. He was going to need a shower, too. Too bad it would have to be by himself.

After helping Rafael to the bathroom then returning him to the couch and the oxygen, Duncan took a shower of his own. He dressed in clothing he'd left on a previous trip, but he wondered what Rebel would be wearing as she hadn't brought anything with her. It was too much to hope that it would be skimpy.

As he descended the stairs and scraped his hair back from his face, he expected to see Rebel sitting with Rafael, but she was nowhere in the vicinity. And neither was Rafael.

"I put him to bed, and she's out on the *portál*," Lupe called from the kitchen. "I'm making my hot chocolate for you. I'll bring it out in a few minutes."

He found Rebel ensconced on one of the settees, with her feet tucked beneath her and covered by a Pendleton blanket.

What a picture she made. After the shower, her hair seemed curlier and luxurious. He wanted to sink his hands into it and pull her closer to him, pull her fragrance into his mind so he would never forget it. The firelight cast a golden glow over her and he paused, absorbing the image of her quiet beauty. He knew he didn't make a noise or hardly breathed, but she turned. A few beats of his heart went missing.

And then she smiled.

And he knew he could *never* be her friend. He wanted way more than that. Especially after that kiss that afternoon had set his blood on fire.

Without directing his feet, they moved him over to where Rebel sat, and he settled beside her. Placing a hand on the back of the settee, his hand tunneled beneath her hair so he could make contact with the skin on her neck. She was such a beauty. Vastly different from the women he'd known from society who'd only seen the prestige in his name and the dollars in his pocket, convinced their beauty alone would win him over.

Rebel had none of those issues. She had others, but he was willing to work on them. She needed a friend, and he wanted to be that for her, as well as something else he wasn't quite willing to name. Lover? Best friend? Partner? He didn't know and didn't want to think about it right now and pushed aside thoughts of his fiancée. Although it had been a long time ago, guilt from his inability to save her resurfaced. Right now, all he wanted to do was put his arms around Rebel and never let go.

"This is lovely. Who knew there would be a need to have a fire on a summer night?"

"Summer nights are the perfect time for a fire." There was a fire in him that he wanted to explore. Leaning closer, he stopped just short of placing his lips against hers. "There's been a fire between us since we met, whether you want to admit it or not."

A small gasp came from her mouth, but she didn't pull away and she didn't deny it. How could she when the proof was in front of her face? The proof was in that kiss and the way her body reacted to his.

Slowly, she moved her hand up and she placed a palm on his cheek. "I'm not the one you want, Duncan." Sadness crept into her eyes again and it maddened him when things were going so well between them. He didn't want to stop, and he didn't want anything to get in his way.

"You *are* the one I want." He hardly had to move and his lips would be against hers. Every breath she took tingled against his skin.

A sudden interruption on the *portál* ended the conversation.

"Here it is. I told you my special hot chocolate would be just the trick to warm you up from the inside out." Lupe hustled across the patio stones and placed a serving tray in front of them. She handed each of them a huge, steaming mug.

"Lupe, this smells incredible."

"It is!" She clapped her hands together once. "This recipe has been handed down for generations in my family. You will love it."

"Thank you, Lupe. How's he doing?"

"He's asleep and looks peaceful for the first time in months." She leaned over and kissed Duncan on the forehead. "Thanks to you, *mijo*." She moved to Rebel and gave her a kiss as well. She smiled and for the first time tonight he saw the fatigue and the fear in her eyes. "Thank you, *mijo*. It's time for bed for me. You two enjoy the evening."

"Goodnight," Rebel said.

Duncan watched her as she stared into the fireplace, cupping her hands around the mug of hot chocolate he already knew was a gift from the gods. "Somewhere along the way, Lupe's family must have made a Mayan sacrifice to get that recipe." He'd been drinking it since he was a child and it never ceased to impress him.

"What?" She frowned. *"What?"*

"Kidding." He clinked his mug gently against hers. "It's magical. The Mayans were the first to use chocolate and chili in their cooking."

"This whole place is magical, Duncan." Hesitation in her eyes, the stiffness in her posture indicated a level of discomfort he wanted to put at ease.

And he really wanted to kiss her.

Clearly there were events in her past that continued to haunt her in the present. If they were going to be friends, or anything else, he needed to know some of them. Patience had never been his way, but right now he knew it was the only way. The way he tended to plow right through things worked in some ways, but not now. Not with Rebel.

She blew on the steaming hot chocolate, and he noticed a tremor in her hands he'd not noticed before. Maybe he made her nervous or just talking about her past made her tense up.

"Want to talk about what happened earlier?"

Shy, she looked down at her mug and avoided the question for a few moments. Then she nodded, as if having come to a firm decision. The mug rattled against the table as she set it down and then turned to face him. "You deserve the truth. To know the truth about me and my family."

"What, are you descended from a line of circus performers, or bank robbers or something?"

She gave a sad smile. "No. Much worse."

"You have the plague?" Seriously? What could it be?

Tears sprang into her eyes, and he had to confront the fact there might be something seriously wrong he'd not been aware of. He dropped the attempt at humor. Obviously, now was not the right time for it. "Tell me what it is. Some things are best told straight out. Why don't you try?"

After a few breaths, she looked at him and held his gaze. "My family has Huntington's disease."

Duncan closed his eyes, immediately feeling sadness for her and understanding her grief—her behavior now made perfect sense. Genetically, it was a death sentence. There was no getting around that. At least for some people.

"I'm so sorry, Rebel. Truly." He leaned closer to her, intending her to see how serious he was. "But you can't give up your life because of an illness that may or may not strike. Have you been tested?"

"No. I don't need to, I know I have it." She looked down, shamed. "I've begun to have symptoms."

"What? How long has this been going on?" That thought sickened him. She was in the prime of her life, and they'd just met.

"It started in the last couple of days. Things like this have never happened to me before, so I'm certain it's the Huntington's." She brushed away a tear that was making its way down her cheek.

"Tell me what your symptoms are. I'm not a genetic expert, but I know a bit about the disease."

"Over the years, I've become one. I've got tremors in my hands, shortness of breath, headaches, and I've been losing control of my extremities."

"How so?" He hadn't seen anything unusual.

"The last few days I've been dropping things more than usual. Paperwork mostly, but I dropped the vial in my lap three times when I was preparing it for Rafael."

"Have you checked your blood sugar? Simple things like dehydration and moving to a higher elevation can make you behave in ways your body isn't accustomed to." The panic in him started to settle down. "You haven't been here long enough to have acclimated. I'm sure it's something like that."

"It's not. It's can't be *just* that. I'm accustomed to

traveling." She picked up her mug again and avoided his gaze. "I appreciate you trying to help, but—"

"But nothing, Rebel!" Anger snapped inside him, and he had to rein it in. He normally didn't have much of a temper, but when injustice occurred in front of him, his temper roared. "You can't just sit here and say you're giving up. Unless you've been tested, you can't know you're going to develop the full-blown illness."

"Haven't you ever just *known* something in your life? I mean, just known it down in your gut without anyone ever having to tell you?" She looked into her mug as if she were going back into her memories, seeing them now as if they were a movie in front of her eyes.

"Of course, everyone has. But I've also been wrong about some of those things too. That's a sign you're thinking with your emotions and not logic." He'd been there and done that, in spades.

"Logic? Research shows a full fifty percent of people develop the disease. The pattern in my family is well over the fifty percent mark. So far, seventy-five percent. There were four children and three have died of it."

"Rebel, you're not interpreting the research properly. A full fifty percent of people then *don't* develop any symptoms and go on to live beautiful lives." He raked a hand through his hair, frustrated at her thinking process and her unfounded belief. "Have you thought that you've got those sort of statistics on your side? Those are quite positive in my book."

"No." She sighed and clutched her hands in her lap. "It's just always easier to believe the bad stuff, you know? How can I even consider thinking I might not have it when the proof is in my symptoms?"

"You are a stubborn one, aren't you?" He sighed,

not wanting to run over her beliefs, but he wouldn't be satisfied until she obtained the proper testing. Her symptoms could be anything from simple fatigue to stress from work.

"Why haven't you gotten the testing done to know for sure?" That's what he would have done, immediately.

"I'm…" Her breathing came in short huffs and tears sprang forth in earnest. Duncan patted her shoulder but remained silent. "I'm *afraid*! God, I'm so afraid to have what I know confirmed." She covered her face with her hands. "I can't take knowing that every tick of the clock is leading me closer to my death."

Duncan pulled her against his side, offering her some comfort as the fire in the *kiva* fireplace snapped and crackled, offering its warmth to her as well. He pressed a kiss to her temple.

"Science may equally *disprove* what you think you know, too."

"I don't know if I want to know. It's like I can feel it coming on, what more proof do I need?"

"What you may be feeling is the stress of unrelenting anxiety from years of worry." Squeezing her shoulder, he leaned back into the settee, pulled her closer, tucked her head beneath his chin. "Tell me about it. Tell me the story that's locking you up inside."

A few minutes passed before she took a deep breath. "My dad died when I was eleven, and he was forty-five. We had no idea what had happened to him, but a few years later when my oldest brother got sick and showed the same symptoms we had a clue it was the same thing." She cuddled against him and allowed her body to relax. One hand drifted over his abdomen, almost shyly, as if she hesitated to hold on to him. He placed his hand over hers and held it against him.

"Then what happened?"

"My grandparents finally told us that dad was adopted and they had no idea what his family history was. But when Ben became symptomatic, we started digging. Mom got all of the boys tested as they were the ones showing symptoms. I didn't have any symptoms yet, so she decided to wait for me." She paused as a tear ran down her cheek. Duncan caught it with the back of his fingers and wiped it away. "Seemed like every couple of years all we did was plan funerals. All of them were dead by the time they were twenty-five." She huffed out an irritated breath. "I have three nephews and so far they are doing okay." She took a deep breath and looked up at him. "They might be okay, then, right?"

"I'm so very sorry, Rebel. That's a lot of pain to go through." He could only give the odds science had already established. The guilt she felt for surviving such tragedy now explained everything. Why she ran from one assignment to the next and why she was so reluctant to make friends.

"I know." She nodded. "It's awful. But it was part of the reason I became a nurse. I couldn't help my family, but I wanted to do something to help someone else's."

"No matter the reason you entered healthcare, you're an excellent nurse." He paused for a second. "But you are entitled to have a life of your own, no matter what your family history is."

"How can I even think of having a relationship or a family with such history?" Anger blazed in her eyes at the suggestion, but it was part of the process of letting go.

"By living your life you honor your family, and you don't let a disease, something you have no control over, live your life for you. That's how." Anger surfaced again, and he struggled to choke it down. Wasting a life was unconscionable. His fiancée had wasted her life, died after a stupid argument, and he wasn't going to let Rebel just as surely destroy herself.

"That's a very different way of looking at it." She turned away and reached for her mug on the table in front of her, clearly not comfortable with that way of thinking.

"I'm challenging your thinking, Rebel, not your commitment, or loyalty, to your family." He pushed her hair back from her shoulder.

"You haven't mentioned your mother at all. Where is she in all of this?" Mothers were a driving force in the lives of children. His had gone from his life entirely too soon.

"I don't know. We haven't spoken in a while." She shrugged and looked away. "It's hard for me to be around her. I think, whenever I'm with her, I remind her too much of everything she's lost."

"She may be sad over her loss, but I think she would be overjoyed at being with you."

"She's married again. She's moved on." She made a face. "I don't think she really needs me."

"Look at me, please?" Her pain was almost tangible, and he wanted to ease it, but he didn't think he could right at the moment.

It took a few seconds, but she turned her face toward him. The anger still blazed inside him, but it was tempered by compassion. "The question really is, do you *want* a relationship and a family? If you don't, then it's simple, you carry on the way you are. But if you do, then you have to make a change."

"I did want a family. I grew up loved, and I wanted that for my own children. But when my brothers died, I knew I couldn't face such pain ever again or bring it to anyone else." She sighed. "I've already tried to have myself sterilized, but no doctor would do it because of my age."

"You don't want children?" That would be a crime.

"I would. I did. I do." She shook her head and her hair caught the firelight. "I gave up thinking about it. It's not like there have been many men lining up, wanting to father my children. All I could do was have the birth control implant placed in case of accidental pregnancy. It lasts for three years. It's a pain, but it works."

"We all have pain. It's just different for everyone." Thoughts of the night his fiancée had died surfaced again, but he pushed them away. It was the past and should remain there, though it hadn't stayed there, ever. She hadn't wanted children and it would have ended their relationship had she not died that night.

"You have an incredible family with a history like something out of a story book." She gestured around the patio, encompassing everything.

"True. But it wasn't perfect." He had to concede that. "You don't know about how many of them were killed or died on the trip to the United States, how many of them died from starvation and disease until the ranch got established, how many died in raids or in gunfights with early settlers, Indians and bandits from Old Mexico."

She smiled. "I can just see Rafael hanging out with Pancho Villa if he'd been around then."

Duncan snorted out a laugh, admiring her spirit once again. "Actually, we have a photo of my *great*-grandfather with Pancho Villa."

"No way!" Astonishment showed in her eyes.

"Way." He pressed a kiss to her temple. "My ancestors not only fought disease but Mexican revolutionaries, as well as Mother Nature. It's not the same thing, but every family has their trials, their grief. My mother and a sister have both died from breast cancer." He sighed, not letting the pain of their loss intrude on this conversation. "It's what you do with the pain, how you learn from it, that counts." He paused for a second. "And growth hurts. It's uncomfortable, but it challenges you in places you'd never thought about, but in the end it's worth it." Like he'd been challenged so many times in his life.

"Wow. I'm so sorry about your losses. I'll have to think about that." She dropped her gaze to her mug again and remained lost in thought for a long time. "It's been quite a day, hasn't it?"

"Yes, it has. Tomorrow will be crazy, because the family is going to come to check on him."

"They don't just call?"

"You've obviously not been involved with a large Hispanic family before." Call? They descended *en masse* from all corners of the state when there was a family crisis.

"Um, no. No, I haven't."

"Just wait. You'll see."

Sipping again from her mug, she realized she'd just

about consumed the whole thing, but clutched the mug like it was some sort of protective chalice.

He caught her gaze. She was frightened, yet curious. Very intriguing mix this Rebel was. And she had his complete attention.

When she lowered her mug, he placed his left arm around her shoulder and drew her close against his side. With his right hand, he lifted her chin and closed the distance between them. Slowly, he pressed his lips against hers when he really wanted to ravage her mouth. Gently, he squeezed her shoulders when he wanted to clasp her tightly. Easily, he parted her lips with his tongue when he wanted to consume her with his mouth.

She was as sweet as any woman he'd ever tasted, but she was such a frightened, delicate thing he knew he'd have to be gentle, though his body insisted otherwise.

When she pulled back, confusion, curiosity and arousal warred in her face. "I don't know what to think about this, Duncan. I'm not a virgin, but if I were more worldly, more experienced, I'd know how to deal with this." This was the first time she'd truly opened up to him, and he didn't want to let go of it.

"With what?"

"With what's going on between us."

"What, exactly, is going on between us?" He knew. He just needed to hear her say it.

She lowered her eyelids. "You know."

"What I know is this has been brewing since the day we met." Truly. From the second he'd seen her in the parking lot, she'd held him captive.

"What, exactly, is that?" she asked, turning his words around on him.

"This attraction. This need to touch you, kiss you. This desire to hold you in my arms and never let you go."

Rebel blinked, uncertain whether he'd just said the words she'd wanted to hear. But she'd never let any man get close enough emotionally to her to say them. She'd always run before she could be disappointed. Could she let Duncan past the barriers she'd erected and held so firm?

"I had a boyfriend in college who I loved dearly. When I finally told him about my family, he broke up with me. Said he couldn't deal with someone who might die at any moment."

"He was an idiot to let you go. And it was probably just an excuse." He reached for her mug and set it aside on the table with his. "Well, it's been a long day. Why don't I see you upstairs, and we'll call it a night, then?"

After removing the Pendleton blanket and setting it aside, he took a look at her, let his gaze wander down over her body, and sighed. Reluctantly, she allowed him to lead her up the curving staircase to the gallery. She stopped at the third door. "This is where Lupe put me, I think."

"It's a nice room." He led the way inside and tugged on her hand, then shut the door.

From the inside.

"Duncan? What are you doing?" She paused, her gaze questioning. She was blossoming right in front of him, opening and tremulous. She was like a new angel just getting her wings.

"Rebel." He stepped closer, his mind and his body aching to touch her, but this was a moment of great importance. If he scared her, if he hurt her, there would never be any turning back. "Let me stay with you tonight." He urged her closer. "Let me hold you tonight and let what happens between us happen." He tilted her face up. "It's been happening since we met, and I don't want to let go of it, of you."

He could see the pulse in her neck thrumming away and his heart raced at a similar pace. He wanted her without a doubt, his body was aching and hard already. But could she accept the intimacy of baring her soul and her skin in one night?

"Duncan." She closed her eyes and rubbed her face against his hand, allowing herself to accept him in small measures. Their bodies were millimeters away from each other. Her fragrance and the electricity surging between them were almost overwhelming. He had to pace himself or he'd frighten her more than she already was. "I don't know what to say."

"Say you want to make love with me tonight."

CHAPTER NINE

WHEN HE CUPPED his hands around her face and tilted it up to his, she didn't resist. She couldn't. How could she resist the one right thing that had happened to her? This moment, this time, this man were all perfect. Pushing away thoughts that she didn't deserve this, deserve Duncan or to be loved fiercely, she brought her hands to his shoulders and hung on.

There was a change in him, a tuning in, a focus that was intense and overpowering. A chain reaction occurred in her, and she was on fire.

With impatient hands, he whisked the black sweatshirt off, over her head, baring her upper half.

"Wow. I hadn't expected that."

"What?" Her breasts weren't big, but they did the job.

"I expected a sensible white bra, not gorgeous pink nipples with nothing covering them." His thumb strayed to tease one.

"I *was* wearing a sensible white bra, but it was wet and I didn't want to put it back on." There was no way to hide the flush that covered her entire body.

Watching her face, he cupped both of her breasts in his hands and stroked her nipples. Tingles of desire raged through her, and her eyelids dropped. She didn't know if she was going to live through this night, but if she didn't, at least she'd die happy.

"I would like to extrapolate on that idea."

"Uh... What?" She was nearly delirious with desire, and he was talking theories?

"Since you aren't wearing a bra, I'm guessing you aren't wearing panties either." His right hand explored beneath the waistband and discovered nothing but skin. "I thought so."

"What?" Brain function minimal. Comprehension vague.

"You are a woman full of secrets." He leaned closer, his breath hot in her ear. "At first look, one would never guess there's such a sexy, passionate woman hidden inside you."

She was about to tell him there wasn't when she realized it might true. At least when she was in his arms. He kissed her deeply, and she wrapped her arms around his shoulders, wanting to draw him inside herself.

Duncan eased her onto the bed and pulled off her sweatpants. Now, naked, anxiety began to surge, and her breath burned in her lungs.

Bouncing up onto her knees, she was about to call the whole thing off when Duncan dragged his shirt off and popped the button of his jeans. His eyes glowed with want for her. She wanted to touch him, feel his skin, put aside any uncertainty of tomorrow and just live in the moment. When her palms touched his chest, all thought of leaving fled.

This was where she needed to be and in this man's arms.

"Rebel," he said, gently holding her face, "let's enjoy right now and let the rest of the world just go away for a while."

There was no need for an answer as his mouth covered hers and plundered. Hot and wet, his kiss took away her breath and her control. Eagerly, she shoved his jeans down over his hips, exposing more of that tawny skin she wanted against her.

Easing her back, Duncan covered her body with his, pressing her down into the cottony softness of the bedding. He slid one knee between hers and parted them gently. The movement gave her the opportunity to feel how hot and hard he was. Kisses ranged everywhere, and he suckled her nipples into intense peaks, hard and tingling with desire. She was on fire. Duncan was both the cause and the cure.

When his hand roamed over her hip and downward to the core of her, she instinctively parted her thighs, giving him greater access. Shyness had no place here. He released her nipple from his mouth and blazed a hot trail of kisses across her ribs and down past her abdomen.

She was the beauty of his dreams. Soft, luscious and passionate. Each stroke of her body, each restless moan that escaped her throat urged him on closer to that moment when he joined with her, when he was able to let go, to let her take him away. Moving downward, he nuzzled his way to the apex of her thighs. This was what he wanted.

When his hot mouth opened over her core, she stiffened, the sensations taking her to a completely new level of arousal. Her hands dropped to the bedding and clutched it in tight fists. Suddenly, her body wasn't her own, and she allowed him to do with her anything he wanted.

When Duncan knew she was his, he dove upward

and kissed her long and luxuriously, exploring with his tongue. He wanted to know every part of her.

Opening her legs wider, he allowed the tip of his erection to ease into her. She was a delicate thing, and he didn't want to hurt her in any way. But he was trembling inside, eager to be inside her, eager to feel her heat all around him.

The demands of his body were growing impatient as he eased inside her slick sheath. Waiting for her body to accommodate to his was sexual torture. Sweat popped out all over him, straining with the effort to control himself.

"Duncan." She breathed his name, and that was all he needed. He kissed her and was lost. He didn't know if he was falling in love with her, but he was definitely smitten when her arms went around him and she clutched his back, her legs raised to wrap around him.

Easing in and out of her was a pleasure he'd never expected. Liquid fire encased his body and was about to take over his mind. Unable to control the sensations Duncan roused in her, Rebel gave up and let the feelings take her under. The sparks that had begun at his first kiss now raged through her and spiraled to an explosion within.

Spasms of pleasure rocked her. As long as he touched her, moved within her, teased the reaction from her body, she responded. Each touch, each thrill bonded her more thoroughly to him and she pulled at his hips, dragging him into her body again and again.

Unable to stop them, cries of pleasure escaped her throat. She buried her face in his neck, trying to quiet the noise.

"Let me hear you, Rebel. Let it go."

She cried out and allowed the experience of Duncan to rock her.

Unable to control his body any longer, Duncan clasped her hips and drove hard into her, taking his pleasure in hers, letting the glorious spasms of her sheath take him over the edge into his own bliss.

He poured his passion into her as sweat broke out over his body and he savored every sensation, every moment with her. He sent light kisses over her face, her eyes, her nose and finally again on her mouth.

Turning onto his side, he dragged her against him, not wanting to let go of her but not wanting to crush her small frame beneath the weight of him.

"Are you okay?" He pressed a kiss to the top of her head. This was Nirvana.

Snuggling against him, she nodded. "Better than I ever expected to be."

"Me, too."

A yawn caught her.

"It's been a long day." He pulled the comforter over them and closed his eyes, allowing the fatigue of his body and the day to overtake him.

Rebel lay for a few moments savoring the sensations of her body and her mind. None of her previous sexual encounters had prepared her for the full onslaught of what she'd experienced tonight. Duncan filled her, mind, body and soul.

She splayed her fingers over his chest, savoring the feel of her skin against his, how her body had fit with his intimately and how they now curved around each other, limbs entwined to perfection. This was a night she'd never forget.

Rain began to fall again on the metal roof, providing

a soothing backdrop against Duncan's regular breathing. Yes, this was a night, and a man, she'd never forget.

Early dawn roused Duncan as a car door slammed shut outside. He smiled. Probably his sister, Juanita, who'd gotten up at three a.m. to be the first to arrive. She really was a drama queen.

Turning toward Rebel, he delved beneath the covers to find her glorious body and pulled her against him. Even in sleep, she aroused him.

The first time they'd made love had been urgent with need. This time, soft sighs and softer kisses fell between them and their bodies joined with ease as limbs entwined and tangled together.

Rebel startled at the slam of another car door. And the sounded was repeated with disturbing regularity.

"What's going on out there? Sounds like an army has arrived."

"There is." He sighed. "You're in for a shock if everyone shows up."

"How many people are in your family?" She could count hers on one hand.

"I have no idea. People keep having babies."

A brisk knock at their door came seconds before it opened and Lupe entered. Rebel squealed and jerked the sheet over herself, but Lupe seemed nonplussed to see her and Duncan in bed together, and naked.

"Here you go. Your clothes are nice and fresh. Get dressed and come down. Everyone's here." She turned and left as quickly as she had come.

"She seriously didn't stay up all night, doing our laundry, did she?"

"No."

"That's good."

"She probably started them last night and got up at five to finish them."

"What?"

"That's normal around here. She gets up before the chickens." He patted her on the arm. "Let's take a shower." Striding across the room naked, Duncan appeared to have no issues with his body, the way women did. In seconds the spray of the shower drew her attention, and Duncan beckoning from the doorway enticed her from the bed.

They dressed and composed themselves. Rebel prepared to meet his family and then they'd check on Rafael, see how he'd fared overnight.

Duncan opened the door and Rebel almost ran back to the room when she saw how many people were down there. She'd never seen so many people in one home before. Or even a stadium!

"This is your family?" She blinked, certain she wasn't seeing this right. "Just *your* family?"

Duncan paused for a look. "Most of them, I think." He gave her a quick hug. "Don't worry. They'll love you."

When they entered the foyer, Rebel noted it had been set up with long tables and was laden with every sort of food she could imagine and some things she'd never seen before.

"Where did all the food come from? Surely Lupe didn't do all this."

"No. Rule is if you want to eat, you bring something to share."

"But we didn't bring anything!"

"You provided a very valuable service last night, so you're off the hook."

Rebel gaped at him. Was he serious? Had he really just said that?

Duncan let out a full-blown belly laugh at her response. "I meant about helping with my grandfather."

"Oh, my. I thought you meant—"

"I know what you thought." His chuckle was warm in her ear. "Get your mind out of the gutter, and let's go see how he is. Then we can eat and enjoy." With a squeeze to her shoulder, he released her.

"I'm so embarrassed." That awful flush she hated race from her chest up over her neck and cheeks.

"Don't worry about it. I'm not offended."

"Okay. So let's go see him before I say anything else stupid."

"Tio Duncan!" a young male voice called out, seconds before a little body launched himself at Duncan. He caught the young man up in his arms with a laugh.

"Pablo! *¿Como está?*"

Duncan spoke in a mixture of Spanish and English to the little boy, then turned to Rebel. "Pablo, this is my friend, Rebel. She's a nurse and helped me to take care of Great-grandpa last night."

"Gracias, amiga." He leaned over and pulled Rebel into a one-armed hug from his perch in Duncan's arms. "Is Great-grandpa okay?"

"We're going to check on him right now. He'll be just fine, you'll see."

"Come here, monkey." Another male voice approached them from behind, and Pablo released his stranglehold on Rebel's neck. The little boy reached for the man Rebel assumed was his father, who placed him on the floor.

"Go find your cousins." Pablo raced off toward a small table set up for the young ones, heedless of the art and artifacts on nearby tables.

A man about the same age as Duncan approached. Instinctively, Rebel drew back a little. The man was intense with eyes that seemed to look deep down inside her.

"Rey, stop scaring her." He gave a handshake, a fist bump and a hug to the man, then turned to Rebel. "He's a cop and likes to intimidate everyone."

"Well, it worked." A hesitant smile covered Rebel's face. "I'm Rebel Taylor."

Rey shook her hand and the cop eyes disappeared as he gave her the once-over in obvious appreciation. "Nice to meet you, Rebel." Then he pulled her into a quick, unexpected hug. "Thank you for helping him last night. He's a tough old bird, but I don't know what we'd do without him."

"Hey man, back off. She's taken, and you're married." Duncan tapped his cousin on the shoulder.

"Okay, fine." He reached for a plate, more focused on the food than Rebel.

"We're going to check on him. Don't eat everything before we get back." Duncan gave his cousin a warning.

"No guarantees." He took a plate from the large stack and got into the line behind his relatives.

"Come on. I'm sure he's been waiting on us since dawn."

"He's an early riser, then?"

Duncan snorted. "Late to bed, gets up early, I don't know how he does it at his age."

After a quick knock on the bedroom door, Duncan pressed down on the handle and pushed the door wide.

"About damned time you two came to see me. I could be dead a week before you'd know." His booming voice thundered through the room.

Duncan grinned. "I see you've survived your night and are back to your usual charming self."

Rebel hid a smile and bit her lips together. It was good to see the man's coloring had improved, the oxygen was nowhere in sight, and he was dressed and ready for the day.

"Charming?" He offered a crooked smile and a foxy gleam in his eyes. "I don't think I've ever been called charming in my life."

"You can be sure of that!" Lupe said from the bathroom. "He's never even *pretended* to be charming as long as I've known him. Maybe my English word is not right, but cantankerous sounds good."

At that, Duncan laughed out loud and met Rebel's gaze. There was something in that moment, a shared intimacy that tugged at Rebel's heart. Then it occurred to her. She was building memories with Duncan. Her heart thumped and her breath hitched. Looking into his eyes, with the laugh lines fanning outward, she knew she was falling for him much harder than she'd ever expected.

Then, in seconds, the moment was gone as he turned to Rafael.

"Let's have a look at you." Duncan opened the medical kit beside the bed and extracted the stethoscope, listened to his heart and lungs and gave a sharp nod. "All that fluid you had in your lungs is gone."

"It damned well better be. I spent half the night in the toilet." He glared at Rebel, but she only raised her brows.

"Yes?"

"No thanks to you." He held his hard stare at her.

"I didn't do anything." The stare was returned with equal intensity. She could handle herself again this morning, and he wasn't going to shake her up like he had yesterday.

"You gave me that medicine." He glared harder, but she was nonplussed.

Rebel snorted and nodded at Duncan. "He told me to!"

Rafael snorted right back. "And you do everything he tells you to?"

"Not hardly. But it was the right thing to do at the time." She raised her chin, holding his gaze, and her confidence strengthened.

Rafael held a hand out to her, and she crossed the room to take it. "Thank you, my dear. I appreciate your help." He leaned over and pressed a kiss to her cheek. "You've made an old man feel good again." He gave a sigh. "And I do apologize for my behavior yesterday. It was uncalled for, and I hope you accept my deepest regrets. Maybe, if you come back, we can have a better time."

Her gaze sought Duncan, and he stood there, his mouth hanging slightly open. A piercing wail from the bathroom drew their immediate attention. Lupe stood, holding her apron over her face, sobbing into her hands.

"Lupe, what's wrong?" Rebel released Rafael's hand to comfort the woman.

"Why didn't you tell me he's going to die?" She covered her face again and sobbed her heart out.

"No, he's not. Why would you say that?" In desperation, Rebel looked at Duncan for help.

CHAPTER TEN

"HE'S NOT DYING." Blandly, Duncan confirmed her statement.

"But…he's being…*nice,* he *apologized*, he never does that!"

Rebel gave an eye-roll and then looked at Rafael. "You really should be nicer."

"Why? She'd cry more then." He glared at Lupe, but softened it with a little smile and held out his hand to her. "Come here, woman. I'm fine."

"Oh, please, everyone. It's just fine. He's fine, and I'm starving." Duncan took Rebel's hand and led her to the door. "Come out so no one thinks you're dying, okay?"

Rafael just grinned. The old goat.

"He's such a pain sometimes." Duncan shook his head but his touch on her was gentle as he took her to the table. They made their way along the line, filling their plates, and Duncan introduced her to entirely too many people. Their names would never stick in her brain, she was certain of it.

After lingering over the meal and sharing coffee with the family out on the *portál*, Lupe approached Duncan and Rebel.

"The clinic is set up."

"Clinic, what clinic?" Rebel had no idea what they were talking about.

"When I come for a visit, I run a health clinic for a few hours. These folks are the poorest of the poor, most of them come from Old Mexico and have never had regular health or dental care. They have issues stemming from lifelong malnutrition and chronic illnesses. We hope we can help them out and the children that are born here will be better cared for right from the start."

"I didn't know any of this." She frowned. New Mexico was not a developing country, but what he was describing certainly sounded like it. "Most people I come into contact with in the ER have health insurance."

"These folks don't." He shrugged and looked away, but she could tell he cared deeply about these people who worked on his family ranch. "Some of these folks have worked here their entire lives. Poverty, lack of education, and cultural biases have kept them this way. Slowly, we're helping change their outlook. The kids are blossoming." He tried to hide it, but a burst of pride pulled his shoulders back. "We even have a daycare and an elementary school on the ranch."

"That's amazing." She leaned I closer to him. "I'm so proud of what you are doing here." Truly she was. She'd never met a man like Duncan.

"I wish we could do more, but there aren't enough resources and it's a seasonal business."

"Well, what can we do today?" Doing things for others had always helped keep her focus off her family tragedy and doing good works never went out of style.

"Let's go see what the troops have set up." Duncan

took her hand in his firm grip and led her out to the staging area.

"During chili season we use this open-air shed to roast the chili and get it ready for locals. There's nothing fresher than produce just picked and roasted within a few hours. Today I have a clinic in it."

"So, what kinds of health issues do you see with your workers?" Though she'd worked in the ER for years, farming accidents weren't something she'd had a lot of experience with.

"A lot of things are farming related, like cuts and other injuries sustained from using heavy machinery. Other things are minor, like tetanus shots, or colds and flu." He shrugged. "The usual stuff."

"You do good work, here, Duncan." Indeed. He was not just some pretty face playing around at being a doctor. He had a heart dedicated to service to others that was very appealing to her.

"I'd like to do more of it, but at the moment there's just not enough of me to go around." That brought some pain to him. This was a group of people who could use his skills, not the people who held fund-raisers and had never set foot in a *barrio*.

They stepped around the large machine shed to a line of people that looked a mile long and her eyes widened. "Wow. That's a lot of people."

"I know." He grinned. "Not doing anything else the rest of the day, are you?" He patted her shoulder, then let his hand linger there for a second. She was so different from women he'd known. That little alarm inside him started to go off, reminding him again that she could leave him at any moment and he'd best not set himself up for getting hurt again. Then he shook it off, reminding himself there was work to do now.

"Uh, no. No, I'm not." She straightened her shoulders, ready for whatever would come up. She was an experienced ER nurse. She could handle whatever they had. Except... "I don't speak Spanish. What do you want me to do?"

"The boys will help with translation for you. You can start with vital signs and triage, get a little info, then send them over to me. You're over there." He pointed to a long table where hand sanitizer, index cards for writing down information, and a blood-pressure cuff lay.

Duncan's area even had a screen so people would have some semblance of privacy.

Jake and Judd stood by, ready to help with translation. With a last look at Duncan as he walked away, she put on her best nurse smile and accepted the first patient into her triage station.

They spent about four hours on mundane issues before a patient of concern surfaced. As Duncan had foretold, the majority of the issues were farm related or other minor complaints. Then a boy with a serious face was plunked down into the chair by his father.

"Hi, there." Her welcoming smile faded. Usually she liked working with pediatric patients because they always had some interesting take on their situation or made up a grand and glorious tale about their injuries.

But not this.

Something was seriously wrong about his situation. She didn't know what, but, watching the boy interact with his father, she knew something was off.

This little boy of about six years old was too thin for his age and bone structure. His hair had been cropped very short, as was the custom, but she could see scratch marks on his scalp, and a little bald spot where the hair was worn away. The child didn't look at her but kept his eyes downcast, a sure sign of insecurity. He was not as frisky as the other children. Then the boy looked up at her and his eyes widened, fixating on her red hair that the wind had begun to tease from its clip.

"What's the problem?" she asked his father, who had distant black eyes. He made eye contact but dropped his gaze quickly.

"He...no..." Frustrated with his attempt at English, he launched into a monologue in Spanish about the boy's problems, pointed to the bald spot on his head and then at the boy's back.

"His father says that he's always hurting himself, falling down or tripping, and then the spot on his head, he keeps rubbing it, and if he doesn't stop is going to be bald before he's seven years old."

A smile curved up her lips at that last statement. "It's okay. He won't be bald, but we do have to figure out the reason he's rubbing the spot." She held out a piece of candy to him. First his gaze flashed to his father, then he accepted it and focused on unwrapping the little sweet. "Kids his age, especially boys, are accident prone. They run full blast and don't see the hazards, so he'll stop falling if he stops running so fast." She waited while Judd interpreted that part.

"What's your name?"

"Alejandro." He bobbed his head politely.

"Is his mother here? I could talk to her about some things she can do to help keep him calm, from a woman's perspective." She'd had lots of training in pediatrics, and now seemed a good time to share some of it.

Judd hunkered over and whispered to her. "Mother's not in the picture. Died last year. He's raising the boy alone."

A sick feeling turned in Rebel's gut. No child should have to suffer the loss of a parent at that age. She knew exactly what it was like. An ache formed inside her, and she just wanted to reach out, gather the little boy against her and never let go of him. He was an innocent victim and his injuries may have been an attempt to gain his father's attention.

"Let me check him and listen to his lungs, look at his injuries and then we'll have the doctor look at him, too." She set about her tasks, but when she placed the stethoscope on his back he winced and cried out.

Rebel pulled up his shirt to look at his back. "Oh!" She nearly cried out in pain for the boy. "What happened?" She shot a questioning look at the father. "This time."

"He fell from the high loft in the hay barn," Judd translated. "He and the other kids were playing a game, and he lost his grip on the rope and fell."

"You're kidding, right?" She reached for the boy's hands. Healing rope burns gave evidence to Pedro's explanation. With a shake of her head, she took Alejandro's chin in her hand and gently tilted his face up until he looked at her. He blinked, as if coming back to himself, and rolled the candy around in his mouth until he'd tucked it into one cheek. "You have to be more careful, little man. You hurt yourself too much."

After Judd had interpreted for the boy, he shrugged. "I...okay," he said, demonstrating some understanding of English.

"You can hurt yourself doing things like that."

He only grinned and resumed playing with the candy in his mouth.

"If his mother is…gone, then what does he do during the day? Who takes care of him?"

The father offered an explanation, which was then translated. "He goes to school during the day, then comes home and one of the neighbor kids looks out for him while Pedro is still working. He won't stay in the daycare."

Rebel couldn't help but imagine what she would do if she were closer at hand. Children were at risk for injuries and death if left unsupervised as they didn't have the capacity to determine risk compared to what the perceived fun would be. She pressed her lips together and tried to resist the primal mothering urge that had begun to surface. If only…

"Pedro says he doesn't know what to do with him. The boy won't stay in the house after school, just runs and runs and runs as soon as he's off the bus. That's why he's so skinny." Judd listened again to Pedro. "He wants to know if there is a medicine or something Duncan can give him to make him behave better."

"I'm sorry, Pedro. This isn't a matter of medication, but may be the only way for him to express his grief at the loss of his mother." Pedro nodded, opened his mouth as if he were going to say something, then pressed his lips firmly together and turned away. Rebel could see the frustration and anger in him. "Children often need to cry in order to get those feelings they don't understand out of them."

Pedro pointed at his son, anger blazing in his eyes. "No cry. He no cry." He launched into another explanation to Judd.

"When Pedro's wife died, it was because she was an alcoholic. He doesn't want Alejandro to cry for a woman who chose the bottle over them."

So misunderstood. Grief had grabbed this family by the throat and hadn't let go. They needed to be in counseling, but how to suggest it to a man still entrenched in the angry phase of grief was beyond her comprehension.

"Duncan, I need your help." Though she spoke to him, she busied herself with taking Alejandro's blood pressure.

"What's up?" Duncan stepped closer and nodded to Pedro, spoke a few words of greeting.

"Kid's got a case of Superman syndrome."

"A what?"

"Superman. Thinks he's invincible, and is into serious risk taking."

"What is he, six?" Duncan glanced at the kid and frowned.

"Still thinks he's Superman. Just needs a cape." After relaying the list of injuries his father had reported and the escalation of them, she turned his hands over to show the rope burns to Duncan.

"So what's really going on?" That was the question. There was always something behind a person's behavior, a motivation, even if they were six years old and didn't know it. She explained the loss of his mother and the emotionally distant father to Duncan as quickly as possible.

He sat with a sigh and examined Alejandro, speaking in Spanish. Pedro seemed to relax a little as he listened to Duncan. Then Pedro stiffened. "No." He grabbed Alejandro by the hand and began to walk away. Rebel let out a gasp of distress and looked at Duncan.

"You can't let him just walk away like that. We have to do something more." There was always something to be done. Alejandro turned to look over his shoulder at her and her heart nearly broke at his big brown eyes beseeching her to do something.

"*Uno momento*, Pedro," Duncan said, and the man stopped, but his leg twitched in his eagerness to get away from the situation. Some men couldn't handle emotion and either ran from it or covered it with anger. Pedro was obviously a runner, so his son came by it naturally. Duncan motioned for the man to return the boy to the chair and spoke to him in Spanish.

Fortunately, the man responded, nodding now and then. Rebel gingerly lifted the boy's shirt to have a better look at the wounds he'd sustained in the fall while Judd translated. "It's okay, little man. I'm going to take care of you, don't worry about anything." She applied a non-sting wound spray to cleanse the open areas on his back and then a soothing ointment to prevent infection. The wounds on his hands were nearly healed, but she was sure they had hurt like crazy.

Responding to her gentle touch, the boy looked at her, hesitation in his eyes, as if he'd not known much mothering in his short life. He reached out to touch a stray lock of her hair. With careful focus, he took the strand and wrapped it around his finger. A curious expression covered his face, as if he hadn't ever seen such a thing, and he probably hadn't. Then he released it and it sprang back against her shoulder, and he grinned.

"Nice to meet you, Alejandro. I'm Rebel." She shook his hand and noted he had a pretty strong grip. But she could tell he was definitely underweight.

He bobbed his head, but didn't take his eyes off of her hair. "*Buenas dias, señorita*."

Duncan patted Pedro on his shoulder. The man still stood stiffly with his arms crossed, his back to the child, but at least he hadn't left.

"What did you say to him?"

"I told him he and the boy both needed some support. We'll pay for it, but we'd really like him to go." Duncan cast a glance at Pedro. "He's not happy about it, but says he will try. At least it's a start."

He took a breath and let it out in a huff. He squatted by Alejandro and spoke to him, getting more information than Rebel could. She didn't know what he was saying, but in a few seconds Alejandro gave a grin and then looked up at Rebel, his eyes sparkling for the first time since he'd arrived.

"What did you say to him?" She played along, pleased to see a light of humor in those defeated eyes.

"I told him you were an Irish fairy come here just to help him." Though his face was stoic, there was a playful light in his eyes she responded to.

"Me? A fairy?" Seriously? At her height? "Aren't they tiny little creatures and have tiny little wings?"

"I told him the only way you could tell a real Irish fairy was that they had beautiful, curly red hair and an impish gleam in their remarkable green eyes, but you had to look closely to find it."

"Duncan," she said. Her heart fluttering wildly at his words. The only glint in her eyes had recently been put there by him. And a fresh beating of her heart.

"Hey, you made him smile again, and that's a beautiful thing." He held her gaze for a second longer then broke away to answer Alejandro's next question. "The other ladies around have tried to offer some mothering, but he hasn't bonded with any of them. Until you."

Alejandro distracted Duncan with another question, and he turned to answer the boy.

"He really likes you, you know?" Judd said, and gave her a playful poke in the arm.

"Well, he's a sweet kid."

"I mean Duncan. He really likes you."

Rebel gave an assessing look at Judd. Was it true? Did Duncan really like her in the way Judd meant or was Duncan just having a good time while she was present and would move on to the next woman when he realized she could never give him what he needed? Was that reality or just her own fears surfacing?

"Oh. Yes. Well." Flustered, she didn't know what to say.

Duncan stood and the moment was over.

The tension that had eased resurfaced again when Pedro collected Alejandro. There was nothing to be done at the moment. Time would heal, eventually, but Rebel wanted to do something else to help him. To take him in her arms and rock him to sleep, the way he should have been all of his life. The boy went reluctantly with his father, casting longing glances at Rebel. As if the Irish fairy could help him.

A pain filled her heart as she watched him walk away.

What had started out as a lovely day had faded into a low hum of concern for Alejandro. Somehow she needed to figure out a way to get back here and help. Something in her called to this little boy, and she wanted to be around for him. Farming accidents were fairly common and if something happened to Pedro, what would happen to Alejandro?

She imagined she and Duncan would be heading

back to Albuquerque soon and this lovely weekend
would be committed to the memory books of her mind.
She couldn't imagine another weekend being more wonderful. Or more impossible to hang on to. There was just
no way she could be what Duncan wanted or needed.
After seeing him, his family, the way they were, this
had to be just a one-time event. She just didn't have it
in her to be what he needed, and there was no way she
would taint this family with her genes.

"Come here, children," Lupe instructed, and ushered them from the heat of the outdoors to the cool in-
terior of the home. Ceiling fans ran in every room and
the windows were left open a few inches in order to
facilitate circulation. The adobe structure needed no
artificial cooling.

Rebel and Duncan settled at a large wooden table
where several of Duncan's older female relatives sat.
Duncan introduced her to the matriarchs of the family,
who all seemed to study her.

"They mean no harm, they're just curious about
you." He took her hand. "As I've not brought many
lady friends here, they are taking the opportunity to determine whether I'm worthy of you." These ladies who
had helped to raise him loved him, but didn't always
trust his judgment in women. That made him laugh.
They were so right. At least up until now.

"Don't you mean that the other way around?"

"No. Once you helped out with Rafael, they decided you were made of gold and can do no wrong."
He grinned. "I'm the one in the hot seat."

"I see. I like them already." Was she really seeing
this? Was his family already taking her under their
wings as one of their own? He looked at her as if he

saw her, saw who she really was. That frightened her.
She sipped her coffee and realized Lupe must have put
a dash of red chili in the coffee as well. It had a nip to
it. Or maybe it was the close proximity to Duncan and
all he represented that made her sweat. The temperature was definitely going up.

"Tell me, dear, where are you from?" one of the
aunties asked her. Before she could respond, Duncan's
phone rang, and he got up to answer it then glanced at
Rebel and moved farther away. That was curious. Made
her wonder if it was work.

Lupe made the introductions as to who was the oldest and the youngest and the ladies began to argue about
who looked the best and who had the best hair and the
fewest wrinkles among them. Rebel couldn't help but
be engaged and put at ease by these women.

The laugh in Rebel's throat caught when Duncan re-
entered the room. Something was wrong. It was in his
eyes, in his walk, in the energy around him. He looked
only at her, and her heart sank. Somehow she knew this
news was only for her.

And it was bad.

She stood, nearly knocking over her chair. "What is
it? I know it's bad, just tell me."

The smile that he'd been suppressing burst out from
his heart. Unable to contain his joy any longer, he had
to share it with the only other person who would understand and appreciate it. He embraced her, and he felt
the trembling of her body against his, as if she could
already read him and know there was something going
on. "I'm sorry, Rebel. I didn't mean to scare you. Eric
was taken off life support this morning." He felt her
go stiff in his arms, and he hurried to tell her the rest.

"He's breathing on his own, and stable." A rough laugh escaped him. He didn't know if it was relief or what, but it felt good to let it out.

"Are you *serious*?" She pulled back from him, her gaze frantically searching his. Unknowingly, she reached out to him, clutching his arms with both of her hands.

"Totally serious. That was Dr. Simmons who called just now. She wanted to tell me the news herself." Another laugh of relief rushed out of him. "I can't believe it. I had little hope for his recovery."

"Oh, my God, Duncan. I can't believe it." She grabbed him around the shoulders and held him close. The feel of her body against his was such a relief, such a wonder. He didn't care if there were fifty witnesses, he wasn't going to let go of her.

"What's going on? Did someone win the lottery?" Lupe asked, reminding him of where they were. He was on such a high he'd almost forgotten. Duncan moved to face them but tucked Rebel against his side, wanting to hold on to her and give her some support. He knew she was as gobsmacked as he was at the moment.

"It feels like it. The little boy Rebel and I rescued from the car last week is off life support." He rested one hand on the table to support himself. "It's such a relief."

"Tell us what happened," Auntie Matilda said. "I didn't hear the story."

Rebel looked to Duncan and made a chagrined face. "You tell it. I'm not a very good storyteller."

"Bah, both of you sit down and tell us what happened. We want to hear how you rescued this little boy. You did it together, no?" Auntie Esmeralda patted the seat beside her and urged Rebel into it. Duncan dropped into the chair beside her and rested his arm on the back of her chair.

"Okay. I'll get it started, but then you have to join in and add your piece of it," Duncan said. "You were as important as I was in this."

"No, I wasn't." She shook her head in that self-deprecating way she had.

"Actually, you were more important because you found him. If you hadn't found him, he would have died."

Saying nothing, Rebel pressed her lips together to keep them from trembling, and he saw the flash of tears before she looked away.

Duncan recounted the tale, with Rebel adding details here and there.

"What will happen to him? And what will happen to the mother?" Those questions were posed by Auntie Esmeralda again.

"We don't know yet, but at his age the brain is very resilient." He certainly hoped so.

"As for the mother, she's probably suffered enough for her mistake." Rebel shrugged.

"We generally don't get so attached to our patients, but this situation…" Duncan tapered off and looked at Rebel. He swallowed a few times, controlling his emotion.

"That's how you met? By saving the life of a child?" Esmeralda leaned forward in her chair.

"Yes." Duncan confirmed her statement.

"You will have a special bond forever because of this."

Duncan held Rebel's gaze. "We already do." His voice dropped and he cleared his throat again, somewhat embarrassed to admit such a thing in front of the ladies, but it was true.

"How about I show you around the ranch now that there are no thunderstorms or medical emergencies?" Duncan was after any excuse to be alone with Rebel.

"Wonderful. I've love to see more of the place since we'll leave tonight, right?"

"Let's see what the rest of the day brings. I'm in no hurry to go back to the real world, are you?"

Shy, she dropped her gaze, but squeezed his hand. "No. I'm not."

That warmed Duncan's heart as nothing else had today. This was a wonderful weekend, and he was so glad he'd convinced her to come with him. With an arm around her shoulder he led the way to the golf cart, which had been charged overnight, and sat out front.

He cupped the back of her head and pulled her closer for a kiss. Her lips were soft and pliant beneath his, letting his tongue search for hers and reveling in the sensations of her passionate response.

After several minutes of lingering kisses, stroking her face and listening to her soft sighs, he seriously wished the house wasn't still full of people. Pulling away, he let his hand drift down her arm to clutch her hand. "Let me show you some sights."

"I think I've already seen quite a few," she said, and gave a quick laugh.

"Are you enjoying yourself?" He placed his boot on the gas pedal, and they lurched forward onto the path to the farthest reaches of the farm. Away from people and truly alone.

"I am." The sound of her voice was a little shy. "I'm

just amazed at how friendly and open your family has been when they don't know me at all."

"They know a good soul when they see one. You will always be welcome here, Rebel. Always." He just hoped she would see it that way.

They rounded a bend in the road that seemed to go off to nowhere. "What's out here?"

"A whole lot of nothing." He knew every inch of this ranch and there was nothing to draw anyone out here for a while.

"Seriously."

"We have some herb fields I thought you'd like to see. Herbs, as you know, are the basis for all medicine, and we still hold on to the belief that herbs grown and used locally are the best. We have quite a few herbalists and aromatherapists who use our plants in their concoctions."

"That's fascinating. I love lavender."

"Then you are in for a treat. We happen to have an incredible crop of it this year. Let me take you to the drying shed. It's amazing in there."

The low building ahead was where they were apparently going. When he pulled to a stop beside it, she knew she was in trouble again. After kissing him again, she wanted more of it. Though she knew this relationship wasn't likely to last, she wanted to immerse herself in every moment of it while she could. To live in the moment because she wasn't sure she'd have a future.

"Take me inside, will you?"

The *double entendre* wasn't lost on Duncan. "Gladly." He paused as she rounded the cart. Something in him changed and intensified as she approached, as he responded to the electricity between them. Each step she

took toward him, each movement that took her closer
to him filled her with desire and longing, the power of
which she'd never felt before. The alarm bells in her
mind grew dimmer.

He took her hand and pulled her closer until her
chest touched his, until she tilted her face upward and
her lips were millimeters away from his. His breath
came as quickly as hers, his focus on her intensifying.

"Is there something going on I need to know about?"

"Yes," she whispered, her breath mingling with his.
"I want to be alone with you." She cleared her throat.
"And naked."

As soon as the words left her mouth his lips were
on hers, his tongue searching, seeking, parting her lips
and devouring her.

Her desire ripped free as Duncan clasped her hips
and lifted her to wrap her legs around his hips. "God,
you're so tall, you fit me perfectly." He cupped her bottom in his hands and held her close as he entered the
drying shed. The dim lighting was no issue as he made
his way through rows and rows of lavender hanging
from the ceiling. The fragrance only added to the primal feelings stirring within her.

He found a suitable place to set her down, whipped
his shirt off, then arranged it quickly on the floor of the
shed. "Come here."

She let him lead her down as he lay back on the shirt
and dragged her willingly over him. Kisses and hands
ranged all over her and soon he had her shirt and bra
off and was working on her slacks. Never having been
an exhibitionist, nerves started to fray as he unclothed
her, but when he pulled back to remove his jeans she
forgot her shyness and reveled in the outrageously glo-

rious image of him completely naked and completely aroused. For her.

"You're beautiful, Duncan." Unable to hold herself back, she nearly launched herself at him. He pulled her hips up to meet his and abruptly joined with her, sinking his erection deeply into her.

She stilled and savored the sensation of him inside her and allowed a moan low in her throat to escape.

"Tell me," he said, breathless. "Tell me what you feel, what you want, what you need."

Hissing her breath in through her teeth, she clutched his forearms while he held her hips, digging his fingers into her flesh. "Oh, God, Duncan. I don't know." Her hair clip flew free as she tossed her head back, giving in to the arousal of her body, of Duncan filling her, of him moving strongly against her as he pulled her hips toward him, then let her rock back.

Each movement, each pulse of pleasure pushed her closer to the edge. Each time her hips moved forward she stroked her sensitive flesh against Duncan's. The pleasure built until the pace moved faster, harder, more intent toward a shared goal.

When it hit, the wave of pleasure overcame her, and she cried out with it, unable to contain the joy of her body and heart joined with Duncan's. Wanting to bring him the same release, she rocked her hips faster and his sensitive flesh responded the way hers had. Explosively. Duncan cried out and dug his fingers into her hips, clutching her tightly to him as the climax washed over him.

CHAPTER ELEVEN

SHE'D HEARD ABOUT SEX as a release of emotion, but she'd never experienced it before. Now it made complete sense as she lay there, contented and at peace in Duncan's arms. Even though they were lying on the floor of an outbuilding, there was no more perfect place to be.

She pushed her hair out of her face. "I still can't believe it. About Eric, I mean."

"Neither can I." He pressed a kiss to her temple and then kept his face close to hers. "I was surprised. Somewhere down inside I thought he couldn't survive, that there was no way. I was never so happy to be wrong about something." He paused a second, touching his forehead to hers and sharing his emotion with her. For the first time in a long time he was able to feel and share it with someone. Someone who knew exactly what he was feeling. Somehow, he knew the more he stepped forward, the more Rebel would step forward, too.

"So what happens now?" She settled against his shoulder, the length of her body against his, as they lay on the floor, looking overhead, soothing him. After today, he'd never get the fragrance of lavender out of his mind.

"I'm sure there will be an investigation. For the family's sake, I hope it's not bad. They've been through enough."

"Something like this can destroy a family." Her voice suddenly changed as if she was recalling a memory, then she shook herself and came out of it.

"We'll likely be called as witnesses, but I'm hoping that Amanda isn't prosecuted. I thought she really just forgot about him."

"Do you think it's that simple?" She tilted her head back as she asked the question. His gaze dropped to her mouth and the intensity of him changed.

"Nothing is ever as simple as it seems." Moving in, he closed the distance between them, pressed his lips against hers and kissed her.

This slow exploration of her mouth, the heat of him against her, the emotional day all sought to rob her of her control, of her rationale, and her will to resist everything she knew she shouldn't have. Shouldn't want. But she did. With all her heart, she wanted it.

Duncan's mouth against hers, his lips soft and hot over hers, his tongue exploring hers, created tangles of confusion in her mind and tingles of desire in her body. Overwhelmed, she pulled away.

"Duncan, I'm so confused by you. You make me feel things I shouldn't be feeling or thinking. Or wanting." Unable to hold his gaze, she looked away. He wished he could impart some of his strength into her.

"Don't be. I'm a pretty simple man." He cupped both hands around her face and forced her to look up at him. "What's going on here is pretty simple, too. It doesn't have to be complicated."

"You mean making love?" Some people thought of it that way.

"I mean everything." How could he tell her he was crazy about her, about her wild red hair and the beauty in her face, the humor in her green eyes and the compassion in her heart? How could he tell her all of that when they'd only known each other for a few weeks?

He didn't fall for women that way. *Ever.* Opening himself up like that wasn't in his rule book. But now it was happening and it had taken him by complete surprise. People were predictable and usually disappointed him. She was everything he wanted in a partner, he only had to convince her of it. And not listen to the voices in his past telling him he was an idiot for falling for an Irish redhead so quickly. Right now, all he wanted was her skin against his, her heart beating in time with his, her breath hot in his ear.

"You're just in time to help put the food on the table." Lupe handed each of them a bowl to take from the kitchen to the table in the dining room. The majority of people had taken off and returned to their homes, satisfied the patriarch of the family was doing well.

Rafael looked as if he was back to his usual ornery self.

After a short dinner, and a lovely walk in the garden, Duncan realized their fairy-tale weekend was coming to a close.

They sat on a wooden bench with the scent of roses, lavender and other things he didn't know swirling around them. It completed his picture of the perfect evening.

"I know we have to go back tonight, but do you think we could see Alejandro again before we go?"

"Yes." The thought of the situation with that family put a damper on his buoyant mood, but it was part of life. It was surviving the bad times that made the good times even better.

"What will happen to Alejandro if his father doesn't go through with the therapy?" She sighed. Concern and resignation flashed in her eyes.

"I'm going to think positively, that Pedro will go, and both of them will benefit." He squeezed her hand. "You know time is the only true healer of grief, and it hasn't been very long."

"I'm sorry his mom died. No kid should have to go through all of that at Alejandro's age. He's so sweet." He knew she was thinking of her own family losses, and he wished he could ease the pain in her heart. Given time, and the opportunity, maybe he would be able to.

Duncan rose from the bench and with Rebel's hand in his they left the garden. When they reached the machine shed and rounded the corner to the row of tenant housing, tension in both of them rose.

They arrived at the *casita* where Alejandro and Pedro lived. Before he could knock, the door swung open, and Alejandro bounded out, a happy smile on his face. *"La mujer está aqui! La hada Irelanda esta aqui!"* He threw the words over his shoulder to his father and raced over to Rebel.

She knelt and gave him a hug. Yes, the giant Irish fairy had arrived.

"Rebel and I wanted to say goodbye before we go. I think Rebel has a soft spot in her heart for him." He nodded to the boy.

Duncan watched Rebel trying to communicate with Alejandro. They needed a little interpreting. The sight of her with the boy invited visions of her with her own child in her arms.

"Oh, Duncan. He's really trying to tell me something, but I just can't get it. If I stick around here for much longer, I'll need to take a course in Spanish."

That was the first indication she'd given about not moving on to another assignment and his heart lightened. "That would be great. We always need bilingual nurses." He stooped beside them and spoke to Alejandro. The boy became very animated in his face, his words and his gestures. Duncan laughed.

"What's he saying? I asked him about his back, and he gave me a two-minute answer."

"He says his back still hurts a little, but he's much better since you, the Irish fairy, applied the magical cream to his back and his hands." He gave her a sideways glance. "He's enthralled with you." And so was he, but he couldn't put words to what he was feeling.

"Only because you told him I'm magical." She gave an eye-roll as if doubting his assessment of her magical abilities.

"To him, you are." Duncan wanted to believe in magic right then, too. He'd learned to mistrust his instincts where women were concerned and the situation with Rebel had *mistake* written all over it. But there was something deep in his gut that made him want to kick his judgment to the curb.

The plane was ready. They just had to get into it and return to reality. He sensed reluctance in Rebel as he buckled her into the seat. She was quiet, her eyes downcast, and she clutched her tartan around her shoulders.

When they were airborne and he had tipped his wings to those watching from below, he spoke to Rebel in the headset. Mostly it was just pointing out land-marks, how the sunset glinted off the Rio Grande and mindless chatter. He wanted to put her at ease, but it wasn't working. Though she nodded and responded po-litely, she had gone deep inside herself again.

The remainder of the trip was quiet except for the whine of the engine. Maybe the little voice in his head was right after all. Rebel was a bad bet. Not just because she was a coworker but because her family model was so different from his, her emotional status was fragile, and she just shut down.

That wasn't how he operated. Although he didn't like to fight, on occasion the situation demanded it. He taxied the plane to its space and cut the engine. Rebel had removed her headset and was reaching for the door.

"Wait. We need to talk."

"There's nothing to talk about. It was a moment in time, Duncan. You'll go back to your life and I'll go back to mine. We'll work together, and that's it." Her eyes remained downcast.

"I don't want that." He shoved a hand through his hair in frustration. "Since we got into the plane you've been withdrawing, and I don't want that either. We need to talk about us."

"There's no us." She shook her head as if trying to convince herself. "You've got a vastly different life than I do. Meeting your family, your *huge* family, has made me realize how different we really are. I appreciate the weekend away and meeting your family and all, but nothing has changed for me."

"What?" Incredulous, he reached for her shoulders to turn her to face him. "*Nothing* has changed for you? Are you kidding me?" She tried to pull away from him, but there wasn't much room in the plane. "*Everything* has changed, Rebel. I'm not going back to my life and pretend nothing happened between us. I don't know how you can."

Her tearful gaze met his for the first time in hours. "It won't be easy," she whispered, then yanked away from him and pushed out of the plane.

No. Way. There was no way he was leaving things like this. He shot out of the plane and the wind slammed the door shut behind him. Monsoon season wasn't over and the wind swirled leaves and dust around them.

She stood beside his locked truck, unable to get into it and unable to avoid him. This was where it all came down to the wire. She had to face her demons and maybe he was the one to *make* her do it.

"We're not leaving things this way." He stood a few feet from her. "What do you mean, 'It won't be easy'? If that's the case, then why don't you at least *try* to have a relationship with me? All I'm asking for is a chance, Rebel." Demons of his own resurfaced at the word. He'd begged Valerie to take him back, and she'd laughed. He'd vowed never to beg another woman to be with him, and he was on the verge of doing it now.

Pressing her face against the glass of the door, her shoulders trembled. Her pain was escalating, but so was his. "I can't do this, Duncan. I can't do it. I don't have what it takes. I can't be what you need, and I can't give you what you want. It's better to end things right here and now, and just say we had a weekend we'll never forget."

"Why? Why pretend? And what makes you think you know *what* I need or *what* I want?" Miscommunication led to disaster, and he was done with that, too.

She turned to him, anger and disbelief in her eyes. "*Really*? I'm not that stupid. One look at you with your family and it was all there. You want what you have, what everyone there has. A home, children, a family. I can't give you *any* of that." Her voice cracked and her lip trembled. "I can't give you children, and you know you want them."

"I do want them. But I want an amazing relationship with an amazing woman first." That was true, and the amazing woman in front of him was drawing into herself, moving further and further away from him. He didn't know if he could bring her back.

She pressed her back to the truck door as he moved closer to her. This was not going to be the end of it. No. Way. "Are you listening to yourself? You've talked yourself into giving up your life, any chance of a happy relationship because of your family history. So. What. Everyone has bad stuff in their lives. It's what you make of it that makes your life worth living." He grabbed her by the shoulders as lightning flashed overhead. "I want that with you. I want to build a life with you, Rebel."

"It's *not* just a bunch of bull, and you know it!" Now she was getting angry and that was good. Time to spew it all out rather than letting it fester inside. "I've lost nearly my whole family. You have no idea what that's like. None! You and your perfect family, have no clue."

"Perfect? *Really?* You think you've cornered the market on despair? I could tell you some stories that would rival your family for losses. I've already told you about my mother and my sister, but what I haven't told you is that I also lost my fiancée. Her name was Valerie and I loved her, she was both my lover and my friend. But we argued. I wanted kids, she didn't, she had her reasons, and I let her drive away knowing she was distressed. She crashed the car and died. I blame myself and I couldn't save her. But I can save you, and make you happy, Rebel. I don't want to lose another woman I love. Please listen to me..."

The closer he got to Rebel, the harder it was for her to get away, to run away from her past when confronting it right here and now was going to heal it. He knew it. He just had to make her believe it. "Don't belittle someone else's experiences because you don't think they're as tough as yours. Open your eyes, Rebel. There's plenty of pain and suffering for everyone. We see it roll through the ER every damned day. There's also enough joy and love and faith and hope for all of us. *Including you*, Rebel. Come out of the darkness for just a second into the light that's right in front of you." Like he was. Standing right in front of her, and she couldn't see him. See the potential right in front of her face.

At that moment lightning flashed again, followed quickly by a roll of deep thunder. The gods themselves seemed to want to have some input into their discourse.

"I. Can't." Tears now fell, and she covered her face with her hands. "Oh, Duncan, I'm sorry, so sorry that you lost your fiancée and for all the pain your family has suffered. But I don't have your courage. It's too painful. Everyone leaves or dies, and I can't take it. I couldn't take it if I lost you, too."

"So you won't even try? You are worthy of being loved, worthy of having the greatest thing ever happen right here, right now." He wanted to comfort her, but it wasn't what she needed right now. He also wanted to shake her to make her see how crazy her thinking was.

He stepped back as the first raindrops fell. There

was nothing else he could say right now to change her mind. He'd put it all out there. There rest was up to her. Vanquishing her demons was within her power. He just didn't know if she would pick up the sword. He unlocked the door to the truck and let her in, then returned to the plane to lock it down and put the covers on.

Soaking wet, he got into the truck and started it, not looking directly at Rebel. She sat with her eyes closed, as if that would prevent her from seeing the world around her.

"I'm sorry you got wet. I should have helped you."

"It's fine." He negotiated the wet streets until he arrived at her apartment complex.

"Thank you for the amazing weekend. I won't forget it." She straightened, then unbuckled herself and opened the door. "I'll see you at the hospital." The smile she tried to paste on was pathetic. His words had apparently had no impact on her.

He watched as she dashed through the rain to her front door, waited until she entered her apartment, then drove away into the deepening night knowing that once again he'd bet money on the wrong horse.

CHAPTER TWELVE

WORK SUCKED. THE SUMMER was shaping up to be one of
the hottest on record. Tempers flared. People lost their
patience on the freeways and crashed like dummies,
drank to levels of idiocy and got into fights with their
relatives, or committed acts of stupidity that landed
them in the ER.

For the next few weeks all staff worked overtime,
gave up their summer fun to take care of the never-
ending stream of patients rolling into the hospital, and
became the most tightly knit group Rebel had ever seen.

"I knew this was a busy place, but this is as crazy as
some of the big city hospitals I've worked in." Rebel sat
at the desk with Herm and a few other nurses, taking
the opportunity to have a quick lunch.

"We're a level-one trauma unit for the entire state.
No one else has the ability to care for trauma the way
we do here." Herm nodded, obviously proud of the work
this hospital performed.

"How long have you been here?" She was curious.
In her life, relationships and jobs were all short term.
People who stayed in one place fascinated her.

"I was born in this hospital, and I feel like I never left!"
Shared laughter warmed a little of the ice in her chest.

The fragrant and distinct smell of green chili got her attention, and she froze as Duncan joined the conversation. A plate of green chili cheese fries sat in front of him as he stood at the counter.

"Hey, Duncan. When's the chili going to be ready?" one of their coworkers asked.

"Very soon. Report from the ranch is that things are looking good." His gaze honed in on Rebel, and he tipped his head to her. "Things are looking very good."

"What's the heat level? I can't find the extra-hot stuff in town." Another person posed the question.

Keeping his eyes on Rebel, he answered the question. "Yes, we have the hot stuff. So hot you'll need a cold shower."

"That's the stuff I'm talking about. I want it to make me sweat."

"Oh, you'll definitely be sweating." Everyone at the table got animated, eager in their anticipation of the new crop of chili. Everyone except for Herm, who raised his brows at Rebel.

"What?" She cleared her throat. "Um…I like green chili, too." The flush up her neck betrayed her lie. It wasn't only green chili she liked, and Herm knew it.

"I see."

And then the moment was gone when the doors burst open with an ambulance crew, fire crew, and police all looking like they'd been at some smoke-filled rave.

Strapped on the gurney lay a firefighter, having succumbed to burns and inhalation of smoke during a structure fire. She'd never seen so many impressive men and women at one time.

"Trauma one," Herm instructed, and pointed to the

room. "Gina and Candy, you're on it. Duncan, you're it for now. Rebel, crowd control, then suit up and come in."

Everyone sprang to action at the direction of the charge nurse. He knew who he had working with them, their skills and where they would best be utilized.

The overpowering stench of smoke invaded the entire emergency room. The highly sensitive sprinkler system clicked on and purged the main area with water from the ceiling.

"Out! Everyone who smells like smoke, take it outside!" Rebel waved her hands to get the attention of the firefighters, whose only focus was on their fallen comrade. "I'm sorry, everyone. Please go outside and ditch the stinky stuff, then come back."

She dialed the operator. "Please call off the 911 alarm, half the department is here. We need Maintenance for water cleanup." She herded the first responders to the waiting area reserved for VIPs. There was nothing like the support of your peers, who in this case were like family, to help through the tough times.

"I want to know what's going on in there." The tallest woman she'd ever seen emerged from beneath protective gear. She was strong, fit, but highly agitated. Her hair was a wild, iron gray and her steel-blue eyes pinned Rebel in her spot. Tension filled the posture of her shoulders and the tightness around her lips. This was a woman who was used to being in control and had suddenly gotten lost in unfamiliar surroundings.

"I'm Rebel, one of the nurses—"

"Kat Vega, Station Nine Commander. What's going on with Jimmy?" There was no handshake, no polite query.

"Right at the moment he's being assessed by Dr.

McFee and the trauma team." She held her hands out to stop the tirade of questions she knew was going to be coming. "I can't answer any more questions, because I just don't know. I'll go in there and check his condition. When I have something to report I'll be back."

"You'd better be, or we'll be coming in there to find you." The woman with pain in her eyes turned away from Rebel. She held her hands out to two of her crew members, who clasped them and pulled her into a tight hug. Though she was obviously tough, she depended on these men to hold her up in times of need.

These people weren't afraid to feel. They embraced every second of it because they never knew if it would be their last. Rebel hurried from the scene and hoped she would have good news to share. Her meager concerns and needs dropped away in the face of real tragedy. She hoped this firefighter was made of strong stuff, because he had a long road to recovery.

"I'm back."

"What's going on out there?" Herm asked. "I heard alarms."

"Those firefighters set off the smoke alarms."

"What?"

"Yeah. Those guys were so hot they set off the sprinkler system. Literally." Rebel contained herself, knowing the situation was serious, but any chance at levity helped people perform better by cutting some of the tension right out of the air. "What do you need?" To prevent the chance of bringing any infection to this patient, she pulled on a protective gown and mask as she entered the room that stank to high heaven of smoke.

"He's got one IV in, but we can't get another one in. Both arms are burned and Doc's going to put in a central line." Herm supplied the information. Though his voice was casual, tension filled the lines on his face and the concern in his eyes. The man was not immune to the stress of the job.

"Have you checked his feet?" she asked, and began the process of removing his protective boots. "Sometimes the feet are good, especially since he's had these big honkers on."

Both boots thudded to the floor, and Rebel reached for an eighteen-gauge IV catheter. In seconds she felt the tip enter the vein. "Got it!" Carefully, she secured it and connected the bag of fluids.

"Get one in the other foot, and we'll hold off on the central line for the moment." Duncan spoke to her from behind his protective gear, his voice calm and professional. "Good job, Rebel."

"Thanks. I worked burns in a few places and the feet are usually a good bet." She grinned, excited to share this moment with him, forgetting she was supposed to be maintaining a wide boundary from him and any emotions she didn't want. He nodded and turned back to the patient. "Need to intubate him right now. I don't like the look of his saturation level."

"He's got soot in his nose and mouth. Sure sign of inhalation injury." Rebel clucked her tongue and shook her head. Inhalation injuries destroyed lung tissues if the fire was hot enough, but inhaling smoke suffocated the patient at the blood level.

"What about a blood transfusion?" Duncan said aloud, almost talking to himself, trying to puzzle out the problem and the solution.

"That would add fresh oxygen-carrying ability right away, wouldn't it?" she asked Duncan.

"Yes." He nodded and smiled at her and gave a nod of approval that made her flush.

"Brilliant idea, Doc! You two are quite the team." After receiving Duncan's nod, Herm called the blood bank. "Need two units of packed cells right now. I'm sending someone for it." He hung up and turned to Rebel. "See why that scavenger hunt is so important?"

She removed her protective gear and dashed toward the blood bank, but skidded to a halt, changed direction and raced back to the waiting room.

"Do you have news?" Kat crossed the room in two strides.

"Yes." Rebel caught her breath. "We've got good IV's in him, I'm going to blood bank now, and we're going to transfuse him."

"I'll go." A blond firefighter stepped forward.

"Me, too." Another one approached.

"I can donate." And another.

Several people rushed her at once, willing and eager to donate their life-giving blood to help their friend. Their eagerness and intensity impressed Rebel. Never in her life had she had friends the way this Jimmy did. And she wanted them. More than almost anything else, she wanted to belong, wanted people to call her own, friends to depend on.

"It might not all go to him, but come with me, and we'll see if they can take your donations now." Rebel led the way to the basement, negotiating the way as if she'd run this route a hundred times.

In minutes she had the two units of blood in her hands, the proper paperwork, and had set up two donors with the blood bank.

Rebel returned to the ER, huffing and puffing, out

of breath. "I have…it…here." She held up the two pints of red stuff.

"Are you okay, *chica*?" Gina asked.

"Out…of breath…for some…reason." She was in good shape. Why running up a few flights of steps should wind her, she didn't know.

"It's the elevation. We're over five thousand feet here, and you aren't used to it yet." Gina verified the blood type was correct with Rebel.

"How long does it take?" she asked, and took some deep breaths, beginning to feel better. At least the stars spinning around her vision had vanished. Maybe Gina was right. Her gut churned. Maybe Duncan was right too. He'd told her the exact same thing and she hadn't believed him, hadn't been willing to believe it. Maybe she was overreacting to symptoms that really weren't related to the Huntington's. Maybe.

"About a month. You might have headaches, hand tremors, too." Herm supplied the answer. "Keep up the fluids, exercise slower and eat more green chili."

"That doesn't help. Don't listen to him." Gina gave her a look of disbelief.

"Okay, but it won't hurt anything, will it?" Rebel asked.

"Green chili never hurt anyone," Duncan said, amusement in his voice.

"Good to know, thanks." She paused and took a step back from him. "Think I'm going to see Jimmy's friends again. Give them an update."

"Oh, his parents are on the way from Belen. The fire chief lady called them." Herm made a notation on his notepad as he spoke.

"Where's Belen?" She had no idea. There were so many little towns around the area.

"Don't you remember? I pointed it out to you in the plane—" Duncan began, then stopped talking when the other staff became very interested in the conversation.

Gulp. Secret out. "Oh. Yes. I remember now." Face flushed, she returned to the waiting room to escape the knowing looks of her coworkers. They had questions she was *not* going to be answering. She would be professional. She would do her job, and she would *not* be caught alone again with Duncan.

Ten minutes later she was alone with Duncan.

She went to the staff lounge for coffee and a short break. Burn patients were always intense. Seconds after she turned the coffeemaker on the door swung open and Duncan entered.

"Oh. Hi." He paused for a second when he saw her, then recovered and approached. "Coffee?"

She didn't make eye contact or even look in his direction, but kept her gaze on the drips of java that came way too slowly out of the pot. "Yes. Coffee." She was *so* skillful at trite conversation. She amazed herself. So *not*! How embarrassing. Did the elevation make her heart beat fast now, too? Or was that Duncan's presence?

"You were great." His voice was low and sexy and rattled her nerves.

"Oh. Thanks." Work related…phew! Then she looked at him.

Mistake.

The longing in his eyes almost brought her to her knees. The feeling was mutual. "Don't look at me that way," she whispered.

"Why not?" With his gentle hand, he reached out and pushed her hair behind one ear. The gesture was so sweet she wanted to cry.

"You know how I feel." Despite her words, her resolve lacked the strength to resist him.

"I do." He stepped closer, his voice dropped. "I know how you feel in my arms. How you feel when you put your arms around me and squeeze me." He moved closer still. Though he didn't touch her, he pressed his face into her hair and spoke into her ear. "I know how you feel when you let yourself go and how you feel when you let me inside you."

"Oh, God, Duncan." She whispered his name in protest. What was he doing to her? "Please don't."

"Don't what? Remind you of how good you felt when we were together? Of how you laughed and how you loved me?" He took her hand and moved it around his neck, his chest and abdomen. "Did you forget what I feel like when you touch me?"

"No, I haven't forgotten." She looked up at him, longing now in her own eyes, but curled her hand into a fist. "But it can never be."

"Only because you think it can't." He pressed a kiss to her palm. "I won't forget how you felt, and I hope you don't forget what you felt like because it was real, Rebel, not just some fantasy for you to bring out when no one is looking."

Tears pricked her eyes. Images of them together at the ranch, in the plane, in the barn in the rain, and snuggled together beneath the covers, skin to skin, bombarded her mind and her heart. This man cared deeply for her. How could she walk away from him, from what they could have? How could she love him and then die too soon?

The door to the lounge swung open, and Herm stuck his head in. "He's crashing."

They all raced to the trauma room where fifteen firefighters stood around the stretcher of their fallen one.

"Everyone back up." Duncan, in command again, pushed his way through the pack of people. "What happened?"

"His parents arrived and there was a scene," Gina said. "His mother got hysterical and fainted."

"Dammit. Let's get him settled down again. Give him some more sedation and pain control." He issued the orders as Rebel ushered everyone from the room.

"Everyone except Kat has to go." She led the woman to the head of the bed. "Sit here." Rebel indicated a stool by the stretcher. "Talk to him. Tell him everything that's going on, everyone is safe, use their names."

"But—" She looked down at Rebel, but sat as directed.

"Just do it, Commander. He needs to hear a familiar voice to tell him everything out there is okay so he doesn't worry and can focus on himself."

Kat began to talk low, directly into his ear. "Jimmy? It's Kat. I'm going to tell you what's going on, like the crazy Rebel nurse said, but you have to relax and let me do the talking and the worrying right now." She took a breath and gave a questioning look at Rebel. "Trust me to take on your burden."

Rebel nodded and backed away from Kat. Even though they were in a room full of people, there was a little privacy she could give them.

"Rebel, you're just brilliant," Herm said as he

watched the scene unfolding in front of him. "His oxygen level is better and his heart rate is slowing down."

"It's probably the sedation." She denied any responsibility for his improvement.

"Every bit helps, remember? And stop putting yourself down. You're a highly skilled, if unconventional nurse, and I'm very pleased to be working with you." Herm patted her on the back.

"Me, too," Gina said, and the other staff nodded. A flush of warmth rose in Rebel's chest at their words and their obvious sincerity. This was what she needed and craved. This was the kind of place she'd been looking for but had had little hope of finding. Could she take the plunge and actually stay put? Stay in Albuquerque and build a life for herself here, instead of running the way Alejandro ran and ran and ran? She didn't know, but it was getting harder to be on the road all the time. Slowing down and resting her head on the same pillow suddenly became very appealing but very frightening, too. Change. She knew it was change that scared people the most.

"We're going out for drinks afterward. Maybe you want to come along this time." Gina nodded as she spoke. "We all can use it."

"Maybe," she said, unwilling to commit to anything yet. Was this an opportunity to make a few friends staring her right in the face, and she'd been blind to it previously?

Finally, the shift ended, about an hour late. Her feet ached, her back hurt, and she had a headache. Gina was right. The elevation took some getting used to.

"Ready? We're going to meet at Roscoe's. It's a dive,

but we like it." Gina nodded toward the door. "Come on, Rebel. You deserve a break as much as the rest of us."

Rebel bit her lip in indecision, but as she watched the staff walking out the door, a bubble of excitement made her stomach squirm. Just like the firefighters, the nurses and other staff were like family. She'd noticed it the first day when she'd met Herm and his fatherly way.

"Okay." She nodded, eagerness bursting inside her, giving renewed energy. "I'd like to come if I won't be intruding."

"Intruding? Where'd you get that idea?" Gina gave a snort. "You're one of us, kid."

CHAPTER THIRTEEN

NERVOUS, BUT EXCITED to be inducted into the group of friends, Rebel followed Gina to the parking lot and then to the little restaurant. It was a low, adobe-style building with twinkling lights in the windows and festive chili-shaped lights hanging from the ceiling.

Everyone straggled in and gathered around a central wooden table that wobbled on its uneven legs. Pitchers of drink were ordered and the servers placed baskets of handmade tortilla chips and bowls of salsa on the table. She was coming to realize this was a staple in all New Mexican restaurants. Chips and salsa. The staff devoured them as if they hadn't seen a meal in a week. People kept plopping into the chairs and then her pulse raced when Duncan took the one beside her that magically opened up. Jokes and stories were told as more people contributed to the conversation. Then something happened to Rebel that hadn't happened in a long time.

She relaxed. And she laughed. And she enjoyed herself. And she began to let go of the tight coil holding herself together. Life was messy, but when you had friends to help clean up, it was okay.

She leaned back in her chair, a smile on her face as she sipped a margarita and watched these people interact. In the past she would have been alienated by such a tightly knit group.

Could she really have relationships like the ones she'd seen in the firefighters? Covertly, she watched Duncan, casual and comfortable, despite the grueling day they'd had.

"Rebel? How about it?" Herm patted her arm.

"What? Did I miss something?" Apparently.

"Yes. Gina asked what your most interesting assignment has been." He snagged another chip and signaled the server for more. There was never enough.

"Oh, sorry." She paused and tucked her hair behind her left ear, remembering how Duncan had done that just a few hours ago and a flush warmed her insides. Or was that the margarita? "Every assignment has its perks, but I have to say Hawaii was the prettiest place I've been."

"I've heard it's really amazing."

"It is. I worked on Maui and when you drive around, the whole place smells like pineapples." She smiled with a fond memory of the islands.

"Well, stick around here long enough and there will be plenty of stuff here to get hooked on. There's skiing in the winter, all kinds of outdoor stuff to do year-round, loads of great food, too."

"Sounds great. I'm here for two more months, then I guess I will have to decide where to go from here." But in her heart she knew there was going to be no other assignment like this one. She didn't want to go, but she didn't know if she had the courage to stay.

"We always have a need for nurses with your skills, so you can stay another three months before deciding." Herm patted her arm. "I already know you want to stay."

Only Rebel saw the small nod he made in Duncan's direction. She leaned closer to Herm. "Please don't say anything about what you think you know." She glanced at Duncan, who was listening intently to another staff member. "I hate to ask you to keep my secret, but I am." Her lip trembled. "I don't even think it's real."

"No worries, Rebel. I'll keep your confidence." He lowered his voice. "Just know that he's a *good* man. He doesn't hook up with women the way you might think." He patted her on her shoulder in a comforting gesture. "Listen to your instincts and do whatever you think is right."

"I appreciate that." The burn of tears flashed in her eyes at his kindness. "You don't know how much." She had no father or older brothers she could go to for comfort or to help explain men to her. She'd not had the best of experiences in love. Muddling through things had been too difficult and so she'd given up on love, just focusing on her career. At least until now. Until coming to Albuquerque had completely upset her goals, and her beliefs about love, life and family. Until Duncan.

Now she didn't know what to think. The one person she wanted to go to for comfort, for love, for friendship and understanding was the person most likely to hurt her. Trust and vulnerability were so hard for her. The universe seemed to enjoy taking people from her.

"I don't know what's been going on between the two of you, but I know neither of you have looked happy these last couple of weeks." He shrugged. "I have three daughters of my own, and I recognize the signs of heartache."

"It's complicated."

Herm laughed. "Every great love story has compli-

cations. Have you ever heard of one that was *easy*?" He
shook his head. "No, my young friend, there are always
issues, no matter who you are or how long you're in a
relationship." He downed the rest of his drink. "Trust
me on that one. If you find someone you can laugh with
and love with, there's no better relationship than that.
The rest, you work out." He patted her hand again. "I'm
going to challenge you to think about what it would take
to get through the complication. I don't need to know
what it is, but you need to think of solutions, not stay
stuck on the problem."

No matter what happened things would be okay. How
had she forgotten that? As her family had disappeared
one by one, it had become harder and harder to remember. Then, instead of trying to remember, she'd tried to
forget. The guilt of surviving hung around her shoulders every day. What should have driven her closer to
her mother, had only driven her further away.

"Hey, you okay?" Gina tossed a wadded-up napkin
at her and struck her in the chest.

"What?" She blinked and realized where she was.
"Oh, sorry. Guess I'm tired or something." Or something.

"You looked like you were out there somewhere."

"Yeah. Somebody said something that made me
think of something. You know how it goes when your
brain takes off on you and leaves your body behind."

"No kidding. Just don't do it when you're driving,
okay?" Gina interjected with an understanding nod.

Rebel shifted her position in the chair, then yawned
and stretched. "This was great, but I'm going to call it
a night." She stood. The day had been long and intense.
Fortunately she was off for a few days.

"I think we're all ready to call it a night." Herm stood and waited for her to extricate herself. "You take care, Rebel."

"You, too."

Herm surprised her by putting a friendly arm around her shoulders and pulling her against his side. "I don't know what's going on between you two, Rebel, but you won't find a better man than Duncan."

Breathlessness overcame Rebel, and she placed a hand over her chest, nodded at Herm and left via the back door. She didn't know what was wrong with her, but she definitely needed some fresh air. Too many things were getting to her all at once, and a sense of panic churned in her gut.

Herm's words, her memories, the day's fatigue, the crowded restaurant all seemed to close in on her. Something was wrong, something was changing. Everything she had known and accepted for so many years was changing. Could she have been wrong about her entire life? Her livelihood and the lives of countless people depended on her making the right decisions in an instant. What if she'd been making the wrong decision in her life over and over and over—

"Rebel?" Duncan's voice made her jump.

"Duncan! What are you doing?"

"You're in an alley alone, at night, in a town you don't know. I'm not going to just let you walk alone." He emerged from the shadows. Lines of fatigue looked as if someone had drawn on him with a marker. These last few weeks had been very difficult.

"I appreciate it. I hadn't thought of it, because I do so many things by myself." Maybe she'd done too many things by herself.

"No problem."

Tension filled the air between them. She didn't know what to say as she led the way to her car a few blocks down the street.

"How are you?"

"I've missed you."

They spoke at the same time, and she turned to face him instead of opening her car door, as she should have. Some part of her wanted to reach out to him, but she'd trained herself for so many years not to touch, not to want, not to need. Just survive. That's all she needed. At least that's all she'd needed until Duncan had blazed his way into her life and set fire to her beliefs.

Without another word, he cupped his hands around her face. He hesitated a second with his mouth just an inch from hers, looked deeply into her eyes and kissed her.

Surprise and the shock of his action shot overwhelming desire all the way from her lips to her feminine core. Oh, the man could kiss. His hot lips opened over hers, and she stroked his tongue with hers, unable to hold back her response.

He pressed her back against the car and his hips pressed into hers. She felt the strength of his body and his erection through the scrubs and wanted him with everything she had in her. Breathless, she pulled away, thankful she was supported by the car. Desire nearly swamped her resolve to stay away from him evaporated.

"Will you stay with me tonight?" His breath came in quick little pants, his desire for her seeping out everywhere.

"What?"

"Will you stay with me tonight?" He was serious.

"Come home with me. Stay with me. I need you, Rebel. I don't want to let you go."

"I don't know what to say." She gave a nervous laugh. "My body says one thing, but my mind says another."

He stepped back from her, and shook himself a little, creating the distance she needed. "When you figure it out, let me know. I'm heading to Hatch in the morning. Sounds like you're off for a few days. If you want to come with me, you can."

"Rafael's okay, isn't he?"

"He's fine. I'm the one who needs you." He took another step back. "I'll be gone for a week."

I need you. I just don't want to need you.

"Okay. Well. Goodnight, then." Fumbling with the door and her keys, she finally got into the car and started it. She watched Duncan walk away through blurred vision. It was better this way. If he wasn't going to save himself, she would do it for him.

The night had to be the longest on record. She sweated despite the cool air in the apartment. Her heart raced despite doing thirty minutes of yoga breathing. Desire filled her body despite her best efforts to channel it elsewhere.

Once she'd had a dose of Duncan McFee, he was in her blood, and she didn't know how to get him out. Finally, after a restless and unfulfilling night, she slept for about four hours, awakening to a bright day full of promise.

And five days off with nothing to do but feel sorry for herself. Her schedule had been arranged by Herm and with a couple of staffing changes she'd agreed to she now had five entire days off. Alone.

Normally she would be excited about exploring the

area, hiking the foothills outside town, taking in museums or movies, but now all of that sounded incredibly boring and dull without Duncan to share it with. She'd never shared anything with a man and now that she'd had a taste of Duncan, she wanted to share everything with him. But how could she when her life was a ticking time bomb?

Had she blown the best part of her life by being alone? Was Duncan right? She didn't want to think so, but some part of her knew it was the truth. She'd turned into an old woman well before her time. Tears pricked her eyes. She was such an idiot, unable to see outside her own pain.

When her phone rang she jumped for it, hoping it was Duncan, but it was work. Maybe she wasn't going to have five days off after all.

"Rebel, this is Herm."

"Hi. Do you need me to come in?" She hoped not, but it might keep her mind off of Duncan.

"No. I want to tell you not to come in."

She laughed. "Why is that?"

"It's Duncan."

It only took a nanosecond for her to imagine the worst-case scenario, and she gripped the phone tightly. "What happened? Has he been in a car accident? God, he didn't crash his plane, did he?" She bombarded him with questions.

"No. He's okay, physically." She heard the concern in his voice, but there was no panic as if something bad had happened.

"Then what's going on?"

"He's gone."

"Yeah, he went to Hatch for a few days." Whew, what a relief.

"He came in, was very serious and the *way* he did things, said things made me think he's not coming back."

"*What?* He loves the ER! Why would he resign?"

"I don't know, but he came in this morning, said goodbye to everyone and left." Herm paused. "Maybe this thing between you two is more serious than you know."

"I'm dumbfounded that he would do that, but why are you calling me?" Seriously. What was she going to do?

"You're the only one who can talk him into staying. We need him here and, frankly, Rebel, we need you here, too. For good." He sighed. "Truly good ER docs are hard to come by, and Duncan is just about the best."

"I don't know what I can do. He'll never listen to me if his mind is made up. That Scottish blood of his is as stubborn as any Irish I've ever met."

"If there's anyone he will listen to, it will be you."

"Herm, what am I supposed to do?" She knew he was going to the family ranch in Hatch today, but that's all she knew. After her refusal of him last night, he might not want to see her. Ever.

"He's always taken a week off during the height of the chili harvest, so I'm sure that's where he will be."

"He told me last night that's where he was going."

"I know it's none of my business, but can't you give the man a chance?"

"It's not just about him or me. It's—"

"Yes, it's complicated. But when isn't life complicated? Don't you want to have someone to hold your hand through those tough times? A shoulder to lean on, and cry on, when you need it?"

Rebel paused, a pulse of regret warming her chest. "I never thought of it that way."

"Well, it's time you did. I've seen your résumé, Rebel, and it's appalling."

"What? It is not. I have an excellent résumé." It clearly outlined all her travel experiences and her references were flawless.

"Clinically it's perfect, but there are no gaps where you took time off for vacation or to climb a mountain or anything like that. That's just wrong."

"I see." She thought about it a second, and he was right. She'd gone from assignment to assignment over the last six years without any pause. "How did you get to be so smart?"

"I'm old with a lot of miles under the hood. Now write this down. I'm going to give you directions to get to Hatch, and you can find the ranch from there."

Rebel wrote down the directions and signed off with Herm. How in the world was she going to talk Duncan into returning to work?

CHAPTER FOURTEEN

AFTER GETTING AN early start, Rebel drove to Hatch, hoping she could find the ranch. Having been there only one time, only by air, she faced uncertainty. Herm's directions were great, but they only led her so far. There was a whole lot of nothing out here for her to get lost in. She knew people died in the desert all the time, and she didn't want to be one of them. In preparation for the trip, she'd tossed a case of water and some snacks into the car, so hopefully she would survive the day.

Then she smiled, her heart a little lighter. All she had to do was ask a local where the best green chili in all of New Mexico was grown, and she was sure they would send her right to Rafael.

The drive was beautiful, following the river south, the massive cottonwoods green and white against the dark shadows beneath and the red clay below.

The scenery, the air rushing in the window brought the scent, a fragrance of things new, fresh and exciting. A memory bubbled up within her that began in her gut and flooded upward, surprising her with the intensity, the passion. She gasped as pain made her heart pause, then race in reaction.

Tears she'd buried, emotions she'd forced down for

years unhinged in her. Braking hard, she pulled to the side of the road, raising a cloud of dust.

Images, hard and fast, raced through her mind. An outing with her brothers, her father, their mother. The joy of the occasion. She didn't even remember where they'd gone that day, but the sense of safety, security, of family overwhelmed her, and she sobbed into her hands.

The pain, the grief, the loss flowed through her and the rock-solid shell around her heart shattered.

That was the last time she remembered them together. And happy.

Ben had pushed her on a swing.

Collin had carried her on his back.

Patrick had played tag and chased her around the park.

The pain she'd held back would no longer be ignored. After the storm of tears passed she rested her forehead on the steering-wheel and caught her breath. All this pain, these memories were thanks to Duncan.

The sound of tires crunching on gravel alerted her that she wasn't alone. Panic emerged on the heels of Duncan's warning in the alley last night. She was on a back road in a place she didn't know. She straightened and wiped her face with her hands, now alert.

A black sedan pulled up behind her. Red and blue lights flashed from the grill of the slow-slung car and a police officer emerged from the vehicle.

"Great. It's always something." She rolled down her window.

"Are you okay, ma'am? You've been pulled over for some time." The man took a wide-legged stance a few feet from the car and rested his right hand on the weapon at his hip. It was probably just habit, as she'd seen many cops take the same pose in the ER.

"Yes. I'm fine." Her voice cracked, and she cleared her throat. "I'm… I was just…resting…for a bit."

"Resting?" His dark eyes narrowed. "Are you impaired?"

Only by emotion. "Am I what? No." She blinked and looked down, wondering what to tell him that didn't include her whole life story.

He gave a long-suffering sigh, as if he'd been through this many times before. "Registration, ID, and proof of insurance."

Silently, she handed the items to him.

His brows went up and the expression on his face changed.

"You're Duncan's girl?" He relaxed his stance and handed her paperwork back. "Yeah, for sure, you're Duncan's girl."

"How do you know that?" This time her brows raised in surprise.

"Rey told me." He grinned. "It's a small town and cops talk, you know?"

"I see. Yes. Well. Hi. I'm fine. Really." Maybe knowing Duncan would get her out of a ticket she didn't need.

"Now, that's not true." He gave her that cop look again.

"Why do you say that?" Was she *that* obvious? She didn't deny it, but she wanted to know how he knew.

"Easy. Pink nose. Pink cheeks. Swollen eyes." He clucked his tongue. "Unless you're having an allergy attack, something's wrong."

"Oh."

"Did you and Duncan have a fight or something?" He gave her a brotherly look.

"No."

"Men can be a pain, you know. But you ladies have to forgive us. It's our nature." He gave a shrug that said it all.

"Your nature?" That was a new one. Now they could blame everything on their DNA.

"We want to be right all the time. So, whatever he did, cut him a break. He can't help it." He patted the window frame twice and stepped back. "Have a good day."

"Okay. Thank you, Officer…"

"Gutierrez. But my friends call me Tito."

She smiled, unexplained relief in her belly. "Thanks, Tito." She held out her hand, and he shook it.

"*Mucho gusto.*" Nice to meet you. He nodded, then returned to his car and drove away, leaving little swirls of red dust in his wake.

Maybe there was something to small-town living she hadn't seen before. She'd spent years running from one big city to another. If an assignment became too easy, too familiar, too tempting, she headed off to the next one.

Looking ahead to the small town of Hatch, she was beginning to wonder if her travel-nurse plan was a good one any longer. She pulled back onto the road with a renewed buoyancy of spirit, with a flicker of hope in her soul that she didn't have to run any more.

But Tito was wrong.

She didn't have to forgive Duncan, and she wasn't going to.

He'd been right all along. She just hadn't been able to face it.

After a few wrong turns and a few course corrections, otherwise known as U-turns, she found her way to the ranch.

But something was wrong.

Something was different.

An unusual and chilling quiet cloaked the land around the *casa*. When she'd been there before there had been activity and noise everywhere, but not now.

Something was very different.

Everything looked the same—the house, the grounds, even the tire tracks through the chili field was familiar—but her senses were on alert. Maybe it was her ER nurse experience or the personal protection classes she'd taken. Learning to be aware of her surroundings had saved her a time or two, and her senses were on high alert now.

She knocked on the front door, but there was no answer. No Lupe coming with open arms to greet her. No Rafael to loom over her. No goofy nephews causing chaos. Mysteriously absent was the persistent fragrance of cooking.

And no Duncan. If he were here, wouldn't his truck be parked in front?

Then a sound she never wanted to hear caught her attention.

She ran toward the sound of a screaming child. "Where are you?" The sound echoed off the buildings, and she ran in circles until she figured out where it was coming from.

Underground.

"Oh, God." It must be one of those old wells Duncan had told her about. Racing forward, she dropped to her knees beside what looked like a bunch of old wood stacked up. Lying on her belly, she pushed aside the planks to see into the dark. "Hello?"

The crying stopped for a moment. "*Señorita? La Irelanda hada?*"

"Yes, Alejandro, it's me."

He began screaming and crying at the top of his lungs and Rebel nearly broke down too. Determined to save this little boy, she pulled out her cellphone and dialed Duncan.

"Hel—"

"Duncan, it's Rebel. We need your help!" Quickly she explained what had gone on.

"Where are you?" The confidence in his voice calmed her a bit.

"I don't know. Somewhere behind the machine shed." She rose up onto her knees, looking toward the main house, and relief struck her as she saw him come out into the yard. She waved with one hand. "I see you." She stood, waving her hand.

"I can't see you. Where are you?"

She placed the phone on the ground, jumped up and down and waved with both hands. "We're over here!"

Duncan responded to her voice and saw her disappear. Fear like he'd never had twisted in his gut and sliced like a knife through his heart. She'd fallen into the hole, too. Prayers that he'd long ago forgotten moved his lips, and he whispered to the saints for strength.

"So, where is she?" Jake asked, scanning the horizon with his hands shading his eyes.

"Go get the backhoe and bring it behind the machine shed. There's an old homestead site there, and I think they've fallen into the old root cellar. We're going to need the horse sling, the winch and cable."

"What—?"

"Just do it!" Duncan raced to where he'd last seen Rebel, running as fast as he could, and his heart felt like it was going to burst. Panic set in when he couldn't see her, couldn't find her. "Rebel! Where are you?" He cupped his hands and kept calling for her. He didn't know if she didn't hear him or couldn't call out. Hastily, with hands shaking, he dialed her number. Maybe it was still above ground and he was close enough to hear the ring. If it wasn't on vibrate.

Dammit. After two tries, he finally got it right and heard the faint music. Listening intently, he moved around, going closer, hanging up and ringing again until he saw the pile of wood that was supposed to have covered the hole from one of the original homes built on the ranch. There was no way she could have known it was there. "Rebel?" He skidded to a halt and fell to his belly, then scrambled to the edge of the opening.

Below was a scene he never wanted to see again. Rebel lay crumpled up, with Alejandro shaking her shoulder and crying.

"Alejandro?" The boy looked up, frightened but not hurt.

"I'm coming to get you. Don't be afraid."

"*La mujer? La hada?*"

"She'll be okay, too, but you have to help me."

The little boy nodded. "I help."

Though Duncan didn't know how at the moment, he knew he had to get them out of there before the whole room collapsed on top of them. The vibrations of the backhoe reached him and he stood, directing Jake.

Workers arrived, hurrying after the heavy machine, and Duncan derived some comfort from having such a knowledgeable group coming to help. Pedro raced ahead of the group, his face distorted with worry and fear. He gasped for breath, trying to question Duncan in between breathing.

"Pedro, calm down." Duncan motioned for the other men to come closer. "We're going to need the ropes and pulleys set up. Strap it to one of the horse harnesses and use the backhoe to be the support." Everything was done quickly and Duncan looked over the edge again.

Rebel was rousing. The little Superman patted her shoulder and spoke to her softly. Duncan noticed spots of blood on the back of her shirt and hoped she wasn't badly injured. With that kind of fall, it was hard to predict.

"Rebel. Honey, are you okay?"

She turned at the sound of his voice then winced. More slowly, she pushed her hair out of her face and looked up at him. "Duncan? How did I get here?"

"You fell into the hole when you called me to help get Alejandro out." He paused to take a breath and calm himself, but his heartbeat thundered in his ears. "Can you tell what kind of injuries you have?"

That information was necessary to ascertain before putting her into the harness. If she had serious injuries, they'd have to get the rescue squad and dig her out.

"I hurt everywhere. My back is scraped, but I don't think I've broken anything." Experimentally, she moved her limbs, testing for injuries, then shook her head. "No, everything seems okay." She took a gasping breath that sliced through his heart. "I'm scared, Duncan."

"Don't worry, darling. I'm here, and I'll get you out."

One of the men called to him. "Hold on. I think we're ready up here. I've got a horse harness I'm going to lower down to you. Put Alejandro into it first, then we'll get you up right after." Though it nearly killed him to do it this way, the child had to come first.

"Okay." She nodded, as if trying to convince herself of the plan. "Okay." Crawling to her knees, she slowly rose upright, swayed, then caught herself. "Just a little dizzy."

"You'll be fine. Once we get you topside, you'll be fine." And he would be too. Everything was in readiness, and the harness was lowered down to her. Though her hands shook, she was able to get it loosely around the boy. He was so small Duncan was afraid he'd fall out of it. "Hold on tight and up you go."

Duncan gave the signal and the men began to pull the boy up. As the rope sliced through the ground at the edge of the opening, dirt and other debris were dislodged and fell down onto Rebel's head.

She cringed and turned away from the dust and dirt, coughing as she tried to breathe. In seconds, though, Alejandro was topside and Duncan untangled him from the harness. Pedro fell to his knees and hugged the boy between kisses and curses.

Duncan lowered the harness down to Rebel. "Put this on somehow and we'll get you out." His heartbeat faded away, his breathing faded away, the sounds of the machine and the other people faded away until all that was left was Rebel. "Come back to me, darling."

Flinching from pain, Rebel was able to get the thing mostly around her torso and gripped it with both hands. She looked up at him and her eyes met his. The trust, the need in them humbled him. It all came down to this moment with Rebel putting her life in his hands. He couldn't, wouldn't let her down. Never again.

"I'm ready. Get me outta here." She gave a thumbs-up signal and Duncan signaled the men. They hauled on the ropes, pulling and easing Rebel up through the opening. Dirt and more small rocks rained down on her as the rope dug into the dry ground.

The second he could touch her hair he knew she was going to be okay. And so was he. "I've got you. I've got you." Helping her over the ledge and onto the ground, he reached for her, and he wasn't ever going to let go again.

"Oh, Duncan." She reached out, still tangled in the harness, and he brought her against him. He was trembling inside. He couldn't help it. The fear he'd had in the last thirty minutes was like nothing he'd ever experienced in his life. And he never wanted to go through that again.

"Oh, my God, Rebel. Are you okay?" He pushed her away from him to look at her. She was a mess. Scrapes and scratches covered her face and arms, and dirt and dust covered everything.

"I think I'm okay. My head is starting to hurt, though. Where's Alejandro? Is he okay?" She clutched Duncan's arms, her eyes wide.

"He's okay. He raced off to his father, so I think he's okay."

"Good." She nodded and pressed a hand to her forehead. "Can we go to the house now? I need to sit down."

"Yes." He unbuckled the harness and ropes as the men gathered around, smiling and laughing, offering good wishes and many thanks for her finding Alejandro. Someone gathered up the ropes. Someone else got the harness and Jake drove the backhoe to the machine shed while everyone else followed them to the house. Lupe met them at the door with a screech and a litany of orders that everyone scrambled to get going. "What happened, *mija*? Oh, you are such a mess."

The tremors he felt from Rebel intensified, her eyes fluttered, and he knew she was going into shock. Moving quickly, he scooped her up in his arms and hurried into the house.

"Lupe! Have one of the boys get my kit from the plane. I need warm blankets and a bottle of whiskey."

"Whiskey or tequila?"

"Both." In a Scottish-Hispanic household both libations were always available.

Lupe gave orders to the women of the household and before he could even get Rebel settled down onto the couch someone had arrived with pillows, an electric blanket, a heating pad and a bottle of electrolyte water.

Judd arrived with his medical kit, and Duncan's hands trembled as he tried to start an IV in Rebel's hand. He missed the vein and the IV blew.

Lupe placed a hand on his shoulder. "Take a breath, *mijo*. It will be okay. You have the power in your hands to heal her. It's not like before. Give her your love, and it will all be fine."

Duncan nodded and, without looking up, he addressed his nephew. "Judd, go get a bit of the herbal mix we use on the horses. She's gonna need some."

"Seriously? The stuff for the *horses*? It stinks. Really bad." He stood, though uncertainty remained on his face.

"Just go." Judd raced off and Duncan took that breath Lupe had suggested, releasing the tension in his shoulders and his hands. He did have the power to heal her and it was right in front of him.

Focusing again, Duncan successfully inserted the cannula into a vein in the back of Rebel's wrist. Relief swept through him as he connected the IV fluids, letting them infuse quickly.

A small hand appeared on his arm. Alejandro stood tearfully beside him, and he hadn't even noticed. Duncan put his arm around the boy and drew him closer.

"*La hada*, she bad hurt?" Alejandro spoke in soft Spanglish. Duncan could see the little man adored her.

"*La hada* is hurt bad, but she's going to be okay." Duncan hugged Alejandro, who tried to hide a wince. "Let me see your arm."

Alejandro shook his head and looked down, holding his left arm across his middle.

"Alejandro, *es bien*. I want to see if you have any injuries." He took a breath, trying to calm the fear and adrenaline racing through him. "You're not in trouble, *entiendo*?"

Tears welled up in the boys eyes as he looked at Duncan. "My fault."

"No, it's not your fault *la hada* is hurt. She came to rescue you with her magic. Sometimes when the magic runs out the fairy has to rest a while, *entiendo*?"

"*Sí, entiendo*." Still downcast, Alejandro held out his arm to Duncan. A purple bruise had begun in the middle of the forearm. Probably broken, at least deeply bruised, but they'd need an X-ray to determine it, which meant a trip to town.

"Lupe? Can you take him to the kitchen and get him some of your special hot chocolate and some ice for his arm?"

"Come, Alejandro." Lupe held out her hand to him, but he refused to take it.

"No. Stay *con* Rebel. *Por favor*?" Trembling, he made the request to remain in the living room with Rebel, the only woman who had put her life on the line for him. Even at his young age, he knew how special she was. Even if she wasn't a magical fairy.

"Okay. Lupe, can you bring those things in here for him?" Duncan nodded to the end of the couch at Rebel's feet. Alejandro climbed up carefully and placed one hand on her foot, patting it gently.

A groan from Rebel and a twitch of her arm indicated she was coming round, which was a good sign after the trauma she'd sustained.

"Can you sit?" Duncan knelt beside her and put an arm behind her shoulders. As careful as he was, she winced anyway.

"Oh. Ow!" She sat up abruptly and put a hand to her forehead. The second her legs hit the floor Alejandro scooted closer to her, not touching, but needing her nearness to comfort him. Pedro plopped into a chair across the room, and dropped his face into his hands.

"Easy, love. Take a few breaths." Though Duncan understood there was an unofficial rule in medicine that you never treated those you were emotionally close to, he didn't give a damn.

With Rebel lying limp and in pain in his arms, he would trust no one else to care for her, even if they had been in Albuquerque in their own ER.

Whatever needed to be done was going to be done by *him*.

CHAPTER FIFTEEN

REBEL RAISED HER HEAD and looked into his eyes. "My back is on fire. Got anything for that, Doc?" Her smile was as stiff as her movements, but she curled her left arm around Alejandro.

"Judd is bringing me a special herb concoction we use on the horses. It will help as soon as I get it on you."

Her brows shot up. "The horses? You're using a horse liniment on me?"

"Sure. If they like it, I don't see why you shouldn't." A small smile lit him up. If she was starting to crack jokes, she was going to be okay.

"Yes. Lupe makes a salve out of the herbs we grow."

Judd arrived, skidding to a halt beside them. "I got it." He shoved the container, the size of a mint tin, into Duncan's hands. "Here."

Lupe arrived at that moment with a tray for Alejandro, laden with her special hot chocolate, a few cookies and a picture book. "Come over here, Alejandro, so Duncan can tend to Rebel."

This time, when she held her hand out to him, he took it and allowed her to lead him to the chair across the room beside Rafael, whom Duncan hadn't even seen come into the room. The great man said nothing, but

Duncan could see the tension around his eyes and in the set of his mouth, firm and displeased. Duncan nodded to him and received a return gesture.

"Let me see your back. You'll be amazed at how well it works. The horses make a fuss at the medicinal smell as it's camphor, but I don't think you'll mind."

Rebel turned her back to him, and he raised her shirt over her shoulders. Red welts covered her back, swollen in places and already deep bruises showed themselves. He dipped his fingers in the salve. Starting at her trim shoulders and moving downward, he applied the ointment. She winced several times, but it couldn't be helped. After settling her shirt again, she sat on the edge of the couch so her back didn't touch anything.

Jake shuffled into the room, carrying two neoprene packs of some sort. "When the horses get hurt we put these ice packs on them. I figured you and Alejandro could use them, too." He cleared his throat and blushed gloriously as he approached Rebel.

Duncan raised his brows. Apparently, Rebel had made quite an impression on the men in the family, no matter what their age. He obviously had some competition for her attention. That made Duncan smile. She'd already been accepted by the family, and she didn't even know it.

"Thanks, Jake." Duncan took the cold gel pack from him and placed it gently on Rebel's back. She closed her eyes and gave an audible sigh.

"That's fantastic. Thanks, Jake." She reached out for his hand without opening her eyes.

The young man shook her hand roughly and turned a florid shade of red, matching Lupe's scarlet trumpet vine on the *portál*. "Glad to help." He dropped her hand, and then she opened her eyes. "I…uh…got something to do." He backed away from her, prepared to bolt from the room.

"What's the status out there?" Rafael questioned, and hit him with a stern stare.

"It was the old homestead foundation, sir."

"I thought we blocked that well off some time ago."

"It wasn't the well, sir, but some sort of storage room. Maybe the root cellar." Jake said. "The backhoe's still out. I can just plow the whole thing over if you like and cover it for good."

"Go ahead. Then we need to start going to the other old home sites and making sure there aren't more death traps we've forgotten about."

"I'll get it done right now." Jake left to do the job.

Rebel leaned against Duncan's shoulder, and he was glad to be her support. Her gentle breathing against his skin was something he wanted to savor for years to come. This woman who had no qualms about putting herself in harm's way for others deserved to be cherished and adored.

He'd been so determined to have his own way he hadn't been able to see there was another way to be had! He'd been so determined to make Rebel see things *his* way, to do things *his* way, he'd nearly driven off the woman who excited him, inspired him, and stirred his passion for living.

Lupe paused in front of him until he looked up.

"She deserves your best, *no*?"

"She does, and she's going to get it." He stroked Rebel's hair and pressed his cheek to the top of her head.

Rafael stood. "Come on, kid, let's go see if you can help me figure out this new cellular phone." Alejandro looked with longing at Rebel. "She's in good hands but needs to rest right now. Come on, Pedro. You too."

"Okay." Alejandro took Rafael's hand and allowed the man to lead him away, Pedro following behind.

"Rebel, you are an amazing woman. I wish you knew that." As Duncan held her, her breathing changed from the easy, restful pace to rapid and anxious.

"Duncan."

She leaned her head back and looked up at him and all he wanted to do was kiss her. So he did, dirt and all.

Leaning in to her, he opened his mouth over her parted lips. Somehow, he wanted to put all his fear and all his love into that one kiss. He cupped the back of her head gently and kissed her. She allowed him to take what he wanted, the glide of her tongue over his assuring him she was no longer upset but needed him as much as he needed her.

Breaking the kiss, he held her close, the tremors surging through him coming as a surprise.

"You can't leave."

"I'm not going anywhere." This was where he wanted to be for now. With a hand that still shook he brushed some of the dirt from her face.

"Herm told me." She sat upright, urgency in her expression. "You love that place. You can't leave."

"What exactly did Herm tell you?" He frowned, puzzled by this. Did she have a concussion?

"He said you resigned this morning. You can't do that."

Duncan smiled and gave a head shake. "He exaggerated a little." Warmth stirred in his chest at her reaction.

"You didn't resign?" Confusion warred with relief in her eyes.

"No. I came in to say goodbye to everyone as I decided to take the rest of the month off to help with the chili harvest. Not resign the whole thing."

"Oh, that man! He made me believe you'd resigned and weren't ever coming back, and I was the only one who could talk you into keeping your job!"

Speechless for a moment, Duncan pulled her against his side. "And you thought you could do that?"

"I thought I might be able to help, yes." She placed one arm around his waist. "You aren't leaving?"

"No, I'm not going to leave the ER, but I do need to spend some more time here. The situation today with Alejandro and the lack of serious healthcare here has made me wake up to where I am needed just as much."

"I see." She looked away. "That's good."

"But we need to talk about us, Rebel." He stroked the hair back from her face, extricated a chunk of dirt. "I know you're in pain right now, but I can't wait any longer." Here goes. This was going to be the hardest conversation he'd ever had with anyone, but for both of them it had to happen, it had to be done. And if he couldn't make her see, couldn't convince her of his sincerity, then he would have to move on. Again.

Her chin trembled, but she nodded. "Go ahead."

"I know you're still grieving about your family, and it sucks." He wanted to touch her, comfort her, but making it easier wasn't going to help either of them.

"Grieving?" She took a deep breath and let out an agonized cry, as if coming to a conclusion on her own for the first time. "I'm not grieving, Duncan. I'm feeling *guilty*!"

"For what? You didn't do anything."

"I. Survived." Emotions choked out of her. "I was

supposed to help my mother, I was *supposed* to make things better for her, and I didn't. I couldn't! All I did was live and remind her every day of what she'd lost." Painful though it was, she stood and began to pace.

"None of that was your fault, Rebel. None of it." He punched a fist against his thigh, unable to contain the temper that ate at him on her behalf. "You were a child. And if your mother expected you to do anything else, then she was out of her mind with grief, too."

"It was my job to be *good*, to be *quiet*, to help take care of them when my mother needed a break." Tears streamed down Rebel's face, making muddy tracks, and the memory took her deep.

Duncan paused, wanting to reach out to her, to hold her, to comfort her, to make it better in some way, but he knew he couldn't. He couldn't take away her pain, but he could be there when she let go. He stood and watched as she moved through the pain that had shaped her entire life.

"I did what I could, and it was never enough. It was never going to be enough. *I* was never going to be enough. Even as a kid I could see that." She took in a breath, her eyes still glazed as she whispered her pain out loud. "I emptied trash cans and vomit basins, and stood up on an old wooden box so I could reach the controls on the washer when I was eight. I went to school in the day, but when I got home I became the mother, the nurse, the caretaker, and my mother went to work."

"So you stayed home with all of them?" Incredulous, he could hardly conceive of the responsibility heaped on the tiny shoulders of a child.

She nodded and reached up to tug on a strand of her hair, wrapping it round and round one of her fingers.

"Yes, but they weren't all sick at the same time. The first one, my dad, went on for three years."

Duncan closed his eyes, unable to fathom the pain and the loss of a vital part of her youth. No wonder she was such a strong nurse. She'd been at it since childhood. "What happened after that?"

"Well, I don't remember much from some of those years. Just going to school and staying up with my dad until my mom got home." She shrugged. "Fortunately, he died at the beginning of my summer break when I was eleven, so I had the whole summer to recover."

"You don't really recover from the death of your father, though, do you?"

"No, I mean from the exhaustion of caring for him. I had a few months to recover before school started again."

"I see." He settled on the arm of one of the couches. "What did you do then?"

"The boys were okay for a couple of years, then when I was about thirteen or fourteen, I don't remember, the boys started showing symptoms, and we got a clue it wasn't just Dad." She let out a heavy sigh. "Ben had a stroke when he was twenty-three. He was the oldest." She shook her head and tears flowed again. "My mother was so proud of him when he got this job working construction. He loved to build things, and she was so happy he was doing what he wanted." A sad smile curved the corners of her mouth upward. "He was in a heavy equipment accident at the construction site where he worked. No one ever figured out if he had the stroke first and then the accident happened or the other way around."

Duncan didn't think it mattered, chicken or egg, the

result was the same. "So that's how you found out he had Huntington's?"

"Yeah. When the neuro symptoms lingered longer than the rest of his injuries, and he couldn't go back to work. After that it was bam, bam, bam." She hit the back of one hand against the palm of the other for emphasis. "They all became symptomatic within three years and died within five." Though her breathing had settled, she inhaled an erratic breath as her body calmed and she told her story.

"The emotional pain must have been excruciating." He couldn't conceive of it. Even though he'd faced his own pain and saw the pain of others on a daily basis, he just couldn't wrap his head around what she'd gone through as a child.

"It doesn't matter now, but there it is. You know what my deal is and why."

Without responding, he stood and placed his hands on her cheeks and lifted her face upward until she looked him in the eye. Hers were the saddest eyes he'd ever seen, and now he knew why. "Did your mother ever thank you, or tell you she was proud of you?"

The green darkened and the tears she'd managed to contain welled again and overflowed. "No." Her chin quivered, and she began to cry in earnest.

Then he did comfort her, held her against him and gave her the support of his body as he held her and let her cry against him, let her cry for the childhood she'd never had and the family she'd lost. "I'm proud of you, Rebel. I'm so proud of the woman you've become, of the humor you've maintained, of the compassion you share, and the insight you've developed. Of your passion when we make love." He stroked her hair and didn't know if she heard him, heard his words or the things he meant when he said them.

"I'm such a mess, how can you be proud of me?" Pressing her face against his neck, she hid her face from him.

"Because I love you, Rebel. With all my heart, and all my soul, I love you." At those words, she stiffened, stilled, and he didn't know if she even breathed. With gentle hands, he pushed some of her hair back and bared her face. "There you are."

"You must be delusional or something." Red, blotchy-faced, with tears still flowing, she was the most beautiful person he'd ever known.

"Why? Because I love you?"

"Yes," she whispered, and the seemingly endless fountain of tears continued. "You've seen the real me, all of me, and you can still say you think you love me?"

Using his thumbs, he wiped the tears from her face and placed a kiss on the tip of her dirty, red nose. "I don't think I love you, I *know* I do. You're one of the strongest women I've ever known, Rebel Taylor, and I want to know more of you every day."

There were no words to describe her feelings. Relief, guilt, loss, confusion, but most of all love for Duncan. The kind of love she'd heard about and read about but had put down to good fiction, wild fantasy, or drunken debauchery. Never in her life would she have thought she could find that kind of love for herself. "I don't deserve you, Duncan. Or this family or—"

"Shh. Yes, you do. From the second you set foot on this property, you've been welcome. From the second you looked at me in the parking lot when we met, I've been unable to get you out of my mind, and you've found a place in my heart. I want you in my life."

"I don't know how you see all of those things in me, but I'm so...glad...you do." She clutched him against her and this time there were tears of joy, of happiness along with the pain left in her, but if Duncan was beside her, she knew she could take at least one step forward to having a normal life, to having a great love in her life and putting behind her the pain of her past, the childhood torn away from her by death and disease. "I don't know how to say the words." She looked at him, begging him to understand.

"The words 'I love you'?"

Nodding, she pressed her lips together.

"Then I'll say them for you, every day, until you can say them to me." He pressed his forehead against hers, holding her, trying to help her see she was worthy of his love. "I love you, Rebel Taylor. Will you stay with me, will you love me, and be my wife?" He felt her stiffen again. "It's not too soon, it's not too fast, it's barely fast enough for me."

Then she smiled, and he knew they were going to be okay. Even if she couldn't yet say the words, she loved him.

"Dr. McFee, what will people think? We've only know each other...for how long?"

"It doesn't matter how long we've known each other." He curved some of that wild hair behind one ear. "People will think I'm damned lucky you agreed to be my wife. Say you will?"

"I will be your wife and stay with you and...love you."

"Will you be part of this crazy family and help me

to open a free clinic here in Hatch? I know it's a lot to ask all at one time, but when you see your dreams right in front of you, how can you not grab hold with both hands?"

"I…I never thought I would marry or have children, so I cut that dream out of my life a long time ago."

"I want to take you on all those trips you never took, and I want to check everything off that long bucket list of yours, and experience with you all the things you've never done."

"Well, that's quite a lot," she said with a laugh, and she knew she would be okay. Really okay on the inside. With time, with love, maybe a little therapy and his support, but she would be okay. Now, she could breathe again and for the first time she inhaled a sense of relief she'd never had.

"Duncan McFee, I will marry you and be part of this crazy family of yours and travel anywhere you want to go. As long as you're with me, it will be home."

Duncan held her close, mindful of her injuries, and the tremor of fear inside him began to subside. All was going to be well with them, and he'd spend his lifetime ensuring she knew it. "I love you."

"But what about children? I can't give you any babies." He knew her history, but would he accept it? That could be the deal-breaker for them both.

"You don't know that. Not for sure." He took her hands in his. "I think it's time for you to know."

"To know wh—? No." She shook her head and tears filled her eyes. "I can't, Duncan. I just can't. I already know."

Though she tried to pull away from him, he held on to her hands. "Darling, you don't know, and neither do

I." He drew her a little closer. "What I do know is that I love you. The results won't stop me from loving you. It will give you some peace, and that's what I want for you more than anything."

"Peace? How can you say that when having the test will determine how long my life is?" Her eyes were wide with fright he'd put there, and her chest rose and fell quickly.

"No, it won't. That test is what it is, and that's all. It doesn't determine how long your life is or how well you live it. I'll be with you every step of the way, and I will love you through whatever happens."

"I've never known anyone like you, Duncan McFee. I can't believe you love me enough to want to know the truth about me."

"I already know the truth about you. You are a wonderful, caring, vibrant woman who loves deeply. *That's* the truth of you. What I want is to bring you peace, to ease your mind, and take away the pain that's been in your heart for too long."

"That's a pretty tall order." One she'd never been able to fill on her own, but now, with his help, his guidance and his love, she could.

"I know, and I may not be able to do it all, but I want to try. And I want to spend whatever time we have on this earth together."

"So what happens if I'm positive? I won't be able to give you children, and you so deserve to be a father." Her voice had gone soft, fear filling it again.

"And you deserve to be a mother. I've seen you with Alejandro, and I know you would love to have your own. I know. But there's more than one way to be a parent. And that's more important than having a pregnancy, isn't it?"

Rebel wrapped her arms around him, feeling like there was hope for her future. "Yes, yes, it is." She took in a deep breath and huffed out the remaining doubts and uncertainty. "If you'll be with me and help me, I can be strong enough to find out the truth."

"You're already stronger than you know." He stroked her cheek. "And I'll be with you every step of the way."

EPILOGUE

TROPICAL BREEZES HEAVY with the smell of the ocean and flowers surrounded Rebel. She emerged from the small commercial plane and was enveloped by the welcoming arms of Jamaica. This was something she'd never imagined, stepping out into such paradise. Now that she'd received the test results, life could go on. Beautifully, peacefully.

She did not carry the gene, as she'd thought she did. She'd been able to tell her mother the wonderful information on her wedding day. What a joy that had been, to be reunited with her mother, introduce her to a huge new family, and share the perfect news of being negative, all in one brilliant day.

"You were so right to tell me I was nuts."

"I never said that." He looked at her over his aviator sunglasses as he had when she'd flown with him for the first time.

"When we first met and I told you Jamaica was on my bucket list. You didn't say it quite that way, but you inferred it." She smiled up at him. "And you were right. This is unbelievable. We haven't even left the airport and I'm speechless."

Duncan stopped and placed a well-deserved kiss on

her lips, then took her by the hand and led the way through the airport. "Our luggage will be delivered to the bungalow, there will be fresh fruit on the table when we get there, with a bottle of rum and a lovely breeze bringing the smell of the ocean through the windows."

"It sounds heavenly." As she let him lead her through the colorful airport, the sun glinted off the ring on her left hand. It was a plain silver band, but she hadn't wanted anything else, much to Duncan's disappointment. What was the use of having money if he didn't spend some of it on her? She'd said he could spend the money on making memories with her, rather than on a sparkly token. He'd taken her at her word and booked the honeymoon trip immediately.

"It is." He kissed her hand then pulled her closer for another kiss. "Just like you."

"My birth-control implant runs out in another few months. Maybe we should think about baby-making." That was another thing she'd never considered before meeting Duncan. But now life had opened up into a new world since meeting him.

"It takes more than *thinking* to make babies." He smiled. "While we're here in Jamaica, I think we could work on perfecting our technique, so when the time comes we'll have it down pat."

She laughed, feeling freer than she'd thought she'd ever be, more loved than she'd ever thought possible, and happier than she'd ever thought she *could* be.

"Thank you, Duncan McFee." How else could she put it? She was grateful for his presence in her life and for the joy he gave her every moment of the day.

"For what?" He stopped and other people in the

airport just moved around them, as if accustomed to lovers stopping spontaneously.

"For loving me." Tears distorted her vision, and she happily blinked them away.

"Always." He put an arm around her shoulders and drew her close against his body, then led her out into paradise.

* * * * *

**Don't miss Sarah Morgan's
next Puffin Island story**

*Some Kind
of Wonderful*

Brittany Forrest has stayed away from Puffin Island
since her relationship with Zach Flynn went bad.
They were married for ten days and only just
managed not to kill each other by the
end of the honeymoon.

But, when a broken arm means she must return,
Brittany moves back to her Puffin Island home.
Only to discover that Zac is there as well.

Will a summer together help two lovers reunite or
will their stormy relationship crash on to the
rocks of Puffin Island?

Some Kind of Wonderful
COMING JULY 2015
Pre-order your copy today

0315/MB507

MILLS & BOON®

MEDICAL ROMANCE™

THE ULTIMATE IN ROMANTIC MEDICAL DRAMA

A sneak peek at next month's titles...

In stores from 7th August 2015:

- **Hot Doc from Her Past** – Tina Beckett *and*
  Surgeons, Rivals...Lovers – Amalie Berlin

- **Best Friend to Perfect Bride** – Jennifer Taylor *and*
  Resisting Her Rebel Doc – Joanna Neil

- **A Baby to Bind Them** – Susanne Hampton
- **Doctor...to Duchess?** – Annie O'Neil

Available at WHSmith, Tesco, Asda, Eason, Amazon and Apple

Just can't wait?
Buy our books online a month before they hit the shops!
visit www.millsandboon.co.uk

These books are also available in eBook format!

0715/03